Also by James Kelman in Polygon

The Busconductor Hines
Not not while the giro
An Old Pub Near the Angel

A CHANCER

James Kelman

First published in 1985 by Polygon Books.
This edition published in 2007 by Polygon,
an imprint of Birlinn Ltd

West Newington House
10 Newington Road
Edinburgh
EH9 1QS

www.birlinn.co.uk

9 8 7 6 5 4 3 2 1

The publisher acknowledges subsidy from the

Scottish
Arts Council
LOTTERY FUNDED

towards the publication of this volume.

ISBN 10: 1 84697 040 7
ISBN 13: 978 1 84697 040 5

British Library Cataloguing-in-Publication Data
A catalogue record for this book is available on request from the British Library.

Typeset by Palimpsest Book Production Limited,
Grangemouth, Stirlingshire
Printed and bound by
Clays Ltd, St Ives plc

I dedicate this novel to my parents, Ronald and Mary; and to my brothers, Ronnie, Alan, Philip and Graham; and also to my parents-in-law, Mary and Pat Connors; and to my brothers-in-law, John and Kevin.

Aside from the low droning noise it was quiet in this section of the factory. In the smoke-area around a dozen men were sitting at a big wooden table, involved in a game of solo. Only four were players but the rest gave it their full attention, each positioned so that he could watch the cards of at least one of them. Although voices were seldom raised quite a bit of laughter occurred, controlled laughter, barely audible beyond the smoke-area. One of the players was a man in late middle age by the name of Ralphie. He wore a bunnet and smoked a pipe. While he was tapping a fresh shot of tobacco into the pipebowl somebody told him to hurry up and get a move on, it was his shout. Ralphie nodded then nudged the youth sitting slightly behind him. This was Tammas; he lifted the cards immediately and sorted them out. You're going a big yin, he said.

Ralphie grinned and exhaled smoke from the corner of his mouth. He took the cards back.

You cant get beat, said Tammas, you're a certainty.

Ralphie laughed at his three opponents. Yous mob better be listening to this boy of mine's, he says I'm a certainty!

A few jeers in answer and then the game continued. About an hour on came the sound of somebody whistling loudly and the solo halted. The cards were covered by sheets of newspaper, the men sitting back on the benches. A couple of them rose, yawning and stretching. And the foreman appeared from behind a large machine; he entered the smoke-area carrying a cardboard box under his left arm. Missed yous again! He smiled: Never mind but, one of these days, one of these days.

He took the lid off the box, began issuing each person present with a wage packet. Once he had replaced the lid and was turning to leave a man called: Any news yet?

Nah, not a whisper . . . And without further comment the foreman walked out of the smoke-area, the box tucked beneath his arm.

Some of the men had their wage packets open and were checking the contents. Others had thrust them straight into their pockets without breaking the seal. And a general conversation started. Almost at once one of the former solo school rose from his seat and walked a couple of paces towards the exit. He was shaking his head. No use kidding yourselves, he muttered, if that bloody order's no in now it'll never be in.

The rest of the men were looking at him.

I'm talking about redundancies, he said, that's what I'm talking about. And yous better get bloody used to the idea.

One of the men shrugged: Ach well, we knew it was coming.

That's as maybe but they should've gave us notice. Formal. It's no as if they've told us anything. I mean all we're doing's fucking guessing and we shouldnt have to be fucking guessing!

Aye but they might no know for sure yet.

Hh! the man frowned then shook his head. He left the smoke-area. A silence followed. An elderly guy coughed and cleared his throat, dropped a mouthful of catarrh onto the concrete floor; he stroked at it carefully with the heel of his boot, at the same time withdrawing a cigarette packet from the bib pocket of his dungarees. Somebody else leaned to lift the newspaper sheets from the top of the table, gathered up the cards and began shuffling them briskly. Come on we'll finish the game! he said. Eh? might as well.

A spectator volunteered for the vacant playing spot but most of the others who had been watching seemed to have lost interest. And within ten minutes the game ended.

As the solo players got up to leave a couple of former spectators returned and some others were bringing out their wage packets once more. Ralphie took the pipe from his mouth and grunted, Yous and your fucking pontoons!

He was answered with jeers and a younger man lunged at him as though trying to knock off his bunnet. Ralphie dodged past, laughing.

Small piles of coins now lined the table and a man was shuffling the cards very thoroughly and now cutting them and cutting them again, and offering them to the guy sitting next to him so they could be cut yet again. And he dealt the cards, one to each person in the company. First jack takes the bank, he called.

Pontoons began. At the outset the stakes were restricted to a 50 pence maximum but the man holding the bank was also holding the initiative in this. Eventually the limit was raised to £1. Later it was scrapped altogether. The deal was now being held by the youth named Tammas. And as he shuffled the cards he shouted, Hey Ralphie – come on and post for me eh!

The older man had been sitting near to the exit in conversation with a couple of folk. He squinted across then grunted something and got onto his feet, rubbing at the small of his back and making groaning noises. He muttered, I hate this fucking pontoons. The sight of all that money flying about. Goes to my fucking head so it does!

A player laughed: You're just feart to open your wages ya auld cunt!

Others laughed. Ralphie glared at the man. You trying to say I'm henpecked or something? Aye well you're fucking right I am!

Tammas held out the cards for the former banker to cut. He said to the other players, Will yous space yourselves out a bit eh!

There was a bit of muttering in response. One of them grunted: Always the same when he gets the fucking deal. We've all got to change about just for his convenience.

Aye! Cause I like to watch what you're fucking doing with these cards!

Ralphie laughed.

One of the other men cried, It's that auld cunt you should be watching Tammas, no fucking us!

Tammas grinned while beginning to deal.

By 7.30 am most of the non-players, including Ralphie, had gone from the smoke-area to the washroom to get ready for clocking out. Some of the dayshift had arrived already. Two of them were involved in the pontoon game although not having received their wages yet their stakes were minimal. The bank had been won and lost many times since the start, and now it had landed back with Tammas. Within five minutes only two men were left in against him. The other had gone to prepare for going home while the two dayshift workers had lost their money and were now spectating. The first cards had been dealt and Tammas was lighting a cigarette while the bets were being made. One man put down £1 and the other put down £5. Then the second cards were dealt and the bank won both bets. The guy who had gambled the £5 shook his head and stubbed out the cigarette he was smoking. He glanced at the other player and frowned, shaking his head again.

From outside the smoke-area somebody shouted: That's the two-minute!

What . . . The man who had lost the £1 bet cried: Jesus Christ! and grabbed his money from the table; he paused to call: See yous on Monday!

Tammas glanced across at the remaining player. Time we were moving as well Murdie eh?

Aye okay, make the next yin the last.

Tammas nodded, he dealt the cards. Seconds later the dayshift chargehand came striding into the smoke-area and raising his right arm he jerked his thumb: Okay – out!

Last hand, muttered Murdie.

Last hand nothing, you'll get me fucking arrested.

The two dayshift men who had been spectating moved away from the table and the chargehand looked at the money lying between the players: it amounted to £20. He snorted and shook his head: I dont fucking believe this, yous pair must be crazy!

Last hand, said Tammas, surely we can play it out.

Naw, can you fuck.

Murdie sniffed, then he glanced round at him. Come on man eh? Give us a break.

The chargehand was silent for a couple of moments. Then he muttered, Stick that fucking dough out of sight . . . And he turned and walked out of the smoke-area. The two dayshift men had gone before him.

When they had taken the money off the table Murdie lifted his two cards, and asked for a twist, he was dealt a 10. He threw down the cards.

Tammas collected them in silence, left them on the centre of the table. He came out from behind the table and sat down on the bench next to Murdie, bending to take his shoes out from beneath it. He unknotted the laces on his boots, exchanged them for the shoes. Murdie had been doing likewise; now he paused a moment, and he said: Fancy a last hand?

Tammas looked at him.

Eh?

It's a waste of time man your luck's right out. Anyway, I'm still waiting for the twenty quid.

You're getting the twenty quid. Dont worry about it.

I'm no.

Murdie paused. Come on, he said, last hand.

Naw, no point.

No point! What d'you mean no point? the fucking money I've lost the night!

Tammas inhaled twice on his cigarette, the last deeply, and he laid it on the floor and ground it out beneath the sole of his shoe.

Okay, said Murdie, a cut. One cut – double or clear.

Naw.

Come on a cut, just one cut.

Christ sake Murdie.

Murdie was about to say something in reply but stopped. The dayshift teaboy had entered and was sitting noisily down on the edge of the bench near to the exit. He grinned over at them: Yous still here yet!

Naw, said Murdie, we're some fucking place else.

The chargie's standing down at the gaffer's office.

Murdie glanced at Tammas: Come on eh? one cut, double or clear.

After a moment Tammas shrugged. And Murdie nodded; and he reached for the cards from the table and he passed them to Tammas: It's still your deal.

Tammas shuffled quickly.

Plus a tenner, Murdie added.

Plus a tenner?

Aye . . . double or clear, plus a tenner.

Fuck sake.

Aw come on Tammas I'm losing a fortune, a fortune, no kidding ye.

Tammas shook his head but he shuffled again, and held the pack towards him. Murdie took it and cut immediately; showing a 3; and when Tammas cut an 8 to win his eyelids flickered shut and he made a sound which resembled a chuckle. The teaboy had been watching it all and now he took a step closer, and he said: Was that for thirty pound?

Neither answered. Tammas was already up from his seat and lifting down his jerkin from one of the nails on the wooden board attached to the wall above the table. And he also lifted the jacket hanging next to it and gave it to Murdie. They left the smoke-area together, walking the length of the section without speaking. Most of the machines were now in operation. At one of the silent ones a man was wiping down a flat bit with a paraffin soaked rag; he glanced at the two and laughed: Did yous sleep in!

They ignored him. They continued on to the timecard board and they clocked out without appearing to glance in the direction of the gaffer's office where the chargehand was standing; he had a cigarette in his mouth, he inhaled and took it out of his mouth, blowing smoke towards the floor. On through the doorway they walked down the sloping corridor, down into the yard and across to the big gate at the works' entrance. They passed out by the window of the timekeeper's office.

When they reached the street they slowed then halted on the pavement. Murdie made as if to speak but he sniffed instead, he stayed silent. A group of primary schoolchildren and three women was approaching. Once they had gone he sniffed again, before saying: I've not got the full thirty Tammas.

Aw Christ.

I thought I did have.

Tammas turned away.

Okay if I owe you it?

What d'you mean the full thirty?

Murdie nodded.

Aw for fuck sake man.

Honest Tammas I just . . .

Tammas turned away from him, he strode down towards the main road. A bus was standing at the traffic lights. He broke into a run for the nearest bus stop.

•••

One of Betty's wee brothers answered the door and shouted back inside: It's him! Come in Mister.

Tammas followed him along the lobby into the front room. The other brother and Betty's two younger sisters grinned at him then stared back at the television. The first boy rushed in and then back out again, and he was shouting: He's got a wee box of chocolates with him. Hey Betty, he's got a wee box of chocolates with him.

The younger sister turned round to say, She's ben the room doing herself up.

He nodded.

She takes ages.

Will I take her in the chocolates? asked the boy.

Ha ha, said Tammas. And then you eat them!

Naw I wouldnt.

Aye you would, said the girl.

Naw I wouldnt.

I'll give her them myself, said Tammas. He brought out a packet of cigarettes and he lighted one. The older girl suddenly rose from the settee and switched channels, and sat down immediately, gazing at the screen. Tammas got an ashtray from the top of a glass display cabinet and he drew over a dining chair to sit on; then the sound of the first boy running along the lobby floor and in he came.

She says she's just coming Mister.

Ta.

The boy grinned and stood where he was for a few moments, before walking to the edge of the settee and bouncing down on it next to the girls. The older one cried: William!

He jumped off, laughing, and sat down on the floor. The other girl and boy were also laughing and they turned to look at Tammas who shook his head and smiled. He put his hand in his trouser pocket and took out some loose change which he held out to the older boy. Here son, he said, away and get a couple of bottles of ginger and some packets of crisps.

The boy grinned with his mouth shut tightly and he made a face at the younger sister when he stood up from the settee. Once he had left the room the first boy jumped up from the floor and said: Can I go with him Mister?

Okay.

The boy laughed and rushed out after the other one. The outside door banged shut soon after. Minutes later Betty entered; she walked to behind the settee and placed her hand on the back of it. What's on? she asked.

The older girl replied, Nothing. That film was rubbish.

Anything coming on after?

The girl shrugged; the other one made no response at all. But then the two of them glanced quickly at each other, they were grinning. Betty turned and said to Tammas, Coming ben?

When they were outside in the lobby she closed the door and whispered, Listen Tammas I'm awful sorry but I've got to stay in the night and babysit.

Aw.

My mammy and daddy asked if I would and I said aye – they've no been out for ages. But I thought it would be alright. We can go in the bedroom; the record player's in there . . . She looked at him.

Och that's fine Betty.

Are you sure?

Aye, it's fine. Here. He gave her the chocolates and she leaned to him, they kissed briefly.

An electric fire was on in the bedroom and the record player sat on a chair beside it; a selection of LP's were on the bed and the floor, and Betty put one to play. When the music started she turned to him and they kissed until the outside door banged open and shut. The footsteps down the lobby was followed by voices coming back the way and then the bedroom door opened.

Tammas dropped his hands immediately. It was the two boys. Betty cried: Dont come barging in here without chapping!

The older one held up the two bottles and the other one was carrying the crisps. Tammas nodded. Away ben and share it out, he said.

You no wanting any?

Naw.

What about you Betty?

No, just go through.

When the door was shut he smiled at her and moved nearer. They were standing beside the electric fire and soon they had to move away; they sat down together on the edge of the bed, arms round each other's waist. Betty said, Are you sure you dont mind staying in?

Naw, honest. He kissed her on the cheek. She leaned her head on his shoulder and he moved to kiss her on the lips; they remained kissing for a while.

Someone was tapping on the door. Betty moved slightly but they continued to kiss. The tapping became louder. It was Tammas who broke away. That's the door, he said.

God sake . . . She walked to the door and jerked it open.

William knocked over his ginger! cried the youngest girl. It was on top of the mantelpiece and he was reaching up!

Betty made no answer. She continued standing there for several seconds. Then she turned and said, I'll be back in a minute Tammas.

When the door was shut she could be heard asking if the tumbler had smashed.

There was a travelling clock on the dressing table. Nearly 8 pm. He got up from the bed, walked to the window, pulled the curtains aside to see out and down the three storeys to the street below. It was now dusk, rain drizzling. He closed the curtains. He looked at himself in the mirror of the wardrobe door, patted his hair down. In the ashtray his cigarette had burned away and the grey ash was about threequarters of an inch in length. He took two drags on it before stubbing it out.

By the time Betty returned another LP was playing and he was sitting on the bed browsing through the sleevenotes on the various covers. I'm really sorry Tammas. She said, It's that wee bugger William. I ended up having to put him to his bed. He's a bloody pain so he is.

Mm.

You never get any peace in this house at all.

Tammas nodded. He opened his cigarette packet and lighted

one. Betty shook her head: You dont know how lucky you are. Sometimes I feel like running away. Just packing my bags and going away, going away from here altogether.

She sat down beside him and he put his arm round her shoulders. And she continued speaking: I've got an Auntie lives in England. She was up in the summer for a visit and she was telling me there was plenty of jobs down there if I ever felt like trying it.

Hh, whereabouts?

Torquay.

Is that no just seasonal work?

No, all the year round.

I never knew that, I thought it was just hotels.

No.

They were silent for a short while. Tammas leaned across to nip his cigarette into the ashtray, leaving the remainder on the side to be smoked later. He grinned: Did the tumbler smash right enough?

It was a china cup! Mammy'll kill him . . . She smiled, put her hand to her mouth and bit at the corner of her thumbnail. She smiled again and added. What like were you when you were a boy?

Terrible.

Honest?

What! Terrible! No kidding ye Betty!

I dont believe you.

I was – ask my sister!

Well I will!

Good! Tammas grinned at her and inclined his head to kiss her on the lips.

She moved away quite soon and she said, It was their fault anyhow because they shouldnt've let him take one of the china cups.

He nodded.

•••

The runners were at the post for the 2.15 at Lingfield. He was standing gazing up at the names of the horses listed on the board. The latest betting show had just come through the speaker and the elderly boardman was still marking up the price changes. Then Donnie appeared in the doorway. He rushed straight over and grabbed Tammas by the elbow, kicking the holdall bag that stood between his feet. Come on ya bastard!

Hang on a minute.

No time man come on they're nearly fucking away... Donnie bent and lifted the bag and pushed him on the other side of the shoulder. Tammas glared at him and strode off to the counter, scribbled out a bet and passed it beneath the grille to the cashier who returned him the receipt when he had paid across the money.

Donnie was holding the door open. They raced along to the subway station, in time to see the others disappear round a corner beyond the ticket office.

Down at the platform a subway was in and they clattered aboard just before the gates shut. The rest of the team was sitting along at the top end of the compartment. Following Donnie down Tammas sat next to him on the side away from the others. Donnie was pointing him out to the man in charge of the team and saying, This is the guy I was telling you about, plays in the midfield, or wherever.

The man glanced along at him and so did some of the team

members. He took out a cigarette and lighted it, he gazed at the floor while exhaling smoke.

Forty minutes later they were at the park and having to rush into the dressing rooms to get changed. The opposing team passed them on their way out.

When Donnie had his strip on he began fixing an elastic bandage round his left knee and he whispered, I'll see him in a minute.

Tammas nodded. He was sitting on the bench with the team stockings and the pants on but had yet to be thrown a jersey. He reached into his jerkin pocket for the cigarette packet, but left it there.

Soon most of the team had gone. Donnie came back. The man in charge was walking towards the exit. Donnie muttered, You've to go sub man sorry.

Aw fuck.

Donnie was silent for a moment. It's your own fault; he chose the team at the station.

Tammas looked at him.

He's just after telling me . . . Donnie pointed to the exit. Christ sake Tammas if you hadnt been fucking about in the bookie's you'd probably've got picked. You were too late.

Too late! I was first there.

Aye well you should've stayed there; that's what I'm saying, he didnt know. How could he if he didnt fucking see you?

You told me I would get a game Donnie.

Well what can I do man? I cant do fuck all . . . He shook his head and turned away, then he indicated the large suitcase in the centre of the floor. Number 12's in there, he said. And he grinned. Come on Tammas ya bastard, stick it on immediately. If he doesnt give you a game before half time I'll strangle him!

Fuck off.

Donnie had reached into the bag and he threw Tammas the jersey, and he laughed. I always collapse at half time anyway, so you can come on in my place!

About midway through the first 45 minutes Tammas zipped up his jerkin to as high as it went, hunching his shoulders. The wind was fierce. And that coupled with the sharp slope from sideline to sideline was causing the ball to travel on long distances whenever miskicked with any force. In company with the substitute from the other team Tammas was having to go chasing after it every few minutes. A couple of old men and wee boys were also there helping. On one occasion he had to run fast to stop the ball interfering with the game on the next pitch and when he ran back the teams were waiting for him and Donnie was there on the touchline ready to take the throw-in. Tammas gave him the ball and muttered, Fuck ye Donnie ya bastard.

Donnie seemed not to have heard. He moved to take the throw-in. Tammas stuck his hands in his side jerkin pockets, he took out his cigarettes. The other substitute approached him. Hey jimmy, he said, you got a fag you could give us?

Tammas nodded and gave him one, and offered him the matches.

Ta . . . He indicated the man in charge of the other team: He doesnt like us smoking when we're playing.

Silly cunt, said Tammas.

The other guy nodded, he was concentrating on getting a match to stay alight long enough to get the cigarette going. Eventually Tammas passed him his own and he got a light from it.

It was nothing each at the interval. When the players came off the man handed round a pile of orange quarters. Tammas left them and strolled onto the park where the other substitute was kicking the ball about with the boys and the elderly men. He kept his hands in his jerkin pockets but trotted over to get the ball when it was passed to him. Then he saw Donnie waving to him and he trotted back. Donnie said: Has he no told you anything yet?

Naw.

Hh, he's not told me anything either.

Tammas nodded, then he grunted: He's no even fucking spoke to me.

Ach. Donnie shook his head. We could be doing with you too, that number 6 we've got's a fucking dumpling.

Tammas sniffed.

I dont really know the guy well enough to eh . . . to say anything. What like is it watching?

Ha ha. Tammas turned and spat onto the pitch.

Donnie chuckled.

The referee was returning to the centre circle; he paused on the way to uplift the ball.

That fucking rain better stay off, muttered Tammas.

The teams were now returning and the referee had placed the ball on the spot and was checking his watch. When Donnie had gone Tammas strolled down the touchline, passing the man in charge of the team, to stand some twenty yards away from him. But less than ten minutes later he walked back to him and said, Listen eh I want to go to the dressing room a minute. I've left something there and that and eh . . . Is the door locked or what?

The man nodded, his attention on the game.

After a few moments Tammas asked: Will I be allowed in okay?

What? What's that? The man frowned.

Have you got the key? to the dressing room?

To the dressing room! Naw, naw son you've got to see the caretaker.

Aw aye. Tammas sniffed. He continued standing watching the game. The winger of the opposing team had the ball and was cutting in towards the corner of the 18 yard line; a player came to meet him and the ball eventually ran loose and was collected by the keeper who kicked it high, and the wind carried it and it bounced out for another throw-in from the touchline opposite. He turned away and blew his nose through his fingers, wiping his nostrils on his wrist; he headed off to the dressing room.

...

Simpson's Bar was crowded. Moving between the bodies he ordered a pint of heavy and carried it to a group seated at the far side. Donnie was standing next to the table, nearby the darts' board and when he saw his approach he roared: Look who's here! The famous vanishing substitute!

Tammas grinned; he sat down on the fringe of the company.

So he isnt skint after all! laughed Billy.

Detained in a betting shop! laughed somebody else.

Ah shite, said Tammas.

A mixture of jeers and laughter greeted this. It was followed almost immediately by a loud roar from the darts game; a match had just ended. One of the guys at the board there shouted the initials of the next player. And while he was rising and crossing the floor the person in question pounded the air with his right fist.

Tammas drank a mouthful of beer and asked, What's happening?

Rab replied, Happening? What d'you mean happening – nothing's happening apart from a chinky, we're all going for a chinky.

I mean the arrangements man, Blackpool.

Hey Donnie will you listen to the boy here! Stoating in at 9 o'clock and he's wanting to know about arrangements! Arrangements by fuck!

Donnie shouted: We're going for a chinky!

O Christ! Tammas shook his head and raised his beer glass.

See what I mean? Rab laughed. You're too late man – everybody's steamboats.

John leaned over the table: We've booked in bed and breakfast Tammas. Seven pound a night and we're lucky to get it. Usually well booked up before the end of August according to the woman, the landlady. That's how it's so dear.

Aye, said Rab, nudging Tammas, there's a guy in John's work could've got us a place at half the price.

All I'm saying's what he told me.

Aye well you fucking tell him to give us the address man and then we'll see.

What is it yous're paying? somebody asked.

Seven notes.

And that's just for bed and breakfast, added John. On top of that we'll have our dinner and tea to pay.

Billy sniffed. That's right enough. And then we've got snacks and bevy on top of that again.

Aye and our fucking travelling expenses, called Donnie.

True. Plus if we back a few losers and all that I mean who the fuck's going to pay that!

John shook his head. You cant get fucking talking in this place.

It's only because you talk so much shite John . . . muttered Rab.

Aye do I!

Aye, laughed Billy.

Tammas had opened a new packet of cigarettes and he offered them about the company. He said to Rab: Saw the result in the paper man – great stuff. Is that yous through to the next round then?

Quarter finals . . . Rab shrugged. And he added, What about the eh . . . you wanting to give us a few quid or what?

A tenner, aye. Tammas withdrew the money and handed it to him. Is that okay?

Well it's up to you man but you're still a wee bit behind. Rab folded the notes and put it into his hip pocket. He had a notebook in his inside jacket pocket and he flipped through the pages, entered in the details, and added, Even Billy stuck in a score!

The others laughed.

Billy called: What d'you mean ya bastard ye!

Nothing, nothing . . . As Rab was returning the notebook into his pocket he said quietly to Tammas, You alright man?

What . . . aye, Christ – I just want to have it all in front of me at the time and that, see how I'm fixed for everything man, see what's what.

Rab nodded.

Some choice . . .

What?

Naw I mean the chinky and that, a Saturday night.

Billy called: A couple of the boys are going up the dancing.

Aye, said Donnie, if you'd been in earlier ya cunt we might've got something organised.

Organised! We can fucking do it the now.

Naw we cant, too late.

Tammas shook his head. Think I'll start going back to Shawfield.

You kidding!

Naw, this Saturday night routine man it's fucking murder.

Aye okay but the dogs! Jesus Christ! You must've a short memory man!

Cause you go to the dogs doesnt mean you have to have a bet Donnie. Plenty of people go there just to watch the actual racing.

Aw aye! Donnie laughed and reached for his beer.

Rab said, Bad enough going to the dump but what like would it be without having a punt? Naw no me Tammas I'd rather have a few jars. And I mean imagine being over the night!

I know, cried Donnie, it's fucking pissing down out there. You wind up going skint man and having to hoof it back up the road cause you've no got the price of a fucking bus ticket!

Tammas was grinning. Hey wait a minute Donnie they give you credit fares remember!

No for Shawfield punters they dont! That's fucking all stopped!

Lying bastard.

The others laughed. Rab said: It'll no affect Tammas anyway. He's just wanting to go and watch!

Aye well it's better than fucking sitting here all night!

I agree, called John.

Nobody's forcing you, Rab answered. He sniffed and lifted his beer, sipped at it while gazing in the direction of the darts' match.

Donnie agreed. We're fighting again, he muttered. Then he rose and added, I'm away for a pish out the road!

There was a brief silence. John turned to Tammas: Ever thought about emigrating?

Emigrating? Course.

Whereabouts?

Any fucking place!

Naw it's just . . . John shrugged. An auld guy in the work, he was saying you dont need to pay if you're under 21 years of age.

John! Billy was shaking his head at him: I keep telling you man that's a load of fucking rubbish.

How do you know?

How do I know!

For one thing, said Rab, Donnie would've told us, cause his da would've fucking found out right at the beginning.

Aye but you're talking about New Zealand.

Australia or New Zealand ya cunt it doesnt matter.

Doesnt matter! Australia or New Zealand!

No for this it doesnt.

What! You trying to say it's the same thing? Australia or New Zealand?

Course I'm no trying to fucking say it's the same fucking thing! Rab gazed at the ceiling and cried: Aw Jesus!

Well it's two different countries man.

Tammas nodded. He's got a point but, the John fellow, Australia and New Zealand man – two different countries! I mean he's right enough.

Rab and Billy laughed. And Billy added. He still doesnt want to go – Donnie.

Ah he's off his head, I'd go in a minute.

Rab swivelled on his seat, seeing Donnie coming from the *gents*, and he called: Hey Donnie, this cunt says you're off your head!

What have I done now?

New Zealand!

Fuck New Zealand! If they send over Ibrox Park I might consider it.

Billy grinned and jerked his thumb at John: This yin's trying to tell us New Zealand and Australia's the same fucking country.

It's no, said Donnie.

Bastards, grunted John, lifting his pint and swallowing a big mouthful. Then he said to Tammas, If you're really interested man I'm thinking of sending away for the details . . .

I thought you were wanting to go to London! laughed Billy.

John looked at him.

Sorry!

Aye well no wonder – you cant get fucking talking in this place!

I agree, said Donnie, give the boy a break for fuck sake.

Hey . . . Tammas exhaled smoke and sat forwards, leaning an elbow on the edge of the table. A suggestion!

Aw naw! cried Rab.

Serious. Tammas sniffed before continuing: Mind that club place I was telling yous about? Where they played cards and that?

Ho! Rab shook his head.

Naw wait a minute . . .

Ho! Rab was pushing his chair back the way and standing to his feet, and he placed one hand on Donnie's shoulder and the other on Billy's, and bending slightly he whispered loudly: Dont listen to one word the cunt says cause it'll fucking cost you! He laughed and strode off in the direction of the *gents*.

Is it that casino you're talking about? asked John.

Aye I mean Christ . . . Tammas shrugged: I was just wondering if anybody'd fancy giving it a go.

John nodded.

If I had a couple of quid . . . Billy shook his head.

Actually man you dont need that much.

You need more than I've got Tammas. Anyhow, they're all fucking sharks in places like that!

Ach away.

You kidding!

Naw for fuck sake Billy they're just ordinary.

Aw aye, ordinary!

Ordinary, aye.

Well that's no what I've heard man – lucky to get walking out alive if you win a few bob!

Dont be silly.

I'm no fucking being silly.

John nodded. I could believe it Tammas.

Ah rubbish! I saw guys walking out when I was there.

Donnie glanced at him. I didnt know you'd actually been inside the place.

Aye. Tammas sniffed.

Billy said, But did you see them walking out winning a lot of dough? And I'm talking about going down the stairs and right out the fucking close.

Billy, the place isnt up a fucking close.

You know what I mean.

I dont, I dont know what you mean at all.

Tch! Billy shook his head and he looked away.

And after a moment's silence John said, It'd be okay but if a few of us went the gether I mean, if we were team handed and that, we'd be okay.

Aye John . . . Donnie raised his eyebrows and lifted his pint.

Tammas laughed.

I'm being serious but, replied John. The kind of guys go about these clubs man they probably carry shooters and all that!

That's shite.

It might not be, said Billy.

Tammas frowned at him.

Naw I mean I wouldnt be too sure.

Ach away for fuck sake Billy.

Naw Tammas . . .

Shooters!

Shooters! What's this, shooters? Rab laughed as he sat back down on his chair. I cant leave yous for a minute for Christ sake shooters! What're yous fucking on about now? Shooters!

Ask them, said Tammas.

Donnie grinned. Tammas is wanting to go to a casino.

I'm no wanting to go to a fucking casino man it's a club, just a fucking club, where they play cards.

A gambling club . . . Rab nodded. Tammas ya bastard if you can afford to go to a fucking gambling club you can afford to weigh us in with a bit fucking more of your Blackpool money.

Exactly! shouted Billy.

Fuck off, muttered Tammas. He stood up and looked about the table, then finished the remainder of his beer. I'm away to buy myself a pint before I die of thirst.

Rain was drizzling down when they came out of the pub, heading along in the direction of Billy's place. They had chipped in for a carry out of beer which John was holding. As they passed a side street Donnie halted, he sniffed aloud. Chips!

Billy cried: Donnie, I keep telling you, my maw'll stick us on a big pot of soup.

Aye, aye, so what, I'll no stop her! Donnie grinned and made to walk off round the corner. Sure none of yous're interested?

Naw, said Rab, you're the only one as usual ya greedy bastard!

Donnie laughed, patted himself on the belly; he disappeared round the corner. Farther along they paused by a shop window; the interior lights were on to display the goods. John placed the carrier bag of beer on the ground inside the shop doorway and stood with it balanced upright between his feet. It's that big belly he's got . . . Donnie I mean, he's got more to fill than us.

Billy nodded. He's putting the weight on.

It's just the bevy, said Tammas. But fair enough, he has slowed down hell of a lot. I noticed that this afternoon at the football.

Ach he was always slow, said Rab. He turned and cleared his throat and spat out into the street.

Still a good player.

Aye but too slow, just too fucking slow . . . Rab put his hands into his trouser pockets and stepped sideways, leaning against the shop window with his shoulder.

After a moment John said: What soup is it?

What soup is it? How the fuck do I know! Billy grinned and shook his head.

Well I hope it's no minestrone. All these wee bits of stuff floating about.

Rab said, You're a dickie ya cunt ye!

Ah well you dont fucking know what you're eating man that's what I dont like.

You're thinking of curry, said Tammas.

Thinking of curry! Billy roared.

Tammas laughed and he made a move as though to punch Billy; then they both crouched to face each other, fists raised.

Seconds away!

Tammas and Billy circled each other.

Hey yous!

Two policemen were standing on the other side of the street. They stepped off the pavement and strolled across. One of them said to Tammas: What's up then?

Eventually Tammas replied, Nothing.

What d'you mean nothing?

We were just kidding.

Just kidding?

Aye, said Billy, honest.

Tammas added, We're waiting on somebody.

The policeman glanced at his companion: They're waiting on somebody.

Mmm . . . The other policeman nodded.

Honest, said Tammas, he's just round the corner for a bag of chips man he'll no be a minute.

Bag of chips man he'll no be a minute. The first policeman smiled at Tammas: What is that? a bag of chips man . . . Heh, he said to the other policeman, d'you know what that is? a bag of chips man. What is it, is it the same as a black pudding?

The other policeman smiled and then he gazed at the carrier bag, and looked at John. John lifted the carrier bag and handed it over to him. The policeman gazed inside; he moved the cans about. When he handed it back to John he said, On your way.

But the mate'll be here in a minute, replied Tammas.

On your way I said, move!

He's just round the corner in the bloody chip shop! cried Rab.

What . . . what was that? The first policeman frowned and he stepped closer to Rab. What was that? What d'you say there? I never really heard you right son what was it?

Rab looked away.

Naw I thought you might've swore there son but I'm no sure. Did you I mean? Did you swear?

After a moment the other policeman asked: Where d'you stay?

Just along the road, said Billy.

I'm no asking you I'm asking him. The policeman pointed to Rab. It's you I'm asking.

Rab sniffed. He was standing away from the window now. He replied, Scotstoun.

Scotstoun. Fine, right, the bus-stop's over the road.

Aye but he's coming up to my house, said Billy.

Naw he's no, no the night he's no, he's changed his mind, he's just going home.

I'm no, said Rab.

Aye you are, you've changed your mind.

I have not changed my mind.

The first policeman grinned: He's steamboats anyhow, look at him, he can hardly stand.

If you ask me they're all steamboats . . . The policeman shook his head. He glanced at Rab: What's wrong? Can you no hold your drink or something?

Tammas stepped over, nearby Rab, and he said to him: Come on man time we were moving.

I'll tell you something, said the policeman, it's time yous were all moving; and if yous are no out of here in five minutes flat I'll do the lot of yous. Ye listening now? D'yous understand?

After a brief silence the other policeman gestured with his thumb: On your way.

Move! said the first one. Then his attention was attracted to John who was pointing along the street. Donnie had appeared. He was walking quite quickly, then he slowed. He was holding the bag of fish and chips in his left hand and in his right he held a chip. He continued on towards them, putting the chip into his mouth.

John said, It's the mate.

Just keep walking, grunted the policeman, just keep walking. And yous go with him, and dont stop, dont even look back.

Tammas nudged Rab with his elbow and the five of them continued on along the street in silence. It was Donnie who spoke first. What the fuck happened?

Billy replied, Tell you in the house.

Dirty bastards, muttered Rab, the dirty fucking bastards.

Tammas nodded. I'm leaving this dump man I'm definitely leaving, definitely fucking leaving.

Okay Tammas you can take my place! Donnie gestured at him with a chip and grinned: You go to New Zealand and I'll just stay here.

Rab swivelled round and grabbed him by the shoulder and shouted: You dont go to New Zealand man and I'll fucking have ye, I'll fucking have ye man . . .

What! Donnie moved forwards, turning and picking off his hand: What d'you say ya cunt?

You fucking heard what I said!

Aye I fucking heard alright!

Ya bastard . . .

What? Donnie was glaring at him, the bag of chips and fish clutched in his left hand.

This is fucking hopeless, cried Billy.

Well what's up with him then? shouted Donnie.

He just had bother with the fucking polis! Tammas said, Did you no notice?

Donnie glanced at him, then poked himself on the chest: Well he shouldnt get fucking onto me that's all I'm fucking saying.

Tammas nodded.

John said, Come on, we better go, just in case they come.

I agree, said Billy.

You always fucking agree, muttered Tammas.

Aye, just get onto me now.

What?

Well, fuck sake . . .

Tammas looked at him. Then he added, Right, sorry; sorry.

Let's just go up the house out the road.

Tammas nodded.

Donnie said, I think I'll just go home.

Naw you're no, you're fucking coming – eh Tammas?

Tammas smiled.

Come on, said Rab. Donnie . . . I shouldnt've fucking . . . He sniffed: Sorry about that. I mean I shouldnt've fucking . . . He shook his head.

Donnie nodded, he squashed the bag of fish and chips into a ball and he threw it into the gutter.

•••

They travelled by hoist up to the 2nd floor. It was quiet here, hardly any machinery. Most of the workers were female. A transistor radio was playing pop music. Ralphie grinned and nudged Tammas; they walked in the direction of the foreman's office, down between rows of long workbenches where women were cutting rectangular sections out of ragged, flat pieces of plastic, the discarded bits being tossed into wide containers beneath the benches. Ralphie paused by one of the women for a chat. Beside her two girls were working and talking together while slicing through the plastic with short stubby knives.

They continued on to the office. Ralphie chapped the door and opened it and entered immediately. The foreman had been studying sheets of paper. He squinted up at them and said: It's yourself Ralphie?

Aye.

Hh! So how's life?

No bad, no bad. Wee McCreadie's retired.

I heard, I heard. He'll be dead in a month!

Ralphie smiled.

Shouldnt say that I suppose! The foreman raised his eyebrows; he folded his arms then sat back on his chair. So . . . what can I do for you?

Ralphie shrugged. Me and the boy here were told to report to you.

Were you? Hh, well well well. He unfolded his arms and sat forwards again, took a tipped cigarette from the packet on the desk; and when he had it alight he sat back, resting his elbows on the chair-arms. He said: Know who I saw last week?

Ralphie shook his head.

Thompson. Mind of him?

Thompson?

Over your way he worked.

Eh . . .

Big heavy set kind of fellow.

Thompson?

Aye, no mind of him?

Eh . . . naw, cant say I do, cant say I do, to be honest.

The foreman grinned. You're getting auld son you're getting auld!

Thanks a lot!

Naw, so . . . The foreman leaned forwards and said: Yous've lost the Belgian order eh! Pity, pity.

Ralphie shrugged.

So what d'you do now?

Ah they're talking about the nightshift coming off for good.

Are they? Aye, I heard that.

Ralphie nodded.

Aye, it's a game! So, yous've to report to me eh! He glanced at Tammas. It must be the shifting they want you on. Nothing else I can think of. The two of yous Ralphie, on the shifting, the lassies' bins – got to shift them out the road when they get full otherwise they cant get working properly. He paused and he took a long drag on his cigarette. When he exhaled he blew the smoke onto the desk, scattering ash from out the ashtray. You take the bins out the back yard, he said. You'll see the pitch when you get there. Okay?

Okay, aye . . . Ralphie paused then turned to leave.

The foreman said: So how d'you fancy this neck of the woods?

In here you mean?

Aye . . . The foreman winked. The lassies and that . . . They're good workers mind you, I'll say that for them!

Ralphie nodded. I know what you mean. By the way, I take it we use a bogie or something?

O aye, aye. You'll get one up in the storeroom maybe, or out in the yard. And Ralphie, mind the bins – you know what like they are in this bloody place! Steal the braces off your trousers if you gave them the chance!

On their way back down between the row of benches Ralphie paused to say something to the woman he had spoken to earlier but she contorted her face and continued to stare at the plastic in front of her, and she whispered: Dont look now but he's keeking out the window!

O Jesus Christ . . . Ralphie smothered a laugh and they walked on at once.

At the top end of the section the two girls were now assisting another woman load a flat trolley with cut plastic sections. The woman said something to them and they laughed loudly.

The hoist arrived and Tammas pulled open the gates; and when Ralphie stepped inside he closed the gates, and pressed the button for the ground floor.

Behind the rear yard the factory was bound by a canal. There were thick clusters of nettles, different sorts of weeds, some growing to enormous heights; twisted in amongst the roots were barbed wire, other wire, strips of plastic and various kinds of rubbish. On the canal surface more rubbish lay trapped in a mixture of oils and solvents.

Ralphie was stuffing tobacco into the bowl of his pipe. Seated between him and Tammas was an elderly guy by the name of Benny who chainsmoked hand-rolled cigarettes. They were sitting on old piping, with their backs resting against the boiler room wall. Benny was the boilerman. When he had lighted a new cigarette he pointed to a part of the canal and said to Tammas: Just there son. I've seen that wee teuchter who works in the blacksquad catch a perch as big as your arm with a bit of wire and a bent pin. Aye and I'm no fucking kidding either – eh Ralph?

Aye.

Tammas nodded.

See son the canal's stowed out with fish. They're no like us at all I mean fuck sake if we fell in we wouldnt fucking drown, we'd die of dipfuckingtheria, but no the fish, not only do they survive they fucking thrive. That right Ralph?

Ralphie nodded. At one time they used to send folk down from the university.

That's right son. See what they were doing, they were experimenting with the oil the fish has inside its body. It's to do with their gut, they've got some fucking thing allows them to separate the good out from the bad.

Hh. Tammas rose from where he was sitting and he stretched and yawned, then sat back down and yawned again: Wonder what time it is?

The back of two, said Benny.

What?

I would say about 5 past.

Christ, it must be more than that surely?

Naw.

Fuck sake!

My watch is through there if you want to check.

Ralphie was smiling. No patience Benny, these young yins nowadays. Same with that fucking Belgian order – they're all up to high doh worrying about it as well. I dont see the point myself.

You're right. I mean it'd be a different story if it affected the whole fucking place but it doesnt, just one fucking section.

Aye, said Ralphie, ours!

Ah well that's as maybe; could be yours could be mine's.

Ralphie chuckled. How could it be yours ya auld fucking fox ye! The boiler room! That's the last place to go. And well you fucking know it!

Naw I'm just saying but Ralph I'm just saying.

Ralphie smiled and shook his head. He put the pipe back into his mouth and sucked, but it had stopped burning. He took out his matches.

Ah! Tammas got onto his feet again and put his hands on his hips and stretched.

Cant keep still a minute!

I'm getting stiff sitting down.

Ralphie shook his head, he struck the match he was holding and began getting his pipe going.

You can blame your football, said Benny. You're talking about being stiff sitting down son it's cause of your football, that's what you should fucking blame. That's the cause of it. Yous all go running about daft every dinner time and then yous stop all of a sudden, and your muscles dont cope, they just fucking stiffen up. Same as these athletes. Their bodies are all highly tuned up. So they've got to run a fucking race cause they've been training. See if they dont son, their fucking bodies, their muscles, they all get fucking knotted up. And sometimes they can wind up catching the flu out it.

Tammas nodded. He took a half smoked cigarette from behind his ear and he struck a match against the brickwork.

•••

He sat down with the *Evening Times* before lighting the cigarette, turned down the volume of the radio a little. Then he laid the paper on the table and placed his elbows on it, resting his chin on his thumbs, his hands covering the front of his face. The sound he made was half sigh, half groan. Withdrawing his hands abruptly he sat back on the chair and stretched his arms, the fingers of each hand outspread; the cigarette fell and he snatched it from out of his groin. The kettle was whistling. He used the boiling water to top up the bowl containing dirty cutlery and dishes and he washed them all and then dried them. He went through to the living room where his sister was watching television. At half past seven he got up from where he was sitting, he strolled to the window and gazed out.

There's a good film coming on, she said, spies or something.

Aw aye, good. I'll be back later.

In his own room he lay on the bed with his hands clasped beneath the back of his head. He stared at the ceiling for a while. Eventually he turned onto his side to reach for the book that was lying on top of the adjacent cupboard but he did not open the pages, he lay back down again with his eyelids shut.

A knock on the door roused him. It was Margaret, asking if he wanted a coffee. He glanced at the clock while telling her to come in.

Coffee?

Eh aye . . . aye Margaret, thanks.

D'you want it ben here?

He shrugged then added: Aye, ta.

She had turned and was going back out when he called, Eh Margaret.

She paused, looked at him.

Any chance of a pound till Friday?

She smiled. I knew it – after you getting everything up to date at the weekend; I knew you would leave yourself short. You didnt have to give me so much.

I thought I would've lasted.

I'll bring it with the coffee.

It's okay, he said getting down from the bed. And he followed her to the kitchen. She opened her bag and took out her purse. After she had given him the £1 she lifted the kettle to fill it from the tap. But he said, Dont bother Margaret, I think I'll just nick out for a pint.

I thought it was for your work.

Ah well I've got to see Billy and that about Blackpool, some arrangements still to be sorted out.

She frowned briefly, and added: There's more to life than *Simpson's* pub you know.

Tammas had stepped to the doorway and he stood there with his hand on the handle. Just a pint, he said.

She sighed, shook her head.

I'll no be long.

Well . . . she nodded: I dont suppose you'd get very far on a pound.

Thanks Margaret. He pushed open the door, and closed it behind him. But she called his name and he opened it again, remaining outside in the lobby.

Tammas . . .

Aye?

You need to go a bit easy you know.

Mm. He sniffed then nodded and closed the door.

•••

He took the remaining cheese piece out of the greaseproof wrapping paper and ate it slowly. There were no conversations in progress. The men were eating or smoking, reading the morning newspapers or staring at the floor or the wall or the ceiling. Sitting next to Tammas the man turned the pages of the *Daily Record* and kept them open at the racing section. Tammas gazed at it and eventually the man moved the paper a little nearer for him.

Anybody for a game of solo? called the teaboy. He was sitting at the table with the cards spread out in a game of clock patience. When nobody answered him he called: Trump?

A man sitting near him said, Sssh.

Tammas finished the sandwich. He screwed the wrapping paper into a ball, chipped it in the air, to land in the big cardboard box where the litter was dumped. He looked back at the newspaper. The man was indicating one of the day's runners and saying, I'm sick of punting this fucking bastard here – owes me a fortune so it does.

Ah it's a bad yin.

You're no kidding. I saw it on the telly a couple of weeks ago. Looked like it was going to win a distance then everyfuckingthing came and passed it.

Tammas nodded.

Should've won out of the fucking park so it should – terrible!

I saw it as well: said another guy. But I had a wee hunch the jockey dropped the reins.

Ah they all drop the fucking reins! said somebody from the bench opposite.

Here we go! muttered the man next to Tammas. And he pointed to another runner. Darktown Lad, he said, What I want to know is how come they're fucking running it in a handicap the day when they stuck it into a fucking seller last week!

Aye, said Tammas, maybe a move on.

Exactly. He shook his head: Best to leave the race alone altogether.

The man from the bench opposite cried: Wish to fuck you'd leave them all alone ya cunt – save you tapping me every time you go skint!

Fuck off.

Fuck off yourself!

The man closed the newspaper and brought out a cigarette packet and he lighted one and returned the packet into his pocket, then he opened the newspaper again.

One of the others yawned and stood to his feet, glanced at his watch and said: I suppose I suppose. Time to do a bit.

Somebody laughed: Listen to him! He's been out getting a suntan on the fucking canal bank all morning!

I'll tell you something, if you want to go out there picking up bits of fucking plastic then you're welcome; I'll fucking swop you any day of the week. Fucking boring man! I'm bored out my head!

Ah, cushy number.

Cushy number! The man shook his head; he turned to the bench and lifted his newspaper and tobacco tin, and then walked out the smoke-area. Gradually the others began to leave.

Tammas said quietly to the man sitting next to him: You got a fag you could lend us?

The man nodded, he brought out the packet and handed it to him.

After dinner Ralphie and Tammas reported to the front yard where a lorry had arrived. The driver climbed down from the cabin and began unloosening the ropes; it was a load of 56lb bags of cement. After a minute Tammas walked forwards; he made to untie one of the knots but the driver told him not to bother. It was me that tied it, he said. I know how to get it done quick.

When he had finished he climbed up onto the rear and manoeuvered the first to the edge. Ralphie glanced round and shook his head. I might've fucking known! he muttered, We're on our fucking tod as usual!

He bent to dunt the ashes out of his pipebowl, stuck it into the top pocket of his dungarees. Okay, he said to Tammas, we better just start.

Aye, replied the driver, it's appreciated – I've got another delivery later.

They worked in silence, the driver dropping then dragging the bags to the edge of the wagon where the two would pull them onto their shoulders and walk a few strides before swinging them down onto the ground next to the wall. More than twenty minutes went by. Then assistance arrived; two men, one of whom was Murdie. And they were followed almost immediately by the yards' foreman. He came to the rear of the lorry and stopped there, he scratched his head and studied the pile against the wall.

Ralphie had just swung down another bag; he took off his bunnet, ruffled the hair on his head and put it back.

The foreman sighed and pointed at the pile of bags. Tell me this, he said, how's the bloody forklift going to shift they bloody bags?

What?

I said how's a bloody forklift going to lift that fucking load there!

Ralphie made no reply.

I mean did you no even think to get a couple of bloody platforms? Christ Almighty you could surely've thought of that!

Ralphie frowned and stared at the ground.

The driver of the lorry was lighting a cigarette. Then he said, Hey is the unloading stopped or what? I've got another drop this afternoon.

The foreman did not answer him. He said to Ralphie: There's a pile of platforms out near the skip. I want you to go and fucking get them. Alright?

Ralphie said nothing.

And yous three, yous three fucking help him. And see when yous've got them . . . He pointed at the pile stacked against the wall. Just take all them and stick them onto them and then after that yous can start unloading the rest off the fucking wagon. Okay? And he turned to the driver and shook his head, and then strode off.

After a moment Murdie grinned at Ralphie: See the bother you get us into!

Away and fuck yourself son, muttered Ralphie. He walked away in the direction of the skip. Tammas and the other two followed. When they had caught up to him he spat before saying: We're fucking machinemen, we shouldnt have to be doing this.

The man with Murdie smiled: Aye, he said, it's a labourer's job! He smiled again.

Ralphie replied after a moment. Ah well you know what I fucking mean.

We're all labourers, said Murdie. That's the fucking point.

Aw thanks for telling me. Ralphie nodded. Thanks.

Well so we are – eh Tammas?

Tammas shrugged.

The quiet man eh!

Tammas looked at him. They continued on in silence to where the wooden platforms lay. He knelt to tighten his boot-laces while the others sorted out the ones to be taken. Ralphie and the third man paired off on the first batch and Tammas took the second batch with Murdie. While they were walking he said quietly: I know you're no really due me anything till Friday and that Murdie but I was wondering if you could manage a couple of bob just now I mean even just fifty pence or something . . . I'm fucking skint. He grinned. Right out the game!

Murdie shook his head. You must be joking Tammas.

I dont even have a fucking fag man.

Neither do I.

Tammas gazed at him.

I dont. I'm no fucking kidding. The busfare she gives me and that's that . . . Murdie lowered his voice as they approached the others; he added in a whisper: Honest.

Tammas nodded.

...

Robert looked up from the book he had been reading, he rose from the armchair and crossed to the television set. He paused there with his hand at the channel switch. Anything in particular . . . ?

Margaret stifled a yawn. I'm not bothered.

Neither am I, said Tammas.

Robert shrugged. I'll see what's on BBC1 . . . He switched channels. He continued standing for a few moments, before slightly reducing the volume of sound and returning to his armchair, where he picked up his book and resumed reading. Margaret had been knitting; her needles and wool were lying to the side of her, she rested her head on the back of the settee, her eyelids closed. Moments later she blinked.

Tammas grinned at her and she smiled. What about some tea and a slice of toast? he said.

O no for me.

Are you sure? He stood to his feet.

Before she could answer Robert said: Look at her! An hour home from my work and that's her off to bed out the road – I'm beginning to take it personal!

Margaret shivered and yawned. She shook her head and

looked at her wristwatch. I dont know what's up with me, she added.

You're tired, replied Robert, that's what's up with you!

She smiled.

Tammas said: You sure you dont fancy a tea?

It'll just keep me awake.

He nodded and sat back down again.

Actually, said Margaret, I think I'll just go to bed the now. Bob, I think I'll just go the now.

Nobody's stopping you!

She tidied her knitting needles and wool before rising, and she added: Are you staying up?

Eh . . . He glanced at his book and frowned slightly. Naw, I'll just eh . . . He smiled. By the time you've done your face I'll have finished this chapter.

She yawned and remained standing by the settee.

Robert grinned. I'll see you ben there in other words.

O, okay . . . Goodnight Tammas.

Goodnight Margaret . . . When she had gone he added: What about yourself Robert, fancy a cup of tea?

Eh, och naw, I'll no bother. He yawned, then chuckled: It's contagious.

I dont fancy doing that backshift, said Tammas. Even worse than the nightshift.

I know, you're right, it's the worst of the three. Robert lifted his book upwards and he looked at it closely, then he glanced at Tammas. Naw, he said, I dont like it myself.

Tammas nodded, he shifted on the settee a bit, inclining his head while gazing at the television screen. Some moments later he got up, saying: Think I'll put the kettle on . . .

Robert nodded without looking away from his book.

Once the kettle was on to boil he went ben to his own room. There were two ashtrays, one on the window sill and one on the small cupboard near to the bed; both were clean. He pulled open the wardrobe door and felt into the pockets of his clothes.

The kettle boiled while he was standing by the kitchen sink, staring out the window over the backcourt. He made himself a cup of instant coffee. When he opened the living room door Robert stirred, he sighed and closed the book, and said: Is she in bed yet?

She's no in the bathroom anyway.

Ah well . . . Robert nodded. He bent forwards to see his slippers, nudging his feet inside them. Never mind, he said, the holiday next week – we'll probably get a heatwave.

Definitely.

Robert smiled. No that it'll bother you.

Tammas looked at him.

Naw, what I mean, Blackpool, you're no worried about the weather; even if it was blooming snowing you've got places to go.

Aw aye . . .

We had a great time when we went. Course we were winching at the time. And that makes a difference. He smiled, walking round the armchair to the door. Goodnight.

Goodnight Robert.

The *Evening Times* lay to the side of the fire-surround, nearby Robert's armchair and Tammas went to get it, opening it at the back pages.

Later on Robert could be heard leaving the bathroom and entering his bedroom; Once the bedroom light had been switched off Tammas turned the television back on. Another twenty minutes and he was checking the meter-bowl on the mantelpiece, withdrawing two ten pence coins. He went to his own bedroom and put on a pair of shoes; along the lobby he opened the outside door gently, leaving it on the latch.

It was raining quite heavily when he left the close and he ran to the corner and along to the cafe. One side of the shop was in semi darkness but the other side was open. Two guys were at the counter, telling jokes to the elderly woman serving. She was glancing at them now and again while turning the chips in the boiling fat with the long strainer. A younger woman appeared from the rear, wiping her hand on a tea-towel. She nodded to him. Eh hullo Marie, he said. You got three singles?

After a slight pause she sniffed and turned to the cigarette counter and took three cigarettes from an opened packet. She took the money and gave him his change.

Thanks, he smiled at her.

•••

Here you are! said the foreman.

Ralphie glanced at Tammas before looking at the men, and he replied, Christ almighty we've just sat down.

The foreman nodded. I believe you I believe you – but come on the now till I show you; I've got a wee job.

They followed him from the smoke-area, right outside the building to the rear yard, where he indicated a big pile of broken wooden crates. A couple of your mates were breaking them up yesterday but they forgot to get bloody rid of them! The foreman shook his head: I told them as well! Anyhow, okay, I want yous to burn it. Alright? A bonfire, but make sure yous keep it well away from anything inflammable.

When he had gone off Tammas said, Thank Christ, I was

beginning to wish he'd stick us back on the machine. Anything's fucking better than nothing.

Aye, it's been a long week son.

You're no kidding.

Never mind. Ralphie lifted his bunnet up off his head for a moment then settling it back again he bent to drag out some of the wood. Watch for nails, he said.

They carted the wood across to a cleared area and also collected in bits of plastic and cardboard which were lying about. Rain began drizzling; soon it became heavier and Ralphie moved to shelter by the factory wall. Tammas continued finding rubbish until the other called him across, and added: You dont get paid to catch a fucking cold.

Several minutes later the foreman appeared at a door some yards away. He gestured to them to come. Here, he said, and handed them two enormous polythene bags. Stick a couple of holes in them and you'll be able to wear them – they'll keep you dry. And here . . . He handed a gallon tin to Ralphie: Paraffin; to start your fire.

The foreman turned slightly and he winked at Tammas. You're doing a grand job Ralph!

Ralphie grunted.

The rain was falling heavily now. When the foreman departed Tammas began pulling on one of the polythene bags but Ralphie laughed briefly and said: For fuck sake son!

He shook his head and grinned at him, then strode out to the big pile of wood and rubbish and emptied the paraffin on top. Tammas trotted out to beside him and watched as Ralphie knelt a little to drop on a match. Then he followed him along the path near the canal, leaving the pile to burn. They walked quickly, hunching their shoulders against the rain.

At the entrance to the boiler room Benny was standing

gazing at the sky. That'll be on for the rest of the day, he said. He stood aside to let them in.

To the back of the room, behind the boilers, there was a large pipe Benny used as a bench, and here the three of them sat down, Ralphie shaking the rainwater out of his bunnet before bringing out his tobacco and his pipe. Benny was already smoking a roll-up. So, your nightshift's been halved? he said.

Ralphie looked at him. How did you know that? Ya auld cunt ye I bet you knew before us!

Benny sniffed before replying. Well, he said, I heard a wee whisper at the beginning of the week there but eh I didnt want to say anything – in case it was just a fucking rumour. You know what like they are in this place Ralph you can hardly believe a fucking word you hear. He nudged Tammas and continued, I'm telling you son see if you listen to everything you get fucking told in this joint you'll wind up in a confused condition. It's fucking notorious so it is! How long you been here now?

About seven month.

Is that all? said Ralphie.

Aye.

Hh. I thought it was longer.

Naw, it just seems like it!

Benny said, Wait till you're here the same as us.

God forbid . . . chuckled Ralphie.

Tammas shook his head. No point worrying about that auld yin – last in first out. I'll be heading the line soon as the redundancies start.

There was a brief silence.

Then Tammas glanced at the boilerman. I was wondering, he said, any chance of loaning me a smoke?

What d'you say?

Naw I was just wondering, if you could lend me a smoke, one of your roll-ups.

Aw aye . . .

Ralphie coughed.

Any chance?

Benny nodded. He took his tobacco pouch out of a pocket in his boilersuit and handed it to Tammas. There's a couple rolled already, inside.

Thanks a lot Benny. Tammas unzipped the pouch and brought one out.

Ralphie passed him a box of matches and added, Look and see if that fire's still going.

Shortly before the dinner break the foreman appeared in the smoke-area to distribute the wages' packets. Minutes later Tammas was walking out through the factory yard, in company with others from his section. It was still raining. Just beyond the gates the teaboy and two other youths were sheltering, they had a ball they were throwing to each other; and the teaboy called: Hey Tammas you coming up for a game?

Maybe . . . He glanced at the sky and shrugged.

The rain's going to go off!

Tammas nodded; he continued on along the street. There was a pub down near the junction traffic lights and he entered, making his way through the crowded bar into the lounge. Ordering a pint of heavy and a pie and peas he walked to where a few of his workmates were grouped. When a gap occurred in the conversation he said: Any of yous seen Murdie?

I dont think he's in, somebody replied.

You mean he's no at work?

As far as I know.

Hh. Tammas shook his head.

He still owes you a couple of quid?

Aye . . . Tammas grimaced then returned to the bar to collect his pint and his food. Afterwards he left the pub and crossed the road to the betting shop.

At 4.45 that afternoon he was stamping his timecard and racing down the sloping corridor to the front yard, and across and out through the gates, and down the street. Others were running also. They dashed into the bookmaker's just as the runners for the 4.45 race were about to come under starter's orders. Tammas grabbed a betting slip and managed to scribble out a bet and get it on just as the race was off.

It was the last race of the day at that particular meeting but there was another meeting on; it had a race coming up at 5 pm and another at 5.30.

•••

Betty had her back to the shop window, staring at the pavement, her head bowed. Quite a few other people were standing about at this corner. He hesitated some yards away. Another girl was approached by a youth and together they walked off round into Argyll Street. Betty raised her head a moment later and she gazed after them. Her head was bowed again when he reached her. He tapped the side of her arm. Sorry I'm late.

She made no reply but linked arms with him.

I couldnt get a bloody bus. Ended up I just walked.

Walked? She smiled.

Aye.

Is it no a long way?

Aye. He shrugged. I do it a lot but, I quite like walking.

She nodded. They continued up Union Street in silence, until Betty smiled: I thought you'd forgotten!

Forgotten?

Have you been for a pint? she said, sniffing near to his mouth.

What – aye.

Is that how you're late?

Naw, not at all . . . He paused; they stopped walking. Am I no allowed a pint on a Friday night!

Tch Tammas, I didnt mean that . . .

He nodded.

I was just meaning if that's how you were late.

Aw, aye.

They were standing at the traffic lights; he had his hands in his trouser pockets and Betty was to his left, her arm linking his. A few other people were there also and they started across Gordon Street as the lights turned to amber. Tammas and Betty followed. After a bit she said, A girl in work was saying that the one in the ABC 2's quite violent.

Hh.

That's what she said, but . . . Betty shrugged, pursed her lips. D'you fancy it though?

Eh . . .

She was looking at him.

Eh, well . . . He sniffed and glanced suddenly across the street, checking slightly in his stride.

When they continued over to the other pavement she smiled at him: You fancy the pub, she said.

Naw. Naw Betty, honest.

Yes you do.

I dont, Christ.

She was smiling. I dont mind Tammas except I just dont like sitting all night in them. Sometimes I go with the people

49

in the work and it gets awful boring, especially if some of them start to get a bit drunk. Rena's the same. She doesnt often go out with them at all. And d'you know something else?

He nodded.

Naw, she said, about Rena?

What?

I'm saying do you know something else, about Rena?

About Rena? He frowned.

No Tammas . . . Betty shook her head, she grinned and tugged on his arm till he brought his hand out his pocket. And he looked at her. She sighed: No Tammas I was just saying, about Rena; she told me she wished Rab didnt drink so much.

Rena?

Aye, she said she thinks he's drinking too much.

Hh!

She did.

He nodded.

Is it every Saturday night he goes to the pub?

He shrugged. No every one, I dont think . . . He paused and she withdrew her arm from his. He took his hands out his pockets. Betty . . . he said. He put his hands back into his pockets and hunched his shoulders.

They had stopped walking now and she was looking at him. Eh . . .

What's up? she asked. She frowned, glanced away, watching someone pass by, before turning to him again. What's wrong? she said quietly.

Nothing, nothing, it's no that, there's nothing wrong. He patted her on the elbow, led her in to stand closeby a shop window. Naw, he said, it's just – I'm skint. He sniffed and poked his right forefinger into the corner of his eye socket, blinked a couple of times, then brought out his cigarettes and lighted one. When he exhaled she asked: What d'you mean?

Naw. Just – I'm skint, I've no got any dough. Well – about . . .
He took some change from his trouser pocket and displayed
it on the palm of his hand. Sixty three pence.

Betty began to say something but stopped, frowning.

Naw, he said, I'm really . . . I just eh . . . He shut his eyelids.

I dont know what you mean Tammas, I dont know what
it is; what is it? what d'you mean?

He sighed. He was gazing into the shop window then he
glanced very briefly at her, and then up in the direction of the
cinema. The September Weekend and that I just eh . . . I was
really behind and . . . He shook his head, inhaling deeply on
the cigarette. He turned to her, putting his arm round her
shoulder but withdrew it at once and shook his head again: I'm
really sorry Betty, honest.

Do you mean you've had to put your money bye for
Blackpool?

Aye well, aye – but no just that I mean . . . you know how
I'm living with my sister and that?

She nodded.

It's just eh, I always like to pay my way and that, spot on,
with the money and that, just to keep it right.

Aw.

I dont like to eh . . . He sighed, then he inhaled on the
cigarette and gazed up Renfield Street.

Tammas. Betty smiled and linked arms with him. Dont be
silly.

Naw, he said. He continued to gaze away from her.

Betty tugged at his arm. She smiled. Come on . . . God
Tammas I've got money, if it's just the pictures, my goodness.
She chuckled.

Naw but that's no fair Betty, hh, Christ.

Tammas, it's alright, honest.

He shook his head.

Come on . . . She tugged on his arm again and then they carried on walking towards the cinema; but before arriving he stopped and brought his right hand out his pocket so that Betty had to withdraw her arm.

He was shaking his head. Naw, he said, and he sighed quite loudly. Betty . . . He rubbed his eyes. This is out of order. I'm sorry, I really . . . He touched her on the arm, just beneath her shoulder, then turned about and strode off across the street, and down the way, without looking back.

•••

His head jerked up from the pillow at the slight tremor of the clock and he switched off the alarm before it sounded. His eyelids closed. They opened, and he groped at the top of the bedside cupboard where the cigarette packet was lying. He left it there and raised himself up, studied the clock. A moment later he slid out between the covers and went through to the lavatory before getting on his clothes.

The house was in semi darkness. He tugged the cord to pull up the venetian blinds in the kitchen, leaving off the electric light. He ate cornflakes and milk, rinsing out the bowl and spoon and drying them, returning them into their places in the cupboard. Then he collected his jerkin and cigarettes from his own room. Back down the lobby he clicked open the outside door, closing it gently behind him.

The street and pavement were damp but the sky was clear and it was a mild morning. Along at the newsagent's shop the man was sorting through his big bundles of Sunday newspapers, a cigarette burning in the corner of his mouth and his eyelids blinking to avoid the smoke. He nodded at Tammas and gave him his ordered *Sunday Mail* without a word.

At the bus stop two men in donkey jackets and denims stood talking together, behind them queued a woman and two children who were clutching thin religious books. A block further on he paused to strike a match, cupping the flame in both hands, the newspaper beneath his right oxter. When he had the cigarette going he flicked the match into the gutter then opened the newspaper at the back pages, he read while strolling. He came to where a plot of grass had been planted in a gapsite; an arc-shaped iron railing surrounded it, and in an inshot a bench had been fixed into a concrete slab. He sat down there for a while.

A bus passed, travelling slowly. Tammas looked after it, the newspaper now lying folded on his lap. From behind his ear he brought the half smoked cigarette and got it alight before rising and continuing on.

Where he was now walking the buildings consisted mainly of warehouses and small factories with occasional TO LET signs pasted on their windows. Very few vehicles were on the roads. He turned off and along, parallel to the river. From where he was it could be seen stretching only as far as Govan. Nearby stood an enormous crane with what looked to be a very large shed on one end.

The rain had started falling by the time he entered the entrance to the pedestrian tunnel. The floor was white with bird shit. Condensation seeped down the walls and roofing and there was a continuous gurgling noise coming from somewhere, also a roaring noise that increased the further downstairs he stepped, until it seemed to block out all other sound.

On the other side of the river he sheltered in the entrance until the rain lessened, then headed along the cobbled dock road. The area to the left was waste ground, where tenement buildings had been recently demolished; here and there foundation work for new buildings seemed to be in progress. To the right of the pavement he was on was a high wall which continued for about a mile. When he reached its other end he took his newspaper back out, glancing at it as he went.

He only had one cigarette left. He lighted it and crushed the packet and dropped it to the ground, but kicked at it just before it landed. Then he brought the box of matches out his jerkin pocket again. It was nearly full. Striking one he thrust it in beside the rest and watched as it all burst into flames, and he bent and placed it on the pavement. Several paces on he turned to look back; the small fire was still burning.

A man was staring at him from a bus stop on the other side of the road.

Half an hour later he was at Linthouse, entering the pedestrian tunnel there; a further forty or so minutes and he had arrived at Rab's place in Scotstoun. His younger brother Alec opened the door, dressed in pyjamas and rubbing his eyes. Tammas, he said.

Is Rab up?

He's no in.

No in?

Naw, he never came back last night. Alec yawned: I thought he was with you and Donnie and them.

Tammas nodded.

How, was he no?

Eh I'm no sure, I never went out last night.

Did you no?

Naw.

Alec yawned again. He'll probably be back soon anyway. Come on in and wait if you want. Maw and da are still in bed. I'll be making a bit of toast.

Eh . . . ach naw Alec I'll no bother – just tell him I came.
Aye. Anything else?
Naw.

•••

Margaret was standing in the doorway, all set to leave for work;
she was frowning.

What's up? he said, resting on his elbows.

What's up! I thought you were away long ago!

He nodded and lay back down, pulling the blankets to his
chin. I slept in, he muttered.

You slept in! Tammas, for heaven sake, you cant afford to
be taking days off your work.

He shut his eyelids.

She continued to stand there. The door creaked on its hinges
then after a few more moments it closed behind her; she could
be heard walking quickly down the lobby and out, banging the
front door shut. Eventually he dozed. Later in the morning he
was carrying a bulky plastic bag to the pawnbroker's. A young
woman came out of the back entrance pushing a small pram;
he stood aside to let her pass to the front close. In the shop he
entered one of the cubicles and brought the suit out the bag
and onto the counter. A girl attended him; without examining
the suit she asked: How much?

Seven.

The girl hesitated.

Tammas nodded. Ask him and see . . . He watched through
the grille as she crossed the floor and handed the suit to the

middle aged man at the table. He glanced at the suit and muttered something to her. When she returned she laid the suit on the counter before speaking. He says three fifty for it.

Three fifty?

Yes.

Mm. He opened the bag and brought out a pair of black shoes, slid them beneath the grille.

The girl shook her head.

But they've only been worn once.

He wont even look at them.

What – I mean, hh . . . He shrugged and indicated the soles: Hardly even scuffed.

They have to be brand new but, no worn at all.

No worn at all?

Yes, they've no to be worn at all.

Just ask him.

No, there's no point, he'll no . . . She closed her lips and shook her head.

Och that's terrible I mean they've no even been worn, just the once.

She nodded.

He sighed, then he smiled briefly. After a few moments she pushed the shoes back under the grille to him and she asked: Do you still want to leave the suit?

Aye. He looked at her.

•••

It was beginning to rain heavily. Ralphie and Tammas were collecting rubbish from the long grass near the canal bank and disposing of it in the skip container. The older man stopped working first. That's that, he said. The boiler room! He started trotting in that direction at once, holding his bunnet down on his head with one hand.

Tammas shouted after him: I'll see you later.

Ralphie paused: Where you going?

Ah – just for a walk.

Aye well you better hide son, keep out the fucking road – know what I mean?

Aye dont worry. He turned and walked to one of the doors into the factory, keeping close in to the wall to avoid the rain. Inside was another door, lying ajar. There was a steady hum from the generator room. He pushed open the door more widely, and entered. It was a small room and there was a youth sitting on a pipe with a magazine open on his lap, leaning on his shoulder was one of the engineers. They glanced at him. The youth grimaced: Dont fucking do that to people!

Sorry.

Jesus sake, said the man, placing his hand on his chest. I nearly had a fucking heart attack!

Tammas nodded. After a moment he said, I was looking for eh auld Benny, you seen him?

They shook their heads. The man added, He'll be in the boiler room.

Aw aye . . . Course . . . He nodded, then he made to leave.

The youth said: You playing football at dinner time?

Aye, you?

If the rain stops.

Aye. Tammas turned but he glanced back: Hey you got a smoke at all?

Naw.

I've got one, said the man. He took a packet of tipped from the top pocket of his boilersuit and flipped it across.

Great, ta – I've been gasping all morning! He withdrew a cigarette, flipped the packet back.

While the man was taking one for himself he gestured at the magazine and chuckled, Horny porny.

Aw. Hh! Tammas struck his match down the wall; he inhaled and exhaled.

Take a look, said the youth.

Tammas smiled. It'll put me off my work!

Ach come on man it's amazing stuff; manky as fuck, take a swatch!

After a moment Tammas stepped forwards, placing one hand against the wall to balance himself while bending slightly. The youth held it to the side a little for him to see. It was a colour photograph covering the two pages and showed three men sexually involved with one woman. Tammas blushed, he continued to stare at it.

The man laughed: Look at his face!

Tammas breathed out; he inhaled on the cigarette, shaking his head; he moved away. That'll do me, he said.

He's had enough! grinned the man.

No fucking wonder! Tammas shook his head.

The youth was grinning and turning a page. Come here and see this yin!

Naw no me man . . . Tammas shook his head again. I'll see you later.

The youth laughed.

Outside the room he nipped the cigarette and wedged it behind his ear. He returned back out into the rear yard and stood close in to the wall with his hands in his pockets and his shoulders hunched. A man in a white coat appeared suddenly at a door farther down, and Tammas was walking along and back into the factory; a brush was lying on the floor just inside the doorway and glancing quickly sideways he collected it and continued walking in the direction of the hoist.

The top floor of the part of the factory where Tammas normally worked was a small storeroom, nowadays used only for the cutting-section. One guy was in charge. Ralphie and Tammas were up helping him shift old packing crates to make space for new stock. He had left them to enter up his written work for the afternoon, but eventually he opened the window of his office and called to Tammas: Make the tea!

Tammas looked at him then at Ralphie who shrugged, and nodded in the direction of the sink. Thanks, he said. I'm a teaboy now.

Ralphie shrugged again and looked away.

During the break the three of them sat in the office in silence. Ralphie rose and he walked to a stack of parcels, began to read their labels. Eights by twelve, he said, I didnt know we still used them?

The storeman nodded. We just keep a few in case.

Mmm . . . Ralphie had taken the pipe from his pocket and was opening his tobacco pouch. The storeman lighted a cigarette, returned the packet into the drawer in his desk. Did you hear? said Ralphie. Auld McCreadie, he's retired.

The storeman inhaled deeply on his cigarette.

Couple of weeks back.

Hh.

Aye, said Ralphie. He tapped the tobacco down inside the pipebowl and got his lighter out, and flicked on its large flame, sucking on the stem while lighting the tobacco; soon it was burning and he put the lighter away and let out a big cloud of blue smoke; he returned the pipe to between his lips. He came to sit back down again.

Tammas stood up. Going to the toilet, he said, and he left the office. There was a toilet on this floor but he passed it by, heading to the back of the area where the fire-escape staircase was situated. He walked down slowly, to the landing between floors, and he gazed out the window, out over the canal to the tenement buildings beyond. After a time he lowered himself to sit on his heels, then he sat on the concrete floor, his back to the wall and legs outstretched and crossed at the ankles.

•••

The smell of cooking was quite strong when he entered the lobby. Closing the door he continued on past the kitchen to his own room. He changed his clothes then lay on the bed. He got up and tugged over the curtains, lay down again, hands clasped beneath his head on the pillow. But he rose moments later.

Margaret was alone. She was sitting at the kitchen table, reading the *Evening Times*.

He went to the oven and lifted the lid off one of the pots, sniffed loudly: Delicious. I'm starving Margaret! He turned the switch a little, so that the flame became higher.

Dont do that, you'll just burn it.

Sorry, I was . . . he shrugged, I was only kidding.

She nodded, gazing at the newspaper. He sat on a chair across from her, with his back to the wall, facing away from her. He said: Did you manage up the hospital?

Yes. Yes, I did . . . Margaret stood up; she walked over to the oven, lifted the lid off the pot, glanced inside.

How was she? he asked, pulling the newspaper towards himself.

Fine. The usual.

He nodded. Did she know you? He shut the newspaper, turned it to the back page. Margaret was taking the lid off the other pot which had potatoes boiling in it, and she tested them with a fork. Tammas said again: Did she know you?

Margaret nodded.

Mm. That's something.

What d'you mean?

Eh . . . Naw – just the last time I was up; remember? She thought I was her brother.

Margaret returned to her chair at the table. He carried on reading for several moments before glancing up, and saying, How was work? Then he dropped his gaze and muttered: Sorry Margaret . . . He looked at her: I'm sorry. The thing is . . .

She had shaken her head.

Placing his elbows on the edge of the table he inclined his head slightly and rubbed the bridge of his nose between the thumb and forefinger of his right hand. I was a bit short, had to put in extra for Blackpool and that. He took his hand away from his face and gazed at her: Coming off the machine Margaret, it means a drop in the wages, no bonus or nothing. Labouring rates just, that's all we're getting – even them that's been in the job for years; hopeless . . . Plus there's a guy owes me a good few pounds. He was supposed to give me it on Friday there but he's on the panel and there's no way of getting in touch with him I mean I was thinking of going up to chap his door and that but I dont like to I mean . . . he shrugged.

You kept out my road all weekend.

He sniffed.

Tammas, you kept out my road all weekend. How did you not just tell me? Her arms had been folded but now she had unfolded them. She looked away, shaking her head a little.

I wasnt keeping out your road. I was in the whole of Saturday night, it was just yous were out. I went to bed early and then got up early on the Sunday cause I had to go to Rab's.

If you didnt have enough money all you had to do was tell me. And then what time did you come in at last night? I never even heard you! Did you come in last night!

What?

Well for all I know it was this morning. Robert didnt hear you either.

I was in the back of 2.

The back of 2?

Aye, the back of 2 . . . He sniffed and glanced at her: I was up at Donnie's.

Why did you not tell me? you could've phoned Mrs Brady up the stair, that's all you had to do. When I dont even know you're coming how do I know about food? How am I supposed to know? Did you go in to work even? Or did you just lie in your bed all morning?

He looked away.

After a few moments Margaret got up off her chair and she crossed to the oven.

Eventually he cleared his throat and said, Donnie's maw was asking for you.

Margaret nodded.

Her and Donnie's auld man, they're really knocking their pan in about New Zealand. She's got lists of her furniture all made up; all ready. It's good – what she's done.

Margaret had been forking the potatoes. She settled the lid back on the pot and glanced at the wall-clock.

Where's Robert?

He's away a message, she replied after a moment.

Naw, he said, she wants to be ready, Donnie's maw – so there'll be no last minute panic once the date comes through.

I didnt know they were going for a while yet . . . Margaret lifted a cloth from the sink and she dabbed at the side of the oven with it.

It's just she wants to be ready, so when the time comes it means there'll be no worries about selling the stuff. It's good but, the way she's made up the lists and that. She's going to stick numbers on everything as well. She's got it all worked out.

Margaret nodded. That's good.

After a moment or two he turned the back page of the newspaper and began to read. But he stopped almost immediately and he got up and crossed to the cupboard, brought three dinner plates, teacups and saucers from a lower shelf, and cutlery from the top drawer. While he arranged them on the table he asked, Did you see any of the nurses? at the hospital?

Yes . . . yes I did.

Which one?

O, that wee one, her from the highlands.

Tammas smiled. He had returned to the chair and was sitting with one elbow on the edge of the table, his other hand in his trouser pocket.

I know she barks at some of the poor old souls but at least she makes sure nobody takes what doesnt belong to them. Margaret smiled. And she can be cheery when she likes. Anyway, before she came to the ward it was terrible; you could hardly leave a packet of biscuits down without there was somebody pinching it. Grannie was always losing things, it wasnt fair.

Aye. Did you no say she was a gossip but?

No. Margaret shook her head abruptly. The wee highland one? No, not at all; you're mixing her up.

Mm.

Margaret turned, her back to him; she switched on the cold water tap and washed her hands. When she had dried them and returned the hand-towel to the rail she glanced at the clock again.

Eh Margaret . . . He stood up, nodded at the pots on the oven while lifting a dinner plate: Mind if I take mine the now? I'll just eat it in the room if it's okay. I've got a book I'm reading.

...

Three men in suits had appeared on the path outside the factory door. They gazed at the canal, one of them talking and the other two listening. Then a foreman came out to join them. Tammas stepped out from the wall, he strode in their direction. He continued past them and in through the doorway. He strode on across the factory floor to the hoist but when he reached it he paused, then carried straight on up the corridor, and he made his way round to the back staircase leading to the small storeroom on the top floor.

The man in charge was sitting up by the hoist with a clipboard of papers on his lap. Tammas watched him for a time, before sidling in from the fire-escape exit, and moving in behind the large stacks of packing crates. Piles of old sacking lay in the corner. When he reached there he felt in at the bottom of some of it and brought out a couple of *Readers' Digests*, and lowered himself down onto the sacking.

A while later the hoist could be heard clanking to a halt, the gates being opened. Shifting some of the higher crates a little he was able to make enough of a gap to see through. Two women from the floor below. A younger one followed them out pushing a barrow; her blue dustcoat was unbuttoned and she had a blouse on and jeans. She was pushing the barrow down towards him while the other two stayed at the hoist gates chatting to the storeman. When she reached a stack about 20 yards off she stopped, and she bent to lift a big cardboard box onto the barrow, lifting one corner only, and then sliding it on; but the weight caused the barrow to move, the box sliding back off to lie on the floor. The girl stood up. She glanced up to the others, she put her hands into the side pockets of her dustcoat and she kicked gently at the cardboard box, making a whistling sound, a tune. The two women were coming. Tammas stood back from the gap between the crates; he lowered himself down onto the sacking.

The man was saying: Naw, I dont give a fucking monkey's; it's wrong. He strode into the smoke-area and sat down facing Ralphie and Tammas. His mate followed him, propped the brush he was carrying against the wall. How's it going?

Ralphie shrugged. Tammas did not reply.

The first man frowned at them. You heard?

Heard what?

Heard what! The man frowned again and he gestured vaguely around . . . These fucking bastards in here. Fucking O.T. man!

O.T.?

Aye fucking O.T. man! They're fucking working O.T. man and we're fucking . . . bastards! He turned and he pointed at a guy who was standing by a machine some distance away. Him and all the rest of the cunts up here.

Heh, said his mate, reaching to him and patting his arm. Take it easy.

Aye no fucking wonder. Make you fucking sick man we're about to get laid off man and these cunts're steaming into the fucking O.T.

Ralphie nodded.

The second man said: Did you know?

Put it this way Fred, I'm no surprised.

Hh! He glanced at Tammas: Did you know and all?

Who me – naw, did I fuck, I never knew . . . Tammas turned to Ralphie.

Different department. The older man shrugged: This wing's nothing to do with us, no when it really comes down to it.

What! The first man gazed at him. What did you say!

I said it's a different department. Here. It's fucking different, it's different from us. He took the pipe from his mouth and he pointed it at the man: Can you work any of their machines?

Course I cant work any of their fucking machines.

The second man glanced at him: Ralphie means cause it's a different machine man, you cant work it . . . He shook his head. Even if they wanted to let you man you couldnt fucking work it.

I know. So what!

Well, fuck sake.

Look I dont give a fucking monkey's man it's out of order. I've never heard of anything like this in my fucking puff. Treat you like fucking shite in this place and you all fucking stand back and let them man – fucking . . . He stopped and shook his head.

Come off it, muttered Ralphie.

Well it's the same fucking factory.

I know it's the same factory.

Aye well you trying to tell me should fucking stand back and watch them steaming into the fucking O.T. when we're getting fucking laid off!

Nobody's getting laid off.

Yet, added the second man.

Ralphie glanced at him. He had the pipe back in his mouth and he sucked on it. He struck a match and began relighting the tobacco. But he blew out the flame and took the pipe back out of his mouth. He dropped a mouthful of spit onto the floor, wiped his boot heel over it. Then he sniffed and stood up. He said to Tammas: Time we were going eh.

Aye. As he followed Ralphie out the smoke-area he called to the other two, See yous later.

They walked in silence to the corner of this wing. There was another stores' section here and they were assisting the storeman clear old stuff away to create space. Some ten minutes later the other two men could be seen leaving the smoke-area. Tammas paused with the box he was passing to Ralphie and he said: I can see his point but.

Good for you son. The older man took the box from him and turned to lay it on the platform.

Tammas had reddened. After a moment he walked away. He went to the nearby toilet and sat in one of the cubicles.

Back in the stores Ralphie was starting on another stack of boxes. Tammas joined him at it without speaking. Eventually Ralphie said, Another two and we'll call it a day.

Tammas made no answer.

Then by the time we get over to our bit . . . Ralphie shrugged.

Tammas nodded slightly.

•••

The room was in darkness. He lay there with his eyelids shut. Footsteps down the lobby, from the bathroom to the front room, and the door being opened and closed. He squinted at the alarm clock. It had stopped, it was not ticking. Pulling off the quilt he swung round his legs and sat for a moment; he was wearing jeans and a shirt and had his socks on. He got up, he stretched, standing on his tip-toes and thrusting out his chest, making a groaning sound. And he walked to the window, drew the curtains enough to peer out. It was still raining, the actual drops of water visible as they fell within range of the glow of light from the street lamps. A man was walking from one pavement to the other and his voice was audible, as if he was calling to someone in Tammas's close. But he was not doing that, he was singing to himself as he walked.

•••

The foreman looked at him when he entered the office.

About Friday afternoon, said Tammas; okay if I get it off? I saw the chargehand at tea-break and he says to ask you.

What is it for?

I'm going away for the weekend.

So am I. So's a lot of folk. It's always the same at this time of year.

Tammas sniffed and stared at him.

What is it you want the afternoon for?

Well the bus, it leaves at half three.

Half three?

Aye. And I'll need to get home and changed and that.

The foreman paused. Then he went on. You shouldnt have got fixed onto a bus that's leaving when you're supposed to be at your place of work. I mean that's daft; it's silly. Christ, if everybody did that we'd be as well shutting down on bloody Thursday night!

Tammas nodded.

A carry on so it is. The foreman looked at him. You had Monday off this week as it is.

I had diarrhoea.

I know you had diarrhoea.

I phoned in.

I know, we're grateful.

Tammas glanced at the floor. Look, he said, I'm going with a few of my mates; it was them made the arrangements.

I'm no denying that. I just think you should've made sure it wasnt going to interfere with your job. I mean some things are bloody more important than holidays.

Tammas nodded.

Away you go . . . The foreman returned his attention to the things on his desk.

•••

The door had opened. He sat up. And rubbed his eyes when the light came on. Margaret was saying: Somebody at the door.

What?

Billy. I thought you came ben here to read?

I fell asleep.

No wonder, with the light out! Margaret was smiling.

Tammas nodded. He yawned.

Stepping outside his room Margaret called: Come on in and get him Billy.

The footsteps and then Billy was at the door, grinning.

Tammas pulled his shoes out from under the bed, slipped them on and quickly knotted the laces. He grabbed his jerkin from the back of the chair and ushered Billy out into the lobby. When the outside door was shut and they were walking downstairs Billy said: What you doing in bed at fucking 9 o'clock at night! Then he laughed: Dont tell me ya dirty bastard ye.

Shut up ya cunt. Tammas punched him on the shoulder. That's my fucking social life you're slagging!

Billy laughed. Naw, he said, I was expecting you in a while ago man.

Hh!

We could've gone for a game of snooker.

Tammas stopped. You kidding?

Naw, Christ – too late now.

What did you no come up and get me for! Fuck sake Billy.

Tch aye, I should've.

Tammas looked at him and shook his head. I mean I take it you've got fucking dough?

Aye. Billy shrugged: I won a couple of quid.

Fuck sake!

Alright alright.

No wonder man.

I said I was fucking sorry.

Aye I know but . . . Hh! They continued on down the stairs and out through the close, heading towards *Simpson's*.

...

At dinner time on Friday he redeemed his suit on the road home from work. He met the others in the pub as arranged, the parcel under his arm. John failed to appear. Donnie was saying: I knew it, the cunt's been too miserable to take the afternoon off.

As long as he makes the bus, said Billy.

Ha ha ha! Rab said: I hope he fucking misses it!

Ah give the boy a break, said Donnie.

Ach!

Who's sleeping with him anyway?

Tammas.

Aw thanks a lot!

The other three laughed.

I didnt even think you were listening! Anyhow . . . Donnie chuckled: You dont have to worry; with five of us it'll mean he can sleep by himself.

Unless it's three to one room and two to the other.

Aye you never know right enough.

Billy smiled. It's alright, I'll sleep with him.

We can toss for it, replied Donnie.

Naw, said Rab, let him if he wants!

He's no that fucking bad.

You kidding! You wouldnt know which way to turn with the cunt!

That right? Donnie cried: In that case I'll fucking sleep with him!

The bus was scheduled to leave Buchanan Street Station at 6.55 pm and they were to meet back in the pub for 5 o'clock. From there they would be taking a taxi to another pub closeby the depot; any latecomer was to go there directly. When Donnie and Rab left to get a bus home the other two strolled along to the betting shop. Billy borrowed a £1 from him. Just for an interest, he said with a grin.

What're you skint!

I didnt want to take any chances man I left the dough in the house.

Fair enough, said Tammas. He gazed up at the formpage tacked onto the wall then he moved along to the next one. The runners for the 2.30 were being loaded into the stalls. He wrote out his selection and strode to the counter. Billy was in front of him. During the race commentary they stood listening by a radiator. An outsider won. Billy laughed and tore up his receipt, That's what I get for backing the favourite for a paltry pound!

Tammas nodded.

Mind you, he added and indicated the form, it could've been backed.

Aye. Right enough . . . Tammas grinned: Funny how you always fucking spot things like that after the result.

Cheeky bastard! Billy turned from the wall, putting his hands in his pockets and hunching his shoulders. You coming?

Nah, think I'll hang on for the next. What about yourself?

Naw man you kidding! Anyhow, if I wanted to stand in a betting shop all day I'd've went to my fucking work.

Ha ha.

Actually I think I'll get the fucking head down man I'm a bit tired.

Okay.

Heh . . . Billy grinned. Watch yourself!

Aye.

When the next race was coming under orders he was standing gazing at the previous day's tote returns and he had to run to the counter, he scribbled a bet on the favourite. At the furlong marker it moved up to challenge but its effort was always being held by the eventual 20/1 winner. He walked out of there and went to the shop two blocks away. The coming race was for 2 year olds and almost half of the field was unraced; minutes before the off one entered the betting at 12/1 and was quickly marked down through all rates to 6/1. He hesitated, strode to another formpage. It went to 5/1 and he scribbled the bet and raced to the counter, taking the price.

The horse led till the distance; then it was passed, it finished unplaced.

His shoulders ached. He flexed them while leaving the premises. He crossed to the newsagent's and bought a packet of cigarettes though he still had quite a few in the packet in his jerkin pocket. He checked his money. Back in the bookmaker's he studied form. Half an hour later he was walking home. Margaret frowned when he came into the living room. She said: You better get a move on.

Ah I'm no bothering Margaret.

You're no bothering?

Nah. He sat down and looked at the television.

Margaret said nothing.

No, he said, I really, I just eh, I dont think I'd be that keen on Blackpool anyway.

But Tammas, you've paid your fare down. And your bed & breakfast – I thought you had paid that as well.

No it all, naw, just part of it.

Still . . . That's money down the drain.

He nodded. She had turned her head back to face the television but after a moment she made to resume speaking. He stood up and yawned: Think I'll lie down for an hour.

Margaret looked at him.

All I'm doing in the factory these days is walking about; its more tiring.

You'll be here yourself for the three days.

Fine.

She shook her head: I think you're silly. Did you have an argument with somebody?

Naw no really.

She shook her head again, shifted on the chair.

He was standing at the corner opposite where the convoy of buses would leave. People were already filing aboard or having their luggage loaded into the rear compartments by the drivers. Ten minutes from time and still they had not appeared, then he saw them. They came from Buchanan Street, running across Sauchiehall Street, suitcases and holdall bags swinging and both Rab and Donnie were carrying large carry-out bags. John and Billy were first aboard. The bus driver was chatting to Rab and then with Donnie the three of them stepped away from the rear and began to look this way and that way but finally they stepped up inside the bus. A few minutes later the first of the convoy moved out from the stance. Tammas edged a little farther back down the lane and he turned aside while their bus passed.

...

Next morning it was dry and once Margaret and her husband had gone he searched the house. He found a pile of coppers amounting to 17 pence. The meter-bowl was empty. Gathering his new suit from the wardrobe he went out and pawned it in a different broker's. He collected a *Sporting Life* on the way home, studied form until early afternoon. His nap for the day was going in the third race at one of the flat meetings. In the betting shop he glanced at the other newspaper formpages on the wall, reading the stable news and any sort of racing gossip. The first race was about due off. The shows of betting had been coming through for some time. He glanced back at his own newspaper then made out a bet for the favourite, laying on what he had. It finished fourth.

He watched the boardman wiping out the old price quotations, tearing down the runners' list and replacing it with the next. Three or four guys hovered near the pay-out window. He did not know any of them. A show of betting came for the next race. He walked to the door. Upstairs in the house he switched on the television for the televised racing, seeing his nap win at 5/2 and hearing the commentators recall how it had won and why it had been well fancied to do so. And the owner being interviewed briefly, receiving a trophy. He turned channels. Motorbikes were racing over bumpy countryside. He switched it off altogether and went ben the kitchen and put on a kettle of water to boil; then he switched off the oven ring. He went to his room, undressed and got into bed, then got back up again and drew over the curtains. He dozed eventually.

•••

Once he had washed and shaved he put on the fresh shirt and his old suit. Taking the jacket off again he began peeling a couple of potatoes but stopped, he went into the front room and put on the television and lay down on the settee with his head on an arm of it. Mrs Brady lived in the room and kitchen on the landing directly above. Tammas had known her most of his life; she had been acquainted with his mother and friends with his grandmother. She rarely left the house; she would be sitting watching television, or reading maybe. Margaret did her shopping quite a lot; and Tammas too, on occasion – even collecting her pension a couple of times last winter.

Going into the lobby he opened the outside door but closed it immediately and went ben the kitchen. The potatoes lying on the draining board at the sink. His cigarettes lay on the floor next to the settee in the living room. Three of them remained. He smoked part of one then nipped it and shoved it back in the packet, and walked to the front door. He left the door on the latch before going upstairs. When Mrs Brady answered his flapping of the letter box he said: Eh Mrs Brady I was wondering if you had a ten pence bit by any chance – the electricity's away and that . . . He sniffed.

She nodded. I think so, wait a wee minute. Then she closed over the door. Back she came with her purse and she opened it in such a way that he could look inside also. I've got a couple, she said, and she took them out and gave them to him. Here's another yin as well Tammas.

Probably one would be enough, he said. He made to return the other two.

Are you sure? Take them, just in case.

Well okay. Thanks. I'll hand them back in tomorrow.

Och there's no rush: she shook her head. As soon as you like, it doesnt matter.

Well . . . thanks.

Mrs Brady smiled: And where is it the night?

He shrugged.

The dancing?

Maybe, maybe. He grinned, turned away, about to go downstairs.

And how's your grannie?

O fine, fine.

You tell her I was asking for her. I would go up and see her if I could.

Okay Mrs Brady.

Mind and tell her now.

I will.

•••

The conductor was standing waiting for the money. Tammas passed it to him and was returned half. The conductor nodded very slightly, not looking at him, not giving him a ticket, before moving on down the aisle. Tammas stared out the window, keeping the money enclosed in the palm of his hand. The night could yet turn into something although in another way he would have preferred the actual ticket. Having this extra bit of dough was a bit of a nuisance. It left him twopence short of the minimum tote bet. Better to have had nothing but the sixty quid he was giving himself. He stuck the change into his trouser pocket. Out of this sixty he was keeping forty for his nap. The dog in question was running in the fourth and it was out of Trap 1. It was a good dog, a fast dog, and he fancied it very strongly. The other twenty quid was just for playing about with on forecasts and small single bets.

The bus was crowded; it had been standing room only downstairs. On arrival at Shawfield Stadium he sat on until everybody else had left; he strode down to the rearmost seat and from there back to the front, peering down into the corners of the floor but nothing at all was lying except a few empty beer cans and other assorted litter. The conductor was reaching to change the destination screen while listening to something the driver was saying; they both glanced at him as he came down the stairs.

He walked on past the vendors of the *Greyhound Adviser*, on up to the entrance where an elderly woman was sitting on a wooden stool, selling pens and pencils. He paid his money at the turnstile and was returned a programme.

Out on the track the handlers were walking the dogs for the first race. Numbers flickered slowly on the totalisator board, few bets ever being struck in earnest for this race; it usually consisted of dogs new to the track or dogs returning after injury. Form rarely existed on it. Tammas leaned on a stanchion studying the programme. Of the twenty quid he was allowing five on this race; he decided to stick it onto Trap 3. The handlers began leading the dogs into the traps and he was aware of the loose change in his pocket. An additional twopence and he had an actual bet. The hooter sounded. The hare trundled off round the rail. Some cheers from the punters. Dog 3 got beat. While the handlers were out capturing them after the finish he wandered off, his gaze to the ground. He reached the wall dividing the track from the enclosure and stared about. The busfare home was not essential. It was not a bad evening, mild. The busfare would give him a bet. Coupled with the cash returned him by the conductor he had enough for a twenty pence bet on the tote, twice the minimum. He could stick the whole lot on a dog. Or split it two way, 10 on the 2nd race and 10 on the 3rd. Or keep the 20 pence for the nap he had chosen; it would be racing in the 4th. Or a forecast, a 10 pence reverse forecast. Or even a place-only bet of 20 pence. No need even to dig out a winner, just one to finish in the first two. It was a safety first bet, that was the thing about it. And if it came up and he had the same sort of bet on the 3rd, then he might end up with something for the 4th, to stick down on his nap. The place-only bet was correct, it was the correct thing to do. And so what if the dog actually won the race instead of just running second, it would not matter, the point was to get a return, to keep getting returns. It made no difference whether it won or was second, just so long as it was placed and he could go up to the pay-out window and be given a return for his money.

He was standing amongst the small crowd directly beneath the row of bookies, checking the form for the race, studying times and weights and distances. Yet it would not matter. The dog he decided on would either be placed or not. Which dog did not make any difference. He glanced at the list again. Nothing striking about the names of the five runners. More punters had arrived and he watched them busying about the line, trying to pick off the best price about their selections. And the vet was now on the track checking the dogs. He gazed back at the punters and the bookies but there was nothing catching the interest, nothing of note. He turned and strode off towards the tote windows and joined one of the queues. There was a woman in front of him, smoking rapidly and continually glancing behind to see if the dogs were about to start racing.

He was going to back Trap 4. The dog coming out of Trap 4, this was the one. The woman left the window clutching her tote receipts.

Tammas sniffed. Trap 4 twenty pence a place, he said to the girl. She stamped out the numbers, took his money and gave him the receipt.

Trap 4.

On examining the form he saw that this dog out of the fourth trap had a good chance after all. He was glad he had gone for it. According to the form notes it had been off the course injured for some time but was now back and expected to do okay. He remembered he still had £15 out of the £20 playing about with money and decided to stick it all on. In fact he felt like sticking the other £40 he was keeping for the nap down on it as well. But no, that was wrong, that was the wrong way. The forty had to be for the nap. The quick route to going skint usually lay in changing your mind at the last minute.

The hooter. Tammas thrust the programme into his back pocket and pulled the half smoked cigarette from behind his ear, he struck a match to light it, was exhaling smoke when the traps crashed open.

He kept silent throughout the race but began nodding as the favourite came wide round the last bend to run on past dog 4 up the home straight, with this dog 4 just managing to hang on for second place from the fast finishing Trap 1.

In the large queue at the pay-out window he listened to

the folk who had backed the winning forecast. He could have backed the forecast. Easy. The favourite to win from dog 4. He could have dug out that forecast no bother. The fact that he went for dog 4 a place proved it. Yet this was nothing to do with anything. What he had done was back the dog to get placed and it had got placed and he was getting a return for his money, and this was the point.

Once he had the money he went into the bar and bought a carton of bovril, carrying it to a shelf at the side of the area. Including everything he now had 57 pence. This 57 pence was good. Another 3 would see him with 60. Without the bovril he would have had 65 and with 5 pence more the round 70.

Leaving the bovril on the shelf he returned to the counter and bought a packet of crisps. This left him with 51 pence. 50 pence was not bad at all. It had come from nothing, nothing. A 50 pence bet was fine.

Along at the tote window he struck his next bet. Dog 2 50 pence a place, he said to the woman.

With the ticket in his pocket he swallowed the remains of the bovril and crumpled the crisp packet onto the floor, and left the bar. The programme was in his back pocket. But he left it there. No point even seeing if the dog stood a chance. That had nothing to do with it now. The bet was made. The 50 pence on Trap 2, no matter what. If it finished first or second he would receive cash in exchange for the ticket. He got it from his pocket and looked at it, it was green, a green ticket; 2. Trap 2, 50 pence place. A 50 pence was not bad. Even for the nap it would not have been too bad. 50 pence the nap would have been fine, it would have been alright. But no matter. It made no difference. Not at all. Nothing. There might have been no 50 pence. A mistake to even think about things like that.

The hooter.

Again he stayed silent throughout the race but he nodded, he nodded at dog 2 coming inside on the rails rounding the third bend and on round the last bend. And staying on really strong to get up and win its race on the line. Trap 2 winning the race. Trap 2 as the winner. But fuck all to do with it, fuck all to do with it. It made no difference. None at all. To have finished placed was the thing, the bet. To finish in the first two, that is what mattered, to get a return on the stake, in exchange for the cash; this is what it is about. And the next race was the fourth on the card, and the nap was going.

Dog 2 paid 2/1 on the tote a place, giving £1.50 in return for the 50 pence. And if he had backed the dog as a straight win on the tote he would have received more than four quid but so what, it was irrelevant, it had nothing to do with it – a mistake to even think it. He had £1.50 in his pocket and it had come from nothing, and that was the only point.

When it came time he made his way to the line of book-makers, letting the 1 pence coin fall from his hand, not looking where it landed. He hovered around the crowd of punters waiting to shade the odds and finally dashed in to take the 7/2 to the whole £1.50. And that was not bad. The morning paper had forecast 5/1 for this dog but he had known such a price was out of the question. 7/2 was fine, it was good. And when he was turning to leave the area he saw one bookie scrub out the 7/2 and mark up 3's. He nodded.

Up at the spot where he had been standing were two middle aged men. He stepped in closer, and another step, until he was in as near as he could manage, without banging into them. He was gripping the programme when the hooter sounded. And the hare trundling off on its way, collecting speed till rounding the bend and now hurtling towards the boxes, and up crashed the trap gates. Dog 1 was the nap, and it walked out its box, and he nodded, there was no chance. It had to get well off its mark to have any chance and it didnt, so it had none. There was no point even giving it a shout.

He watched the dog chasing after the pack, making up a fair bit of ground down the back straight, coming inside the dogs directly in front and eventually running on into third place. If the thing had trapped properly it would have guyed it, no danger. But it had finished third. Dog 2 had won and dog 5 was second. From somewhere behind him somebody cried: That fucking 5 dog should've pished it.

Tammas turned and shouted: You fucking kidding! Dog 1 was a fucking certainty – if it'd trapped it'd've fucking guyed it. Bastards. He shook his head and strode off and up towards the exit.

An attendant was standing there and he unlocked the door for him. Some boys were waiting outside and they glanced at the man as he closed the door.

He continued striding till beyond the car park and outside the ground he walked more slowly. Approaching the bridge he paused, taking the bookmaker's ticket from his pocket. He began to tear it up in rectangular sections, and then scattered them over the parapet, watching them as they landed on the river.

•••

On the following Tuesday morning he rose from the bench and walked from the smoke-area, down to the short flight of steps up to the gaffer's office. He walked up and chapped on the door, and opened it immediately. The chargehand was there, sitting on the edge of the desk. He was talking to the gaffer who was leaning back on his chair with his hands clasped behind his head. The two of them frowned at Tammas. He sniffed and said: Eh I want to leave, on Friday, I want to lift my books – I'm chucking it.

After a moment the gaffer nodded. Fine, he said.

He did not acknowledge the chargehand. He turned and went back out and down the steps. In the smoke-area he saw where he had been sitting previously, and he smiled. He nudged the man next to him: You got a spare fag at all?

The man said, Aye. And gave him one from his packet, and gave him a match.

Ta . . . Tammas lighted the cigarette and exhaled, he looked across at Ralphie and winked, smiled again. Ralphie nodded.

•••

It was 9 pm and a Friday evening, and he was in a pub up the town. From there he strolled along to the dancing. The doorman scarcely glanced at him as he entered and paid his money. At this time of night females and couples were the main people present. Nobody at all was on the floor dancing. Tammas bought a bottle of beer and he carried it upstairs to the balcony. He sat at one of the empty tables, taking an *Evening Times* from his side pocket; he glanced at the racing results then turned to the page with the following day's race programme. Across from him, a few tables off, sat a couple. While the girl sat with her elbows on the edge of the table the guy kept bending and kissing the nape of her neck. Eventually Tammas shifted on his chair so that he was not facing in their direction, turned a page of the newspaper; then he brought out his cigarettes and matches, but he stopped there.

John was approaching.

He was making his way over from the top of the staircase, a glass of beer in one hand and pointing at Tammas with the other, and laughing quite loudly. Ya bastard! he was saying. He put the glass down on the table and settled onto the chair opposite. So this is where you've been fucking hiding yourself!

How's it going John?

Ya bastard! John laughed and shook his head. D'you know something? You're bad news!

Tammas sniffed. He lifted his own glass of beer, sipped at it.

Naw no kidding ye man, bad news! John drank another mouthful of beer and he laughed once more. Heh you been in long? Christ – imagine finding you here!

Tammas nodded; and he turned slightly to gaze over the balcony rail, down onto the floor. A few people were now up dancing.

You should've told me Tammas. I've been wanting to start coming for ages. Same as the night I mean we're sitting in fucking *Simpson's* as usual and I says to Billy, d'you never get fucking sick of this man! Bad enough having to come every Saturday night but every fucking Friday night as well!

Tammas looked back at him, then added: Hh.

Aye, went on John. So I just ended up I got fucking up and walked out.

Did you . . .

Aye. Fucking browned off man, just sitting about there all night, week in week out . . . John frowned and he leaned closer to Tammas and he whispered: How the fuck do they ever expect to get a lumber man? I mean fuck sake – *Simpson's*!

Tammas chuckled.

Naw I mean even trying to get them to go up the fucking town for a change; new pubs, new scenery, the discos – anyfuckingthing!

You've got a point John.

They both drank from their glasses of beer. John grinned across at him. So this is where you've been hiding! You're a fucking fox Tammas – see if Donnie knew!

Tammas smiled.

But what about yon lassie? Betty – what about her?

He shrugged. Ach, just passing the time. The now I mean, being up here.

Aw aye. John nodded. Are you still going with her like?

Eh . . . I dont think so, no really.

Aw, aye . . . John nodded again then lifted his glass and swallowed a mouthful of beer.

The queue at the bar had lengthened and he had to wait a while to be served. Everybody was having to shout their orders to be heard above the general noise. Tammas bought four bottles of beer. Back upstairs he told John, It'll save time.

Good thinking. John took his first one and poured it into his glass. Then he leaned forwards across the table; he sniffed and whispered: See them along at the next table up from the pillar. He nodded his head in that direction and added, One of them's got a blue blouse and black hair. What d'you think man?

Tammas wrinkled his nose. Wait a wee minute yet.

Aye okay, but I'm just saying man I mean . . .

Aye but we're no in a rush.

Naw I know that but eh – no fancy it man? Eh? they're no that bad. I mean it doesnt matter if we get a knockback.

Tammas looked at him.

Naw I mean Christ, everybody gets a fucking knockback now and again.

I know that John; fuck sake, I'm no worried about that.

Well then, Christ, just to get started.

It's only fucking ten o'clock.

John nodded and looked away. He lifted his glass and held it, not drinking, staring down at the people dancing below. When the song ended he continued staring down for several moments, until the next one began. He turned to Tammas: Hey man I heard you'd chucked the job?

Did you?

Aye.

Hh.

Billy was telling us the night; he met your big sister or something.

Tammas nodded.

So he said.

More people were getting onto the floor now. Some were coming from upstairs, including the two girls sitting along by the pillar. John pointed them out below and he made to say something, but Tammas nodded and stood to his feet. Okay, he said, and he grinned and rubbed his hands together.

Great! John got up at once then hesitated, indicated the beer. What d'you reckon?

We'll chance it, come on.

The girls were dancing together, not too far from the edge of the floor, where there was now a row of tables and chairs. Tammas and John walked forward, strolling round the side of each one, and began dancing, without saying anything. The girls moved slightly from facing each other, so that they were more in the direction of Tammas and John. And John began to call to the one with the blue blouse and dark hair, attempting a conversation. Soon afterwards Tammas had edged his dancing in such a way that he and his partner were facing away from John and the other girl.

He gazed to the side of his partner's head, towards the band, watching the female vocalist as she sang the chorus at one of the guitarists. The girl he was with was taller than John's. She had yet to look in his direction. For a time he looked at her but still she stared elsewhere. At the end of the song he said: You staying on the floor?

She shook her head. He nodded and walked off immediately. John was behind him, tapping him on the shoulder: See mine! he was saying; Terrible! No kidding you Tammas, trying to chat her and that man like talking to a brick wall so it was, fucking murder man – what about yours?

Tammas continued on up the stairs to the balcony. Their beer was still lying on the table and nobody was sitting there. John made straight for the rail and sat down on the seat nearest, gazing over. There they are, he said. See them?

Tammas nodded but remained where he was; the position he was in it was not possible to see over. He lighted a cigarette, glanced round about, then said, How's the time?

I've no got my watch on. Still early but . . . John returned his attention to the dance floor, and added: Would you ask them up again?

Would I fuck.

Naw, neither would I man. There's plenty other yins but. John sat around and raised his glass and drank the rest of the beer, and he reached for his second bottle, poured it in.

Tammas sniffed. To be honest about it John I think I'll get going I mean I actually only came in to pass the time.

What, how d'you mean?

Naw man I just eh, came in to pass the time, I wasnt going to stay.

Tch, fuck sake Tammas.

Naw – Christ, that was how I came, just in out the rain for an hour, Trying to keep out the boozer!

John nodded. Then he stared over the parapet.

Honest man, I'm going somewhere else.

Are you?

Aye, Christ. Tammas had poured in his second bottle of beer and he drank most of it in one go. He rose, I'm just leaving this.

Where is it you're going?

Eh it's a club.

Aw.

Well no really a club man a kind of casino, it's a kind of casino.

A casino? Is it that one you were telling us about already?

Aye, probably. He pointed at his glass, the beer that was left in it. I'm just leaving that . . . I mean if eh . . .

John nodded. He had lifted his own and was now drinking it all down. He stood up afterwards, wiping his lips. I'll come with you, he said.

Tammas looked at him.

Naw I'm no fucking doing anything anyway man I mean it looks like it's going to be fucking rubbish here I mean . . . He shrugged and went on. See sometimes you start off bad you feel things arent going to work out I mean that fucking lassie with the blue blouse man you could tell she wasnt fucking interested. I knew it right away – no fucking point even trying man.

Fine.

•••

89

Rain was falling quite heavily and neither had an overcoat. They walked quickly, occasionally trotting, keeping in as close to the buildings as possible. When they arrived down the lane Tammas rang the bell next to the POSITIVELY MEMBERS ONLY notice while John remained out beyond the small entrance lobby in the shadows. He had to ring the bell again. There was an orange light contained inside it which went out once the button was pressed. He glanced at John, pursing his lips and shrugging. Then the door opened. The doorman was more than 6' tall. He said: Aye?

Hello, replied Tammas, and made to enter. But the doorman stood where he was.

Where you going son?

Well I was going to go inside. Is it alright I mean can you sign us in or what?

Sign you in? The doorman frowned. You been here before like?

Aye, a couple of weeks ago.

The doorman shook his head.

Well more than that. But I definitely got in and I'm sure it was you done the signing for me – there was three of us.

It wasnt me signed you in son, it must have been one of the ones you were with. The doorman glanced sideways along the lane. Then he muttered: Who was it you were with anyway?

Murdie McKinnon, and a guy called Rankine, I cant mind his first name.

The doorman nodded. I know wee Murdie . . . He looked at John and added: Many are you?

Just the two.

Ah right you are then okay . . . The man stood to the side, opening the door for them. But mind, no noise or fuck all. And you better get yourself a membership card in future.

They walked along a short corridor into a fairly narrow

room where a woman was serving coffee and tea and a variety of snacks from behind a counter. Half a dozen tables with about four chairs round each stood near to the opposite wall. Mostly women were there, young women, sitting chatting or else gazing up at the large television set on a high shelf up from the counter. John had ordered coffees and two chocolate biscuits; he carried them to where Tammas was standing, and he indicated two empty chairs. No fancy a seat? he whispered.

Naw. Tammas took the coffee and the biscuit from him, headed towards the door at the top end of the room. When he laid his hand on the handle John frowned and said quietly, Tammas, no fancy sitting down in here?

Naw, no here.

John murmured, All the women and that I mean . . . see that wee blonde sitting down there near the door – naw man no kidding ye but she was looking, she was looking, no kidding ye, when I was up there at the counter and that, honest man I'm no kidding ye.

Tammas nodded as he opened the door. They're all brass-nails, he whispered. Every one of them man they're on the game.

What?

Aye . . . He held the door ajar for John to come in then closed it quietly.

The other room had been quite noisy because of the television and this room was also noisy, but the noise came from the game of cards taking place. Some twenty or so men were grouped around three sides of a horseshoe table; at the fourth side sat the dealer between his two workers, one of whom was wearing a bunnet while the other wore a sort of fedora. Several poker tables lay idle; at one of them a man sprawled, asleep, his head cradled on his folded forearms.

When they finished the snack they put in £1.50 each for their joint stake. Tammas was to play the cards. The game was *chemin de fer*. He stood behind the row of spectators who were standing just out from the table. He stood for more than twenty minutes. At first he replied when John spoke but gradually he stopped it and edged in closer to the table. Now that the pubs had closed it was becoming more crowded in the room. Tammas held £1 in his hand. The next chance he got he leaned across one of the seated players' shoulders and laid it down. And the worker wearing the fedora covered the bet immediately. Tammas stepped back.

About quarter of an hour later their £3 stake was up to £8. John tapped him on the arm. He was holding another two coffees. Thought you might be a bit thirsty, he said.

Aw aye. Ta . . . Tammas took the cup; he stood for a moment then he raised it to his mouth but the worker with the fedora waved him way from the table and called: Just in case you spill it son.

Tammas nodded. As he moved away from the table he muttered, I wasnt really feeling like this John.

John led the way to one of the poker tables.

Tammas lighted a cigarette and then sipped at his coffee, gazing back across at the game. John grinned and shrugged. Hey, he asked, much we winning?

Eh, about a fiver I think.

A fiver. Great, great stuff. No fancy splitting?

Tammas smiled.

Naw serious man I mean, no fancy it?

I thought you were kidding.

Christ Tammas when you think about it, Christ, we might end up losing it back again. Fiver's a fiver I mean that's two and half each man.

Tammas took the money out of his trouser pocket and peeled off four singles, and gave them to him. John sniffed while lifting them, he put them in his trouser pocket. Then he brought them back out. Look, he said, are you wanting to hang on or what?

Aye.

Okay then I mean . . . He shrugged and returned the money.

You dont have to John, I can carry on on my tod.

Naw, he said, naw.

You sure?

Aye. Tell you what, give us a pound back; you take yours as well; so's if we lose then we're only losing 50p. Eh?

Good, aye . . . Tammas grinned. That's sense. He stood up and returned to the chemmy.

John was tapping him on the shoulder. It's after 1 o'clock, he was saying, I'm going – make sure I catch the half one bus from the Square.

Okay man; if I get a turn I'll come up your place the morrow afternoon.

Today afternoon!

Aye . . . You alright I mean or do you need another couple of quid for the fare?

Naw naw, it's okay Tammas.

You sure?

Aye.

Outside of the immediate space round the table the gaming room was deserted now; but among those present a few were spectating, mainly losers. Tammas was sitting on a seat at one of the smaller sides of the table. From a peak of £24 his money had declined to £1, and it had been more than twenty minutes since he had managed to get a bet on. The bank travelled back to him. About to let it pass he shrugged and tossed in one of the 50 pence pieces. The dealer grimaced. The worker wearing the fedora hat – his name was Deefy – turned to mutter: It's getting a bit late for fifty pence pieces young yin. It's just prolonging the agony.

Tammas hesitated.

A man sitting farther along smiled suddenly and pushing three singles £1 notes onto the centre of the baize said: Since you're no everybody son.

The other worker returned the man the 50 pence piece. The dealer nodded: Fine Erskine . . . right lad it's a three pound box.

The bet was covered at once and he flicked the first card of the bank to the man called Erskine; but he passed it straight on to Tammas, face down. And the second was flicked to him directly.

The bank's opponent asked for a card and was dealt a 10. Tammas showed a pair of 2's and won. He won the next hand also, and the bank now had £12 going onto the third round. Erskine gave him a wink as he reached for the cards. Two 4's. Turning them face up immediately he called: Natural.

Is a winner, replied his opponent, throwing his cards in.

The dealer collected the £24, deducting £3 house-puggy which he folded and slid through a slot on the edge of the table. Okay lads, he called, there's twenty one quid to go; all or any part.

The previous loser quickly bankoed the sum. On receiving his cards he asked for another; he was given a 7.

Tammas was showing 6; after a moment he also asked for another card and he was dealt a 5. Aw Christ, he said.

The other man shook his head and grunted: Dont worry about it son. And he threw down his cards, a 3 and a 10 to go with his 7, which all totalled 0.

Brilliant play: laughed Erskine. Your one's a winner kid – you did the right thing taking a card. Here . . . He opened a packet of thin cigars and tossed one across the baize.

Tammas grinned and struck a match to light it.

The loser was counting a wad of notes onto the pile in the centre of the table. The dealer raised his head, he turned to Tammas: What you doing son, you wanting any money out?

Naw, it's alright.

The dealer glanced at the loser. Okay Davie, you've got the bet.

When the cards had been dealt the man spread his calmly, showing two 4's. Natural, he said.

Same. Tammas showed a 3 and a 5.

Jesus Christ!

The dealer frowned at him.

Deefy called: It's a good paddle Davie.

Good paddle! Hh! The guy turned his head, he reached into his pocket and got out a cigarette, and lighted it.

Okay . . . The dealer tapped the table then dealt the cards from the shoe. He looked at Davie who shook his head, and he turned to Tammas who spread his two cards on the baize, showing 7.

Aw for fuck sake! Davie stood up from his seat and threw in his cards. He sat back down again, put his elbow on the table and laid his chin in the palm of the hand.

The money and the cards were still lying on the baize. The dealer and the two workers had sat back on their seats and were lighting cigarettes. Eventually the dealer sat forwards, put the cigarette in his mouth and lifted the money, counted it, extracted the puggy and folded it into the slot. He glanced at Erskine.

Erskine nodded. Pass mine, he said. He smiled at Tammas. I'm passing son, it cant last forever.

Tammas shrugged and inhaled on the cigar; then he nodded and turned his head to blow out the smoke, coughing slightly. And he watched the dealer count the bank's money into four piles, and pass three of them plus part of the other one, up to Erskine.

Okay kid, the dealer said, you've got fifteen quid – what you doing? Want to withdraw anything?

Tammas was staring down at the money and made no answer.

The dealer looked at him. Listen, you were only in for a sixth of what was there – half a quid to Erskine's two and a half. As it is I've had to stick you in a couple of bob to make up the round fifteen.

Aye, said Deefy. You've got to mind there's a puggy coming off.

Tammas shrugged. Might as well leave it all in then.

The previous loser bankoed the money immediately. Tammas won again and the man bankoed once more, on the £30. When he lost he sat staring at the money for some time, he was still holding his wallet in one hand.

Davie . . . The dealer asked, What you doing?

The guy looked at him.

You wanting eh . . . ? The dealer nodded his head at the money on the baize.

Naw. Davie slid the wallet into the inside pocket in his jacket and got up off his seat, he walked across the floor and out of the room.

The dealer raised his eyebrows and pursed his lips; he glanced quickly at Deefy and shrugged. Then he put the cigarette in his mouth and taking the puggy from the bank he said to Tammas, You've got fifty four quid son.

Give me a score.

Once he had passed him it the dealer glanced round at everybody. Thirty four quid lads, all or any part.

There was an immediate rush from the punters. Apart from the previous loser nobody had managed to get a bet on since the third round of the current bank. Both workers moved quickly trying to see that those who had stuck their money down first were covered, but even so there were a few grumbles. The dealer remained silent. He sat back on his chair smoking, one hand behind his head. Then he put the cigarette in his mouth and leaned forwards, tapped the table and flicked the cards from the shoe.

The man who had made the largest bet of the punters was given the cards; and he asked for another. The dealer gave him a 2. Tammas turned his and stayed on 4 to win. He inhaled the cigar and coughed, he pulled over an ashtray and ground it out then lighted one of his cigarettes. The dealer was looking at him, indicating the money. Tammas said, Give us thirty; split five for the workers; the rest goes.

The dealer smiled. He counted the £30 swiftly and passed it over, then he gave Deefy the additional £5. Deefy nodded to Tammas. And the other worker called: Ta son.

The cards were dealt. Tammas won again and waved his hand when the dealer glanced at him. And the dealer paused a moment, gathered up the money and called: Okay lads, there's fifty eight quid here says there's a bet for every one of yous.

After the initial flurry of money there was a fairly quick dwindling of it. The dealer grinned: I'll take it in coppers!

A few of the men laughed, and began digging into their pockets. One of them brought out a ten pound note, some lesser stakes were laid down; then nothing. The dealer glanced at two men who were sitting next to each other. They had not placed a solitary bet since Tammas had taken the bank. The dealer pushed the shirt cuff back off his wrist and he examined his watch, muttering, Could be the last hand this, if we dont get moving soon.

One of the pair sniffed; the other one nodded, he placed five fivers on the baize.

Pony's a good bet, replied the dealer, and he looked round at the rest of the players. Another tenner and we go.

One of the spectators stepped forwards; his hand came out of his coat pocket and he tossed two crumpled £1 notes onto the table.

Deefy lifted them and smoothed them and he winked at the guy. Stopped raining anyway Tommy – nice night for a walk!

The guy laughed. And soon the remaining £8 was taken by different punters. And the dealer was tapping the table and calling: Okay lads, we go . . .

The major bettor was given the punters' cards. He looked at them for a couple of seconds before saying: No card.

Tammas asked for one and the dealer flicked him a 7. That's it, said Tammas, and he showed his other two – both facecards.

The opposition tossed in his cards and shook his head: I've got 7 as well!

Another good paddle! called the worker with the bunnet.

Him and his fucking paddles, muttered a man.

Somebody from behind called: You cant beat that boy.

Then Deefy said. It's only a draw lads it's only a draw. Good yin but! He glanced at Tammas and winked.

The dealer had folded his arms and leaned back on his chair, gazing round at everybody. The conversations going on were quite noisy but eventually those doing the talking began to stop, and to look at the dealer. He sighed and grunted, Is that us got a bit of order at last?

Once the cards had been dealt the punters' man glanced at his and made to speak. But before he did so Tammas was upturning his own pair and calling: 9 – natural!

Deefy grinned and he lifted the cards and put them next to each other on the centre of the table. A good 9, he said.

The reaction was not as loud as on the paddle; but three men left the game immediately and a couple of others moved away to sit at one of the poker tables. The dealer opened his cigarette packet and lighted a fresh one from the burning end of the old one. He passed one each to the workers, then glanced at Tammas but closed the packet when he saw he was smoking already.

All the money and the cards were still lying in a heap towards the middle of the baize. Deefy and the other worker had moved their chairs back the way and were conducting a conversation behind the dealer.

Tammas had borrowed the following morning's *Daily Record* from a man and was reading the back pages. After a bit he turned to the racing, and noticed the workers now leaning to take in the cards. They began shuffling for a new shoe. He shut the newspaper and returned it to the man.

Okay, said the dealer. Much you wanting son?

Much have I got?

Hundred and sixteen.

Tammas frowned at the money on the baize.

The dealer smiled: Want me to count it? He sniffed and began to do so immediately.

It's alright.

But the dealer continued, sorting it into wads of £20. A hundred and sixteen it is. Much you wanting.

See what you can get on.

Okay . . . The dealer paused and smiled before saying: Right you are lads, quite a bit to go now.

A few grunts greeted this. Then a voice saying: How much exactly Jake?

Eh . . . The dealer glanced up. It was Erskine back.

Much is it? For a banko.

The dealer glanced sideways: You sure you dont want something out son?

Eh naw, eh what about the workers maybe? Give them the odd six quid. And the puggy as well? What about it?

Fuck the puggy! The dealer grinned and extracted six singles and passed them to Deefy. Then he smiled at Erskine. You've got a hundred and ten.

Erskine nodded. He had taken a thick wad of notes from his trouser pocket and began counting. But one of the two men who had lost most of the last bet suddenly stood up. Wait a minute, he cried, this is fucking ridiculous. I just done a forty there! A forty – and you're trying to tell me I've not to get a chance to get my money back!

The dealer stared at him.

Fuck sake Jake!

A silence followed. Then Erskine said: Fair enough. Let them get as much on as they like – I'm no bothering.

Well it's up to you, said the dealer. But as far as I'm concerned you've bankoed the bet. And a banko's a banko in this club.

Erskine shrugged.

The other man nodded and sat down again. He and his mate counted exactly £40 out and deposited it on the baize. Deefy quickly covered it with £40 from the bank. The dealer called: Okay lads, get the money down!

And wee bets were laid and covered, some of them coin stacks which Deefy and the other worker checked through methodically. As soon as there was a pause the dealer said: Finished. That's it.

Seventy two quid, said Deefy.

Seventy two, called the dealer.

Erskine nodded: It's a bet.

The dealer stuck the cigarette back in his mouth and he dealt quickly, sliding the cards out from the shoe, keeping his right forefinger on each. One of the punters at the front took the cards and kept them face down, neither looking at them nor letting anyone else look at them; he passed them up to Erskine who asked for another. The dealer flipped him a 9, then he glanced at Tammas. Tammas turned his two cards over, two 2's. Beat it, he said.

Erskine shook his head. I cant; I cant beat it. He shrugged and tossed in his cards.

Fucking hell, muttered somebody.

And somebody else sighed. Apart from that it was silent for several seconds.

Tammas put his hand in his pocket to get his cigarettes, and noticed he had one still burning in the ashtray, but it had almost burned down onto the tip. He tapped the ash off then ground it out. A cigarette landed beside his hand. It had been thrown by the dealer. Ta, he said.

The dealer nodded. He turned to the other worker and whispered something to him, and the man got up off his seat and walked ben the snacks' room. Then he turned back to Tammas again, and he gestured at the piles of money and pursed his lips. Take it son, he said. Unless . . . he glanced up towards Erskine.

You joking! Erskine smiled. No me Jake. The boy's a machine.

The dealer nodded; he glanced briefly round at the other punters and shook his head. He pointed at the money again. On you go son . . . they're finished.

Tammas nodded.

Both the dealer and Deefy helped him tidy all the money, separating it out into the different denominations. There were a few pounds in silver coins. Tammas took the notes and left the rest lying. Eh . . . he shrugged at the dealer, indicating it. The workers, eh . . . he shrugged again.

The dealer nodded. He sorted out £5 in 50 pence pieces and gave it to Deefy, leaving the rest in the centre of the baize. Okay lads! He called: Okay lads . . . there's about six quid here for the first Jack, the first Jack for six quid!

Most of the previous punters and most of the spectators all returned to the table.

Tammas left his seat quickly, stuffing the notes into his trouser pocket and keeping his hand inside.

In the other room Erskine was standing chatting to the doorman and the woman who served behind the counter. The very boy, he grinned. Hey son, d'you play poker?

Just a wee bit.

Ah well that's where I'm headed the now if you're interested. You're welcome to tag along.

Eh, naw, I'll no bother. Thanks but.

Suit yourself, suit yourself. Erskine smiled. I'll see you then, cheerio.

Tammas nodded and continued to the door. The doorman was there before him and he followed him along the short corridor.

A girl came from the Ladies toilet and she looked at him as she passed.

Thanks for letting us in, he said to the doorman.

No bother son.

This is eh . . . Tammas gave him £5 and walked off but when the door shut he began trotting. And when the reached the end of the lane he started to run quite fast, not stopping till he saw a taxi for hire, and he signalled the driver.

•••

He woke up suddenly. The curtains were not drawn and the room was bright. The alarm clock had stopped. He got out of bed, crossed to the window and peered out. Quite a few folk were on the street. He turned to the cupboard, tugged on the bottom drawer. The thick wad lay in the corner beneath his socks. He took it out and counted it, threw it on the bed; he dressed in moments, grabbed the money and raced downstairs and along to the betting shop. It was approaching 1.30. The first race of the day was about to begin. Tammas scanned the board, strode to the wall to study the formpages; but when the next show of betting came through he went to the side of the counter and beckoned across Phil, the elderly man who worked there as cashier on Saturdays.

I want the second best to eighty quid, he said quietly.

Phil nodded. He walked off behind the partition to where the manager was. When he returned he accepted the money without comment. Tammas strolled to a radiator to stand. A guy he knew approached and started to chat about the race. He had stuck 50 pence on the same horse. Tammas nodded when he told him this, then he shook his head and stared at the floor. Before the race was due off he left the place and trotted along the couple of blocks to another bookie. The race was over when he arrived. The favourite had won and his selection was not in the first three. The boardman ripped the page down and stuck up the next. Tammas called: Hey what happened to the second best there?

The boardman shook his head, spat onto the floor. Never in the hunt, he said.

Tammas lighted a cigarette. Another show of betting began and he went to one of the formpages but without looking at it he turned away and left, and he hailed the first available taxi.

John was still in bed; his mother led Tammas into the living room. About five minutes later John entered, wearing a dressing gown; he slumped onto an armchair, swung his legs over its side. Tammas threw him a cigarette, gave him the burning matchstick.

John coughed on the smoke. He groaned and inhaled again. Cheer up, said Tammas, taking the wad from his pocket. He began dividing it into equal piles on the rug in front of the fireplace . . . One to you and one to me, two to you and two to me, five to you and five to me . . .

John's eyelids parted more widely and he gaped at the money, sitting upright on the chair now and with his arms tensed. For fuck sake, he was saying.

. . . and one to you and one to me. And Tammas continued counting. While he was doing so he started detailing the events of the night. Finally he sat back, smiling. I told you man. I knew we'd knock it off. A wee bit of patience.

John was nodding.

I've never felt anything like it man, No kidding ye it was fucking – Christ! You should've been there to see it.

John nodded. Then he frowned at Tammas for a moment. He said, Eh . . . see that you were saying there man . . . was that no – what you were saying, were you no saying it was more than two hundred quid?

What?

Naw I mean at the chemmy, when you won that last yin, was it no for two hundred quid or something?

Two hundred and twenty. Tammas nodded, he glanced at the two piles on the floor. By the time I gave out tips and that, and eh . . . aye, I stuck a few on a fucking mule – finished third.

How much?

Eighty. Eighty quid.

Eighty quid! Eighty quid! John had sat forwards on his chair and now he sat back the way, leaning against the side. Fuck sake Tammas! Eighty quid!

Okay.

Naw I mean Christ that's fucking – I mean it wasnt your fucking money. John sat forwards again and he pointed at the money on the floor: Fifty two and a half quid each you're saying?

Aye, fifty two and a half each, aye.

Fuck sake.

What?

What! Christ sake Tammas it wasnt your fucking money to stick on a horse, it was mine, it was the two of us, it wasnt just fucking yours – I mean that should be a fucking hundred I'm getting. I know it was you that won it and all that, but eighty quid on a horse! A tenner aye but eighty! I mean that's fucking . . .

Tammas looked at him. Then he shook his head and he bent to lift one of the wads which he folded and thrust in his trouser pocket. He walked to the door. I'll see you, he said.

Tch Tammas, wait a minute.

Nah.

Och come on for fuck sake! John was off the armchair and coming towards him with his hands raised palms upwards.

Naw. Tammas continued on down the lobby. I'll see you

later, he said and he opened the outside door and stepped out and closed it behind himself immediately.

•••

Two guys were sitting on the second bottom step of the flight up to the labour exchange, one held a bottle of wine and was wiping his lips when Tammas got out of the taxi. He paid the driver. They watched him as he approached, and continued watching him as he stepped roundabout, and on up into the place. He joined the queue at his box number, taking the newspaper from his side pocket and unfolding it.

When it came his turn to sign the clerk told him nothing had come through yet and asked if he wanted a B1 form for the social security office.

No, ta.

Along the street he met Brian McCann, a regular from *Simpson's* who was heading down to the job centre. It was crowded inside. McCann went directly to the vacancy board while Tammas walked over to the thick, upholstered seats near one of the interviewer's desks and he sat there reading the newspaper. McCann called him eventually and they left. On the pavement McCann muttered, Fuck all – unless you want to count Welwyn Garden City.

Hh. Tammas gave him a cigarette and paused to strike a match.

They're wanting electricians but. McCann smiled briefly; he bent to take a light; he exhaled. Aye, I'll tell the wife to pack this afternoon.

Tammas grinned. He stopped walking at the bus stop but McCann hesitated. Dont worry about it, said Tammas, patting his pocket.

McCann shrugged. He nipped his cigarette and stuck it behind his ear.

Tammas was pointing to one of the day's runners on the racing page of the newspaper. That Mint Julep, he said, I fancy it quite strongly.

Mm, aye.

If I mind right it won a handicap up at Haydock a month or so ago, eh?

I think so. McCann nodded, looking up the road. He brought the half cigarette from behind his ear and gestured with it to Tammas who handed him the box of matches. Ta . . . eh . . . He sniffed: Eh Tammas, any chance of a pound till the weekend?

Aye Christ fuck here. Tammas got one out and gave him it. Course, dont be daft.

Naw it's just for a packet of fags and that.

Christ. Tammas shook his head. Not at all man, hh, a pound! He inhaled deeply, looked back at the racing page. Naw, he said, I think I'll leave them alone the day – maybe go to the pictures or something, stay out the road.

McCann chuckled. He cleared his throat and spat into the gutter. No seen Billy this morning?

Naw, I waited for him as well; must've slept in – unless he signed early or something.

They dont usually allow you to – fucking strict about things like that; in case you've got a casual or something.

Aw aye.

Which in his case is fucking right anyway! McCann laughed: Lucky wee bastard so he is, I wouldnt mind the chance of marking a board myself!

Trouble is he's no lifted a full fucking wage since he started!

Tch, is he still punting? I told him to screw the fucking nut about that. I mean a job like he's got! You'd just wind up working for nothing if you werent careful.

That's what he's doing. He's no backed a winner for weeks.

Mad! McCann shook his head, he looked back up the road. There was a bus in sight. Come on we'll walk, he said.

What?

Mon we'll walk . . .

Walk?

Aye. McCann upturned the collar of his jacket and set off without further comment.

Okay.

They walked steadily. After ten minutes a drizzle started and they quickened the pace. When they approached the corner of the street where *Simpson's* was Tammas said, Fancy a pint?

Eh – I've to meet the wife at the Post Office.

You sure?

Aye.

Honest?

Aye. Fuck sake. McCann was frowning at him.

Naw I mean if it was just cause of the dough and that . . .

Naw.

Tammas nodded.

McCann continued on by himself.

•••

I bumped into that girl earlier on.

What was that?

Margaret shook her head. You never told me you'd stopped seeing her.

Are you talking about Betty?

Well I didnt know you were seeing anybody else!

Mm . . . Tammas looked away. His cigarette was lying smouldering in the ashtray; he puffed twice on it, before stubbing it out and swallowing what was left of his coffee. He returned his attention to the television.

I dont think it's right.

He made no response.

Tammas, I dont think it's right. Surely you could at least see her and tell her if you dont want to go out with her. I mean she was upset the girl, it's no fair.

Margaret, God sake.

Well you dont treat people like that.

He turned his face to her: Like what? I've no done anything.

Tch! You walked away and left her standing in the middle of the street.

Did she tell you that?

Yes, who else? you never say a word.

Tammas sniffed.

Did you?

What?

Just leave her? in the middle of Renfield Street?

Look Margaret I mean what is this at all . . . He resumed watching the television.

After several seconds she said: Well will you at least see her?

He nodded slightly.

Really?

I was going to anyway.

Were you?

Margaret, God sake.

Well if Robert had ever treated me like that!

Like what? I mean Margaret . . . He groaned and got up off the settee. Shaking his head he grabbed his cigarettes and matches from the coffee-table and he frowned at her while passing on his way ben the room.

•••

In *Simpson's* bar Auld Roper was scowling at McCann. That's us having to avoid a granny! he said, A granny!

Ach stop your moaning for fuck sake. Shuffle the doms. Anyhow ya silly auld cunt ye, if you hadnt hung on to that double blank we wouldnt fucking be in this fucking position. McCann glared at him and raised his pint glass to his mouth, sipped at the lager. He glanced at Tammas and winked: Eh? Want to swop mates?

Ho!

It's they auld yins, laughed Billy, they never fucking learn!

Never fucking learn! What you fucking yapping about? Auld Roper shook his head: The luck yous two are carrying! Jesus Christ Almighty I wish yous'd fucking fill in my coupon – eh! Lucky pair of . . . ! He sniffed and reached for his tumbler.

Skill, said Tammas.

Skill! Skill! That's a bloody good yin right enough. Eh McCann? D'you hear him? Skill for fuck sake! He wouldnt know what skill was if it jumped up and punched him one on the fucking chin!

The other three laughed.

Come on, shuffle the doms!

It's your turn, replied McCann.

Auld Roper turned to him: I'm going for a fucking pish – if it's alright with you that is . . . And he moved his chair backwards, rising with the aid of his stick. Tammas also got up and went to the bar to order a round. The argument had resumed by the time he carried the pints across. Auld Roper had also returned; he grinned at him and pointed at McCann. He's away in the fucking cream puff! Imagine that? At his time of life.

My time of life! Ya auld cunt, what you blethering about!

The elderly man shook his head; he leaned back the way to put his hand into his side pocket and bring out his cigarettes. He took one out, lighted it, put the packet away again. McCann was frowning at him. So generous, he said, so fucking generous.

Well what am I supposed to do! Hand them round the bloody pub!

I'm just after buying you a pint! said Tammas.

Auld Roper looked at him. I said thank you . . . His gaze was on the dominoes he had lifted; he was sorting through them, the cigarette in his mouth, his eyelids blinking occasionally to avoid the smoke. Then he muttered, This is a terrible hand this. Ah well McCann, prepare yourself for a granny, we've no chance!

Lying auld bastard, said Billy.

I'm no lying son; the worst hand I've seen for twenty years – tell you something but, we'll still fuck yous! Eh McCann?

Shut up and play your doms.

Aw give us peace ya crabbit swine ye!

Billy said to Tammas: Just let them fight among themselves.

Tammas smiled. He had been studying his own dominoes.

He laid them on the table and ripped open the cellophane on the new cigarette packet, offered it about. Then the game continued. Towards the close McCann put the two pieces he had left on the edge of the table. He waited a moment before saying, That's me finito, no fucking point.

You have to play it out, said Tammas.

McCann was staring at Auld Roper: How come you cut the fives? A simple question, there you are. I mean you must've fucking known I was holding the double. You must've, surely?

Auld Roper drank beer.

A simple question, come on.

Auld Roper looked roundabout and began to whistle quietly between closed teeth, then he studied his own dominos. And Billy said to McCann: You've got to finish the game.

I'm giving yous it, I'm surrendering.

Surrendering fuck all! shouted Auld Roper. There's two of us here! Just play your doms like a man. Come on!

I'm chapping ya fucking pest.

Chapping? Hh. Might've known, it's all you've done all morning.

Tammas was next in line and he played a domino, followed by the elderly man then Billy. Back to McCann who banged the board with his fist, causing several pieces to jump out of order. Chapping, he said.

You've no even looked, muttered his partner.

I dont have to fucking look, I know what I've fucking got.

Ach! Auld Roper shook his head and he threw his dominoes onto the table. I'm no fucking playing!

McCann laughed.

Aye, that's all you're good for. You're a joke ya cunt. First granny I've suffered in years and it just had to be with you.

Ho, listen to that! McCann glanced at the other two. The trouble with this auld cunt is he's fucking senile.

Billy had turned their dominoes face up and he said: Yous were beat anyhow . . . He started shuffling them.

Aye, said Tammas, tapping a finger on the edge of the table. And we're still waiting for our ten pence.

Ten pence! What d'you mean ten pence? That game was a bogey. Pub rules son, if a game doesnt get finished all bets are cancelled. Eh McCann?

Aye, course. Tell you what but we'll give yous a double or clear.

Aye, said Auld Roper, starting to shuffle the domino pieces. Twenty pence or clear. That's just fair.

Cheating bastards, said Tammas. He leaned forwards and helped the other shuffle.

But Billy said: I better get going to my work – only half an hour to the 1st race . . . He raised the beer to his mouth, glanced at Tammas. You coming with me or what?

Eh . . . he shrugged, might as well. Naw, fuck it, on second thoughts.

Wise man, said Auld Roper.

Billy was nodding. He began swallowing down the beer, getting up off his seat.

I'll see you the night, added Tammas.

•••

He was one of the last to enter the dressing room. He sat down immediately on the end of the bench, just inside from the door. Most of the team had been playing the other time he had come and a couple nodded to him. Donnie was injured and unable to play; but he was assisting the man in charge. The two of them arrived later, carrying in the big travelling bag between them. They distributed the jerseys, stockings and pants to each of the team. Tammas was thrown the number 2. The guy sitting next to him asked: You Donnie's mate?

Aye.

Paul's the name.

Tammas.

Tammas?

Aye . . . he leaned down to take off his shoes and socks, leaving his cigarette balanced on the edge of the bench. Then dragging deeply on it he stubbed it out and undressed quickly. Members of the team were heading to the door now, laughing at something, the studs on their boots making skliffing sounds across the concrete floor. Somebody pushed the guy in front and he lurched forwards, and Tammas had to jerk sideways to avoid being struck into. One of the team cried: Foul, referee!

Right yous! The man in charge said, No wanting any blooming injuries before we get out onto the park!

The door banged open and shut and open and shut, rocking on its hinges.

Noisy bastards, muttered Paul.

Watch the language! called the man in charge. It's Mathieson reffing!

A few groans in reply to this.

Tammas waited for Donnie. The two of them followed out the man and just before leaving the building he passed Donnie a cigarette and whispered: Half time . . .

Donnie palmed it at once. Then he pointed to Tammas's right boot. Its lace was trailing.

The wind was quite strong and he knelt on the gravel path. It had been raining earlier, a few puddles had gathered here and there. He knotted the laces and walked after Donnie. He had begun to shiver, and soon his teeth were chattering uncontrollably. He turned side on into the wind as he went, clenching the cuffs of each sleeve in his fists. There was a game of football in progress, the average player seemed about 14 years of age. He hunched his shoulders and folded his arms, watching the play while walking.

Donnie stopped to wait. You're chittering!

Aye well it's fucking freezing.

No that much man it's nerves.

Is it fuck nerves.

Aye it is! Donnie grinned. Dont worry but – it's supposed to be a good sign!

Fuck off.

Keep moving, get the blood going.

Tammas glared at him but he started trotting, keeping his arms folded, his shoulders still hunched up. When he reached the field they were due to play on he slowed to a walk, and he halted near the 18 yard line. The ball came towards him and he attempted a first time shot at goal but miskicked and it went bouncing off onto the neighbouring pitch. While it was being collected he turned his back to the others; he began jumping on the spot, fists clenched on the cuffs of each sleeve again; his teeth resumed chattering and he was making loud shivering sounds.

In the centre circle the referee now stood with a ball tucked beneath one elbow. The captains were with him, one calling the toss when the coin was flipped into the air. The other team won it and their captain chose ends, selecting the one opposite where the teams were now positioned; this meant each set of players having to walk down to the other half of the field. Tammas passed their number 11, he looked to be well over 6 feet tall and was very skinny, his socks seemed scarcely to reach above his ankles.

Soon the whistle was blown and the ball kicked off. One of the opposition lunged at it, booted it high into the air. The ball travelled right down and over the touchline for a goal kick. When it had been positioned the keeper turned his back to measure the run then he turned sharply and signalled to Tammas and kicked the ball to him. He raced in to trap it but was a yard short in meeting it, it canoned off his knee. He chased after it, just failing to stop it crossing the line for a throw in.

While one of the other team's players gathered the ball Tammas looked for the number 11 and marked him. When the throw was taken the ball was shied to the tall fellow and he tried to flick it on as he turned but Tammas was right behind him and his studs caught in the guy's sock, taking the foot from under him and he went crashing down, the ball returning out for another throw in. Tammas reached to help him up but he shook off his hand and muttered: That was fucking ridiculous.

I didnt mean it, replied Tammas.

The winger ignored him; he was rubbing the side of his back and shaking his head.

Tammas walked to his side, almost behind him completely, his hands on his hips and breathing quite harshly. The ball was shied in almost the same way as the last time but just as the winger trapped it Tammas stuck his boot between his feet and managed to deflect it out for a further throw in. The winger grunted unintelligibly; he strode down the park some 20 or so yards, keeping nearby the touchline. Tammas went after him. The winger stared away from him, keeping his gaze to the player shying the ball, then he signalled to him in some way Tammas was not able to see. And the ball arrived about 3 yards short. As the winger moved forwards to get it Tammas slid in from behind, upending him. The guy landed back the way, right on top of Tammas; he rolled off at once. Fucking hell, he cried, I wish you'd keep out the fucking road.

What you talking about!

You're fucking . . . ! The winger shook his head and trotted off down the touchline.

Tammas trotted after him. But this time the player taking the throw in shied the ball towards the middle of the park. From the touchline Donnie called: No bother Tammas!

Tammas made no response. His breath was coming in short gulps. He coughed to clear his throat and spat while breathing out. He put his hand to his chest and coughed again. The ball was with the forwards in his team and he set off trotting as far as the halfway line where he stopped and looked on. The ball had gone for a goal kick. The opposing left back booted it out and down the middle, where it was booted straight into the path of the big left winger who raced onto it at once, arms flailing and head downwards. Tammas was across to meet him immediately. Some yards from him the winger looked up but he kept on running as though to go right over the top of him but at the last moment he flicked the ball inside and made to carry round Tammas on the outside but Tammas went in the same direction and took the full force of the winger crashing into him. They both fell heavily and Tammas lay winded for quite some time.

The referee had blown for a foul against him. The man in charge came on with Donnie and soaked Tammas's neck and forehead with a wet sponge. Unlucky there son, he was saying.

Tammas nodded, easing his breathing as Donnie placed his hands on his chest and counted slowly. When the man had returned to the touchline Tammas gasped: I'm fucked.

Donnie shook his head. You'll be alright man, just get your second wind.

Tammas looked at him; then he moved his head to see the big winger hobbling into position for the free kick. Donnie helped him to his feet before returning to the touchline. Tammas walked after the winger, studying his right thigh as he went; it was bruised quite noticeably and some gravel seemed to be stuck in it.

The winger had his hands on his hips, he did not look in Tammas's direction, keeping his attention on the player taking the throw in.

The ball was shied to the rear and one of the opposition struck it high into the air, away to the far wing.

At half time he lay at the touchline with his hands clasped behind his head, a few yards away from the rest of the team. Donnie handed him the cigarette but he had no matches and Donnie had none either. He got up, he walked down to the other team; one of their supporters was smoking; Tammas received a light from him.

When he returned the guy called Paul passed him a piece of orange and asked, How's it going?

Ah okay.

Quite a hard game.

Aye.

Paul grinned at the cigarette: Give us a drag eh?

Tammas handed him it then he lowered down to sit on his heels, he ate the orange.

Donnie came over. How you doing?

Tammas shrugged.

That winger's no going near you now!

Naw.

See if we can keep it nothing each . . . ! Donnie laughed briefly. They'll be asking you to turn professional!

Hh. Tammas turned his head, glanced at the other player who had a last puff on the fag before giving him it back.

•••

He was limping slightly when he arrived in the lounge bar that evening. Rab and Rena and Betty were sitting waiting on him. Betty smiled and pointed at Rab: That's the two of you – he hurt his knee!

Aye, said Rab.

Tammas grinned. He remained standing, his hands on the edge of the table. I saw your result in the paper – hard lines.

You no sitting down? asked Betty.

Eh . . . he frowned. We dont have that much time.

Rena laughed: I'm really excited!

So she is! chuckled Rab. Then he glanced at his wristwatch: Sure you cant have a pint?

Eh . . .

Go on, said Rena. I feel like another martini. So does Betty.

Aye okay then.

Tammas had sat down on the spare seat beside Betty but when Rab rose to get the drinks he went to the bar with him. Thanks for coming, he said.

Aye, it's a real chore.

Naw man, serious.

Dont be fucking daft.

Tammas sniffed. I'll just have a half pint . . .

Rab looked at him. The barmaid was serving someone else

and he had yet to give the order. We dont have to have one at all, he said.

Ah well . . .

Rab turned, strolled to the table: Okay girls, let's go.

We no having another drink?

Tammas shrugged. We'll get one at the track.

O! I didnt know they had a bar, said Betty.

Aye, Christ, all the mod cons!

At the large carpark outside the stand the taxi stopped and a wee boy pulled open the door. Ta son, said Tammas and tipped him 10 pence. When he had paid the driver he guided the others across to the entrance, buying two *Advisers* on the way, one of which he gave to Rab. He bought two pencils from the old woman at the turnstiles. She's a millionaire, he said, but never mind!

He went through the gate after them, pushing Rab on to stop him paying the entrance money. I told you, he said, I'm getting it.

Dont be daft man.

Naw, replied Tammas. He passed the money across the counter to the man and received the four programmes in return.

In the upstairs lounge bar overlooking the track they managed to squeeze in at a table close by the tote grid. He handed £2 to Betty. This is to have a go – you and Rena.

I've got my own money! answered Rena. She grinned pointing at Rab: His!

Well I'm no putting two pound on a dog! Betty said, Definitely not!

Tammas smiled. It's to last you the whole bloody night!

Heh. I thought we were only staying till the 5th race? Rab was frowning.

We are. Tammas sniffed; he brought out his cigarettes, lighted one.

I would stay later, said Rena after a moment.

Naw, said Tammas, I'm no bothering.

Rab shook his head: Christ I'm no bothering either man, whatever you like . . .

Tammas grinned. Probably be skint by then anyhow!

It was not until the 4th race that he left the lounge. He had been betting in small amounts only, and doing it via the tote. But he had one he quite fancied now and he wanted to see how it figured in the ring. While he stood watching the bookmakers as they watched the punters and each other he suddenly spotted Deefy, the worker from the club; he was wearing the fedora hat, standing amongst the crowd below the row. And then he strode away to the side, to the second last bookmaker, and he handed him what looked like a thick wad. And the bookmaker accepted it without returning Deefy a receipt, and scored out the 5/1 price of the 2 dog. The other bookmakers were offering 4/1. But instead of marking up 4/1 the fellow left it blank, and then marked in 3/1. Immediately Tammas trotted up to the nearest bookmaker and backed the 2 dog at 4/1.

The dogs were being loaded into the traps as he left the betting enclosure and he started running up the stairs. In the lounge Rab was standing near to the window to see the race. Tammas joined him.

Then the hooter sounded and the lights round the stadium were extinguished, leaving the track brightly lit. When the hare flashed past the traps Tammas said, On you go the 2 dog!

Rab frowned at him. I thought you were backing 5?

Naw.

They watched the race, dog 2 just failing to catch the favourite, the dog coming out of Trap 3. Tammas shook his head and tore his ticket into pieces.

I would probably have backed that! said Rab. But I let you chat me onto the 5 dog!

Tammas shrugged.

At the table Betty was laughing and holding her tote tickets in the air. Tammas! I got it! Number 3!

So she did! laughed Rena.

Hh . . . Tammas nodded. Did you back it as well?

No, tch.

What about you Tammas? What did you take?

Eh . . . a mule.

A mule!

What yous wanting to drink?

The bar was busy. Once he had shouted his order to one of the barmaids he concentrated on the form given in the *Adviser*. His nap for the night was going in this the 5th race. He had selected it that morning, as soon as he had seen the *Daily Record*. When he carried the drinks to the table Betty asked for a loan of the *Adviser* and she read it for a few moments. Rab grinned at her. You better give Tammas your tip!

Betty laughed. As a matter of fact, she said, I'm going to. Tammas – number 5. Real Sunshine.

Real Sunshine! Rab nodded. That's what I fancy myself!

What d'you think Tammas? asked Rena.

Eh . . . It's got a chance.

What one do you want to win?

The one I'm backing.

The one you're backing?

Rab said, In other words he's no telling you!

O thanks a lot Thomas.

Sorry, naw, it's nothing personal.

I'm glad to hear it!

Tammas lifted his glass and sipped at the beer, then inhaled on the cigarette he was smoking and muttered: Actually I'm going to back the 1 dog.

Honest?

Aye.

Well well well, the 1 dog eh . . . Rab gazed at the race in his *Adviser*.

Can I do yours with mine? asked Betty.

Course.

Aw good. Betty took the purse out of her handbag and gave him 40 pence. Can you do it for me?

Course, aye, 5 and 1 you want – fine, I'll reverse it too.

Betty looked at him.

The forecast, I'll reverse it for you . . . Tammas had got up from the chair and he indicated Rab: He'll tell you what I mean. I've got to go down and eh . . . He sniffed; he walked away quickly but Rab came after him. And once they were outside he muttered, Hey Tammas you okay?

What, aye, what d'you mean?

I dont know, you seem to be fucking – a bad mood or something.

Och naw it's no that. While they continued on downstairs he added, To be honest with you Rab I'm just eh . . . Betty and that . . . He shook his head. I dont know man I'm just eh . . . My leg's a bit sore as well.

Aw aye . . .

Tammas glanced at him. Then he gave him the 40 pence: You stick it on for me eh? I want to punt 1 dog with the bookie.

He left Rab outside a tote window, and moving in towards the centre of the crowd grouped beneath the row of book-makers he gripped the notes he had left and stood waiting.

The odds against his nap winning the race were 5/2. Then he saw one of the bookies mark it out to 3/1. But he continued to stand there. Gradually the crowd thinned as the time of the race approached. He turned and left the enclosure, the money still in his pocket.

The hooter sounded while he was climbing the stand steps to the lounge bar.

He stopped, halfway up; and he nodded as he watched the dog he had napped win comfortably. He lighted a cigarette. Out on the track beneath the big totalisator board the handlers were catching the dogs to take them back to the kennels. The punters surrounding him were discussing the result and how the race had been run. He nodded slightly, and walked downstairs and along, and into the bar beneath the stand. He ordered a bottle of beer, stood there drinking it steadily.

Rab was at the tote pay-out window when he returned upstairs to the lounge. Your woman's caught the forecast! he called, grinning. Well done man! Good nap!

Tammas nodded. He carried on across to the table and sat down, giving his attention to the *Adviser*. Betty and Rena were smiling at him. Aye, he said, eventually. Well done Betty! Good forecast.

Ninety three pence.

Great.

Did you win much?

Eh . . .

Rab was approaching.

. . . aye.

Aw good, replied Betty.

And it won so easy, said Rena.

Tammas smiled, getting up from the chair, folding the *Adviser* and sticking it into the side pocket of his jacket. Anyway, he said, time we were heading off.

We'll stay if you like.

Naw, I'm no bothering, let's go.

Rab looked at him.

While we're ahead . . .

They went to a lounge bar in the centre of the city where a band performed but it was packed and the amplifiers seemed to be full on. At Tammas's suggestion they left for a quieter place.

When the last bell had gone the two couples shared a taxi as far as Betty's close and she and Tammas got out, waved to the other two as the taxi moved off. There was a bit of fog around and when they breathed out it came as steam. Betty linked arms with him. You should be wearing a coat, she said.

Ah I'm okay . . . he hunched his shoulders, keeping his hands in his trouser pockets. Through the close they walked, the glare of the light reflecting the heavy condensation on the walls.

I enjoyed the night, Betty said.

Did you.

An experience. Quite exciting.

On the first landing she lagged behind, gazing out the window, over the backcourt which was in total darkness. It's really quiet, she murmured.

He nodded, he put his arm round her shoulder and she turned immediately, and they kissed. When they broke it off Betty was shivering and he drew her in closer. You cold? he said.

She nodded.

Never mind, a nice hot fire up the stair!

She nodded again.

Okay?

Yes.

He stepped back from her, gazed at her eyes, taking out his cigarettes at the same time, and he lighted one.

I wish you could come in the house, she said.

Och.

No I mean Tammas if I could I would, it's just my mum and dad – they dont, well, they're not getting on. Sometimes I wish I was away from here altogether.

Torquay.

Just to get away from them, all of them.

Ah! I dont know Betty at least you've got company. Half the time I dont see anybody. The sister and brother-in-law – I dont always like to sit in with them you know? give them a bit of privacy and that.

O aye.

He shrugged.

Betty sighed.

Come on. He put his arm round her shoulders. They started to walk towards the next flight of stairs.

•••

The crash of the plug and chain of the toilet cistern awakened him. It was just on 9.30 am. He got out of bed and pulled on his jeans and his socks, and a tee shirt. Robert was supposed to be on a mid shift, beginning at 2 pm. But he would be starting early, doing some overtime. He was drinking tea at the kitchen table when Tammas entered. Cold yin this morning Robert, eh? He rubbed his hands.

Aye. Tea in the pot by the way. Might still be hot enough.

Cheers . . . Tammas felt the sides then poured a cupful, gestured with the pot towards Robert's cup.

Naw no me, I better be shoving off.

Tammas nodded. He sat down facing him. Overtime?

Aye.

Good. Handy . . . Tammas sipped at the tea but it was luke-warm only; he drank it all in a oner and made to rise, but he did not; instead he asked, Eh Robert, I was wondering, any chance of a pound till the giro comes?

What?

A pound, any chance of loaning me a pound; just till I get the giro on Friday morning.

You must be joking.

Tammas looked at him.

The way you've been carrying on! Hh! Think I dont know the score or something!

What d'you mean?

You know fine well what I mean. You must think I'm a right bloody monkey.

Aw please yourself then.

Aye you're bloody right I'll please myself. Working all sorts of hours to try and save a few quid while you're out wining and dining! Eh? You must think I'm a bloody idiot!

For Christ sake! Tammas sat back on his chair, folded his arms.

You listen son . . . Robert stood up, one hand on the edge of the table and pointing at Tammas with the other. You want to go and ask that sister of yours how much I take to myself out the bloody wages!

What you on about? I'm no interested in your bloody pocket money. All I did was ask you for a loan of a pound, that's all. If you dont have it then fine, fine – but what you handing me all this stuff for? Jesus Christ!

I'll Jesus Christ you! Dont you use that kind of language in this house!

Tammas got up off the chair and for a second they stood glowering at each other, then he strode out and ben the room where he sat down on the bed. Not many more minutes and the outside door banged shut. Tammas sat on, staring at the wall.

Around 1 pm he was sitting in the living room with the radio playing, drinking coffee. He had checked through every pocket in his bedroom. He considered trying the pawn with his old suit – the new one had gone back in a couple of days ago. But there was no chance of them taking the old one. The radio was the only true possibility; aside from the watch Margaret had given him as a birthday present some months ago. He rarely wore the thing anyway. Usually it lay on top of his bedroom cupboard. In fact he had no real need of a watch. But the problem was she would notice its disappearance.

The meter bowl contained four 10 pence coins. Tammas had dropped in a couple of quid's worth less than a week since.

He got up from the settee and peered inside again. Then he withdrew three of them and quickly grabbed his jerkin, put on his shoes, and went straight out. He walked into town to a snooker hall he occasionally played in with Billy. It was situated between a pub and a betting shop, down below street level. Before entering he laid a 20 pence bet up in the bookie's.

The hall was mobbed. Every table occupied and a queue of more than twenty guys for a game. An attendant watched him come in the swing doors; he walked to the cashier's desk and had his name added to the list.

It'll be maybe an hour and a half till you get on, she said to him.

Ach well . . . he shrugged. He remained for more than an hour, spectating at different games. As he turned to leave he said to the guy next to him: You got a spare fag at all?

The guy brought out a packet and gave him one.

Ta.

The guy made no response.

Upstairs in the bookmaker's he strolled to the board with the results. His bet had lost. He stared at the results for some time. Then he walked home and thoroughly searched the house, finding a tiny amount of halfpences inside a vase on top of the living room mantelpiece.

He lay outstretched on the settee then got up and went to the bedroom and setting the alarm for 5 o'clock he got undressed and into bed. But he leaned over to the clock and pressed in the alarm stopper a moment later.

•••

He was standing at the bar with the half pint of beer when in walked Phil, the elderly man who did occasional work in the betting shop down the road. They exchanged nods. He glanced at the half pint and gestured at it to the barman. Pint of the same for the boy there, he said.

Right you are Phil.

Tammas smiled. Cheers. How's it going?

Ah no bad no bad. Yourself?

Eh, struggling, struggling.

Aye . . . I thought I saw steam coming out of your beer!

Tammas waited for the barman to serve the drinks before saying, Results are murder!

Results are always murder. You should know that by now. I heard you were getting a turn these days but?

That was last week! They build it out of all proportion anyway.

Phil nodded. He was drinking whisky and a pony of beer; he called for another whisky, swallowed what had been left of his first one. He said. Aye son you're best to say nothing. Never tell a soul. Nothing. The best way.

Aye.

Phil drank the second whisky, followed it with the remainder of his beer, set the glasses firmly on the counter beside each other. I'm away, he said, before the crowd shows up.

Thanks for the pint.

Phil frowned and raised his right forefinger to across his lips: Ssshh. Then he reached out to shake hands with Tammas, and left two £1 notes inside his palm. Mind now, he said. Say nothing.

Thanks Phil.

He had moved to a table near the darts' area when John and Billy arrived. Donnie came at their back, pausing to collect the dominoes and the board from behind the bar. Me and you, he said to Tammas. Eh? Will we take them on?

And sitting down he upturned the box onto the board, the dominoes coming tumbling out. He began shuffling them with both hands spread widely, his elbows sticking up in the air. And he said to John: So it's Manchester eh!

Aye what's this we've been hearing? asked Billy.

Nothing, I'm just considering it.

Tammas glanced at him: I never heard.

That's no surprising, replied Billy. We never fucking see you!

Nah, went on John, I'm just fucking fed up with it here. A guy in work was telling me the nightlife's brilliant down there. And the money as well, it's supposed to be brilliant too. Big big wages he says.

Great – when you going!

Soon, dont fucking worry.

Look John if Manchester's as good as all that then how come that cunt in your work isnt down there right fucking now I mean . . . ? Eh! that's what I like about these bastards, tell you all sorts of rubbish!

He spent years in Manchester.

Well what did he come fucking back for?

I dont know, a change I think – he's married.

He's married! What the fuck's that got to do with it? Billy laughed.

Aw shut up.

Tammas said, Aye come on, give the boy a break. Let's play dominoes.

Billy was last to lift his six pieces: He turned to Tammas: That big 20/1 shot winner man did you see it? This afternoon? This wee fellow, comes stoating into the shop the back of 2 o'clock . . .

Less speech play! called Donnie.

I'm telling the boy something.

I'm no interested anyway. The last thing I want to hear about's big fucking 20/1 winners!

Billy grinned.

Aye, said John, come on.

When Billy placed his first domino on the board Donnie

jeered: Hey Tammas that's us won. Look what the daft cunt's played!

Ah fuck off, replied Billy. Me and my mate'll win this no danger, no danger – eh John?

Load of shite, said Tammas. Easy money Donnie easy money!

John frowned. Here, nobody says we were playing for money!

Aw Christ . . . Donnie laid his dominoes face down on the board, he clutched his forehead. Where am I? Hey Tammas, where are we? I could've swore we were sitting in *Simpson's*!

All I'm saying is if you're going to play for money you want to tell people first, no wait till you're halfway through the bloody game.

Billy grinned. Dont worry John, we're certainties anyway.

Aye but that's no the point. I mean I'm no caring one way or the other. I just like to know what's happening.

Aw John . . . Donnie put his hand back onto his forehead again. I've had a hard day – eh? going to fucking give us a bit of peace? Eh? Please?

Aye but all I'm saying . . .

Shut your fucking mouth!

John looked at him.

Donnie smiled in reply.

When he entered the close he paused to position himself in the middle of the way, then continued, walking in a straight line. Going up the stairs he canoned off the wall and halted, steadied himself.

Margaret came from the living room. You wanting a sandwich?

Aye. Hh . . . he smiled at her, carried on down to the bathroom.

After urinating he filled the washhand basin and dunked his head in it twice, the second time keeping it submerged for a count of ten seconds.

A slice of square sausage was sizzling in the frying pan, the kettle of water almost boiling. Margaret had put it on for him. He got a slice of bread from the bin, spread the margarine on.

In the front room Robert was on his armchair and Margaret was on the settee. Tammas closed the door, carried his tea and the teaplate to sit down next to her. He had the sandwich in his mouth and he bit a big chunk off before taking it out. Anything good been on? he asked.

Earlier. A play, quite good – wasnt it Bob?

Robert did not respond. He had the newspaper on his lap.

Tammas moved his head a little and grinned, covering his face with his hand.

Margaret said, Did you go to the job centre?

No, I was a bit late.

Late?

Aye, I was a bit late. Hell of a long walk.

You're a lazy bugger!

Robert grunted something.

Tammas paused before saying: I'll go the morrow, I'll be fine the morrow. Aye, different story then, get the giro and that, be able to take a bus.

Okay! Robert had swivelled round on his seat to gaze at him. What is it? If you've got something to say say it!

Tammas sniffed. I've no got anything to say.

Bloody liar – he tried to tap me for a pound on Tuesday morning Margaret. You were wondering what was up with me, mind? Right? That's what was up with me. He tried to tap me for a pound and I wasnt having any. That's it Tammas eh!

No.

Ah ya liar ye! Robert sat back forwards again, the newspaper falling from his lap.

These things dont bother me.

Robert glared round at him but said nothing for a few moments. No, he went on, these things dont worry you – wee things, like money, they dont bother you, Only when you come trying to tap me or your sister.

I wish you'd get your facts straight Robert. I think about once in the past two years or something, that's the number of times I've tried to tap you.

Listen son . . .

Margaret interrupted. Why dont the two of you stop it! I wish you would just stop it.

Well, cried Robert, I dont know how many times he's taken it from you!

That's rent money, said Tammas.

Rent money!

He always pays it back, said Margaret.

Robert was saying: What d'you mean rent money? It's our money, it belongs to me and your sister. So never mind what the hell you call it. And as far as I'm concerned when you dont come up with that on a Friday night then it's a hell of a sight worse than borrowing. And what about that bloody meter bowl? Never a bloody tosser in it once you get through with it. You couldnt care less whether we've got enough electricity or no. O naw, nothing like that bothers you. Just wee minor details!

Aye. Tammas leaned to lay the unfinished sandwich on the teaplate, and he looked about for his cigarettes and matches. He saw the packet beneath the corner of the settee and soon was smoking; he exhaled at the ceiling. It's all coming out the night, he said.

Aye and high time too if you ask me . . . Robert shook his head at Margaret: Look at the state of him! He tries to tap me for a pound and then he can still come marching in here half drunk and looking for you to make his bloody supper!

I didnt look for Margaret to make my supper at all.

Ah!

Tammas inhaled deeply and he exhaled before continuing. And if you're wanting to know about the money, somebody gave me it – no loaned me it, gave me it – and I never asked, never bloody asked, he just gave me it.

O goody, it's always nice to know people who give you their money. I've always thought that myself – eh Margaret? Nice that isnt it! People who go about dishing out their money every time you're skint. Wish to heaven he'd stick down their names and addresses so we could get paying off the mortage on this bloody house!

Margaret was staring at the television.

After a moment Tammas said: People like him dont give money to anybody Robert; sometimes they dont even speak to people.

Ah . . . fine . . . Robert was silent. Eventually he nodded. Well Margaret, I think he must be talking about the big timers. Eh son? Is that who you're talking about? The big timers?

Exactly. Aye – he used to be. Won and done more cash than you'll ever see anyhow!

Right then that's enought! cried Margaret.

Naw it's alright. Robert had raised his hand and he smiled. I want to hear about the people that give away their money.

I'm talking about auld Phil over the road in the betting shop. He doesnt have to work in there you know he just likes to do it, to keep in touch with the game.

O, I see.

Aye, he doesnt need to work.

Mm, just like you . . . Robert frowned and he shifted round on his seat to be facing away from him. Away and grow up son.

I might and I might no – have to watch it in case I turn out like you.

Tammas! Margaret was staring at him.

Robert held his hand up to her. It's alright Margaret . . . He glanced at Tammas: I've got one thing to say to you: why dont you pack your bags and go. The trouble is you *have* grown up, you *are* a big boy. You just dont act like one. And I think it'd be best if you went, and I mean that.

Aye. Dont worry about it. Tammas was getting onto his feet, gathering his cup and plate and the cigarettes and matches. Soon as the time comes I'll be off, away, dont worry about that. He was at the door and he paused to add, Goodnight folks, pleasant dreams.

Robert shook his head. God, you give me a pain in the neck, so you do.

•••

The cubicle door banged shut behind him. He read what it said on the receipt then stuck it into his pocket along with the £6. A small woman appeared from through the close, she bustled past him, carrying a baby in the crook of an arm, a bundle of LP records under the other.

Outside was cold and foggy. He walked quickly along to *Simpson's* where he stood with his pint, near to the gasfire at the wall, reading a morning newspaper. Racing had been abandoned, waterlogged; and there were no dog meetings scheduled for the afternoon. Billy came in shortly before 1 o'clock. He was skint. Tammas bought him a pint of lager. Gulping the first mouthful he backed in as near as possible to the fire, placed the pint on the mantelpiece and rubbed his hands together. Fuck this for a game, he muttered, I'm definitely searching for a job man. This no racing no wages is murder. Freezing too – you'd think it was the middle of fucking winter!

Tammas nodded.

You holding?

A few bob.

Ach! Billy shook his head. What a life. I'm fucking sick of these horses man I'm no kidding ye, honest, fucking terrible. That bastard Donnie as well; couple of weeks and he'll be lapping up that sun – fucking bastard! Naw, I'm definitely going after a full time job. A nice warm factory or something.

Ha ha.

Naw I'm no kidding ye Tammas you were mad jacking yours.

Shite.

Naw, honest. Hey, something else man, that auld man of mine's – he was telling me they're going to be starting people in the copper works after Christmas. I think I'll apply. Eh? Fancy it? He'll stick your name down as well.

D'you think there's any chance like?

I dont know, according to him. Sometimes he rabbits on but. Hey, that place you were in – would they no let you back if you asked nicely?

Would they fuck.

Maybe they'd start me.

Not at all man they were speaking about redundancies the last I heard.

Aye but things fucking change.

Tammas shrugged. Drink up and we'll go a walk.

A walk!

Aye, up the town, maybe get a game of snooker or something. I'll stick you in for a game. Eh, see if you can win us a few quid!

No danger . . . Billy grinned.

They travelled by bus. The tables were full when they arrived, with a large crowd queuing. At the top end most of the spectators were watching a tournament involving about eight players; each game used three reds and all the colours. Billy and Tammas settled on a ledge, until eventually the winner had been decided. The entry fee was 50 pence and Tammas dropped it into an empty tobacco tin. Somebody placed the tin on top of the shade above the table. When the lights went out the electric meter would be fed by one of the coins from the tin.

Billy got knocked out in the first round of both this and the following tournaments. Tammas dropped in the third 50 pence and told him it was the last. Billy won his way through to the final. There were ten players which meant a kitty of £5, less electricity. The guy he was playing against looked about 30 years of age. After they had tossed for break and one of the losing players was setting the balls Tammas lighted a cigarette and stepped nearer to the man and said quietly: Want to save a pound?

You kidding! Hh. The man shook his head and walked off to the end of the table; he began chalking his cue. He potted the first red and took the blue with it, but he missed the next red and Billy got it, taking a pink and then the last red with a black; then he missed the yellow after having positioned himself quite well on it. He shrugged at Tammas. Tammas looked away.

His opponent potted the yellow, the green, the brown, and he left the blue on the dyke. Billy came to the table and without hesitation slammed the ball very hard, it flashed off three sides into the middle bag opposite, his cue-ball following through to allow him a reasonable shot at the pink into the other middle bag. He potted it smoothly then reached for the tin containing the money.

The defeated player passed Tammas on his way to return the cue to its case. Tammas muttered, On you go!

What was that?

Nothing.

Did you say something there?

Naw, no me.

The man stood watching him. Then Billy came across and he said, Hard lines.

The next tournament was being prepared for. The man glanced at Tammas. Okay, he said, you still wanting a bet?

I wasnt wanting a bet the last time. I was just wanting to save a pound – know what I mean?

Aye, I know what you mean.

Tammas nodded.

Billy was looking from one to the other. What's up? he asked

Misunderstanding, said the guy. And then to Tammas: You still wanting a bet but?

Suit yourself.

Two quid says I go further than your mate.

You're on.

My mate'll hold the money . . . He gestured to one of the onlookers.

Tammas shrugged.

When the bet had been struck Billy and the other player joined the rest and soon the tournament was under way. The other player got knocked out in the first round. Tammas collected the £4 from his mate.

Eventually Billy got through to the final and he won again.

•••

From where he stood high in the stand he was in direct line with the finishing post. He looked on at the 1st, 2nd, 3rd and 4th races without laying a bet. During the intervals he drank bottled beer in the bar below, marking the form of each race once it had ended. He had come to back dog 4 in the 5th. Both it and the one out of trap 5 were set to receive 10 metres from the scratch dog. This scratch dog – trap 1 – was a good racer; it had to be fast otherwise it would not have been giving away such big starts. But as far as Tammas was concerned it was a two dog race, traps 4 and 5. If 4 trapped well enough to lead at the first bend then he reckoned he could start walking to head the queue at the bookie's pay out. But if 5 got out and managed to hold off 4 to the first then he could leave the track immediately, because 4 would have no chance. When 5 dog got its head in front round the first bend very few dogs could ever pass it – but its starting ability was no-torious, it usually required a couple of yards before it began to race.

Dog 4 did look good.

And according to the betting market most people at the track had reached the same conclusion, the bookies were laying the dog at 6/4. The scratch dog was next in at 5/2. The dog out of trap 5 stood at 7/1. Tammas was surprised. All it needed was a fast trap and he would not have minded having a couple of quid down on it to stay in front to the line. But it usually trapped really badly.

He edged his way forwards, to the head of the crowd waiting beneath the row of bookmakers; he was gripping the £30 wad in his right trouser pocket.

Nobody seemed interested in the favourite. Each bookie showed 6/4. Occasionally they would glance along the line at each other, then call out the odds. One of them knocked the 1 dog out to 11/4 and quite a few punters rushed in to take it. But the main body still watched and waited, one or two turning to note what the tic-tac men were signalling from their positions at the barrier.

The vet was checking the runners' girths. The handlers preparing to walk them to the boxes and begin the loading up.

Then a bookie called: I'll lay 10's the bottom! 10's the bottom!

Dog 5 at 10/1. It was a great bet. Tammas shook his head. All it had to do was trap properly and it would lead from there to the line. 10/1 was a great bet. And suddenly some muttering began and one of the bookies had scrubbed the 6/4 away altogether and was glancing about and now marking in 5/4, 5/4 from 6/4. And another bookie was scrubbing out the 6/4. And now the rush was on, the punters crushing forward onto those bookmakers still offering 6/4. Tammas was carried along to one who had wiped out the 6/4 but without marking in anything else and he was frantically accepting the bets of those directly beneath his stool. Then he stopped and shook his head. No more! he cried. The 6/4's away, it's away! Tammas flung himself forwards, almost over the shoulders of a wee man standing in front of him, and he thrust the thirty pounds into the bookie's face. To thirty quid: he shouted.

6/4's away son, it's away!

But while he was saying it he had taken the £30 and was dropping it into the satchel and muttering to the clerk: Down to the boy thirty quid, one and a half.

Ta Sid . . .

He walked quickly away, trying to reach his place in the stand before the race started. He overheard somebody saying the favourite had further shortened to 4/5.

He arrived just before the off. He rubbed his hands, brought out a cigarette. Around him men of all ages were hunching their shoulders and stamping on the spot, hands in their pockets and cigarettes clamped in their mouths. It was a cold and damp night and a quite heavy mist had arisen; when the stadium lights dimmed and the floodlighting round the track came on the whole area seemed enclosed in it. Yet on the actual track the green of the grass and the muddy brown at the inside rail were distinct.

And the hooter sounding. In the silence that followed the whirr of the mechanical hare was quite loud as it staggered into motion, to go lurching along the outside rail. It gained momentum rapidly till when it rounded the final bend it was hurtling on to the traps, and the bang of them opening, and dog 4 had a flier, a flier. Tammas had cupped his hand to his mouth and was roaring EEeeeesssaaaayyyyy!

•••

He had rung the bell. When the doorman opened he said, How's it going son?

No bad.

Nothing's started yet.

Ah well. Tammas followed him along and into the snacks' room. He ordered a coffee and a roll and sausage, and sat down at one of the empty tables, reading the next morning's *Daily Record*. At the far end of the counter, near to the door into the gaming room, the dealer was standing chatting to a couple of folk. And the television was on, its volume quite high, being watched by some of the women.

Getting on for 11 o'clock more men had arrived, some entering the gaming room, others ordering food and drinks at the counter. Then the gaming room door opened and three young guys came out. One of them asked loudly: When does the chemmy start in this place?

The dealer glanced at him. He sniffed and continued listening to what somebody in his group had been saying. But moments later he swallowed what was left in the cup he was holding and strolled to the door into the other room. Many of the men followed but Tammas was amongst those who remained. He was still eating his roll and sausage. Two men were now at his table and were discussing the evening's results at Shawfield with a couple of other guys at the neighbouring table. One of them was saying: Five favourites! Punters must've done okay.

Aye but three of them were the last three races, half the punters would've been fucking skint by that time!

True, true.

Tammas glanced across at them. A couple of other winners were well fancied but.

Mmm.

Were you over bye like yourself son? asked one of them.

Tammas nodded. I left early right enough.

Aw, like that was it!

Naw. I had my one and it won; I just came away.

Aw. Good. The man nodded, That's the way to do it. He looked at the man next to him: What am I always telling you eh? Back your winner and then get home, just like the boy here. All you need's a bit of will power. There's always another night.

Every cunt knows that!

So what?

So fuck all. I'm just telling you; we all know you need a bit of fucking will power. So fucking what? What does that mean? That means fuck all. The man glanced at the others in the company.

Because we all know it doesnt mean it isnt fucking right, said one of them.

Aw aye, and *you* know! Give us a break ya cunt you never go anywhere near the dogs!

Aye and I'm no fucking likely to either! Fucking mug's game.

There was silence. Somebody passed out cigarettes and grinned suddenly. I was just thinking there: know the last time I was at fucking Shawfield? That night they were going to burn the fucking place down. Any of yous remember? Fair Friday night, about 1964.

Actually I think it was 66, one of them replied.

Naw, naw, that's definite, 64, I mind it well. I know cause the wife had just booked us a holiday at the last minute, and I never even knew and I'd went off to fucking Shawfield with the holiday pay in my pocket and all that! He laughed: I could've fucking lost the lost! Lost the lot! As it turns out I didnt, I think I broke about even that night. But the point is, Christ! They were going to burn the fucking place down . . . He turned to Tammas: No kidding ye son! They were going to burn the fucking place down!

Big Cowboy was there and all that night. No wonder they were going to burn the place down but! Fucking stroke they pulled. He shook his head at the others: It was an Open Event, dogs up from England and all that. Fair Friday I mean so every cunt's there with a fortune in their pocket. Me with the *lot* in mine. And the fucking wife with the holiday booked at the last fucking minute and I dont know, I dont fucking know!

Tammas smiled. He got up, still smiling, shaking his head slightly while the conversation continued.

The game was quite noisy at the horseshoe table. He stood at the rear, beside the spectators, hearing someone whisper that it was about time the bank won, that it hadnt been winning at all so far.

When its losing run eventually did end the bank was being held by one of the three young guys from earlier in the snacks' room. As soon as the third round had been won Tammas stretched over the heads of those sitting at the front and bankoed the £20. He lost and *suived* the £40. He lost that too. He had two single pound notes left in his trouser pocket. He noticed the dealer looking at him. Deefy, sitting next to the dealer, was also looking at him. He shook his head and the bank's money was split for other punters. While the cards were being dealt from the shoe he turned and left the room.

He hailed the first available taxi. At his close he said to the driver: Listen will you wait a minute for me? Eh? I'll be just a minute.

The driver hesitated.

Tammas smiled. Sorry . . . and he gave him the two singles. Honest, I'll just be a minute.

Okay. The driver folded away the £2.

He raced upstairs. Margaret and Robert were in the front room, viewing a late night film on television. Carrying onto his own room he collected the rest of the money from the bottom drawer of the bedside cupboard. Back in the lobby he paused by the living room door. Then he opened it and he said: Hullo . . . Eh, I'll no be too late! He grinned and shut the door immediately.

The gaming room was still crowded, every chair was occupied and a line of men behind. He had decided to bet only with the bank. If it won he would allow it to go the five coups, then he would withdraw all the winnings and just let it pass.

When the opportunity arose he threw in £5 and it lost on the first round. The next in line put in £2 for the bank and Tammas threw in £5 alongside it. It lost. He had suspected he would lose that one too but all he needed was one winning bank. One winning bank would return him the losses plus a fair profit. In fact, he could afford to lose seven straight £5 bets with the bank and still be £40 ahead on one winning 4 timer.

By the time the bank had travelled round the table and arrived back with him he had £10 left in his pocket; he leaned across and put in on the baize. He lost again. Soon afterwards he was walking home.

•••

Rab's younger brother opened the door. What happened to you? he asked. You're hell of a late.

I got detained. Tammas grinned as he stepped inside.

That lassie's here – Betty – are yous two winching?

Naw, we're just good friends.

Rubbish! Yous going to get engaged as well?

Tammas looked at him. How's the party?

Och it's no really a party man they're all just sitting about – except my maw and Uncle Gus. They're steamboats. So's the auld man – he's in the kitchen giving Rab a lecture!

Tammas grinned. He took the bottle of vodka from the carrier bag and held it in his left hand so that it would be partly concealed when entering the room.

Alec whispered, Tammas, going to bring us ben a couple of cans of lager? I'm in the bedroom with a couple of the mates and that.

You're too young to drink.

Fuck off.

It'll cost you – fifty p. each.

Away you go!

Tammas punched him lightly on the shoulder then clicked open the living room door, edged his way inside, shutting the door quietly behind himself. The folk were arranged in semi circle round the fireplace. Rab, Rena and Betty were not among them. A man of about 40 years of age was singing a country and western song. This was Rab's Uncle Gus. He sat on a wooden dining chair, his eyelids were closed and he was holding his head raised, his face almost parallel to the ceiling; his adam's apple was very prominent, jutting backwards and forwards as he sang.

To his left, Rab's maw was kneeling on a cushion on the floor. Her eyelids were also closed and she held a wine-glass to her lips which were moving very slightly.

Tammas waited a moment before lifting an empty tumbler from the top of the glass display cabinet. He knelt slowly down, unscrewed the cap on the bottle and poured a small vodka, leaving the bottle on the floor in beneath the wall next to the cabinet. Then he stood up, got some lemonade to mix in.

The song ended and a little round of applause greeted it.

Rab's maw was saying: That was smashing Gus smashing, it was, smashing.

What about an encore? asked an elderly woman who was sitting on an armchair close to the corner of the fire.

Uncle Gus shook his head. We'll spin the bottle missis, everybody's to get a shot.

No me! laughed the elderly woman. She folded her arms and nodded to another elderly woman. Are you Jessie? Are you going to sing!

Tch!

Aye yous are! cried Uncle Gus. Then he noticed Tammas and he called: There's a boy can sing!

Rab's maw got onto her feet and was saying to someone, It's Tammas – he's been Rab's pal since they were wee boys the gether. Come on over son, bring your drink with you.

And one for me while you're at it! cried Uncle Gus. I'm bloody well dying of thirst!

He grinned when Uncle Gus rose to meet him and they shook hands.

Where you been hiding yourself Tammas?

Ach around, around. He turned to Rab's maw and they kissed each other on the cheek. Hello Mrs McCorquodale.

She gripped him by the elbow and guided him to the end of the settee opposite where they were standing. A middle aged couple was sitting looking at him. This is Tammas, she said to them. And to Tammas she said: This is Rena's mum and dad.

Aw! Tammas nodded and smiled. Hello. And he shook hands with them.

You're awful late! called Uncle Gus from across at the glass cabinet.

I got held up – these buses! Tammas had half turned to reply; then he saw Rena who had just appeared in the doorway.

She was smiling at him. He winked. Then Betty appeared behind her. He nodded to her.

I know your name said Rena's dad. Tammas, eh? I heard Rab mention you.

Aye, continued Mrs McCorquodale. She glanced at the slight space between the couple and quickly they parted for her to sit down. Yes, she said, I've known the boy all his life. We were neighbours before we flitted to here. Werent we Tammas?

Aye.

Mrs McCorquodale had turned to Rena's mum: Me and his grannie were good friends.

Rena and Betty were standing across at the glass cabinet. Rena was holding a can of beer and pointing at it. Tammas said, Eh I'll see you in a minute Mrs McCorquodale, I'm just eh . . . He stepped over her feet and made his way round between the settee and the fireplace, gesturing to Uncle Gus as he passed: Just going for a can of beer . . .

Right you are son. Uncle Gus winked at him, indicating the one he was holding. And he patted the top pocket of his jacket; some cigars were standing upright inside: You want one of these?

Aye I'll eh just get a drink and that . . .

No bother. Heh you! he said to a young woman seated behind the company on a dining chair. It's your turn for a song! Come on! On your feet!

Hh! She looked away, grinned at a man who was standing nearby. The man raised his eyebrows, tilted his head and swallowed a mouthful of beer.

Tammas laid his tumbler on the cabinet and took Rena by the sides of her arms and kissed her briefly on the mouth. Congratulations, he said.

Thanks Tammas. And thanks for coming. And thanks as well for the records. They're great; we're playing them all the time.

Ah!

No, honest, they're terrific! She kissed him on the cheek then raised her hand suddenly: The ring! You've no even seen it yet! My ring – Betty! He's no even seen it yet!

Betty laughed.

Tammas smiled. He stared at the ring for several seconds. Aye, he said, it's a beauty right enough. Sparkling stones eh!

Rena nodded.

It really is beautiful, said Betty.

Rena made a face and murmured, Cost a fortune! I told him not to. Men!

Tammas grinned.

How come you were so late? asked Betty.

Buses.

O.

Tammas pulled out the ring-opener on the can and he swigged a mouthful of beer.

Tch! Rena gave him a glass. While he poured the beer into it Rena said, Tammas, would you do me a favour? would you go ben the kitchen and get Rab away from his dad.

Tammas groaned.

Honestly, the two of them have been in there for ages. I dont want them fighting Tammas, not the night.

Aye, Christ.

Rena sighed. She glanced generally at the others in the room and whispered: They need livening up. Maybe get them dancing or something. Rab should be here.

Tammas nodded. The other people in the room were now talking in different groupings, or sitting in silence. Uncle Gus was chatting to the elderly woman next to the fire. Tammas nodded to Rena, he lifted the bottle of vodka from the floor and he chuckled: I'll take this with me!

Mr McCorquodale was seated on a high stool at the break-fast counter. He was speaking, using his whisky tumbler to emphasise a point. Rab stood quite close to him, his head inclined as he listened, a beer can in one hand and the other in his trouser pocket. Tammas! he cried.

Well well well, said Mr McCorquodale.

Better late than never! Tammas grinned, walking forwards and shaking hands with the man. He nodded to Rab: Well done.

What d'you mean well done!

Getting engaged and all that!

Aw aye.

Mr McCorquodale was gazing at Tammas and he reached out to shake hands with him once more. So how's life on the broo? he asked, and he maintained the grip on Tammas' right hand, firmly but without increasing the pressure.

So so, the usual – want a vodka?

A vodka! Mr McCorquodale frowned, staring at it; he relin-quished the grip. It's no bloody Hogmanay son, you didnt need to bring your own bloody drink.

Aw eh . . . it was just . . . No want one?

Vodka? Naw no me Tammas – Scotland's own, Scotland's own . . . He lifted the bottle of whisky from the side of the breakfast bar. Come on, you have one with me instead of that Russian stuff.

I'd rather no mix it Mr McCorquodale.

Ah come on for God sake son you're the bloody guest remember!

Da . . . Rab said: Leave him alone eh?

What d'you mean? And anyway, you shouldnt be drinking at all, you're in training. Mr McCorquodale gestured at him while saying to Tammas: This yin isnt to get anything, cause he's in training.

Rab laughed briefly. Look at him! Totally blotto, can hardly sit straight on the stool and he's trying to lecture me about training. Training by fuck!

Heh you less of that language if you dont mind, you've got a mother ben the room.

Awful sorry pater.

It's no pater son it's pahter. Should've sent you to a fucking fenian school; at least they'd have taught you latin! Mr McCorquodale uncapped the whisky bottle, poured himself a drink. He glanced at Tammas: So how's life on the broo then Tammas?

Da you've asked him that already – Christ sake!

Tammas grinned. Rab – Rena says will you go ben the living room.

Did she?

Aye, I think she wants you to liven up the proceedings or something.

Rab frowned then shrugged. I'll sing them a song.

Aye, you better do something son! Mr McCorquodale raised the tumbler to his mouth and sipped at the whisky.

Rab stared at him for a few moments then he sniffed and said to Tammas, I'll see you in a minute.

When the door closed Tammas was breaking the cellophane on a new packet of cigarettes and soon he was smoking, putting the matches back into his side jacket pocket. Mr McCorquodale was watching him. And he asked, So how's it going son? How's life on the broo treating you?

Ah no bad, no bad.

A bit daft chucking your job but eh? I mean when you didnt have one to go to. Would it no have been better making sure there were going to be redundancies first?

Eh, I suppose so, right enough . . . Tammas smiled, sipped vodka, inhaled on the cigarette.

Strikes me that'd have been more sensible. Course I'm aware – your age – sense doesnt always come into it! Mr McCorquodale was smiling.

Tammas nodded. Terrible job but. Really boring.

I thought the wages were alright though – according to Rab anyway I mean that's what he told me.

No bad.

Mind you, I like a boy with the philosophical approach – when in doubt jump on the broo! Mr McCorquodale laughed, drank the remainder of the whisky and reached for the bottle. Tammas glanced at the door. The sound of fast music and a few thumps from dancing feet could be heard. And then a voice, probably Uncle Gus, singing very loudly, *Chicago*.

Mr McCorquodale was pouring whisky into Tammas's tumbler; a fair amount of vodka had still been in it. He poured one for himself, the neck of the bottle balancing against the rim of the glass. Did Rab tell you about the offer? The offer son, did he tell you?

Eh, naw, what's that?

An offer, he's had an offer. Hull City.

Christ sake!

He never told you?

Naw. Christ, that's tremendous!

Mr McCorquodale nodded. He sniffed. Aye, he said, they're wanting him down as soon as possible.

Great news.

Mr McCorquodale nodded. Know what he says to them? I'll think about it. I'll think about it! God sake, you think he'd jump at something like that!

Aye. Hh. I dont know. Tammas shrugged. Maybe it isnt a good offer or something.

Isnt a good offer? You dont even know what the bloody offer is son so how do you know!

After a slight pause Tammas said, Naw, I'm just saying. Just thinking – about Rab I mean you know, the way he might see it.

The way he might see it! Mr McCorquodale smiled, shaking his head.

Well I mean . . . Tammas paused, he shrugged, swallowed a mouthful of the alcohol in his tumbler and coughed, spluttering a little. He inhaled on his cigarette immediately.

Mr McCorquodale was looking at him. Course, you're no really a player but Tammas, are you. I mean I'm no being cheeky or anything. I dont want to hurt your bloody feelings! Mr McCorquodale smiled. What I'm saying is this but; if you dont know the ins and outs then how d'you know what's a good offer and what's a bad offer? You cant, no really – no that I can see. I mean he doesnt either. Rab! What does he know, he doesnt know fuck all hardly. I mean he might be able to play the bloody game but what does that go for I mean he doesnt bloody know about the other side of it.

Tammas nodded; he reached to flick the ash from his cigarette into the sink, he ran the cold water tap to clear it down the drain.

Mr McCorquodale was looking at him. Son, he said, eventually, that Blackpool carry on was bloody ridiculous.

Mm.

I'm no kidding ye – losing all your bloody money like that. And then what you seem to forget, you're leaving the rest of the boys to pay your digs' money. I mean that's what you forget, that's the bloody consequence Tammas, that's what you dont think about. All your pals son they've got to fork out on your behalf. God sake! I couldnt do that.

Tammas scratched his head.

Mr McCorquodale had pursed his lips. He leaned back a little on the stool, placing both hands on the edge of the breakfast counter. He lifted his whisky, sipped at it, his forehead wrinkling. He frowned: See that punting of yours! and couple it with the broo! Well I'll tell you something; you're beat before you start. Christ, I dont like saying it, before you even start.

After a moment Tammas stepped to the sink, flicked ash into it. The tap was dripping and he turned it tightly, cutting the water off. From the living room the volume of music increased suddenly, then decreased; then increased again. Tammas had a last drag on the cigarette, he doused it in the water which was gathered at the drain. There was a rubbish bin beneath the sink. He dropped the cigarette down into there. And the living room door opened and closed. And now the kitchen door; and Rab was there. He paused, then came across to the sink. Tammas made way for him.

Rab ran the cold water and sluiced his face and neck with it. Aw that's better, he muttered. He got a wee towel from a rail, glanced at Tammas: You no coming through?

Aye. Hey what's this about Hull City?

Rab continued drying the back of his neck. He sniffed. Big time eh!

His father grunted. Listen to him.

Rab returned the towel to the rail. Da, he said, I think you should go through as well. And put a word in maw's ear while you're at it. Her and Uncle Gus are taking over. I mean it's a bit early yet for sing songs! People're still wanting a dance.

Embarassing you are they? Mr McCorquodale was gazing at Rab, and he added: Mister and Missis Jesus Christ in the corner above that sort of thing?

What you talking about?

Ah!

If you're talking about Rena's maw and da, they're no bothering, they're just happy sitting.

Mr McCorquodale shifted on the stool, he pursed his lips, raised the whisky tumbler. Bloody biblethumpers.

Rab nodded to Tammas who walked to the doorway, and continued through.

He paused by the living room door. A woman's voice – not Mrs McCorquodale – singing quite quietly. He walked down the lobby into the bathroom, snibbed the door shut behind him. There was a small cabinet with a mirror door above the washhand basin. He stared into it with his two hands clasped over his nose, thumbs together beneath his chin. Then he sat on the lavatory, elbows on his knees, hands covering his nose again. He sat like this for a while. Someone chapped the door.

It was Betty. She called, Tammas?

Aye!

You okay?

Aye. Just be a minute.

You okay?

Aye – I was just sick there.

What did you say?

I was just sick there!

Sick?

Aye! He got up and walked to the door, unsnibbed and opened it. They looked at each other for a few moments.

Betty said, Are you okay?

Fine, I'm fine. I was just sick there. He sniffed, I'm going to go home.

Home?

Aye I've got a splitting head . . . He rubbed at his forehead. Will you tell Rab for me?

Aw Tammas.

Naw I'm eh . . . he shook his head. I'm no feeling that well; I think eh . . . He stepped to the outside door and opened it.

Aw Tammas.

I'm sorry Betty, I'm really no feeling well. He shook his head, stepped out and shut the door. He walked down the stairs quickly.

•••

Excluding expenses he had £10; not a lot to bet with but enough. The train was crowded. Even so he had found a seat by the window. He placed the *Sporting Life* folded on the table, began unpeeling a large orange.

When the train arrived in Ayr Station most of the passengers disembarked and Tammas was amongst those heading to the racetrack. Eventually he started trotting. The first race was due off quite soon. And when he made it into the ground the runners were at the starting post. At the tote window he laid an outsider for 50 pence and was vaguely relieved when it did not reach the first three places. He bet another outsider in the 2nd race. Afterwards he adjourned to one of the bars.

His nap for the day was going in the next race. Its name was Rimini.

The probable favourite for this the feature race of the afternoon was trained in the midlands of England and had an obvious chance on form. On its last two outings the horse had won quite comfortably. Both races were fair class handicaps, and according to racecourse gossip it had not travelled north for nothing. But when the bookies marked it in as a 7/4 chance Tammas was surprised. The race was a handicap hurdle and 18 runners had been declared. No matter how far the horse had travelled this 7/4 was a bad bet. He strolled along the row of bookmakers, glancing at each of their boards. He was still a bit early and not all of the runners had a price marked against them. Rimini was in that category.

Then he saw 14/1 being laid against it. He stepped in front of the bookmaker in question and stared at the board. It was amazing. The *Sporting Life* had forecast 8/1 and now here it was, 14/1. It was almost too good to be true. He had the money in his hand, he stepped up to the bookie and took it to £2.50, returned the rest of the money to his trouser pocket. He stuck the betting ticket into his inside jerkin pocket, turning his back on the bookie and heading back to the bar. He had meant to bet Rimini for more than £2.50 but 14/1 sounded a bit too good. He hesitated. But no, something about it, it was too good. And nearly quarter of an hour to go before the race even started. And then he saw 16/1 being offered. A bookie in the centre of the row up from the last. 16/1. If 14/1 was too good to be true then this 16/1 definitely smelled. Something was up. He continued on and into the bar but then he about turned and raced back to the bookie and took the 16/1 to £1.50.

At the bar he hesitated before ordering a bottle of beer. The more he thought about it the more he knew he was right. Rimini was the one and that was that. All along he had been expecting 8/1 and hoping to catch 10's with a wee bit of luck. Now here he was with 16/1 and reneging – just having a safe £1.50. A price like 16/1 was wrong. And the favourite was definitely a bad bet at 7/4. If Rimini was trying then – Christ; all it needed was it to be trying and it was a certainty.

He struck a match and lighted a cigarette while striding back outside. There was no 16's to be had. He strode along each row but nothing, and now 12/1 seemed the best on offer. And away along to where he had taken the 14/1 the bookie was offering 10's. 10's! Tammas turned and raced back down the row and grabbed the first 12/1 he could get about his remaining £5.

That was that now. And yet it was something – win, lose or draw, he had come and done what he had set out to do. Rimini was the nap and that was it.

While the Starter called the jockeys to the tapes Tammas manoeuvered his way up the steps of the covered Stand. The wind was sharp, stinging his ears, causing his eyes to water.

And the field had jumped off; he could spot his horse, the amateur rider settling it down behind the leaders. He waited there until passing the Stand on the second circuit he moved it up with the leaders. Round the back straight and turning for home he kicked on and Rimini quickly opened up a gap of about four to five lengths. Approaching the second last and the horse was coming under pressure, its lead being cut back to between two and three. Going towards the last flight of hurdles a loud cheer arose from the crowd as the black and white hoops of the favourite could be seen emerging from the chasing pack. And now another horse had come from the pack and together with the favourite the two of them were just about matching strides with Rimini as they met and jumped the last. The favourite pecked on landing but within moments had regained its rhythm to go after the other two. The amateur aboard Rimini had the whip going hard and the horse appeared to shy a little but only a little and he dropped the whip immediately, keeping the horse going with hands and heels only.

The three went past the post in a line.

Tammas continued to stare at the post as the other horses passed. Around him the punters were discussing the outcome. A photo-finish was announced. Then the announcer added: Stewards' Inquiry. Please retain your tickets.

Aye I bet you there's an objection as well! muttered a man beside Tammas.

You think so?

O Christ aye son. No see the way that Rimini was swerving? Favourite had to snatch up.

Tammas nodded. He put his hands in his pockets, hunched his shoulders and strolled down the steps and along and into the bar. He had enough for a bottle of beer. While waiting to be served he tried to get engrossed in the form for the next race, but all about the folk were discussing the last one. He moved down nearer the end of the counter where it was a bit less noisy. Then a guy barged in past him and shouted to a barman and the barman came at once. Tammas was still holding the money in his hand without having managed to order. He watched the man turning and shaking his head at a group of people sitting at a table at the wall. And he recognised one of the men there. It was Erskine. And he was looking over; Tammas waved and he stared back, then he smiled and waved in reply, gesturing at him to come across.

Tammas went. Hello, he said.

Hello yourself! Erskine turned to his company: This is the guy that takes you in as partners and then turns round and beats you for plenty! Come on, sit down. You wanting a drink?

Eh naw, no thanks. I want to find out how the objection went.

Objection? I didnt even know there was one . . . Erskine called to the man at the bar immediately: Objection Charlie, how did it go? the result through yet?

The man was frowning. There wasnt any bloody objection – there should've been but there wasnt. Bloody disgrace so it is!

Erskine nodded. What about the Inquiry?

According to them it doesnt even affect the winner, it's just to do with the second and third! Charlie shook his head and returned his attention to the bar, where his drinks were now being served by the barman.

Tammas was chuckling. He stopped it and raised his *Sporting Life* as though about to read it, but he started chuckling again. Then he stopped it once more. He glanced at Erskine and shrugged: I've backed the winner.

One of the women in the company grinned: Well done son.

You backed Rimini? said Erskine.

Aye.

Hh!

Form horse.

Form horse! Erskine laughed and shook his head.

The other man was returning from the bar with the drinks on a tray. Tammas rose from his chair. There were three women in the company, the one who had spoken plus another of a similar age; the third was much younger, probably in her early twenties. I better go and collect, he said to Erskine.

By the time he had been to the last bookie betting on the following race was well under way but Tammas was leaving it alone. A novice chase; the favourite would be backed odds on. Not a race to bet on at all. When he returned to the bar most of the customers had gone. Erskine's table was empty. Tammas bought a packet of nuts & raisins to accompany the bottle of beer, and he spread the *Sporting Life* on the table. Eventually he heard the roars, heralding the start of the race, but he continued to sit there, sipping the beer, smoking a cigarette. He checked through the wad of notes he had, went up to the bar for another packet of nuts & raisins. Hardly anyone was about.

Erskine was one of the first to arrive. The race had not finished. I dont know what the punters're still hanging about for! The favourite's gubbed. Down the field. Three fences to go and it's got no chance, no chance at all.

Hh.

Odds on too and you want to have seen it jumping! Hardly looks as if it's ever been schooled.

Bad race.

Aye you're no kidding. What about yourself, d'you no have a bet?

Naw. Want a drink?

Eh aye, okay son I'll have a wee brandy. By the way, my name's Joe.

Joe. I'm Tammas.

Right son, fine. A wee drop of water in the brandy.

Tammas moved to the bar quickly as more customers began arriving. Soon it was as busy as before and Joe's company had returned led by Charlie, who seemed angrier now. When Tammas put the glasses on the table he was grumbling about the favourite; it had finally finished 2nd after the horse that had been leading fell at the last fence. Tammas waited a moment, not sitting down, and he asked, Anybody want a drink?

One of the women began declining but Joe grinned: It's alright, he's winning a fortune!

Charlie muttered. Dont tell me he backed that bloody winner as well.

I didnt have a bet.

Joe was still grinning: He says it was a bad race Charlie.

They're all bad races, replied the woman.

Charlie looked at her. The woman's name was Ann; the other woman of the same age was called Milly and the youngest of the three was known as Vi. The third man in the group sat beside her; he did not speak, his name was Stan.

Sure yous dont want a drink? asked Tammas.

Ah go on then, said Milly.

Joe laughed: three bacardis and coke, and two whiskies.

That's no fair! Ann said, Are you sure it's okay son?

Tammas nodded and shrugged. Up at the bar he bought another beer for himself; as an afterthought he bought four packets of potato crisps. When he was taking the things from the tray and laying them out he put the crisps into the centre of the table and muttered, Crisps if anybody wants them . . . And he sat down and took out his cigarettes.

Charlie was looking at him. You trying to tell me you thought Rimini was form horse?

Tammas sniffed.

Granted it had a chance but God sake, if you're going to try and tell me it had the beating of the favourite on the book then ha ha, I dont know, I just dont know . . . He shook his head; he put a cigarette in his mouth and craned his neck, to take a light for it from Stan.

Is it okay if . . . ? The youngest of the women, Vi, was speaking to Tammas. She pointed at the crisps.

Aye, Christ . . .

I mean it was never form horse!

Och! Tammas shrugged. Vi was looking at him. Aye, he said, it depends.

Depends! Charlie took a mouthful of the brandy.

I mean I mind him winning a 3 mile handicap hurdle at the end of last season – Haydock or someplace. Good class it was as well.

Last season but, aye.

And look who they've stuck on him the day, that amateur – 7lb he's claiming. And he's no bad I mean he's won a couple of hard yins I've seen on the telly.

Aye but you're still no going to tell me that makes it form horse I mean fuck sake son! Charlie turned to Joe and frowned.

Come on you less of that language, muttered Ann. She

turned to Milly and shook her head. If he doesnt back a winner quick it's going to be terrible listening to him.

Charlie glared at her.

Well you're a crabbit so and so, she said, you're picking on the boy just because he's winning and you're no.

What! He glared at her again. What you talking about? I'm just bloody asking him a bloody question, what you on about?

Tch! Ann shifted on her chair, to be facing Vi. And I'm freezing as well! Standing about watching these bloody stupid horses – we'd have been better off going to the bingo.

Hey Ann! Joe smiled at her. This is supposed to be a happy day out among friends. Come on!

Well Joe look at him, look at his face . . . Ann turned and shook her head at Charlie. Make you greet to see him so it would.

Make you greet! I'll bloody make you greet! Charlie got up from his chair and he strode off and out the bar.

After a moment Ann shrugged.

Then Joe began whistling. He stopped and smiled. I better go and see if I can catch him!

Leave him go!

Think we should?

Och, tch, I dont care. Ann rose from her chair. I'm going to the Ladies.

Milly also rose: I'll come with you.

When they had gone Joe glanced at Vi and the man with her. He grinned: Some day out eh!

The man shrugged.

Charlie's awful bad tempered, said Vi.

Aye but do you no think she's needling him too much?

I dont, said Vi and she added: Not really. She sniffed very slightly and opened her handbag, brought out a paper tissue and dabbed round her nose. And she's dead right about it being freezing.

Well we're going for a meal in a minute – eh Stan?

Suits me.

Vi was gazing about her. The bar was still crowded with folk discussing the last race and the one to come. She said to Joe: Even a bit of music would liven the place up. I mean it's so boring.

Joe glanced at Tammas and raised his eyebrows.

I saw you, she said, reaching for another packet of crisps.

Apologies. Apologies. Joe smiled.

But everybody here's only really come for the horses anyway, said Tammas, I mean they're no really bothering about other stuff.

She looked at him.

Joe was nodding. He lifted his tumbler, swallowed all of the brandy that was left. I'm going to find Charlie, he added.

Tammas continued to sit there. He drank his beer steadily. Soon the bar was becoming less busy and he stood up, nodding in the direction of the exit . . . Going to see the race.

The horse he fancied finished third. He was watching the race from the side of the stand and he could see Joe and Charlie about 30 yards away. During the race, especially towards the closing stages, Charlie's voice had increased in volume as he roared on his selection and it sounded as if he had backed the winner, but he had not, he had backed the second. Tammas arrived at the foot of the steps ahead of them and he shrugged. Beat!

And us, said Joe.

Charlie muttered, Fucking favourites; you never learn at this place, I'm no coming fucking back.

Joe chuckled.

They continued on through to the bar and along to their

table. Joe was about to order a round of drinks but Milly said,
To be honest Joe, I think we're really feeling like going into
Glasgow now.

Well . . . he nodded.

Charlie shrugged.

Fine then, we'll go and eat. Joe stepped aside to allow Milly
and Ann stand up from their chairs and he said to Tammas:
We're no waiting for the last race son we're just going for a
meal and then I dont know, going up a casino or something –
you're welcome to tag along if you like, eh Charlie?

Aye. Charlie shrugged, stuck his hands in his trouser pockets
and he turned, headed the group towards the exit.

Tammas followed at the rear.

Little was said during the walk to the cars. There were two,
driven by Joe and Charlie, parked in a side street off the main
Glasgow road. After a moment's discussion Joe waved Tammas
into his car, into the rear while Milly got into the passenger's
seat. Vi was first into Charlie's car, with Charlie holding
the door for her. Joe waited for the other to drive off and
he said to Milly: We'll no see him now, no till we reach the
restaurant!

Milly chuckled.

From the back seat Tammas reached across with his cigarettes and when Joe slowed to a halt at the junction of the
main road he struck a match and they each got a light. Joe
said, Eh son if you're fancying coming along to the casino
with us you'll need to get a shirt and a tie. He laughed
briefly: It's no like eh . . . He cleared his throat in a signifi-
cant way.

Tammas had given Joe instruction on reaching his street. He
raced upstairs and put on his good suit and a shirt and tie

and he called a cheerio to Margaret who had just returned home from work. Dont make me any tea, he said as she looked out from the kitchen.

She raised her eyebrows but then smiled. He closed the door, trotted back down the stairs and out through the close. Joe had kept the engine ticking over.

The other group had almost finished eating when they arrived. It was at an Indian restaurant on Sauchiehall Street. From there they strolled along to a lounge bar. An hour later they were walking upstairs and into the *Royal* casino. Tammas had to sign his name and enter his address in a big book that lay open on a table in the entrance lobby. The doorman wore a tuxedo and watched him write.

Inside there were roulette tables and blackjack tables and one for craps but there was no chemin de fer being played, and no table set aside for it. Quite a lot of people were about, both sexes, the women standing mainly at the roulette wheels. Vi and Stan and the other two women were among them. Joe and Charlie had vanished. Tammas walked around for a few minutes but without seeing them. Eventually he stopped by one of the blackjack tables and after watching for a wee while he made a bet. Ten minutes later he had lost about half of what he had returned from the races with. He went to the coffee lounge.

Some time later he looked up from next morning's *Daily Record*. Vi was there. Thought you had left, she said, sitting down at the opposite side of the table.

Naw. Sudden death in there! I just came out.

She nodded.

Too fast. You hardly have time to think.

Mm, you're telling me . . . She glanced around the room. After a moment she continued, Ann and Charlie are away home – still fighting.

He smiled, lowered his gaze to the newspaper then added, I thought Joe told me they played poker in this place?

They do but it'll no be for a wee while yet. Vi yawned; she glanced at the page Tammas was reading and muttered. Horses horses horses – d'you think you could get me a coffee please?

What – sorry, aye . . . he slapped the newspaper on the table surface as he rose but she shook her head: Dont bother.

What?

Dont bother I said, I dont want one.

Tammas hesitated.

I dont.

He shrugged, sat back down. He took his cigarettes from his pocket and offered her one. She accepted it and then took the light from him. Did you lose at roulette? he asked.

You must be joking. I dont have any money to lose at gambling. I only came to keep Milly company.

Aw aye.

Not that she ever wins. And then she's going on at Joe for more money all the time; it gets embarassing.

Are they married like?

Vi laughed.

He shrugged slightly and smiled. He gazed upwards in the direction of the electric wall clock.

Are you playing poker? she asked.

Who me, naw, no the night. He sniffed: What about you? what do you do? Do you wait till they're finished or what?

Finished! I'd be here all night! No, just till Stan's lost his money at blackjack or roulette or whatever it is . . . She had gestured vaguely in the direction of the gaming room. Now she glanced at him: He's my brother-in-law – alright?

What?

Vi frowned. I said he's my brother-in-law. He follows me

about like a guard dog. Anyways, she added, I wouldnt worry about it, I dont fancy getting done for babysnatching.

Tammas was staring at her. She had opened her handbag and was looking in at the contents, her head bent to it. Then he was blushing; and he sniffed, inhaled on his cigarette. He shut the newspaper. I'm off eh . . . He stood to his feet. If you can tell Joe for me and that I'll eh, see him again.

Vi looked at him.

Cheerio.

Cheerio. She shrugged.

•••

Donnie was frowning. He looked round the table at the others. I dont know what we wanted to come here for anyhow, he said. He swivelled on his seat, stared across at the counter: I mean imagine going up to that bent shot behind the bar and asking for a set of dominoes! Eh? Can you imagine it! What a fucking dump!

Rab laughed: A place is a dump if they dont play dominoes!

Aye, well . . . Donnie raised his pint glass, swallowed the remainder of the lager. Then he placed the empty carefully in the centre of the table; he cleared a space round it amongst the ash and spilled beer.

Hint hint, said Billy.

Aye John come on for fuck sake, muttered Rab.

What d'you mean?

Donnie glanced at him. Dont tell me it's to be this kind of

fucking carry on! Tonight of all nights! My testimonial John – eh, fuck sake!

As far as I knew we were having a kitty.

Aye, said Rab, as soon as you weigh in with your round we're getting one going.

We still dont have to stay here, said Billy.

Donnie glared at him. We're no going to fucking start that again. We're here and we're staying. I didnt want to come here in the first place but I did, I did, and now I'm going to fucking stay – so sit on your arse.

Tammas grinned. Come on man for Christ sake surely it makes a change from *Simpson's*?

Fuck all wrong with *Simpson's*.

We dont want you telling every cunt in New Zealand there's only one pub in Scotland.

Only one pint by the looks of it!

Aye John for Christ sake!

Come on John!

Aye ya cunt ye get the round up.

Fuck off! replied John but he got up and walked in the direction of the bar.

Billy was looking roundabout and he said: Still and all but Donnie, nice to see a couple of birds once in a while. You must admit.

Admit fuck all! What's up with auld Mattie? Nice as looking a bird as you'll see anywhere!

Clatty Mattie! Rab gaped at him. Then he laughed: Hey, we should've brought her with us. Go down a bomb in here man – a couple of glass of eldee inside her and she'd be up on top of the bent shot's bar doing tricks with a guiness bottle.

Aw shut up for fuck sake!

They were still laughing when John returned with the beer balanced on a circular tray which he set down. He began passing out the pints. You've no to go the bar for the bevy in future, he said, you've to get one of the waitresses. The barman told me.

Aw John, you're as good as a waitress any day!

I'm just telling you what the guy says. I dont give two fucks what you do!

You tell him, grinned Tammas.

Billy said, It was your fault in the first place Tammas. You were supposed to be keeping notes on who was buying what.

True.

John had sat down on his seat. He swallowed the last of his old pint before saying, Nobody has to take notes about me. I'll get my round in same as the next man. I'm no one of them . . . I've got my money and I dont fucking mind spending it! He reached for the new pint and drank from it.

Heh! Billy frowned.

Tammas nodded. The boy's trying to tell us something.

Quite right and all, said Rab. No wonder the country's in the state it is with cunts like yous two walking about.

Lazy pair of bastards, said Donnie.

I wasnt fucking meaning that, cried John.

What were you meaning then? asked Tammas.

No that anyway.

Ha ha.

John glared at him: I wasnt, I fucking wasnt.

Billy said: Aye you were ya cunt.

Naw I wasnt.

Tell the truth, said Rab.

What d'you mean fucking . . . !

That's it! yelled Donnie. What is it with yous fucking mob! This is my last night, my last night, my last bastarn fucking night. And I'm no going to sit and fucking listen to this! Either you shut up or I'm going. I'm no kidding ye I'll be fucking offski.

Quite right too, said Tammas.

Aye . . . Rab nodded. It's that cunt John's fault.

What d'you mean! Look . . .

Look fuck all! cried Donnie.

Towards the end of the evening Donnie had gone to the lavatory. In the middle of the table lay some untouched drinks but none where he was sitting. Rab said, Aye, that's one thing about the Donnie fellow, he never falls behind with the bevy. Another thing, he hardly fucking shows it. I mean I've seen the cunt drinking I dont know how many pints and see at eleven o'clock!

Billy nodded. Sober . . . He pointed at Tammas: He's the same.

Tammas! Rab gazed at Billy, shaking his head. You must be fucking joking!

Tammas laughed.

Rab was wagging a finger at him. Is he fuck the same as Donnie, he just plays it wide, he takes one to our fucking two. You have to take notes with the cunt. Exact same at school as well so he was. I mean dont let him fucking con you Billy. Listen, how many rounds we had?

I dont know.

Ten, murmured John. He sat stiffly forwards on his chair.

Rubbish, away back to sleep!

He is, said Tammas. Look! Hey John, are you awake or what?

Ach I'm just . . . He shook his head.

Rab continued to Billy: Naw, dont tell me about Tammas man cause I know, I know.

What d'you know! Billy winked at Tammas who was laughing.

And Rab grunted: No point fucking winking Billy no point

fucking winking; cause that's you beat before you've even started, eh Tammas?

Where's fucking Donnie? that's what I want to know.

Terrible, said John, we're splitting up, we're all splitting up, we're all fucking splitting up.

He's like a record player the cunt, muttered Rab.

John shook his head: It'll never be the same again but.

He's right, said Billy.

Thank fuck . . . Tammas grinned.

Ya bastard! frowned Rab. I fucking hate you when you say things like that.

So do I, said Billy and he winked at Tammas again.

And Rab shook his head: He thinks I dont see him winking . . .

Here's the cunt now, said Tammas.

Were you away for a shite? cried Billy.

Shut up ya bastard. Donnie glanced about as he sat down on his seat. I hope yous mob havent been causing a disturbance with the fucking lieges!

Billy laughed.

What's he fucking talking about! cried Rab.

Lieges, said John.

Ah Donnie Donnie Donnie, it'll break my heart to see you away. Tammas pursed his lips and sighed: New Zealand by fuck! That's terrible, terrible.

Rab was nodding and he turned to Billy: See what I mean? That's it been said now – Tammas, Tammas has said it. Eh? Hey Tammas come on ya bastard we've got to shake hands with you cause of that, eh?

Tammas put his hand out and they shook, then he did likewise with John and Billy.

Rab was saying: Donnie, you're a bastard. What you going away for?

I'm no going away.

Aye you are, fucking New Zealand.

You're going away as well.

Aye but fucking England, that's all man, Hull City.

It's just down the road he's going, said Billy. No like you man, you're going fucking thousands of miles away.

Two days to get there, said John.

Donnie laughed briefly. I'll be back, dont worry. Old Firm games, Wembley and all that. Fuck sake! Think I'm going to miss the England match! We'll take 6 off them.

Aye but what you going away for? asked Billy. There's no need for it. No when you think about it, no really. I mean you've got a good fucking job man and you like it here.

It's no as simple as that, fuck sake!

The family and that, said Rab. Eh Donnie?

Donnie shrugged.

Is it cause of your family? asked John.

Donnie shrugged again.

Tammas opened his cigarette packet and offered to the others: Tell you something, he said, I fancy it. New Zealand. Bags of sun and that.

Aye but there's no betting shops! Billy laughed. Got to give your bets to the fucking barber!

Numbers racket, said John.

Donnie grinned, pointing at him.

Tammas exhaled smoke, shaking his head: Can you imagine it but? lying on the beach all day, big blondes and bottles of bacardi.

There he goes! cried Rab.

Naw but no kidding man, no more fucking signing on at the shitey fucking broo. Christ sake. White sands and blue skies. Clear water to swim in. No coats or fuck all and the women all walking about in scanty clad bikinis. Nude fucking swimming at midnight.

Pubs shut at six o'clock, said Billy.

Do they fuck, replied Donnie.

Well that's what I heard.

You're thinking of Australia.

Billy shrugged. Same thing.

Naw it's fucking no man.

Tammas shook his head. Who cares? Forget it.

Forget it? Donnie frowned.

Rab began speaking: My auld man, he was telling me they've all got their own basements in their houses and every basement's got its own wee bar. And that includes gantries and all sorts of bevy, barrels of beer man, the lot.

Fucking hell.

Some of them've even got pool tables built in man, fucking saunas and all that.

Tammas was nodding. That's right, he said, I read about that in a book the other night. Canada it was but.

Canada! Donnie stared at him.

Billy burst out laughing, spluttering half a mouthful of beer across the table.

Donnie frowned at Rab: You trying to take the piss ya cunt? Who me! No me!

Cause I'm no in a fucking mood to be trifled with man I mean this is my testifuckingmonial, my testifuckingmonial!

Billy whispered: Ssshh. Too loud man.

Too loud! My last night! Donnie glanced at Tammas and grinned. What's up with that cunt! I cant even get talking loud on my last night man, eh?

Disgrace!

What time is it? said John.

Time! Donnie frowned: Aye, right enough . . . And he swivelled on his seat, signalled to a waitress. But either she did not hear him or else she was ignoring him. He called: Hey Miss . . .

You're too late . . . Billy gestured at a wall clock: It's away past time.

What?

Five past eleven.

These pub clocks are always fucking bammy but.

Rab pointed at his wristwatch: This isnt.

Here, said Tammas, lifting a three-quarters full pint of lager from the middle of the table.

John had started up from his seat. That's mine Tammas!

Ah John, surely you're no going to grudge it to the boy on his testimonial?

Naw, course I'm no! John sat back down: Welcome . . . you're welcome.

I really appreciate that, replied Donnie. He stared at the pint and then began to drink it all in a go. When he had finished he burped loudly. We better be getting a move on anyway, he added. That auld man of mine's got a couple of his cronies coming up. So's the young sister ya dirty bastards any nonsense and yous're out the door!

The other four roared.

I'm warning yous! Donnie placed both hands on the edge of the table and he cried: And another thing, the maw's cooking a big feed. Know what like she is and all that, a couple of pots of mince and tatties or something so yous better be ready! And spewing in the lavvy's barred!

Donnie Donnie Donnie . . . Tammas reached across the table to shake hands with him.

Donnie laughed and he shook hands with each one of them. Then the waitress had appeared and was lifting all the empty glasses onto her tray. Well after time boys, she said.

Sorry Miss.

Sorry.

When she had gone Rab muttered, It's fucking out of order but – spent a fortune in here so we have.

Donnie nodded. One question and one question only: would it have happened in *Simpson's*?

You're fucking right, muttered Billy.

At least we're entitled to sit, said John. I mean we are, we're at least fucking entitled to sit!

Tammas nodded. John's right, we're entitled.

Fucking right we are.

Aye, we're entitled. Tammas folded his arms and sat back on his seat.

Aye. Rab was smiling. We definitely are fucking entitled. The boy's quite right.

He is that, said Tammas. Hey John – you're entitled.

Billy and Donnie were laughing.

Tammas glanced at Rab: Dont know what they're laughing about when the boy's entitled!

Aye but are you sure he's entitled?

Course he is. Hey John, sure you're entitled?

Fuck off.

Ah leave him alone! cried Donnie. He's just gave me his last pint!

Rab shouted: Keep the fucking glass for a souvenir!

TIME GENTLEMEN PLEASE.

Listen to the bent shot! said Donnie, glaring in the direction of the bar.

Still and all . . . Billy raised his pint glass to his mouth: We're about the last yins here. Better drink up.

Rab reached for his but Tammas passed what was left of his over to Donnie and said: Seeing you're no everybody!

That goes for me too, said Rab and he poured his into the other glass.

Thanks lads. Donnie lifted the near full pint and he gazed at it, and he rose to his feet. Watch closely! Tilting his head back he swallowed the beer in a oner; he wiped his mouth with the cuff of his sleeve and then burped and added, I hope yous mob are taking notes.

Billy laughed. No bother to the Donnie fellow!

I wish to make a speech!

No wonder! said Tammas.

John started to applaud and the other three joined him in it.

Donnie grinned. Thank you friends it's highly appreciated. I have got to say that in all my years kicking a ball about this is the first fucking testimonial I've had and I can tell you I'd just like to say how pleased I am.

Hurrehhh.

Hurrehhh.

Three cheers for the boy!

On you go the Donnie fellow!

The Donnie fellow's a dancer!

Hip hip!

HHUURREEHH.

Right yous: The barman had arrived at the table. That'll do, he said, or the polis'll be in here in a minute. And you dont want to end up getting huckled now eh?

Give us a kiss, said Donnie.

A silence followed. John spoke first. He said to the barman: Do you know how much we've spent in here the night!

What did he say there? The barman was staring at Donnie.

Nothing.

He didnt say anything, replied Billy.

Give us a kiss, said Rab.

Aw naw . . .

Right then! cried the barman and he turned and strode

towards the door that separated the lounge bar from the public bar.

After a pause Donnie said: Watch closely. And pulling back his arm, he took aim with the pint glass and then heaved it against the wall opposite.

One of the waitresses screamed.

Donnie was grabbing for one of the carry-out bags of beer from below the table and racing for the exit. The sound of voices and a door slamming shut. Then the other four were onto their feet and lifting the other carry-out bag and running after him. Out on the pavement they ran to the left side of the building, down a lane of cobbled stones, their footsteps echoing round the high tenement buildings. Donnie was standing at the end of it, waving them on, one arm clutching the carry-out bag against his chest. He roared a laugh and then set off running once more.

•••

It was Margaret, calling him and chapping the door. He turned onto his side, tugging the quilt to his chin. She was telling him tea was ready. Okay, he said. And once she returned along the lobby he got up off the bed. He sat on the edge for several moments, eyelids closed. He yawned and looked about for his socks; they were lying beside his shoes on the floor and he pulled them on. He was already wearing his jeans and a tee shirt. He put on a jersey, glanced at the top of the cupboard; a box of matches lying by itself next to the alarm clock.

In the washroom he doused his face and neck with cold water and grunted while towelling himself dry.

She was dishing out the food onto the three plates when he went ben the kitchen. He sniffed and sighed.

She muttered, Flatterer.

Naw, he said, honest – it smells great.

Tch!

He grinned; and when she had finished he lifted two of the plates, carried them into the front room. The television was on, the volume down low. Robert was reading a paper.

The three of them ate in silence, gazing at the news programme.

Robert made as though to collect in the empty plates afterwards but Tammas was up from the settee immediately. I'll do it, he said. Smashing dinner Margaret!

It was! grinned Robert.

No that good.

Aye it was, honest.

God, she said, the two of yous're at it next.

Tammas was switching on the transistor radio while closing the kitchen door. He filled a kettle and set it to boil, arranged the crockery and cutlery in the washing-up bowl.

When he had cleaned and dried everything, and generally tidied the kitchen he returned to the front room with a book he had been reading earlier. The television was being watched by Margaret and Robert. A quiz programme. Eventually Robert said to him: I know what it is now! Go on the broo and stop smoking!

Tammas glanced at him, then he smiled briefly.

You should be encouraging him, said Margaret.

I am! He's doing terrific!

Are you trying to stop smoking right enough? she asked.

Aye, a bit.

A bit?

He shrugged turned a page in the book.

Start training and get back into the football, said Robert. He smiled. So where is it the night anyway?

Tammas gestured at the television.

On a Friday night!

Tammas grinned.

Heaven sake man you're letting the side down! A Friday night and you're staying in! What are you married or something!

Hh! Margaret turned her head from him. Chauvinist pig! She leaned across and punched his shoulder.

That's sore!

She chuckled, getting up from her chair; and she walked out the room. Robert glanced at Tammas: You staying in right enough.

Aye.

Robert nodded. He shifted on his chair, put his hand into his hip pocket, and brought out a small wad and rapidly peeled off two single £1's. Here, take it quick.

Tammas hesitated.

Come on, before your sister gets back.

Tammas took the money. Thanks.

•••

The bank had reached five winning coups and the man holding it nodded at the dealer then proceeded to withdraw all the money lying. He folded it neatly away and rose from his seat. He nodded again, before leaving the gaming room.

The dealer smiled and shook his head, tapped his fingers on the edge of the horseshoe table. What d'you make of that Deefy?

Deefy nodded.

An elderly guy who was sitting to the side said, The cunt's a millionaire too. I dont think I've ever seen him lose.

He's no skint anyhow! muttered another punter.

The dealer was sitting back on his chair and he yawned and then stretched. Never mind, he said, an early bath'll do us all a bit of good.

That us finished? frowned a man.

How, are you wanting to take the new bank?

It's a winner!

I know it's a winner, put your money in.

The man sniffed and looked away.

Anybody else? asked the dealer, and he looked about at the others. Most of those left in the room had been spectating for the past half hour or so. The dealer's gaze settled on Tammas for a moment.

Tammas shook his head. Then he got up and walked through into the snacks' room and ordered a roll and sausage and a cup of tea. He was eating it while reading tomorrow morning's *Daily Record*, when Deefy sat down at his table. After a moment he said to Tammas: How d'you do son, alright?

Couple of quid I won.

Good.

Want a cup of tea or something?

Deefy looked at him.

A cup of tea?

Naw son, no me.

Tammas nodded, he drank a mouthful of his own tea and added: I was thinking of taking a walk up the *Royal*, see if there's anything doing.

The *Royal*. They'll be playing poker.

Aye, I was thinking of taking a walk up.

Deefy nodded.

Fancy coming along?

Aye, no bother son. Deefy patted the tie he was wearing. You okay? Will I get you one?

Ta, aye.

I'll get you one. Deefy glanced about at the folk in the room and stood up.

Tammas ate the last piece of food, swallowed the last of his tea.

Outside in the lane frost glinted on the brickwork and close in at the foot of the walls white showed on the tips of some weeds. Deefy tugged the hat down onto his ears and adjusted a woollen scarf about his neck. You'd think it was the winter already, he grunted.

Tammas nodded, upturning the collar and lapels of his jacket.

At the *Royal* the doorman greeted Deefy and allowed them both entry without mention of signing the book. The casino was almost empty. But there was a small crowd gathered at the barrier round the poker table. Joe was one of the players. The man called Stan was not amongst the spectators. Tammas glanced to the side, then he left Deefy talking to the doorman. He lighted a cigarette before walking slowly along and into the coffee lounge. And Vi was here.

She was with Milly; they were at a table nearby the door. Milly looked to be dozing. Tammas approached the counter, looking to where the woman would stand who usually served behind it. Then he said, Hullo – I didnt expect to see you here the night. He inhaled on the cigarette and smiled briefly, glanced back across the counter.

Vi had clicked open her handbag. She took out a cigarette.

I never saw that guy, Stan.

Did you no. That's because he's no here.

Mm. He never came?

No.

He nodded, he glanced back across the counter then shrugged and he walked to her table, nodded at an empty chair, and sat down on it.

Sit down, she said.

What?

I said sit down, on the chair.

He nodded, sniffed, inhaled on the cigarette. Milly had opened her eyelids. It's you, she murmured.

Tammas smiled. Hullo.

She blinked at him.

Did you win at roulette?

Me?

Aye, did you win?

Milly sighed and said to Vi: Give us a fag hen.

Vi gave her the packet and she extracted one. Tammas had the matches out and he struck one for her. She accepted the light without comment. She glanced at Vi: I'm away to see how Joe's getting on.

Vi made no response.

Tammas watched Milly leave, closing the door behind herself. After a moment he inhaled deeply, looked over to the counter. He coughed slightly, cleared his throat.

Vi said, I'm going home.

You're going home?

That's what I said.

He stared at her.

She returned the stare. I dont want to keep you from the cards.

He nodded. I'm no bothering – the cards, I'm no bothering. Poker and that . . . he shrugged: You need a score to sit in. I'm short of a couple of quid.

O, sorry.

What?

I said sorry. O God! Vi shook her head and she clasped her handbag to her side and got up from her chair.

You definitely going home the now?

Yes.

Christ Vi. You take the needle hell of a quick.

Well no wonder, your stupid bloody questions!

Tammas began rising from his chair. Vi had walked to the door. She tugged on the handle and opened it and walked out, She crossed to where Milly was standing and she whispered something to her. Tammas waited by the coffee lounge entrance for her. He followed her through to the wee cloakroom where she lifted a barrier to collect her own coat. Glancing to the side she muttered, What do you want?

He looked at her.

I said what do you want?

What do I want, nothing. I'll see you to the taxi.

What taxi?

Are you no getting a taxi?

She made no reply, pulling on her coat and adjusting her hair while gazing into a large mirror on the wall.

I'll get you a taxi, he said.

You neednt bother.

Look Vi . . .

Look yourself.

He went after her, meeting the doorman in the lobby. He nodded to him, continued on downstairs.

On the pavement Vi was waving down a taxi and he arrived in time to open the door for her. She got in without looking at him. When he made to follow she held her arm up and frowned at him: Where d'you think you're going?

Can I no get seeing you home like?

Tch! She shook her head.

The driver called: Where to?

Hang on a minute, said Tammas. Look Vi . . .

O look yourself!

Come on . . .

Come on what!

Hey jimmy! The driver was frowning at him: You annoying the lassie?

Naw. He sniffed and then stepped inside, sitting down beside her.

The driver was waiting.

Eh Vi, going to tell the fellow the address?

She said nothing.

Come on Vi.

She shifted on the seat, stared out the window.

The driver said, You okay hen?

She turned, puffed on her cigarette and stubbed it out in the ashtray. Then she cleared her throat and gave him the destination. The journey took more than ten minutes. Nothing was said during it. Tammas sat gazing out the near window. Occasionally he noticed the driver watching him in the rear mirror. At her closemouth he tipped the driver before following her in and upstairs; she lived on the second top storey. She muttered unintelligibly while fumbling on the front door key. Neither had spoken to the other since leaving the taxi. But now, with the door ajar, she glanced at him. She said: I told you no to come.

He nodded then shrugged and about turned. The door did not shut immediately, not until he had reached the first landing. And he paused a moment before carrying on down the stairs and out through the close.

The south side of the city was unfamiliar to him. Aside from the name of the main road he recognised nothing. He walked quickly. The windscreens of parked cars had frosted over and his breath came out in puffs of steam. In a gap site piles of rubble and different stuff had been heaped as though for a bonfire and the frost showed on the edges of it. He halted at a doorway to light a cigarette. Then the sound of a taxi approaching.

•••

McCann was crossing the road, glancing sideways and moving quickly to avoid a big lorry. Reaching the pavement he brushed the sides of his trousers, shaking his head and gazing after it. These bastards try to splash you! he cried.

Tammas nodded.

They walked on together, detouring to the corner of the street where Billy lived. While they were standing waiting McCann asked, Any fags?

Naw . . . Tammas brought a cigarette dowp out from behind his ear. This is to last me till Christmas.

McCann smiled. That wife of mine's, she's started hiding her handbag!

Another five minutes passed before Billy appeared. They strode along the main road, pausing occasionally to look in at the displays in shop windows. It was Billy stopped at the jeweller's. Still there, he said, pointing to a gold watch with a white face and black Roman numerals.

Billy! McCann shook his head. D'you think there's only one

of the fuckers! Christ almighty, they'll have half a hundred of them through in the back shop.

What?

They'll just take a fresh yin out whenever some cunt buys one.

Hh.

Maybe no, said Tammas. A lot of jewellers like just to have a couple of things at once.

McCann was about to reply but his attention was attracted elsewhere, and he muttered, See yous in a minute . . . He crossed over the road, watched by the other two. He approached a man and woman who were standing outside the post office.

He'll be trying to tap them, said Billy.

Tammas nodded.

McCann and the pair were chatting now and the other man could be seen laughing at something said by him and then putting his arm round the woman's shoulders.

Tammas said, Come on.

They started walking, halted about fifty yards farther on, at a corner beside a pub. Tammas took the dowp from behind his ear and struck the match, got it going. Billy asked, Give us a drag man?

Tammas gave him it.

Billy dragged twice on it and returned it. See the results at Shawfield last night?

Naw, no yet.

Only two favourites. Punters must've took a hammering.

Maybe.

No think so?

Depends.

Billy nodded.

McCann was walking along on the pavement opposite now.

When he made the crossing he did so without looking in their direction. The other two fell into step with him. He winked and led them into the next tobacconist's. Billy laughed: You're a genius.

Think nothing of it, replied McCann.

After signing on they headed round to the job centre but Tammas halted at the entrance. See yous later . . .

What d'you mean? asked Billy.

I'll see yous later.

Where you off to?

Just a message.

Aw aye . . . Billy glanced at McCann.

Look, said Tammas, and he smiled, held his hands palms upward. I'm away to see if I can get a few bob. If I can I'll fucking send you a postcard, alright!

No want us to come with you?

Naw, best no.

Billy shrugged.

Just as he was about to walk off McCann brought his cigarettes out and gave him one. Hope you're lucky!

Tammas grinned. Ta.

A few guys in boilersuits were standing about talking together at the junction of the main road and the street leading up to the factory. He recognised a couple of faces but made no acknowledgments. He stood with his back to the wall of the pub for a time. Eventually he entered. A man stared at him and smiled: How's it going? You got a job yet?

Naw, said Tammas.

Through in the lounge he spotted Murdie immediately; he

was sitting at a table with another man towards the rear of the room. Tammas, he said. He looked at his companion: Mind Tammas?

Aye. How's it going Tammas?

Ah no bad.

Take a seat.

Naw, no got much eh . . . I just come in when I was passing and that – Murdie. That message? Mind?

O aye. Murdie nodded.

Can I see you about it?

Outside! grinned Murdie.

Naw, I dont eh . . . Tammas sniffed: Just for a minute.

Actually, said the other man, I've got to go for a slash.

Tammas sat down as soon as he had gone.

Want a fag? said Murdie, opening the packet and giving him one.

It's that twenty quid man. Tammas paused, accepting a light. He exhaled smoke.

Murdie was shaking his head. I know. I've been meaning to fucking weigh you in long before this. But listen Tammas dont fucking worry about it I mean at least you know you'll get it.

Tammas nodded.

I mean I gave you that tenner.

Murdie that was fucking ages ago.

Aye, I know, Christ.

I mean I'm right out the fucking game man . . . Tammas sniffed and stared at the table.

Murdie sipped at his beer and grimaced. Tammas, he said, I've got three fucking weans. Christmas is coming – know what I mean?

Tammas frowned at him then glanced away. He had noticed the other man coming from the lavatory.

Murdie was saying: I know it's out of order but what can I do? I'm owing half the wages this week as it is. I mean I'm no kidding you. I was up at that chemmy a couple of week ago and took a right fucking hammering.

Tammas looked at him.

Honest.

When am I going to get it then?

Soon.

Soon! Tammas shook his head, inhaled on the cigarette.

At least you know I'll give you it.

Hh.

The other man was returning. Tammas got up and moved out from the table. Murdie asked, Have you seen auld Ralphie?

Tammas made no reply. The other man had sat down and was sipping beer. Murdie continued: He was talking about you the other day, wondering how you were getting on and all that.

Tammas nodded.

I'll tell him I saw you.

The other man gestured at the pint of beer he was holding: You no having one yourself?

Naw, said Tammas.

•••

He blinked and shielded his eyes from the glare of the electric light. The book he had been reading lay closed; it dropped into the hollow left by his elbow and he raised himself to see the time. It was just after 3 am. He got off the bed.

Rain was falling. He stared out the window, watching some of it gather in a puddle on the ledge. He drew the curtains, went to the bathroom and to the kitchen. He filled a kettle to make tea and put on the grill, toasted a couple of slices of bread. When it was prepared he returned with it to the bedroom and got undressed and into bed. He had a cushion which he packed in beneath his pillow, opened his book at the page he had left off reading earlier. Then he reached for a slice of toast.

•••

After he had cashed the giro he went home and reckoned out the money, leaving different sums arrayed on top of the bedside cupboard. He took enough for a couple of pints and a game of dominoes. About 1 o'clock he was involved with Brian McCann and some others in a game of knockout when Phil from the betting shop came in. He waved Tammas over.

They exchanged hullos. Phil went on, Quite a decent boy that nephew of mine; he lets me skip out for a half now and again! He smiled and sipped at his whisky, and added, You're looking a bit healthier than the last time I was in here.

Tammas grinned, indicated the whisky: Want another yin?

Naw son I'll no bother – got to keep the head clear. He drank the rest of his whisky. Then he cleared his throat and lowered his voice while saying: The 6th son, keep your eye on the 3 dog.

Tammas frowned slightly.

I'm talking about this afternoon's card. 6th race trap 3 – at least you'll know it's been trying . . . Phil patted him on the side of the shoulder.

Christ, Phil, thanks.

It's no problem son. And by the bye, I dont have to tell you . . . He tapped the side of his head: Say nothing.

Tammas nodded.

O and son . . . Phil smiled: Mind and bet it in another bloody shop.

He returned to the domino game when the elderly man had gone. McCann was looking at him. One of the others said, A nice auld guy that.

Phil, aye. Tammas nodded.

He played one more game of knockout before leaving the pub. Upstairs in his bedroom he collected all the money from the top of the cupboard. He travelled by bus to the bookmaker's Billy worked in. The closing stage of a horse race was in progress when he arrived, a neck and neck struggle developing between the favourite and a big outsider. The shop was very busy. As the big outsider began to forge ahead on the run to the line the muttering from the punters became an angry outburst. Up on the passageway beneath the boards Billy was standing waiting to mark up the returned odds; he was shaking his head. Down below a punter was calling to him: These results are fucking out of order!

Billy nodded. When he saw Tammas he grinned then shook his head again.

Tammas stood to the side. He kept the wad of notes in his pocket right through the remainder of the horse racing programme and on to the 6th dog race. He told Billy of the tip. But Billy was skint; he already owed half the week's wages. Tammas loaned him £4 to make the bet. This reduced his own to £16, but dog 3 won the race at 7/2 and his return amounted to £72.00 less tax. Once he had been paid he remained near to the pay-out window, leaning on a ledge, gazing at the form-pages. Billy signalled him over and handed him his betting receipt without a word. Tammas stared at it. He had not bet dog 3 as a single bet. Billy had wagered the £4 he had given him on a losing forecast.

After the last race he helped him sweep the floor and generally clean the premises up. Then they went by bus to *Simpson's*. It was just on 5.30 pm and quite empty. They carried their pints to a table near the darts' area.

Fancy a game? said Billy.

Cant be bothered. Tammas peeled the cellophane off the new packet of cigarettes, gave one to him. They sat without speaking for a time. Tammas had a morning newspaper and he brought it out, began reading. Eventually Billy asked, You going to Shawfield the morrow night?

Naw.

With that wad in your pocket! Billy grinned. You sure!

Tammas sniffed. What about you, are you going?

Me! Naw . . . I'm skint man.

I know, I know you're skint.

Billy looked at him for a moment. Hazards of the job. Ever hear of a rich boardman!

Tammas did not answer. He continued to read the newspaper. Soon he folded it up again. He laid it on the table and drank a large mouthful of beer, shifted position on the seat so that he was facing the television screen.

Billy said: What's up?

What's up? Fuck all's up.

Aye there is.

Tammas shrugged.

Is it because I backed that forecast?

What?

Nothing. Billy inhaled deeply and he blew out smoke at the ceiling. Then he stared in the direction of the television.

The first time auld Phil's ever gave out a tip and you've got to go and fucking blow it man. I mean the first time he's ever . . . !

Ach I get tips every day of the week in that fucking job.

No from auld Phil you dont.

Billy closed his mouth tightly and he sighed. He dragged on the cigarette, began drumming his fingers on the edge of the table, staring at the television.

I want to ask you a question Billy, straight: when did you last get a turn?

What? Billy frowned at him.

A turn, when did you last get a turn? I mean you must be the only cunt in Glasgow that never fucking gets one. I mean never! You never fucking win! When did you last win?

Billy lifted his pint glass and sipped from the beer.

What I mean man Christ! that was a good tip, a good fucking tip.

Aye cause it won.

Aye cause it fucking won, aye. Auld fucking Phil gave us it man. I mean I went all the way out to fucking give you it. I gave you four quid. You were skint. And then you turned round and bet a forecast, a stupid fucking forecast. I mean Billy I brought out the dough to bet the one dog, just that one.

I'll give you it fucking back.

That's no the point but.

Billy swivelled round on his seat and cried, Will you give us a break eh! He shook his head and swivelled back again.

Tammas continued to sit for a few moments. Eventually he muttered, I'm away up for my tea.

Billy did not respond.

•••

The Royal was crowded approaching 1.30 am and being a Saturday night the casino would have to shut its doors at 2 o'clock; but the poker would continue in a private room. The roulette and blackjack tables were all in use and there was a small crowd round the craps game. Tammas walked on through to the coffee lounge. He sat at an empty table with the following morning's *Sunday Mail*. On an inside page at the back he found a tiny report on the match Rab had been playing that afternoon though apart from the team list his name was not mentioned.

I thought it was you!

Tammas glanced up, grinning when he saw Joe coming towards him. Hullo Joe, how's it going?

Here! What you been doing to that wee lassie?

What . . .

Joe had sat down facing him, and he chuckled. I dont think I've ever seen her in a bloody casino as much in my life! About three weeks on the trot she's been here! Did you no see her?

Naw but I've no really been through yet.

Joe grinned.

Tammas peered in the direction of the gaming section.

She's at the roulette with Milly. And I'll tell you something son; never teach a woman how to gamble unless you're a masochist cause they'll ruin you! No kidding!

Tammas offered him a cigarette but he declined. I'm trying

to stop it, he said, a couple of cigars a day I'm down to. It's bad for you ye know!

Tammas grinned, but he shut the packet without taking one for himself. He tapped the junior match report and turned the page for Joe to see. That's a mate of mine Joe – McCorquodale – he's just signed senior with an English team.

Aw great – that's smashing! Get him away from this place eh!

Hull City.

Joe nodded. Great.

Tammas turned the newspaper back round and after a moment he asked, What time'll the poker be starting?

Directly. How? D'you fancy your chances?

Eh . . .

Have you ever sat down before like?

Naw, no in here. I used to play at work sometimes – plus with the mates and that.

Aye but it's not quite the same thing son. And it's stud they play here as well remember.

I know.

Mm. Joe nodded, then indicated his wristwatch. Okay, well, if you are wanting a seat you better be smartly out the boxes cause there might be a rush! Joe had risen from his seat while talking and as he turned to leave he added: By the way, what age are you?

What age? Me?

Aye.

Tammas nodded. Twenty two.

Twenty two. Aye, that's about what I thought you'd be. Joe smiled.

Once he had gone Tammas got up and purchased a cup of coffee. He opened the cigarette packet, thumbed through the newspaper. About five minutes later Vi appeared in the doorway. He watched her approach. She was showing him something in her right hand – a big pile of casino chips, which she placed untidily on the table in front of him. Count them for me, she said.

He did so immediately. Twenty one quid. Christ sake Vi you've done great. Much did you start with?

She shrugged. It's all winnings. Plus I gave Milly five pounds.

Hh. Christ! He grinned, then pushed the coffee towards her: I just got this for myself but I'm no really thirsty.

Neither am I.

Aw. He nodded, took two cigarettes out and gave one to her; he struck a match and she leaned to take a light from its flame. And she asked: Did you get home alright the other time?

The other time?

You were away so bloody fast! I didnt even know if you had enough for a taxi.

I did. Hey d'you fancy something to eat?

I'm no hungry at all. You do if you want but, you get something.

I'm no bothering. But I mean if you wanted something . . . He shrugged.

I dont, thanks.

Mm. He sniffed, dragged on the cigarette and exhaled at the floor.

Are you playing poker the night?

Ah I'm no sure.

Joe says you carry a bit of luck.

Does he?

Aye.

Honest?

Vi nodded. She lifted her handbag onto her lap and opened it, and footered with something inside.

Actually I was going to play – give it a try anyway.

He says it's quite hard, Joe – a lot of good players.

Hh.

It'll be right if Joe says it.

O aye I know, I wasnt meaning that I just – it doesnt really matter if I go skint, I'm no really worried.

Vi looked at him.

He sniffed, inhaled on his cigarette. What I mean is that I've got enough to lose without worrying about it.

She shrugged slightly, gazed back down into her handbag.

I'm no actually bothered anyway. About playing I mean.

Vi's cigarette had been smouldering on the edge of the ashtray and when she lifted it a length of grey ash remained behind. She glanced at him and then across at the counter.

D'you fancy going like?

What d'you say?

Tammas shrugged. I was just wondering, whether you fancy just going, just now I mean.

Vi made no answer.

Is that guy Stan with you?

No.

Good then I could see you home. Eh? Eh Vi?

She shrugged.

Can I see you home?

If you like.

•••

With the door unlocked she paused before pushing it open and stepping inside, into a tiny lobby. She waited until he was beside her then put on the light, closed and locked the door. He followed her into a room; it was a kitchen, with a bed in a wall recess. There were a small table with two wooden chairs, a two-seater settee and a television set on its own legs.

Vi filled a kettle at the sink, switched on the electric cooker and put the kettle on a ring.

On the bed, at the foot of it, sat a big doll and a weer one. Other toys were on the floor to the side of the fireplace. Things belonging to a girl. On the mantelpiece was a photograph of a baby in a sort of babychair.

Vi had switched on the electric fire and was now preparing two mugs of coffee. Tammas was sitting on the edge of the settee, he turned to say: Does she sleep ben the room? the wee lassie?

Vi frowned. Ben what room! Anyhow, d'you really think I'd leave her by herself while I was away out gallivanting?

He nodded.

She passed him a mug of coffee and came round to sit down on the other side of the settee, putting the mug down on the floor. She kicked off her shoes and reached to massage her toes. She's across the landing . . . In with Cathy, my neighbour.

Aw aye.

In fact, I think I better go in and see how she is. Vi pulled a pair of slippers from beneath the settee and she slipped them on. She took a key from the mantelpiece. I'll just be a minute.

Fine, aye.

When she had gone he took off his jacket and then took off his shoes, and he lighted a cigarette, stretched his legs so that his feet were just to the front of the fire. Then he nipped the cigarette into an ashtray. His coffee was untouched. He carried it to the sink and emptied it down the drain. Back on the settee he put a cushion in at the small of his back and he stretched out once more.

It was nearly half an hour she was gone. He heard the outside door being unlocked, opened, closing and being locked again; all very quietly. Vi entered. He had his eyelids shut and he did not move. She waited by the door for a long time. She came forwards, very quietly. Another few seconds and she began humming a tune, began moving about the room. On two occasions he was aware of a breeze when she passed close bye, her skirt perhaps.

Then the click of the light switch and he opened his eyelids. He could hear her undressing behind the settee. And then the mattress jolting. And after she had settled he listened to her breathing, irregular at first.

When he awakened he felt really stiff, his shoulders and neck and legs all cramped. And he had been lying on his cigarette packet. He leaned to turn off the electric fire, sitting until the bars stopped glowing. He lifted the half cigarette from the ashtray and found his matches on the floor. He did not smoke it. He knelt on the floor and stared across at the bed. Vi's shape was easily recognisable though he could not hear her breathing. He stood up.

She was on her back, and the shape of her breasts, rise falling pause, rise falling pause. She lay close in to the wall. After a moment he returned to between the fire and the settee and he took off his clothes but left on his underpants. At the bedside he raised the blankets and the sheet very carefully, very slowly, until there was enough space for him to climb inside. He lay on his back close to the edge without moving for a period, gradually inclining his head in her direction, becoming more aware of her warmth, a smell of perfume or soap. Then he turned a little, to touch her shoulder with his left hand, the material of her nightdress nudging his fore-fingernail.

He watched her and listened but except for her breathing there was neither sound nor movement. She was asleep. He kept on watching her.

The next he woke up the kettle was boiling, whistling; and the smell of bread toasting beneath the grill. He lay in the same position as he had awakened, watching her. She did not notice. He continued to watch her for a wee while then he said, Hullo Vi. And he raised himself up to rest on his elbows.

She poked her tongue out at him, turned to check the toast. He grinned and got out of bed. About time too, she said and she glanced at him, and glanced away immediately. He had an erection. He coughed and grabbed his trousers, pulled them on at once and went ben the lavatory. He pissed eventually but got another erection. After a moment he took out the wad of notes from his hip pocket and he counted it, studied the numbers of each one.

When he returned to the kitchen she was sitting on the settee munching a slice of toast. Yours is under the grill, she told him. Tea's in the pot – unless you want a coffee . . .

Doesnt matter, thanks; tea's great. He lifted his shirt from the wooden chair and took it with him to the sink. He washed his hands and face and neck. There was a mirror to the side. When he glanced in it he saw Vi looking at him. Then she looked away. He smoothed his hair down with his hands. What time is it? he asked.

Ten, about.

Is that all. That's good. He had turned to the oven, bending slightly to pull out the grill-pan. It made a sort of grating noise.

Vi smiled at him for a moment then she looked at the fire.

He put the toast back down. He stepped towards her and he took both of her hands in his and leaned to her but she rose from the settee. They put their arms round each other, clinging together, then he kissed her neck, and upwards to the lobe of her ear, and she moved her head a little, till they were kissing each other's lips; then they broke away and clung with their arms round each other again and Vi chuckled.

Vi, he said. He sighed and lifted her up off the floor, walked forwards still holding her.

Put me down, she said and she had to raise her feet to avoid kicking something.

He laughed but continued towards the recess and as she toppled onto the bed he went with her, landing almost on top of her and they were kissing again. She arched her back from him when he attempted to unloosen the strap of her bra but tugged her jumper back down when he pulled it up. She pushed him from her and he stood down. It's okay, she said. Just . . . we'll go into bed first.

Aw, Christ. He shook his head and turned away. She had begun to tug the jumper over her head, the bra cups lying half off her breasts.

I dont mind you looking, she muttered.

He shook his head. Then he glanced at her.

•••

The Art Gallery & Museum would not be opening for another hour. They walked on round the building and along behind the bowling green, across Kelvin Way and into the park. They walked down by the river. The trees were bare and the river was quite swollen. Keeps the smell down, said Tammas. Gets hell of a pongy in the summer. Hey, come on up the duck pond and I'll show you the rats!

Vi laughed.

The child's name was Kirsty. When they arrived at the pond Tammas lifted her down from Vi's arms and he held her so that she was sitting on the bevelled railing surrounding the bank of the pond. He squatted next to her, pointing at the island: Under the bushes there Kirsty, just watch under the bushes, just at the edge. You as well Vi.

I cant see a thing. Apart from the ducks!

Patience, patience . . . He continued to squat, balancing the girl with one hand while pointing out to the bushes. Then there was movement and he whispered, See it? the bush shaking . . .

Where?

At the edge, just keep watching.

I cant see anything. Eh Kirsty? can you? Can you see anything?

The girl made no response, but she gazed in the direction of the island.

Definitely rats there, said Tammas.

At that moment about half a dozen birds flew down to settle on the pond.

Tammas said, Should've brought some bread with us Vi, the wee lassie would've liked to feed them. And the ducks as well right enough. Hey . . . Look . . . Now, the bushes.

Vi moved closer to him, her gaze going with the direction he was pointing in. She shook her head.

O Christ, he said, Vi – you cant miss it! Biggest I've seen for years! Big grey yin! See it? Look! Kirsty, Kirsty, can you see it? Can you see it? the big rat? O Christ, a beauty.

I cant see a thing . . .

After a moment Tammas said, It's away. He stood up, lifted the girl from the railing and returned her to Vi.

I think you were seeing things.

Naw, you kidding! You wouldnt've missed it either if you'd been looking properly.

What d'you mean looking properly? I was looking properly. I was looking properly for the past ten minutes and I'm bloody freezing!

Ach . . . Doesnt matter. Come on, we'll go to the swing park – eh Kirsty? want a shot on the swings? He lifted her back from Vi again and attempted to raise her so that she could sit on his shoulders but she kicked with her feet and he had to duck and then land her on the ground.

Vi took the girl by the hand. Sometimes she's a bit funny. And I dont think she likes being up high either.

Tammas nodded. Okay Kirsty? He winked at her, stepped round the way so that he was walking with the girl inbetween himself and Vi; and gradually he took her by the hand. When they reached the swing park he stood behind one of the swings while Vi sat the girl down on it, fixing her hands to grip onto the iron chains which were attached from the swing to the cross section above. He lighted a cigarette and gave it to Vi, lighted one for himself. This is great, he said.

She raised her eyebrows at him.

Naw, honest.

Dont be daft.

Naw, I mean it Vi; it's the best day I've had for years.

She looked at him.

He smiled briefly. If you had seen the rat right enough, that would've topped it. He shook his head and glanced away from her, inhaled deeply and blew the smoke away over his shoulder.

Kirsty said: Mum . . . And she withdrew her hands from the chains, holding them out to Vi who lifted her off immediately.

The shute, said Tammas. Fancy it?

Vi shrugged, she was holding the girl so that her back was to him.

Think she fancies it?

Ask her and see.

Tammas walked round the back of Vi and he winked at Kirsty. Fancy a shot on the shute?

I think it'll be too damp, said Vi, after a moment.

Mm.

No think so yourself?

He shrugged. Suppose it will be.

Vi smiled. We'll go to the Art Gallery. She cuddled the girl and murmured. Eh Kirsty? will we go to the Art Gallery? get nice and warm!

You'd think it was cold to hear you.

Cold! God! It's bloody December! And I dont know how you survive with just that daft jacket! Vi shook her head and she turned and walked off in the direction of the Art Gallery.

Naw, he said, hey! Hey Vi – mon we'll go to the cafe across the road!

As long as it's warm.

Course it's warm. He put his arm round her waist but she twisted to settle Kirsty more comfortably in her arms, and he stepped aside, put his hands in his trouser pockets.

Tammas . . . do you mind if we just went home?

Naw. He shrugged.

D'you mind?

He looked at her. Me as well like? I mean have I to come with you?

She raised her eyebrows.

He grinned; he took her by the elbow.

I'd rather you didnt – it makes it hard for me to carry Kirsty.

Sorry.

It's okay. There's bacon and eggs in the house. And I can put out some chips.

He shook his head.

Is that alright?

Aye. Aye. It's great. God, great.

During the early part of the evening, after they had eaten, Vi was washing clothes at the sink and Tammas was sitting to one side of the settee, gazing at the television. Kirsty was sound asleep, outstretched on the other side of the settee. Every so often he turned to watch Vi, smiling when she became aware of him. She placed her hands on her hips and said: I hope you're satisfied!

Tell you something Vi, that was the best meal I've had in years.

O I know, bacon egg and chips – very unusual.

Aye fair enough but it was really good, I mean really.

Shut up! She turned back to the sink, immersing her hands in the washbasin, wringing an article of clothing. Tammas had got off the settee making very little noise and he came round behind her, encircled her waist with his arms, placing his chin on her right shoulder and his cheek to her cheek.

You're putting me off.

Sorry. He moved his head round and kissed her on the mouth. Salt, he said, licking his lips.

O thanks! It's probably yours anyhow.

He grinned, put his arms round her again, and she turned to face him. They kissed, clinging to each other. Then she broke from him: We better put the cot up . . . She nodded at Kirsty and at the space between the side of the fireplace and the bed-recess. It goes in there.

Once they had done so Vi began getting the girl ready for bed. She did it very gently and very carefully and Kirsty seemed hardly to know what was happening; and she was back sleeping again when Vi laid her inside on the cot. She pulled over the blankets and stared at her. Then she bent and kissed her on the forehead. Kirsty smiled.

Tammas shook his head at Vi as she straightened. He returned to the settee while she plugged in a table lamp, switched off the main room light. She lowered the volume of the television before sitting down next to him. He put his arm round her shoulders and she leaned her head onto his. They were gazing in the direction of the television. The adverts came on around the middle of the programme. Tammas moved his head slightly. Heh Vi, he said, what're the scratches on wee Kirsty's stomach?

She continued gazing at the television.

I noticed them when you were changing her for bed.

Vi shifted away from him, she reached across to the mantelpiece for her cigarettes. He got his matches and struck one before she had a cigarette in her mouth. She accepted the light from him, then lifted her Sunday newspaper from the floor, began reading the front page.

Will I turn off the telly? he asked.

She shrugged.

I'll keep it on if you like?

She turned a page: I dont mind what you do.

He nodded and waited a moment. D'you want me to go away?

She shrugged again.

Just say the word if you do.

Do you want to go away? she asked, with her gaze still to the newspaper.

No, I want to stay here.

Then I want you to stay here as well.

He put his hand on her shoulder. She continued gazing at the newspaper.

•••

Closing the front door he began to stroll along the lobby to his own room but the kitchen door jerked open and Margaret was there. Where've you been? she said.

Tammas could see Robert behind her, sitting at the kitchen table. I'm sorry, he replied. Honest Margaret, I meant to get in touch with you yesterday.

So you're back? called Robert.

Aye, I'm sorry, I meant to get in touch yesterday but eh . . .

You forgot? called Robert.

I'm sorry Margaret.

Tammas we were really worried.

Wait a minute . . . Robert had got up from his chair and he came to stand next to Margaret. You were worried hen, no me. Eh? Just as well I never called in the polis!

We thought something serious had happened.

Tammas shook his head: I'm sorry, honest, it was a daft thing to do. He brought his cigarettes out and he lighted one quickly.

Robert pursed his lips and patted Margaret on the shoulder, and he left them to go through to the living room. Then

Tammas followed his sister into the kitchen. I really am sorry, he was saying, honest Margaret.

She looked at him.

He took a wad of notes from his hip pocket and counted a sheaf, laid them on the table. That's the rest of the money I owe you Margaret. It puts me up to date now. He laid down some more money: This makes me go two weeks in advance. Okay?

She made no answer.

He had taken his jacket off and now he sat down, unlaced his shoes.

Margaret said, I see you're wearing your watch.

My watch?

Where've you been?

Ach . . . I was just – nothing bad if that's what you're thinking.

Tammas.

Honest Margaret I wasnt doing anything bad.

Well where did you get the money then?

The money?

God Tammas I'm asking you.

Where I got the money? He inhaled deeply on the cigarette, coughed slightly. I just got a wee turn. I was owed a few bob as well. No mind I was telling you before? A guy from the factory? Owed me a lot of money.

Tammas! Margaret shook her head.

Honest.

They looked at each other. Then Margaret said, What have you been doing?

Nothing.

We've no seen you since Friday at tea-time.

Well I was here on Friday night.

You were here?

Aye – Friday night. I slept here, I was in my room.

Well it must've been late when you came in then.

Dont know.

And Saturday, and Sunday, and today – it's nearly half past nine at night Tammas. That's three days; three days you've been away.

Three? He frowned at her.

Saturday Sunday Monday. Three; one two three.

Mm.

I'm asking where you were.

Ach – I was just staying with somebody.

Who? It wasnt Rab because he was up for you yesterday afternoon and it wasnt Billy because Robert met him in the street.

Tammas nodded. What was Rab up for?

I dont know. Margaret had been standing with her arms folded; now she walked to the sink, turned the tap on then off. She came to sit at the table, facing him.

Tammas sniffed. I should've phoned Mrs Brady and asked her to tell you I was okay. I'm sorry, honest. The person I was with doesnt have a phone either.

Margaret looked at him. She shook her head: Tammas, I dont think you would've phoned even if you'd had the opportunity, because I dont think it would've even crossed your mind.

He stared at the edge of the table, reached to tap ash into the ashtray.

After a moment Margaret got up and left him. When the living room door shut he rose, went to his room and changed clothes. He lay on the bed. Then somebody chapped the door. It was Robert. Okay to come in? he called.

Aye.

Ta . . . Robert closed the door and he strolled to the window with his hands in his pockets. He blew a sort of whistling noise between his lips, a tune, while gazing down into the street below. He sighed. You're getting too old for this kind of carry on. It doesnt matter to me what you get up to – it's your sister; she's no your mother you know.

Tammas nodded. He was sitting up on the bed now.

She took the day off work by the way.

Aw. Tch.

What d'you expect but I mean she's been heck of a worried. Eh? Surely you could've at least phoned? Robert glanced round at him, shaking his head.

I'm sorry. I really am Robert I just . . . I never actually knew I wasnt coming back till too late. I didnt want to phone the auld yin up the stair in case it got her out her bed.

Robert nodded. He stared out the window again, hands in his pockets still, his shoulders rocking slightly.

Look eh Robert, could you tell Margaret, let her know and that, it was nothing bad, I mean, I'm no getting up to anything bad, if that's what she thinks – actually I mean I think she does, I think she does think that.

Well no bloody wonder! Robert had turned back round again and he said: One minute you're pinching ten pences out the meter-bowl and the next you're taking taxis to the bloody broo! I mean what do you think people's going to say? Eh?

I'm no thieving.

I know you're no thieving. If I thought you were you'd be out the door in two seconds flat, never mind what your sister had to say about it.

Tammas sniffed.

Listen, I'm no thick; I go in for a pint to *Simpson's* now and again myself. Aye! some strange places you're running about these days – according to what I hear anyway! Gambling dens?

They're no as bad as they're made out to be.

Robert was gazing at him.

Honest, they're no.

What d'you sing hymns or what! Robert shook his head then he smiled briefly.

Tammas cleared his throat. He reached for his cigarettes, glanced at his brother-in-law: I'll be moving out shortly anyhow.

Robert nodded.

Soon as I find a place.

I'll no force you Tammas. But maybe it'd be for the best.

Did you tell Margaret? about what you heard in *Simpson's* I mean.

I did not, no, it's no my place to tell her it's yours.

Mm. He sniffed, struck a match and lighted the cigarette, exhaled: D'you think I should?

I dont bloody know. You're a big boy now. She's no daft but, she's obviously got some idea.

Tammas nodded.

Why dont you find yourself a job?

No so easy.

I know it's no so easy – that's how people hang on to the ones they've got.

Tammas sighed.

Look I dont want to give you a lecture but that was really daft, chucking your job in.

I hated the bloody thing.

Robert shook his head. Then he muttered, Aye, probably best that you think of moving. Seriously Tammas, for your own good. Mind but, I'm no telling you to go.

Tammas nodded.

His brother-in-law had arrived by the door and he waited there with his hand on the doorknob. I wouldnt do that, he said, I wouldnt tell you to go.

I know.

Robert shrugged. Unless I lost my temper! Naw but it's just Margaret, you know what like she is, she's a heck of a woman for worrying and when you're here and she doesnt know what's happening and the rest of it . . . Well, she just starts worrying and worrying and it's hopeless.

Okay.

•••

The taxi stopped at the side entrance but before he could open the door three wee boys rushed forward, scrambling to reach the handle. Will yous fucking stop that! yelled the driver.

While Tammas was paying the fare one of the boys was banging shut the door and he gave him some change. Split that between yous, he told them.

In the bar underneath the stand he ordered a bottle of export and he stood reading the evening's programme in the *Adviser*. The 1st and 2nd races were over. Once he had chosen the like-liest winners he asked a man closeby to tell him the results.

Then he swallowed the rest of the beer and went to the other counter, ordered a hot pie and a carton of soup. Then he spotted Billy and John; they were standing by the door peering about. He shouted to them, waving them over.

What a surprise, said Billy; finding you here!

Is there something up?

Billy winked: Just thought we'd come over and keep you company!

Want a pint? said John.

Eh naw, I'll just stick with this . . . He indicated the pie, and soup carton.

You sure?

I've just finished one.

Okay man – what about you Billy?

Aye, a lager.

John crossed to the bar. Immediately Tammas glanced at Billy: What d'you bring him with you for? He always puts the fucking mokkers on me?

It was him had the dough! Billy grinned: Better be careful, he's here to ask you to go to England with him.

What?

Aye.

Fuck sake! Tammas bit a mouthful of the pie.

Billy nodded. You dont fancy it then?

How do you?

I dont know. At least there's work – Manchester he's talking about. Supposed to be a stack of factories and industrial estates and all that.

I thought your auld man was getting you into the copper works?

Billy shrugged.

After a moment Tammas said, D'you actually fancy England?

A wee bit man, aye, I must admit.

Hh! Tammas bit another mouthful, and he sipped at the soup. Better than beer on a night like this! he said. Hey was it really his suggestion to come over?

Aye, Christ, it wouldnt be mine anyway man I'm fucking skint.

Tammas nodded, grinned. The usual!

Cheeky bastard! Billy frowned slightly and turned to glance at the bar.

Probably fucked off home cause it's his round!

Billy grinned.

A few minutes before the off for the 3rd race Tammas had left the bar and gone to the betting enclosure. Very soon after he saw Billy standing just below the row of bookmakers. And then John was there beside him. Tammas went over. He slipped a £5 note to Billy.

John was saying, Favourite looks good Tammas eh?

He nodded.

D'you fancy it yourself?

It's got a chance.

You backing it like?

Who me?

Aye, the favourite.

Naw . . . Tammas glanced at Billy who was smiling. He added: It has got a chance but. I wouldnt chat you off it John. Ran a great race last Tuesday.

Last Tuesday?

Were you here on Tuesday? asked Billy.

Aye.

John said, Did you win?

Naw. What is this – fucking question-time! Tammas frowned and he peered at the track where the dogs were being held by their handlers for the vet to check them. Yous better hurry if yous want a bet, he said, and he left them there, made his way up to the part of the Stand from where he tried to watch most of the races.

He lighted a cigarette, put his hands in his trouser pockets and hunched his shoulders. There was a wee man with spectacles two terracing steps in front of him. Tammas leaned forwards: Hey Shuggie, fucking freezing the night eh?

Ah you're no fucking kidding son! The wee man was smoking a roll up; he brought it out of his mouth and turned sideways to drop a mouthful of spit onto the ground. What d'you bet? he said.

Fuck all.

The wee man nodded. Hard race. I fancy the F.A.V. right enough.

Aye, it's got a chance. So's the 4 dog but.

Ran a good race on Saturday. Mind? came wide at the 3rd bend? Would've won out the fucking pack if it hadnt!

No danger. Tammas rubbed his hands: The backmarker's got a chance as well!

I was thinking that myself. Any trouble round the 1st and it'll be right up with them!

Tammas nodded, standing back up a step. Billy had appeared at his side, breathless, and whispering: Hey man thanks for the handful . . . I mean it, honest, thanks.

Ssshh.

Then John appeared behind him. And the hooter was sounding, the stadium lights dimming. John stepped round the back of Billy and Tammas both, and he began speaking. It's no as big a crowd as I expected. According to what I hear they really get great crowds at that White City track in Manchester.

Tammas laughed.

Naw I'm no kidding but.

Then the loud roaring as the dogs raced for the 1st bend. Tammas was watching and saying, The backmarker Billy, look at it go look at it go! It's a certainty.·

On you go the 1! Billy had his hands cupped to his mouth and yelled: On you go ya beauuttehh! 1 dog you're a fucking moral!

The wee man turned and shouted: It's a dancer! the backmarker! Favourite's fucked!

The dog from trap 1 hit the front shortly before the last bend and it won easily. Billy threw his arms aloft and jumped at Tammas, flinging his arms round him and yelling: I got 6's too ya fucking beauty! 6's! 6 to fucking 1!

I didnt even know you had money! cried John.

He didnt! The bastard! Tammas laughed: I loaned him a fiver!

A fiver! What did you have on it? asked John.

Aw just a pound, said Billy, just a pound.

Still and all . . .

Billy laughed.

After he had collected the winnings he paused a moment while John walked on, and he said to Tammas: Here, I'll give you the fiver back.

Dont be daft! Hang on and see how it goes. Tammas grinned, It might be your night – you've fucking waited long enough!

And when you go into a pub it's bitter you ask for, no heavy. That right Billy?

True. Billy grinned.

Aye but these Blackpool pubs, said John. I mean they were brilliant. And you thought the same as us Billy so dont give us it!

Naw I agree, I agree.

John shook his head. Even the lassies Tammas – and this pair we met, from Stockport they came. They were telling us Manchester pubs were the best you could get. Cabarets and all that as well. That right Billy?

Defintootly.

Ach shut your fucking mouth!

Wait a minute John I'm agreeing with you!

You're no fucking agreeing with us at all!

Aye I am.

Heh, said Tammas, stop this fighting. We've got to dig out a winner for this next yin. Okay Billy, what's it to be?

I'm divulging nothing.

Ach divulge man for fuck sake?

Naw, you're not on.

Ach please?

Nope.

See yous pair! John shook his head. How come yous never tell any cunt what you're betting?

The mokkers John boy the mokkers. Billy grinned: Never heard of the mokkers?

Seriously but.

Seriously! Well!

Tammas said, I dont mind telling you John – as long as you wait till after the thing's won or got gubbed. I have to admit as well right enough, I dont even want to fucking talk about this race cause the nap's going in it.

Your nap?

My nap.

Billy said: I know what it is.

What d'you mean you know what it is?

I know what it is man, that's all.

Do you fuck.

I do man – you let it slip in *Simpson's* last night.

I wasnt even fucking in *Simpson's* last night!

Aye you were!

Was I fuck!

Well it must've been this morning then.

Ach . . . John had opened the *Adviser* and was reading the tipster's comments on the race. This guy fancies Real Smooth, he said to Tammas, what'd'you think man?

It's got a chance.

Tch, according to you everything's got a fucking chance!

John! that's the whole fucking point!

Billy laughed.

Down in the betting enclosure Tammas made his bet quickly and was walking up the steps of the Stand when the other two came out from the bar. They arrived next to him just as the lights dimmed; then the hooter was sounding and the dummy hare railing towards the boxes. As the traps crashed open Tammas had his hands cupped to his mouth and he was roaring: On the Mona's! On the Mona's! Easy the Mona's! Then he muttered, Bastard . . . Mona's is beat. Dog 3's a stonewall.

What? cried John. On 3! On 3!

And Billy was yelling Go on the 3 dog! On the 3 dog! How far the Smooth! Go on the Smooth!

After the race Billy and John were pumping each other's hands. John shouted: I put my money on at 5 to 2! 5 to 2!

Same with me. Ya fucking beauty! Billy began jumping on the spot: Ya fucking beauty! A fiver I had on it Tammas!

Tammas nodded. Mind you man you were a bit lucky. If the limit hadnt come off the rails then Mona's would've came inside and end of story. He was fighting for it too – brave wee dog. Tammas shrugged: Then yours's got a clear run right up the centre of the track. Still – a good winner.

He went to the bar immediately, leaving the others to collect their money. He was sipping at his beer when they entered. John was laughing and he said, It was a fucking great race but!

Aye, said Tammas, I just dropped a fifty right enough.

What?

After a moment John glanced at Billy who peered along the bar, then waved at a barmaid. John frowned at Tammas: Fifty quid man?

Tammas offered them from his cigarette packet without replying.

Christ Tammas you bet too much for me. The same when

we won at the chemmy – mind? you turned round and stuck eighty pound on a horse?

Did I?

John looked at him.

Tammas smiled. Only kidding . . . He stepped from the bar saying, See yous in a minute; I'm going for a slash.

He made his way through the crowded room in the direction of the lavatory but bypassed it and went outside.

It was far too early yet for betting on the next race. Punters were standing about chatting and reading raceforms; some wee boys dodged about playing games; two men leaned over the wall separating the enclosure from the racetrack, in conversation with a man in a white coat, a dog trainer.

Tammas had lighed a cigarette and he strolled along to the fenced off section, where the ordinary terracing started. He stood there for a time, until the cries of the bookies yelling odds had been happening for several minutes. He walked quickly to the betting enclosure. It was crowded. He moved in at once to lay his bet and was up in his position before the vet checked the greyhounds.

John was first to arrive. What happened to you? he asked. Billy bought you a drink. Still lying there on the bar.

Good. Nobody'll touch it.

I wasnt fucking meaning that.

John, I wish you'd give us peace a minute . . . Tammas turned away from him and he stared in the direction of the totalisator board. He sniffed and took out his cigarettes, gave one to John without speaking.

Are you losing a lot?

Naw am I fuck. Tammas shook his head; he sniffed again and glanced at him. Naw . . . he shrugged.

John had his cigarette-lighter out and he flicked it and Tammas bent to take a light. John said, I dont know if Billy mentioned anything to you man but I was going to say if yous eh, the two of yous and that, if yous wanted to, it'd be good if the two of yous came down to England and that as well – cause I'm definitely going. Maybe next week.

To England you mean?

Aye. Manchester. There's bags of work. And the night-life, it's supposed to be really fucking brilliant man. I really fancy it. I think it'd be great. I mean this place is dead Tammas you've got to admit it.

Tammas shrugged. He glanced down the steps, seeing Billy appear, making his way in a hurry towards them.

John was saying: Even things like buying drinks I mean a guy in the work was telling us that the women down there, if you're in a boozer with them they're happy with a half pint of lager or a bottle of mild beer – no like here man, fucking bacardis and coke and all that! And with the three of us into it we'd get a decent flat.

Sounds interesting, said Billy.

The lights in the Stadium dimmed and the crowd hushed as the hooter sounded. From the traps the dogs could be heard scrabbling against the metal gates and then the hare was whirring past and the crowd roaring. Tammas stared at the dogs breaking and racing to the 1st bend. He was nodding, and he continued nodding as they rounded it and headed up the back straight. He dropped his programme to the ground; he turned and muttered, See yous in the bar.

•••

He wakened early on Christmas morning; ben the front room he switched on the electric fire and the television. There was a packet of cigars lying on the mantelpiece, a present from Robert and Margaret. He unwrapped the outer covering and extracted one, smelled it quite closely from end to end before inserting it in the corner of his mouth. And he gazed at himself in the mirror. When he struck the match for it he inhaled and coughed on it, and began to sneeze. In the kitchen he blew his nose, made a cup of instant coffee. He doused the cigar in the water gathered at the drain in the sink.

A film for children was beginning on television and he settled to watch it, sitting in Robert's armchair, stretching out, his stocking soles to within a foot of the fire.

Eventually he dozed.

A lot of shouting and bawling was going on down in the street. A group of kids chasing after a girl on a bike. He watched them; one wee girl tossing what seemed like half a brick at the other girl's back and it glanced off her and the handlebars could be seen jerking sideways but the girl managing to correct it and she cycled on, putting a good distance between herself and the rest of them. And the rest of them yelling after her. He drew the curtains and collected the partly smoked cigar from the kitchen but he left it on the mantelpiece, and walked to the front door and opened it, and he put the latch on and went upstairs quickly and chapped Mrs Brady's door. He chapped it again. He folded his arms, shivering. He began moving from one foot to the other. Then he bent to lift the flap of the letterbox and peered inside. There were no lights on at all and the doors off the lobby were all shut.

He flapped the letterbox quite loudly, before returning downstairs. In the kitchen he filled a kettle to make a pot of tea. When the kettle boiled he switched on the grill and he toasted two slices of bread and cheddar cheese. And afterwards, sitting on the carpet in front of the fire, he relighted the cigar and watched television, eating some of the chocolates Robert and Margaret had given him.

•••

The elderly attendant pushed open the door for the pair to leave and as they walked up the stairs Billy began whistling. Tammas paused on the first landing and he shook his head, cleared his throat and spat to the ground. And he muttered, Fucking beats me how you can whistle man it really does.

Ah! Billy smiled: Got to be an optimist in this life. Anyhow Tammas dont worry about it, it was my three quid.

Tammas stopped walking. They were approaching the exit out to the pavement. He said: That's a fucking good yin right enough – your three quid! Well well well.

What's up?

What's up? Fuck all up.

Billy had his hands in his trouser pockets and he hunched his shoulders and coughed slightly. Okay okay, he said, I'm still owing you some dough, if that's what you're fucking on about.

Naw, that's no what I'm fucking on about.

Billy nodded. He sniffed and spat out onto the pavement. That's no what I'm on about.

Well what fucking are you on about then for fuck sake! Billy had turned sharply to face him, his face reddening.

After a moment Tammas replied. Nothing . . . nothing at

all Billy nothing at all. And he stepped out onto the pavement and started walking down towards Argyle Street.

Billy caught up with him. What you on about?

Tammas looked at him. What am I on about? You ya cunt. *Your* three quid. *Your* three quid. Christ sake man we've been helping each other out for fucking years and then you turn round and start that kind of fucking patter! *Your* three quid! Hh! fuck sake!

Billy made no answer and the two of them continued without talking for a while. About five minutes passed. They paused to glance in the display window of a men's clothes shop. Tammas indicated a pair of trousers and muttered, No bad them.

Billy nodded. When they were walking on he said, Look Tammas I didnt mean it like that, about my dough and the rest of it.

Ach!

Naw but . . . Billy nodded again, then he added: But I'm no kidding ye man sometimes I think you take it too serious.

Naw I dont. I dont take it too serious at all.

I think you do but, sometimes man.

Mm.

Naw but I'm no kidding ye.

Tammas nodded.

They were approaching a junction; the traffic-lights showed red and some people stood waiting the change but Tammas and Billy walked between them and crossed immediately, dodging a couple of motor cars. On the opposite pavement Tammas sniffed and he said, I'll tell you something Billy, being honest, I'd rather take it too serious than the way you fucking take it – whatever that might be cause I dont fucking know.

Billy glanced at him. What you on about now?

Tammas shrugged. I'm telling you straight man.

Dont talk shite.

I'm no talking shite Billy.

Aye you are.

Naw I'm no man listen, see that fucking blue you missed? I'm no kidding ye, a five year old fucking wean could've potted it. Christ sake! I know everybody misses now and again but that was fucking ridiculous! And the pink was hanging too! Right over the middle bag man if you get the blue the game's finished, finished.

Billy was nodding. Aye, it was a bad yin; I should never've missed it.

And it would've got us the dough too! And I mean . . . Tammas grinned and shook his head: After that fucking brown! I mean that brown man! Christ! What a fucking shot! Length of the table man and you stopped the white dead! That's one of the best pots you've ever done!

Billy nodded.

Position was perfect! Tammas stopped for a moment and felt behind his ear, and muttered: Thought I had a fucking dowp.

You smoked it.

Did I? Bastard! Tammas frowned and raised his right hand palm upwards and he gazed at the sky. It's raining!

Naw it's no – too cold; if it was going to rain it'd fucking snow.

That's the fucking rain alright! Tammas shook his head, zipped his jerkin up to the top. Come on we'll run.

Billy shrugged.

We'll get soaked man!

Ah I cant be fucking bothered. I'm just walking.

Dont be daft! Tammas began trotting, a little way ahead he stopped and called: Come on ya cunt!

Nah! Cant be bothered.

Fuck sake Billy! Tammas turned, shaking his head, and he began to run, his head bowed as the rain started falling more heavily. Thirty or so yards on he slowed to look round once more; Billy was walking in a methodical manner, gazing at the pavement. Tammas continued running.

•••

He was dressed in his good suit and was wearing the shirt his sister had got him for Christmas. On his way out the bedroom he lifted two brown-paper packages from the cupboard. Margaret was in the kitchen, seated at the table, listening to the radio. When she glanced at the packages he said, Just a couple of things.

Presents?

Eh . . .

A bit late surely?

He shrugged.

Anybody we know?

Eh . . . no really Margaret. He paused, touched the collar of his shirt and smiled briefly: Ta.

She nodded. Will you be back?

Will I be back?

Tonight I mean . . . Margaret sighed.

Aw, eh . . .

Never mind.

Simpson's Bar was quite busy. He carried his pint to a seat near a dominoes game in which McCann and Auld Roper were playing. Auld Roper pointed to the packages: What's that?

Packages.

Are they presents or what?

Aye.

Hh! Bit late for fucking Santa Claus son are you no?

Tammas shrugged; he peered to see the value of the dominoes that Roper was holding. Play the 6.4, he said.

Shut up.

McCann called: D'you back that Border Rover this afternoon?

Did it win?

Aye – fucking 10 to 1 the bastard!

10 to 1!

Aye, I thought you'd have backed it! Especially after that last race you hit it for.

Ah! Tammas shook his head. He took the cigarette McCann was holding out to him.

Where you off to?

Tammas shrugged. Just going to see somebody.

Wee Betty?

Tammas looked at him. He drank a mouthful of beer.

Auld Roper laughed: Wee Betty! Is that the name of his girl-friend? Wee Betty! Eh? Fuck sake! I didnt know there was any lassies called that nowadays!

McCann winked at Tammas: Dont worry about this auld cunt he's went senile!

He got a bus into town and cut through St Enoch Square for another. Upstairs he sat on the front seat, the packages on his lap. When the bus pulled out from the terminus he was the only passenger on the top deck and after a moment he went downstairs and said to the driver: You passing Baird Street?

The driver nodded.

Back upstairs he lighted a cigarette. He was staring out the front window until suddenly he recognised this part of the road and he jumped up, lifted the packages and went quickly down, but not in time for the driver, and he had to get off at the next stop after.

There was a small general store just before the corner of Baird Street. He bought a packet of cakes and some children's sweets. Going into Vi's close and up the stairs he paused to light a cigarette. He stood on the landing beneath the one where she lived and he gazed out the window into the back-court for several moments.

He rang the doorbell. He flapped the letterbox. He rang the doorbell again. There was no reply. No sounds coming from inside. He bent to peer through the letterbox vent. It was pitchblack. Not a sign of light beneath the kitchen door. He stood for a time then banged the door again and rang the bell, and he flapped the letterbox. And the door across the landing opened noisily. A young woman, frowning at him. She switched on the light in her lobby, stared at him. Can I help you? she said.

What . . .

Can I help you? Are you wanting something?

Eh . . . He nodded at Vi's door: I was wondering eh – what is she away out or what?

Who d'you mean? Vi?

Aye, d'you know where she is?

She continued staring at him but did not answer.

Eh, are you Cathy?

Do I know you?

You look after Vi's wee girl.

She nodded and frowned again: Are you Thomas?

Aye. He smiled. Did she leave any kind of message?

I didnt even know she was expecting you?

Eh naw she wasnt but eh, I was just wondering and that if eh . . . He nodded.

She beckoned him across. Come in a minute, she said, there's a hell of a draught coming up the stairs.

Nah it's alright Cathy I'll just eh . . . He raised the packages and the paperbag containing the sweets and the packet of cakes. And he handed them to her. Will you give them in to Vi for me?

Yes. Cathy glanced at them.

Just a couple of presents.

She nodded, and added: Are you leaving a message?

Naw eh I'll no bother, just – I was here and that. Okay?

Fine.

•••

The grey figures had stopped dancing and singing and the picture of a clock on a church tower flashed onto the screen. As the chimes began Robert, Margaret and Tammas were onto their feet, each with a glass in hand. On the twelfth chime Robert said, That's it then.

He and Margaret kissed on the lips. The grey figures were now singing *Auld Lang Syne* with their arms linked. Tammas and Margaret kissed each other on the cheek and then he and Robert shook hands, and they clinked glasses and raised them, made the toast to the new year. Then they drank and Tammas said: Refills! And he took their glasses to the table and poured another one each from a bottle of vodka.

And I'm sticking off that bloody goggle box! cried Robert.

Margaret laughed: He's away with it already and we're no even out the house yet!

What d'you mean away with it? Just because I'm turning off the blooming telly! Robert grinned, taking the glass from Tammas.

When Margaret had hers she sniffed it and wrinkled her nose: Vodka!

Aye, said Tammas, you've got to take one.

Not me; I'm sticking to the sherry . . . She moved towards the table but Tammas stood blocking her way, grinning at her.

Naw, he said, you've got to otherwise it's bad luck!

Robert laughed: Right enough Margaret!

O God. Well . . . she shook her head: At least put some lime or orange into it. And I'll have a bit of shortbread to wash it down.

Soak it up you mean! Robert laughed.

Shortly after 12.30 am they were locking the outside door and stepping downstairs and into the street. Quite a few people were about and music came from different windows up the tenement building. On the pavement opposite a middle aged couple who lived up the next close called: Happy New Year! and each of the three replied with the same call.

The streets were damp though it had not been raining for a while. There was a slight fog about. They walked into George Square for the all-night bus services. Tammas then split from them. See yous the morrow, he said.

Take care, Margaret answered, frowning a little.

Tammas looked at her.

I keep telling her you're a big boy now Tammas but she'll no pay any attention! Robert winked.

I know what you mean!

Well, replied Margaret, all I'm saying is take care.

Take care yourself, said Tammas. And he grinned: Have a good night.

And you.

He brandished the vodka bottle, still grinning, before continuing on across the Square to where his own bus would be leaving.

•••

At the foot of the staircase in Vi's close he uncapped the vodka bottle and swigged a mouthful. How's it going Vi, he said, I just thought I'd first-foot you! He grinned and capped the bottle, stuck it into his side jacket pocket, brought out his cigarettes and lighted one.

Outside her door he took the bottle out again but then put it back into the pocket; he rang the bell and stood with his eyes closed.

There was loud music coming from somewhere up the stairs. After a moment he rang the bell once more, then bent and lifted the flap. No lights, no sounds. He thudded his fist on the wood. Then he glanced hurriedly about and he rubbed the back of his head. He lowered himself down, sat on his heels, his back to the wall beside the door. He inhaled deeply on the cigarette. He took the bottle from his pocket and stood it on the floor. He stared at its label. A movement from Cathy's house across the landing. And then a cistern emptying and someone's foot-falls on the floor inside.

He finished the cigarette, stubbed it out on the wall; he

rose and stepped to Cathy's door and chapped it loudly. An elderly man answered. Come on in, he said and he returned inside, leaving the door open. After a moment Tammas followed him, shutting the door quietly behind himself.

Some people, mainly middle aged, were in the front room chatting. They looked at him as he entered.

Happy New Year, he said.

Happy New Year, replied a couple of the people.

And a woman said: What time is it son?

I'm no sure.

It's nearly bloody half one! muttered a guy who was wearing a tartan bunnet.

Dont be so bad tempered, she told him.

Bad tempered! Hh! The man turned away from her and he glanced over at Tammas.

I was looking for Cathy . . .

You're no the only one!

Sssh, muttered the woman.

Well no wonder.

She's up the stair with George, the woman said to Tammas. She'll be down in a minute.

One of the other women pursed her lips and shook her head: They've been up for nearly an hour as it is.

Sit down, said a man.

Naw it's okay thanks. I better just eh go up and have a word. Actually I'm looking for somebody that lives across the landing.

Aw. The man nodded, lifted a tumbler, sipped from it, frowning at the guy with the tartan bunnet. And he said: Give the boy a drink.

The boy can get a drink if he likes.

It's okay, replied Tammas, going to the door. I better go up the stair.

Remind them there's visitors down here and they're having to be going soon, muttered a woman.

Tammas nodded. He went upstairs and chapped on the door of the flat where the music seemed to be coming from. A young girl of about 13 answered and rushed back inside without acknowledgment. Then a woman appeared. I'm looking for Cathy, he said.

Cathy! the woman called down the lobby: Somebody for you!

Cathy appeared, holding a drink in one hand. She frowned at first and then smiled. Thomas! Happy New Year, she said.

Happy New Year. He leaned to her and they kissed on the lips briefly. I'm looking for Vi.

She's over in Milly's. Do you know where she lives?

Naw.

Cathy nodded, coming out from the house. Come on, she said, I've got the address downstairs.

He waited in the lobby while she went into her kitchen to find it. There seemed to be no one speaking in the front room. When Cathy gave him a slip of paper with the address written on it she smiled and added, You've got time for a quick yin first!

Eh naw Cathy naw, I better no.

Och come on!

Naw, honest, I better just eh . . . He grinned, patting the neck of his vodka bottle. Got to keep sober! And you've got company in there as well Cathy.

Tch! She made a face and whispered: Is that what you call it!

He smiled.

She paused at the door, touching his wrist: Look, see if you dont get a bus or that, if you cant find a taxi – just come back; we'll be going for a while up the stair. Especially when that mob through there decides to leave!

Great.

Honest, I mean that, just come back. And no too late or I'll be drunk!

Okay . . . he grinned: That's a promise!

•••

Tammas had been walking for some time. His knowledge of Paisley was limited to the main roads and the driver of the bus had only been able to offer him the general direction of Milly's street. Since the Glasgow city boundary traffic seemed fewer and not many taxis passed. Two had appeared for hire but they were travelling on the opposite side of the road and did not stop when he hailed them. There were three youths up ahead, younger than him. They watched his approach. One of them said, Hey jimmy you got a light?

Tammas was smoking. He took the cigarette from his mouth with his left hand and he gripped the neck of the vodka bottle with his right. What was that? he asked.

You got a light? A match?

A match . . . He sniffed. He passed the cigarette to him.

The youth used it to light his own cigarette then passed it back. Ta, he said.

Tammas nodded. He looked at them for a moment. He walked on at the same pace, without looking back. About five minutes after this a taxi slowed to round a corner at a junction ahead of him. He hesitated, then began running, following it along the street. It halted halfway up and a couple got out. They paid the driver. Tammas shouted: Hey! Taxi!

The man and woman stared at him. They were entering a garden, walking the path to the door of a semi detached bungalow.

Can you take me to this address? he said, showing the driver the bit of paper.

Ah sorry son, replied the driver, I'm going back to Glasgow.

Come on and take us eh? I'm walking in circles.

The driver shook his head. Sorry.

Aw come on eh? I'm lost. I've got to get. Honest.

The driver looked at him. He sighed. Okay, but hurry up.

Aw ta, thanks a lot.

Where is it?

Tammas handed him the bit of paper.

Less than five minutes later and they were there. A garden surrounded the house and when he pushed open the gate it swung back smoothly. There was a porch at the front door and a light was on in it; lights were also on inside the house. But no noise could be heard. After a moment he uncapped his bottle and swigged at the vodka. He said, Fuck – and then he pressed the doorbell.

Vi opened the door. She gazed at him. He was grinning. Tammas, she said. What you doing here?

First-footing! He brandished the vodka ... Am I to get allowed in?

She shook her head slightly, released the doorhandle and stepped to the side so that he could enter. She shut the door softly and guided him into a kitchen. They stood in silence. Tammas stared about at the different things. Then she said, They were lovely presents you got. You shouldnt've bothered.

Ach! He shrugged. He added, Christ! What a time I had getting here! Terrible! He nodded at her. He laid the bottle on top of one of the cupboard units and he took out his cigarettes, offering her one but she shook her head. He struck a match for his own, staring about the room again. Big place, he said. Milly's?

Belongs to Joe actually.

Aw. Aw aye.

It's worth a lot . . . What did you no get in touch with me for?

Sorry, it was just eh. He sniffed and inhaled on the cigarette.

Vi had folded her arms; she was gazing at him. She shook her head and she turned and walked slowly to the window over the sink and she looked out through the slats in the blind. How did you know where to come?

Cathy. I thought you might've been there if you werent in your own place . . .

Vi made no answer.

There was a few people in her house.

You shouldnt've come Tammas.

What?

You shouldnt've come. Vi was still looking out through the slats in the blind. She had spoken very quietly.

After a moment he said: What's up?

She sighed. You know you never even told me you wanted to see me again – when you went away; you never even said you wanted to see me again.

What?

She turned to face him; her arms were still folded and she was leaning with the small of her back against the sink. I mean you didnt even get in touch with me.

He nodded.

Vi sighed again and she smiled slightly, shaking her head. She strolled to the cupboard unit next to the refrigerator and she handled some of the glasses there. She was wearing a longish dress. She stood about three yards from him. He cleared his throat and dragged on the cigarette. I'm sorry, he said. He nodded. That's a nice dress Vi, it's nice.

She glanced at him. What did you come for?

Just first-footing you! He grinned.

She shook her head and looked away.

That was daft, no getting in touch with you, honest Vi, I'm sorry.

She nodded. What made you come away out here?

I told you first-footing.

It's a long way.

Aye you're no kidding – even worse when you've got to hoof it!

Hoof it?

Aye, Christ, took us ages to get a taxi. Walked for miles!

She nodded, looking at him.

D'you want a vodka? He patted his jacket pocket.

I'm drinking gin – I've got one through the room.

Aw . . .

Vi glanced at her wristwatch.

Is Joe and Milly in there?

Milly is but Joe's in his bed.

In his bed! Tammas grinned.

Vi shrugged. He said he was tired – and he's going to Ayr Races the morrow afternoon.

Christ aye, I forgot it was on. You going as well?

Hh! Sitting about in that bar! She glanced at the wristwatch again.

After a moment he said: Is there something up?

No.

He nodded. Sure you dont want a vodka?

No, I told you.

Aye, sorry. Tammas glanced at the length of grey ash at the end of his cigarette and he tapped it onto the palm of his left hand, walked to deposit it into the sink. He took another puff on the cigarette then doused it; he pushed it through the drain. When he returned to where he had been standing he did so without looking at her. And took out his cigarette packet.

You've just put one out, she said.

Aye it's this drinking, makes you thirsty . . . He glanced at her before striking the match. He blew it out and put it back inside the matchbox. I dont suppose you've got a can of beer at all?

I'll get you one.

He watched her walk round him and out through the doorway, shutting it behind herself. Minutes passed. He was across by the window looking out by the time she returned. Remaining by the door she gestured him over: Come on ben.

He frowned at her.

It'll be okay.

He sniffed and followed her without speaking.

It was very warm in the other room and the lighting was dim. Charlie, the guy who had backed the losers at the race-track, was dozing in an armchair and Vi's brother-in-law Stan was sitting next to Ann on a long sofa. Milly was there and so too were half a dozen other people. There was a hi-fi system and a Frank Sinatra song was playing quietly. Vi patted him on the wrist, indicating a laden dining table in one corner of the room. She gave him a can of export and pointed at the empty glasses, then left him; she walked over to sit down behind Stan. Another man who was sitting nearby leaned closer to begin chatting. The others were talking among themselves. One of the men was accompanying the singer on the record, but only by mouthing the words.

Once he had poured the can of beer Tammas stuck the empty beside a pile of others and he hesitated for a moment, looking across at the folk, and he waited there, before going slowly to a dining chair at the side of the table. He nodded at Stan who had gazed at him. He sipped the froth off the beer, inhaled on his cigarette and lifted an ashtray down from the table, placing it on the floor near his feet. Eventually he glanced around the room at the different things on display, at the pictures on the wall and the large curtains reaching from the ceiling to the floor. The song ended and another one started, also by Frank Sinatra. And then one of the woman stood to her feet; she was saying something to Milly about the weather and she finished saying it before coming across to the table. She smiled at Tammas as she lifted a large plateful of sandwiches in one hand and a smaller plateful of cakes in the other. She offered them about to the people in the room. When she returned the plates to the table she said to Tammas: Help yourself.

No thanks, he replied. He continued sipping at the beer, not gazing at the others in the room. When the record ended one of the men put on another one in the same style. Tammas brought out his cigarette packet then returned it immediately. He shifted on his chair and glanced at the assortment of stuff on the table. Then Vi was rising from the sofa. Her feet were bare. She yawned, coming over to the table, to lift a sandwich; she bit a piece, looking at him. It's warm in here, she said.

Aye . . . He took out his cigarettes again, and offered it to her. She shook her head; a moment later she went back to the sofa. Tammas put the cigarette in his mouth, the packet back into his pocket. He brought out the matches and struck one, lighted the cigarette. He stared at the floor, aware of the blood going to his cheeks. His face was getting really red. He unloosened the knot in his tie and opened the top two buttons of the shirt. Then he glanced towards the others and bent forwards a little, leaning his forearms on his knees. There was only a wee drop of beer left in the glass and the bottle of vodka was ben the kitchen; he inhaled on the cigarette, staring at the carpet, at the floral pattern on it; different kinds of flowers with stems and leaves, different thicknesses of stalks but the green colour was the same throughout. He glanced up at the wall again. There did not seem to be any clocks in the room. He shook his head and stood up, and walked to the door and out into the lobby; he pulled the door shut. He stood for a moment. It was much cooler, almost cold. He walked along peering into the rooms there for the bathroom; he found it near the top end. It was large inside and there were magazines on a stool within arms reach of the lavatory seat. He took off his jacket and tugged back his shirt cuffs, and he washed his hands and arms and his face and neck. The towels were thick and quite rough on his skin. He stared at his face in the mirror, patted his hair down at his ears, then wet his hands again and smoothed his hair. He tightened his tie and buttoned the shirt up to the top. Vi was standing in the lobby when he left. Is that you going? she asked.

Aye.

She nodded. I'll see you to the end of the street.

Nah, he said, dont bother.

No, I will.

Nah it's okay Vi dont bother.

Yes . . . She was nodding as she walked past him, into one of the bedrooms. She came out with her coat over her arm. He entered the kitchen before her. A couple of minutes later and she came in. She had the coat on and she was wearing her shoes. That's me ready, she said.

He looked at her. Are you coming with me?

What d'you think I've got my coat on for?

Aye, I'm no talking about the end of the street but.

Tammas, it's past three o'clock in the morning.

Christ sake Vi.

She pulled back her sleeve to see her wristwatch. She glanced at him. How did you no get in touch with me?

He was looking at her.

I mean even writing a letter . . .

A letter?

Even a letter – yes, aye, that would've been better than nothing.

I'm sorry.

Tch. She shook her head, frowning.

After a moment he muttered, Nobody even spoke to me in there. He gestured sideways with his thumb. Made me feel as if . . . I dont know. What was it for? I mean how come?

How come?

Aye I mean, Christ, no even saying a word I mean Christ sake – Hogmanay and that and nobody even says a word to you. That's really out of order. What was it for?

What d'you mean what was it for?

Tammas stared at her until each of them looked away; then he said, Are you coming with me?

No. I've just put the coat on cause I was cold.

Christ sake Vi.

Well you're always asking these stupid bloody questions.

He looked at her.

So you are, stupid bloody questions.

Okay then aye, but all I'm asking is if you're coming and I'm no talking about the end of the street I mean I'm talking about are you coming with me, if we're going out away from here, away from this dump of a bloody place, that's all I'm asking; it's a straight question.

Dont lose your temper with me!

I'm no losing my temper!

O are you no!

Tammas sniffed. Then he added: Christ sake Vi. He took out his cigarettes and offered her one.

I've stopped. Did you no notice?

Naw, Christ – stopped smoking?

A fortnight ago. Sixteen days to be exact.

Christ sake!

Tch. I wish you'd stop saying that all the time.

He reached out and he took her left hand in his, and he stepped in close enough to kiss her; and they kissed each other on the mouth. Come on Vi, he said; come on we'll go away.

She gazed at him and closed her eyelids and they kissed again for a longer period. He put his arm round her shoulders and cuddled her tightly. Christ, he said, hh. He shook his head. I'm sorry I didnt get in touch Vi.

It's okay Tammas. I just wish you had though so I knew what was happening – I just didnt know.

He pulled her to him, her head over his shoulder, her body tightly to his. He got an erection and moved away from her. Neither spoke for several moments. Then he lifted his bottle of vodka and inserted it in his side jacket pocket. You ready? he said.

She nodded. Think we'll get a taxi?

Och aye.

I could phone one from here?

Naw, I'd rather just get out . . . She was looking at him and he shrugged: Okay?

She nodded. Then she raised her hand, put it onto his forehead and she rested it there for a few seconds, and she frowned. Do you know that you've got a temperature?

A temperature?

I'm no kidding.

Hh. Must've been that room in there, I was beginning to get really sweating – like you're going to faint or something.

She sighed, shook her head. You're a poor soul . . .

He looked at her.

She laughed and strode to the door. You're a wean! she said. Come on!

Are you no going to say cheerio?

She made no reply. He followed her in silence to the front door and once they were outside she closed it very gently, but still its noise was fairly audible. Tammas laughed and cried: Quick! And he took her hand as they ran down the path to the gate; and out onto the pavement, letting the gate swing back to clatter against its snib lock.

Where're we going?

I dont know! Tammas was laughing. Somewhere but!

I want a dance!

You'll get a dance!

I'm no kidding! she cried.

Neither am I!

They carried on running for some forty or so yards until they came to an abrupt halt, both were puffing and panting and Tammas had to hold his sides, gasping in an exaggerated manner.

We're both crazy! laughed Vi.

He laughed, grabbed her arms and kissed her on the forehead, and they walked on with their arms round each other.

•••

Tammas squinted and moved his head on the pillow. Vi was saying: I'm going for Kirsty now Tammas.

He frowned, raising his head upwards, resting himself on his elbows.

It's okay, she said, just stay in bed – I'm going to get Kirsty.

Vi had on her coat and she was all set to go out, now lifting her bag from the kitchen table.

When'll you be back?

Soon! She smiled across at him, then came over.

Soon . . . he nodded, sitting up and putting his arm round her waist. She leaned to kiss him and he raised himself up further.

That's enough, I've got to go.

So what time'll you be back?

Soon I said – and you need a shave, desperately.

Hh! He rubbed his chin, grinned at her. Take a taxi.

A taxi!

Aye, I'm no kidding, both ways as well Vi.

Ha ha. Think I'm made of money! She had walked to the door and she swung her bag in a circular movement.

Naw! Honest! It's alright Vi – I've got it . . .

She had opened the kitchen door and she called: I'll no be long!

Then the outside door opened and shut.

Tammas continued to sit for a time, before lying down, his hands behind his head on the pillow. He stared at the ceiling. The ceiling was greyish. It could have done with a lick of paint. And too above the window and sink and oven, it was a kind of yellowish – plus the woodwork. A fresh white right across the whole lot. The walls themselves needed something. The one where the fire was had been done in a lightish brown and the others had a striped wallpaper while in the recess where the bed was the walls were painted in a blue colour to make it look like a different room. But the blue did not make it look different at all. In fact it did not look very good, it looked wrong – better to have done the whole thing in a fresh white and that would make it nice and airy looking. No venetian blind either. That just stopped the light coming in the window. The whole place could have done with a different arrangement. There was no dressing table. All of Vi's stuff seemed to be standing along the big old fashioned mantelpiece or jammed together on top of the tallboy. A mirror was there, a small adjustable one and next to it a framed photograph of the wee girl when she was a baby. No other photographs at all. None. The whole room including the ceiling done in a fresh white paint and all the woodwork done in a fresh white gloss; that would be fine, it would make a big difference to the place.

He got out of bed. A carton of milk was over near to the window and he drank a couple of mouthfuls straight from it. His cigarettes and matches were on top of the electric fire, and so were his socks, which Vi had washed for him. He switched on the fire and turned, glancing at the jumper on the back of the settee. It had a sweetish smell about it and it was a bit tight. His shirt had been sweaty and Vi had given the jumper to him although he had said no, he would have preferred not to put it on; but eventually he had to put it on. There seemed to be no other men's clothes in the place. And there was no shaving stuff. He rubbed his chin again and he lifted his cigarettes, lighted one and returned to bed, bringing the ashtray with him. He propped the two pillows together so that he could sit up against them, drawing the blankets and sheets upwards.

The television was on but he was watching Vi feed the wee girl her evening meal. The two of them were laughing. It was a game: Vi trying to put the spoonful of food into her mouth while the girl would snatch away her head, causing the food to bang against her cheeks or the sides of her lips. Vi was holding the spoon in her right hand and her left grasped Kirsty by the back of her head and neck and probably she could have forced her into keeping her mouth in the correct position. When she noticed him watching she said: Spoiled daft so she is.

Tammas smiled.

Vi frowned briefly. It's because it's just the two of us. I mean just because it's only the two of us. Tch! She shook her head. What I mean is that if I started to get angry with her I'd just end up feeling stupid. Is that right you? she said to Kirsty. And then held the girl's head a bit more firmly so that the spoonful of food went into her mouth.

I know what you mean.

Vi nodded. She glanced at him: How do you find it with your sister? do you find yous do a lot of arguing the gether or d'yous manage to avoid it?

He shrugged.

She probably stops herself.

He shrugged again.

No think so?

Maybe.

Probably she does! Vi grinned: Because you're her wee brother and she's got to look after you!

Tammas looked at her.

I'm only kidding, said Vi. She had dipped the spoon back into the bowl of food and she fed it to Kirsty, and went on: Does she do all your laundry?

My laundry. Aye . . . He reached for his cigarettes and he sniffed before withdrawing one from the packet and then striking a match on the box. She does it when she's doing her own, hers and her husband's.

It's still good of her.

He exhaled smoke and nodded, looking at the television. The next time he raised the cigarette to his mouth he yawned.

He shook his head, gazing in the direction of the screen. Tired, he said.

When Vi did not respond he glanced over. She was involved in cleaning the wee girl's mouth, dabbing at the corners of it with a cloth.

Vi.

Mm . . . she turned her head to look at him, a very slight frown on her face.

After a moment he said, Would it be okay if I stayed the night as well?

The night?

Aye, would it be okay?

She nodded.

I'll go first thing in the morning.

She smiled. It's okay Tammas.

Naw I mean . . . he nodded, and shrugged.

•••

It was just after midday and he was eating a mince pie and beans in a pub down the street from the snooker hall; a pint of heavy at his elbow and he had the *Sporting Life* spread on the table.

The bar began filling up and when two men in dungarees sat by him he lifted the newspaper so they could put down their pints. He folded it and stuck it into his side pocket.

Downstairs at the snooker hall the *full up* notice was hanging on the inside of the swing doors and when he pushed his way inside the elderly attendant grunted, Can you no fucking read?

I'm just looking for my brother – I've got a message for him.

You better be fucking snappy then.

Tammas continued on in between the row of men and youths whose names were down on the waiting list for a game. At one of the top tables a three-red tournament was in progress. He walked behind it, into a corner, and he sat on the ledge there, yawning as he brought out the *Life* and squinted at it in the light filtering from the strip beneath the shade of the nearest tables. He turned the page to the racing card for the day's only meeting not postponed because of waterlogging. He had his nap picked out but also fancied a couple of others. He trapped the paper between his elbow and his right knee while lighting a cigarette.

Hey john . . . A guy had approached him: Fancy a game? I've got a table booked; I think I'm next on.

Naw man sorry I've eh – I'm just passing the time.

It's no for money or anything, just a game.

Nah – actually I'm going up the betting shop in a minute.

The guy nodded and moved off to somebody farther along the ledge. About quarter of an hour later Tammas was getting down off the ledge and heading for the exit. The elderly man was still attending the door but he ignored him as he pushed out.

He had less than £40 in his trouser pocket. The horse he fancied was paper favourite and it appeared as favourite when the actual betting started. He was going to do it for £5 but when he wrote out the line he had written it for £20; and when he passed it beneath the grille he paid the additional £2 tax in advance.

On the *off* they were laying 11/4 against the favourite. It was a race for novice chasers over a trip of two miles. The favourite jumped off in the lead and was still showing ahead when the others closed to challenge between the last two fences. But over the last and on the run in the horse steadily drew further and further away, eventually winning by some dozen or so lengths. There was no objection lodged by the runners-up and there was no inquiry by the stewards; and then the jockeys had weighed in and Tammas was at the pay-out window to receive the £75.

He studied the other newspapers tacked on the wall for the coming race. The opening show had the favourite in at even money and it was quickly taken down to 4/6; scribbling out his line he rushed across to the counter and asked for the board price to £90.

The *full up* sign no longer hung inside the swing doors. He pushed them open and entered. At the top table the tournament had ended but he recognised two good players at another table and he walked to join the small group of guys watching. It happened that if these two went into one of the tournaments a couple of other players would immediately withdraw. Tammas knew their first names, as did most of those watching and some bantering took place. The pair never seemed in earnest when against each other, kept looking to see who else was around. After a few minutes he went to the lavatory for a piss. He ran the tap at the sink then drank some water. He checked the cash in his trouser pocket; less than two pounds.

Upstairs in the bookie's a group of folk had gathered at the results' sheet. He peered over a man's shoulder and saw that the favourite had won. He nodded and smiled very slightly, took his cigarettes out and struck a match and got it lighted, while walking to the small queue at the pay-out window. The man in front turned and said, You got a fag jimmy?

Aye.

When Tammas had given him it and the matches the man nodded as he inhaled the first puff of smoke, passing him the matches back. Good favourite, he said.

Aye. Tammas opened the *Life*, gazed at the declared runners on the next race. The horse he fancied was listed at 6/1 in the forecast betting. On the ledge of the pay-out window lay a pile of betting slips. He reached to take one and he wrote out the name of the horse and then he made the bet out to £135. The female cashier had begun paying the winners and when she gave him his £135 in exchange for the receipt he went immediately to one of the pay-in windows and handed it and his betting line straight across. It was another woman cashier and she peered at the line and at the stack of notes and replied, Hang on a minute son. And she got down off her stool and carried it through to where the settler worked behind a partition. The settler came out and looked at Tammas for a moment. Then the woman returned; she checked the stack of notes and issued him with the receipt, which he checked, before folding it away into his trouser pocket.

6 5's 30 and 3's 18; 18 and 3 21; 6 1's 6 and 2's 8; 810, eight hundred and ten quid; plus the stake, equals 945. £945 less tax.

One more point and the return amounted to one thousand and eighty, one thousand and eighty quid. A grand. All it required was one more point. 7/1.7 to 1 to the 135. £1080, less tax. Even better with the 15/2, that extra half point making sure it was more than the grand even after tax. One thousand pounds.

He checked the time through shop windows while he walked. He was walking at a steady pace. He passed other betting shops. He kept walking until he arrived at where he lived but he continued past the shop old Phil worked in, to

a shop he only went into now and again. He glanced up at
the board, the boardman was chalking in figures on the next
race. His nap had finished third at 4/1. 4 to 1. His nap had
finished third at four to one. Third at four to 1. Even if it
had won he would not have reached the grand – nowhere
near it, five hundred and thirty fives, it did not matter. £700
though. That would have been fine. Seven hundred quid. Six
hundred. 675. Less tax, six hundred and seventy five ten
pences.

He was walking in the direction of his own street but he
remained on the main road and he walked back up the town
and into a picture house.

...

A couple of girls glanced at him. At the counter he ordered
a roll and sausage and a cup of tea, and was given the tea
immediately. He sat at one of the empty tables. There were
four girls in the room, sitting beside each other. A man was
snoring at another table, his head cradled on his crossed forearms, snoring quietly. Otherwise the club was deserted, the
room where the chemmy took place in total darkness. He
lighted a cigarette and stood up, and said to the girls: Fancy
the telly on?

If you like.

He pulled a chair to the side of the counter and climbed
onto it, reaching to switch it on. Later the woman came from
the kitchen with his roll and sausage; he ordered another tea.

A play had begun on the television and he was watching

it along with the girls and the woman. The doorbell rang. It rang again and the woman muttered, Tch, bloody door . . . And she left to answer it. Moments afterwards she was followed in by four men, two going straight into the card room and then the kitchen. One of the other two said: Anybody seen Frank Callaghan?

No one replied. Tammas and the four girls continued staring at the television screen; the man at the table was still asleep, still snoring.

The other two men came from the kitchen with the woman. They had been speaking with her and now they walked back out again, going quite quickly. The one who was talking said to Tammas, How long you been here son?

About an hour.

The man sniffed and nodded. When did Frank go out?

Tammas shrugged.

He was here but?

I dont know.

The man took a handkerchief from his pocket and he blew his nose. He said to the girls: What about yous – you seen him?

No, replied one.

Then the man glanced at Tammas again: You a member of this club?

Who me? aye.

Glad to hear it. The man nodded, then nodded at his companion. He indicated the guy who was asleep, pursed his lips and shook his head. A moment later they had gone.

One of the girls called: That's Frank then Alice eh!

The woman behind the counter nodded in reply. She was smoking a cigarette, holding it to her mouth in her right hand, her left forearm resting beneath her breasts. She stared at the television. But suddenly she moved: she shook her head and she stuck the cigarette into her mouth and she turned and said, I'm bloody sick of this. She strode round into the room and over to the man at the table, shook him by the shoulder. Away you go, she said, I'm sick of your damn snoring.

What . . .

Away you go!

Aw Alice . . .

No aw Alice – away you go bloody home.

Will you no give us a coffee? As he spoke the man had half risen from the chair, balancing himself against the edge of the table and moving in a sort of circular fashion. The woman was about to say something but the phone rang and she went quickly to answer it. Less than two minutes and she appeared in the kitchen doorway. Closing, she said.

The others all looked at her.

Closing, she said, stepping to the counter and lifting a couple of dirty plates; I'm closing for the night.

The man called, No even a coffee for the road Alice?

She glanced at him without speaking and he began grumbling unintelligibly while heading for the exit. And you lot can do the same, she said to Tammas and the four girls.

He followed them, along the corridor and out into the lane. The wind was quite strong and he turned up the lapels of his jacket. At the corner he paused as the girls stopped. Two of them went one way and he walked with the other two the opposite way. I'll get yous along the road, he said.

Neither answered for several moments, until one replied, It'd be best if you didnt.

O aye, aye, sorry.

Naw, said the girl, shaking her head.

Tammas nodded.

Cheerio.

Aye . . . He smiled and shrugged, walked quickly on by himself.

•••

He was lying full length on the settee, his legs protruding over the end arm; although the television was on at its normal volume he was staring to the side of it, in the direction of the curtains at the windows. The main living room light was off but in addition to the light coming from the screen there was a red glow from the electric fire. He yawned and glanced over the settee at the ashtray on the floor, there was the half of a cigarette lying in it; he picked it out and reached for his matches. He rose when he had it burning, leaving it wedged in the corner of his mouth, and he stared into the mirror above the mantelpiece, the shadows there affecting the way his face looked. Then noises from outside on the landing and he moved rapidly, switching off both the fire and the television, going along and into his own room, clicking shut the door, not putting on the light. It was his sister and brother-in-law. Once they had locked the outside door they went into the front room and then into the kitchen and their own bedroom, back into the kitchen; and the sound of the kettle being filled from the tap, and soon they were in the living room.

Not long afterwards Tammas got up off the bed, he stepped to the window and peered out. Down below the streetlamp lighting showed rain pattering steadily onto the wet tarmac and the concrete paving; it was around 10.30 pm.

•••

Tammas grinned. He shut his eyelids and shook his head, his elbow on the edge of the table and his chin being propped by his hand. He looked at Rab again, and he laughed. The two of them were sitting in the lounge of a pub in the city centre. It was threequarters full and a band was performing, using quite strong amplification. He drank some beer and put the pint back down, leaned slightly nearer to Rab: Next month!

Aye, next month.

To Rena you mean?

Naw, her maw.

Fuck sake! Tammas laughed. He drank more beer, shook his head again. What does your auld man have to say about it?

Fuck him. As long as I dont turn a pape he doesnt give a fuck. And he likes Rena as well – thinks she's too fucking good for me!

So she is ya cunt! Tammas shook his head once more. Lucky bastard!

Rab grinned.

So you are man!

I'd have been fucking luckier if I'd still been amateur but I mean these cunts'll be lifting a right few quid out the deal.

Minor matters!

Minor matters?

Well how much are they getting then?

Fucking millions man!

Aye but you'll no lose on it . . .

Naw. Rab lifted his own pint glass and sipped at his beer.

What about Rena? what does she think about it all?

Okay – her maw and da arent too keen but; they were wanting us to wait until the summer. Far as Rena's concerned the sooner the better. Me as well man; I just want to get it over and done with and fuck off to England out the road. I wasnt that bothered before, but now . . . !

Tammas nodded.

So will you do it or what?

Aye, course. But I dont know anything about it. I've never even fucking been to a wedding before.

Honest?

Naw, Christ, no even as a boy.

Ach – there's nothing to it; just hand me the ring and make sure I get to the church on time.

Is that all?

Rab nodded: Apart from shagging the bridesmaid!

Tammas laughed.

O . . .

What?

Rab sipped at his beer before saying, She maybe invite Betty for it.

Och away man for fuck sake!

Eh . . .

Honest?

I'm no sure. She'll definitely be coming but I know that.

Tammas was shaking his head while taking a cigarette out and lighting it.

What can you do I mean she's Rena's mate!

I know, Christ, it's fair enough . . . Tammas exhaled then grinned: Could she no ask that cousin of hers instead?

Wee Julie for fuck sake ya bastard she's only seventeen!

She's a woman but!

Rab grinned and shrugged. I'll see what she says. I know she's no made up her mind yet anyway.

Tammas nodded. Hey listen man what about your da? have you told him you were going to ask me?

Course.

What did he say?

Who else. He said who else. I told him and he says, Who else! Rab laughed briefly. It's a love hate relationship yous've got.

Aye, he fucking loves to hate me!

Naw, said Rab, reaching for his beer; according to my maw he just worries about you.

Hh!

Seriously.

Aye.

Rab grinned. He gazed round the interior of the lounge and began shaking his head, and he murmured, Years we spent fucking about in *Simpson's* man and see when you think about it . . . amazing, how the fuck we ever met a woman I mean, Christ, look at the talent man it's brilliant, fucking brilliant.

Aye, it's nice.

What about this new yin you're winching?

Tammas sniffed.

After a moment Rab said, I mean if you want to bring her then . . .

To the wedding?

Rab shrugged.

I'm no sure.

Well definitely I mean it'll be alright.

Tammas nodded.

Okay . . . Rab turned abruptly as a waitress walked past: Heh miss! Miss! And when the girl arrived and was standing with her pen and notebook . . . Pint of lager and a pint of heavy. Once she had gone he finished the last of the beer he had and he sighed, glancing across at Tammas. While since the two of us've been out for a bevy together.

Life is passing.

Rubbish.

Life isnt passing.

Fuck sake Tammas.

Well ya cunt you're beginning to sound like John!

Still and all but you cant deny times've changed. I mean the team we used to run about with! Christ!

There was a lot of us right enough.

Aye, there was a lot of us.

Headcases man, you're no wanting to run about with a bunch of fucking headcases are you?

Fuck sake Tammas, all I'm saying is there was a lot of us. And now there's no.

So what?

Fucking so what, so nothing! Rab shook his head and he lifted his empty pint glass. Where's that fucking waitress?

Tammas had almost a third of beer in his glass and he brandished it. Doesnt pay to rush your drink, he said.

Aye. Rab looked at him. Just as long as you're pint for pint with me.

Pint for pint with you! Tammas grinned. You should've told me in advance man and we could've fucking made a bet on it.

Rab smiled.

Anyway ya cunt, you shouldnt be fucking guzzling beer if you're supposed to be taking the game seriously!

I always take the game seriously, that's how I'm so fucking good at it! Rab shook his head. He lifted the empty glass again and upturned it, standing it in the middle of the table. He stared across to where the waitresses were leaning at the bar with their trays, watching the band performing on the small raised platform. Then he muttered, No a bad band.

Tammas brought out the cigarettes and lighted one, sipped at his beer. Aye, he said. He was looking at Rab, and he added: You okay man?

Okay?

What's up?

What's up? Rab was frowning at him. Fuck all up.

Tammas nodded.

Naw I mean . . .

It's alright.

Naw, I just eh . . . Rab sighed. I cant be fucking bothered man.

What d'you mean?

Ah nothing.

Tammas sniffed, inhaled on the cigarette and he exhaled to the floor. The waitress was arriving. She leaned to place the tray on the edge of the table, passed the two pints out. Rab dropped the money onto the tray and told her to keep the change and she nodded in reply.

Tammas was looking at him.

Naw, he said, its just . . .

Just what?

Naw, fuck, just – Hull City man! Rab smiled and looked away. I just wish it was some other cunt – that got into the 1st division now and again!

Aw aye. Tammas nodded. A few moments later he glanced at Rab and he asked: Is that all?

Is that all? How what d'you mean?

Tammas shrugged. Is that all?

Rab looked at him, frowned: I dont know what you mean Tammas.

Aw, okay.

Naw, I dont.

Okay.

Naw but what're you fucking – what d'you mean?

Ah well . . . Tammas shrugged. If you were waiting for the Gers or something . . .

Waiting for the Gers?

Tammas glanced at him.

Naw, was I fuck.

Tammas grinned. Donnie once told me you might! I told him he was wrong!

I wasnt fucking waiting for the fucking Gers man! Rab shook his head and he raised the pint to his mouth and swallowed a big mouthful of lager. You kidding!

Hh!

What're you fucking hhing at ya bastard?

You ya cunt I'm fucking hhing at you – waiting for the fucking Gers man! Hh!

What d'you mean?

Tammas smiled, He dragged on his cigarette and blew smoke to the ceiling. Then he said: Honest man – were you waiting for the Gers right enough?

Rab sniffed, then he shrugged.

Tammas nodded.

Naw, no really, I wasnt. It's just eh – I'll tell you something for nothing: I never even thought about it till fucking about a week ago. I mean never, no since I was a boy. Honest. Christ I mind when I started playing junior two seasons ago there was this baldy bastard playing alongside me. I think he was about fucking thirty or something. But brilliant, fucking brilliant. I'm no kidding ye man you could never understand how he wasnt senior. He could've went anywhere as well – except the Gers, cause they never fucking asked him. Every other cunt in Britain fucking asked him except them. Sad. Peter Wylie. Still playing the now. Fucking star man week in week out.

Hh.

It's in ye but, that's all I'm saying. Cause you're brought up a protestant. I mean these fucking Saturday afternoons man when we all used to go over on the Govan ferry and get lifted over the turnstiles. Christ Tammas no mind that? And the fucking turf, that first time you see it coming down from the top of the terracing! Eh? Christ, what like was it at all!

Rab laughed: his shoulders were waggling as he spoke . . .

And the two teams man. All the colours: trotting out with the ball. And the big roar! O ya fucking beauty! And going quiet when the ref blew the whistle and then that fucking cheer once the ball was kicked off. I used to get the shivers man I'm no kidding ye, I used to get the fucking shivers!

Hh! Tammas grinned. So did I. And I can fucking mind even the now what like it was!

So can I! I mean . . . Rab was shaking his head, he sighed, then shrugged.

But you wouldnt want to play for them surely?

How no?

Well I mean what they always say about going there and trying to get a game man – it's alright if you get transferred for big money and that but dont sign as a boy or you'll wind up in the reserve squad, for the rest of your life!

Rab shrugged. Fair enough, I know that – even the auld man said that to me. It's just the fucking . . . He shrugged again, gazed off in the direction of the platform. The band had stopped playing and were on an interval break.

Tammas gestured at Rab's pint: Another yin?

Aye, you okay but? for the dough and that?

Tammas nodded. Then he grinned suddenly: Hey listen, guess where I met that lassie!

Rab smiled.

Naw I'm no kidding man.

What d'you mean?

Naw, guess where I met her – just where I met her.

Guess where you met her?

Aye.

Rab shrugged.

The fucking track man!

What d'you mean Shawfield!

Naw for fuck sake Ayr, the horses.

Ayr?

Ayr Races, aye.

For fuck sake! Rab laughed loudly. You're fucking crazy ya cunt!

Tammas laughed.

Around midnight they were in an Indian Restaurant. Rab had been staring at his half stuffed paratha and he noticed Tammas watching him. Naw, he said, it looks a wee bit greasy.

Come on man.

Naw eh . . . You can have it.

Tammas glanced at Rab's plate, the pile of food still lying on it. Aye, he said, you've got a lot to swallow right enough! Fucking give us it! He laughed and snatched the paratha half from the plate, dipped it into the curry boat and ate it in a couple of bites.

Naw I know. Rab nodded. He was poking at the rice on his plate with his fork. I just . . . d'you ever think about it all man, the parathas and the chapatis and all that, piles and piles of it, all the curry I mean, all of it man . . . Rab leaned forwards a little and he closed his eyes, pointing with his thumb to the side, to where three tables were positioned together, accommodating a party of fourteen people. Plates and bowls of all kinds of food were spread throughout and two waiters were handling a portable sort of oven on top of which lumps of chicken meat lay cooking.

Aw shut up for fuck sake, muttered Tammas.

It's fucking getting to me but.

Cause you're letting it.

I'm no fucking letting it.

Aye you are . . . Tammas sniffed, wiped his mouth with a napkin and he swallowed some water; he lighted a cigarette and sat back on his chair. Best curry I've had for years! You having a coffee or what?

Rab reached for the water jug and refilled his own glass. He gulped a mouthful immediately. He wrinkled his nose. He cleared his throat and muttered, Naw but that poor cunt down the stair man; him that does the fucking dishes and the rest of it, having to scrape off all the fucking leftovers man, into a big fucking dustbin.

Aw Jesus Christ Rab. Tammas leaned to whisper: You fucking sound as if you're trying to make yourself sick.

Naw. Naw, it's no that . . . Rab rubbed his forehead, just above his eyebrows, his eyelids were shut. He opened them and smiled slightly. Sometimes I get the horrors man. I dont even know what they are, just fucking – it's the horrors man; I dont know, these big bins of grub man – imagine lying at the bottom of it, being fucking smothered, no being . . .

Tammas had screeched back his chair on the floor and he coughed loudly, blew his nose on the napkin. He looked at Rab.

Rab was staring at the plateful of food he still had in front of himself, then he was gripping the edge of the table with both his hands, steadying himself a moment, before pushing himself upwards. The bill, he was saying, I need to get the bill. Fresh air man, fucking . . . better get it quick, fresh air and that man . . . He fumbled some £1 notes from his trouser pocket and he put them on the table. He turned sideways and he peered across at the party of folk at the three tables.

You alright? Tammas frowned.

Naw I'm fucking – all wrong man. The head, spinning like fuck so it is. Hurry up and . . . Rab pointed at the money; he walked off at once, his hands at his sides, as though he was wiping his palms on his trousers. Some of the other customers in the restaurant were watching him. A waiter signalled to the man at the cashier's desk but Tammas called: It's okay. And he strode over to settle the bill.

Down on the pavement he found Rab supporting himself against the wall of the tenement building. You alright? he said.

Rab grunted in reply and he stuck his hands into his pockets and hunched his shoulders, pushing himself away from the wall. You'll no fucking let us down now man . . .

What?

You'll no fucking let us down. Tammas, you'll no fucking let us down . . . Rab stood facing him, shoulders still hunched and his hands still inside his pockets.

Course I'll no fucking let you down.

I'm talking about best man, letting us down. We're fucking finshed if you do man, telling ye, that'll be that. Rab shook his head and he started walking away.

What're you yapping about? Tammas went after him. And when he caught up to him Rab put his arm out as though to ward him off. Tammas chuckled: What is that you going to start fucking boxing or what!

Rab kept his arm raised. I've known you for years man but we're fucking finished, finished; and I'm no kidding ye.

Hey come on! Nobody's letting you down.

I know you too fucking well man. Rab had started walking

again and he almost bumped straight into a middle aged couple who had to stop and go sideways. Rab seemed not to notice. He was saying, I dont give a fuck about things like Blackpool but this is different, this is fucking different, it's no a fucking holiday Tammas it's no a fucking holiday.

Christ sake Rab.

I could get other cunts to do the job but I want you.

Christ Rab ... Tammas was shaking his head. Then he stepped forwards and grabbed him by the hand. I'm just fucking, I mean, just glad you asked me and that Christ it's an honour, it's a fucking honour man. I'll no let you down either Christ I mean I wish you hadnt fucking said that Rab, you shouldnt've said that.

Naw Tammas I've got all sorts of mates; you know that, the team and the fucking work man I've got all sorts – it's no that but, I mean, Christ.

Tammas nodded. I know. I know Rab. I know that.

Aye well.

I'm just fucking – it's an honour.

They shook hands.

Honest.

Rab nodded.

Tammas let go his hand. He turned and cleared his throat, spat into the gutter, took out his cigarettes and lighted one, chipping the match out into the street. He glanced at Rab: Dont worry about it.

I'm no ... Rab shrugged. It doesnt matter. As they continued walking he said, You dont have to come to the Stag Night cause there'll be plenty there anyway – the guys from the team and that; you dont have to bother man.

Naw but I want to come.

Aye but you dont have to, that's all I'm saying.

I want to but.

Rab nodded. After several moments silence he said, And we'll have the dress suits to get on the morning as well man that's another thing.

Aye, no bother.

•••

The meter-bowl contained one 10 pence coin and he replaced it on the mantelpiece, going from there to another bowl on top of the display cabinet; it too was empty. He looked along the window sill and other parts of the room and then he went into the kitchen and searched there, but he found nothing. He returned to the living room and lifted the cup of coffee from the arm of the settee. On the floor, in the ashtray, were the dowps of four cigarettes. He picked one out. He straightened it, smoothing the tip and the fraction of unsmoked tobacco. His matches were on the floor. He struck one, angling his head to avoid the flame of the burning match; and he had it alight in two puffs. Another two puffs and it was finished. He straightened the other three, positioning them along the rim of the ashtray, swallowed down the remainder of the coffee and got up onto his feet, and he walked into the lobby. He stood at the door of Margaret and Robert's bedroom; he clicked it open, moved his head to peer inside. The curtains were still closed but it was fairly bright, this room obtaining the sun for a good part of each morning. The bed was unmade. When he entered he kept the door open wide. On the dressing table a tidy assortment of articles belonging to Margaret, one a box with a cluttered pile of beads and necklaces; hanging from the top of one of the wardrobe doors a folded shirt and a striped tie, and other clothes over the back of the only chair in the room. Between the chair and the bed were a radio and cassette recorder plus a couple of paperback books and magazines. Tammas continued to stand not far from the door and then he went back out again, closing it behind himself, returning ben the living room. He smoked the largest of the three dowps. About quarter of an hour later he collected his good suit from the bedroom and folded it into a plastic bag.

•••

McCann had laid his dominoes face down on the board and he glanced at Tammas and indicated Auld Roper, tapping the side of his head with his right forefinger.

The elderly man was rising from his seat with the help of his walking stick and he began moving in the direction of the lavatory, looking back and waving the stick as a mock threat.

Tammas started shuffling the pieces but McCann said, Dont bother.

Tammas shrugged, he lifted his cigarette packet, took two and handed one to him; he struck the match. McCann exhaled, saying: You think about what I was saying?

Eh.

I'm no rushing you.

Naw it's just . . . Tammas looked at him. I dont know man. I'm no sure.

Naw . . . McCann nodded, he stared towards the television. It's a thought but.

Aye.

That guy I was telling you about, he says it's a certainty.

Tammas nodded, raised his pint glass and he swirled about the small drop of beer at the bottom. What about Peterhead? he said. Have you heard anything more?

Naw no really – except they'll be taking on all sorts. Different contractors involved; it's a really big fucking job.

I think I'd be interested and that if eh . . .

But no the other thing?

Naw, I'm no saying that.

Are you worried about it?

What?

McCann nodded. You dont have to be. Kenny, he's alright, he knows the game.

Tammas looked at him and then at his pint glass, swirling the liquid about. He dragged on his cigarette, nipped the burning tobacco into the ashtray and wedged the remainder behind his right ear.

Be more than a grand there he says. McCann raised his eyebrows, sipped at his beer, observing Tammas over the rim of the glass.

Tammas shrugged.

Think about it anyhow, added McCann, then he sat back on his chair.

Auld Roper had returned with a glass of sherry which he set on the table at his place while exchanging greetings with two elderly guys sitting nearby.

We no best to get up there quick? asked Tammas.

Maybe.

Auld Roper glanced at them as he sat down: What yous talking about?

Peterhead.

Aw aye. The old man nodded, he sipped at his sherry.

I'm saying to Tammas they'll be starting to clear the site soon.

Auld Roper frowned at him: Then yous better get up there quick then! Jesus Christ McCann, once they stick these notices into the job centres the cunts'll be coming from all over the shop! Telling ye son yous better no fucking hang about.

No sweat auld yin, no for a wee while yet.

Roper shook his head and he said to Tammas: Peterhead's nothing nowadays. Fucking Lapland they'd go to if the money was there.

Tammas smiled.

I'm no fucking kidding ye son.

Well it's him . . . Tammas pointed at McCann: I'm just waiting for him to say the word!

He'll no say the word, no him.

McCann grimaced.

He'll no leave Glasgow.

Dont be so fucking daft, I've been out of Glasgow dozens of times.

Aye have you! Roper sipped at his sherry again, took out a cigarette and fiddled with his matchbox. After a few moments he glanced at Tammas: What about that mate of yours in New Zealand son you ever hear anything?

Naw.

No even a Christmas card?

Naw, nothing.

He was a good boy that.

Donnie, aye, he was good . . . McCann nodded, inhaled on his cigarette and he glanced around the pub interior.

He didnt want to go, said Tammas.

Auld Roper frowned: If he didnt want to go he wouldnt've fucking went.

Tammas shrugged.

I mean nobody fucking forced him son.

The rest of his family were all going.

Roper shook his head and added: What's that got to do with it?

Aw give us peace, muttered McCann. You never fucking stop.

Naw but if he didnt want to go he would've stayed, that's all I'm saying. Deep down he wanted to go, to have an adventure or some fucking thing.

Adventure my arse. It's just like Tammas says, the boy's family went and he went with them.

Ach! Auld Roper lifted his sherry and drank a mouthful, sat back on his seat and struck a match, lighted his cigarette and puffed a cloud of smoke over the table. Shuffle the doms, he muttered.

Fuck the doms.

Aye fuck you too.

There was a moment's silence. It was followed by Tammas swirling the beer about in the bottom of his pint glass and tilting his head backwards to swallow it down in a gulp. I'm off, he said, I've got a message to go.

Mind what I was saying! called McCann.

Tammas nodded.

•••

There was a rolled newspaper on the floor nearby the leg of the table. Yesterday's *Daily Record*. He settled back on the ledge with it, but the light was too dim now that the snooker had finished.

A game was still in progress a couple of tables away but other tables were also empty as the daytime players went home. It was about 5.30 pm. In an hour the hall would again be full. He continued to squint at the racing page, at the racing results of the day before yesterday, trying to see the tote returns. But soon he gave it up. He closed the newspaper, stuck it into the back pocket of his jeans and strolled round to the nearest game. It was terrible. Two absolute beginners by the looks of it. He brought out the *Record* again but put it away immediately.

At the top of the stairs he remained in the entrance lobby, staring out over the street. The traffic was still busy; a great many pedestrians hurrying along. Rain drizzled but there did not seem to be much of a wind. He zipped up his jerkin and stepped out onto the pavement.

In shop windows the SALE signs were still pasted up although most of the bargains had gone. There was a sports shop. Tammas stopped to look in. Then a hand clapped him on the shoulder. It was Deefy. Heh young yin, he said, how's it going?

Ah no bad.

Doing alright?

Aye, okay.

That's the game son.

What about yourself?

Deefy nodded. Then he shrugged: Aye, no bad, got a wee turn this afternoon.

Great.

Aye, a few quid.

Smashing.

I was thinking of going to the dogs. Deefy turned his head, sniffing; he touched the brim of his hat.

The dogs?

Blantyre.

Blantyre?

Deefy nodded. You fancy it like son? I mean tagging along. Eh . . .

It's no a bad wee gaff. Flapper. Deefy sniffed again and he looked off in the direction of Central Station. Makes a change from Ashfield.

Naw it's just I'm skint Deefy. Tammas held his hands palms up.

Ah. Deefy nodded. That's what I'm saying; I got a wee turn this afternoon. You can tag along if you like. Get a bus down Anderson Cross. Fancy it?

Well . . . Tammas shrugged and nodded, grinning.

We'll grab a pint first. Come on . . . He led the way into a pub down Hope Street and ordered himself a whisky and a half of heavy, a pint for Tammas. He passed out the cigarettes.

They had to wait quarter of an hour for a bus. When they arrived in Blantyre they headed straight into the first chip shop and Deefy ordered fish suppers, which they ate while walking to the track. And later, just before the betting began on the first race, he gave two £5 notes to Tammas, putting them straight into his hand, tapping the side of his nose with his forefinger.

Tammas said, What's this?

Deefy shook his head; he held up the evening's programme, indicating the form figures. No that it'll do me any fucking good, he said. Last time I was here they gambled a fucking dog from 6's to evens in the space of about ten fucking seconds and I shoved my tank on the bastard. Stuck up 2nd! You wouldnt fucking believe it son!

I'll owe you it, replied Tammas.

Another time I'm standing here and there's this fucking favourite and the vet's there checking the girths and all that and out comes an announcement: Favourite's withdrawn, favourite's withdrawn! And d'you know how? Deefy was shaking his head: Cause the owners couldnt get a fucking punt on the bastard! I'm no kidding ye son; they were there to put their fucking money down but some cunt must've blew the whistle and the bookies were no giving more than 3's on. 3 to 1 on. So what do they fucking do? They turn round and withdraw it! I'm no kidding ye! Warned them off the track right enough – told them no to show their faces ever again.

Hh. Tammas nodded.

Some place! Deefy clapped his hands together, the programme tucked beneath his left elbow, moving his shoulders back and forwards, stamping from foot to foot. Bloody cold, he muttered.

Tammas backed the favourite in the first race and it won. He backed the next two winners also and by the time the betting began on the fourth he had £70. But Deefy had yet to back a winner. Then on the fourth they found they had backed the same runner. Their spectating position was as near plumb to the finishing post as they could manage and they watched the dog win in a photo. My last tenner on it! shouted Deefy. You sure it's won?

Tammas laughed. Easy. Short head. No danger!

That's what I thought myself.

When they approached the cluster of bookies they heard one of them calling odds on the outcome of the photograph. There was no dispute about the winner but the bookie was laying 6/4 a *short head*; 5/2 a *neck*; 8/1 a *half length*. Since he was not taking any bets on the winning margin being a *head*, the bookie was obviously convinced that a *head* WAS the winning margin. Tammas stared at the price for a moment. Then he cried: Christ sake! and he grabbed the money out of his jeans' pocket and passed £20 to Deefy shouting: Get it on man! And then rushed up to the bookie: To twenty quid the *short head*!

The bookie took his money and wiped out the 6/4 immediately. Tammas turned, smiling. Deefy was still standing where he had been previously. Quick! called Tammas.

What?

Quick!

I'm no sure son.

Christ sake!

Deefy was holding the £20 in his hand. There was a rumbling on the loudspeaker and then the winner and placings were announced. The dog had won by a *short head*. Deefy returned Tammas the £20.

Tammas muttered, Christ sake Deefy.

Deefy shrugged. He sniffed, took the cigarette from his mouth and dropped a mouthful of spit on the ground. He nodded towards the bookie he had placed his bet with and walked to receive his return. Tammas followed him, collecting his winnings from both bookies. When they met up Deefy said: You staying for the next?

How, are you?

Deefy shrugged. Back to Glasgow I think eh?

It's your decision.

Outside the ground Tammas hailed a taxi. They sat in silence for a few minutes. Tammas had bought a packet of cigarettes and he offered one to Deefy and also passed one through to the driver. And then he added: Look eh . . . And he started checking the wad of notes he had. More than £140. He counted £70 and handed it straightaway to Deefy.

Deefy thrust it back to him.

Aw naw Deefy please. Tammas shook his head, holding it to him: You've got to take it man honest.

Naw. I dont. Deefy held his hand raised, warding off the bundle of notes.

Please.

It's your fucking money son no mine.

I was out the game but, till you showed up I mean . . . fuck sake Deefy. Half the dough, come on, that's fair.

Deefy sniffed.

Christ sake I mean I've never even been to their fucking track man and I've backed four out of four. Plus the photo! Tammas shook his head and he grinned.

Deefy hesitated. Okay then. Halfers . . . He put his hand into his own pocket and brought out £28, gave Tammas £14 and accepted the £70 in exchange.

Let us know when you're going back!

Hh. Deefy frowned. I'll no be going fucking back. Fucking pitch!

How what's up?

Naw son I mean I'm no getting at you or fuck all but tell me this: how can a man lay 6/4 when it's a short head?

Tammas looked at him.

He cant be a bookie son, no a real yin. I mean there isnt any bookie in the whole fucking world would lay that kind of bet.

Ach away man that's daft. Anyhow, it's a flapping gaff.

A flapping gaff! I know it's a flapping gaff. So what but? They're supposed to be wideys these cunts. That makes it even fucking worse so it does.

Tammas shrugged.

Naw I mean . . . Deefy sniffed and he turned slightly, to gaze out the window. I wouldnt go back there again. No me.

Och!

Deefy shook his head. As they approached the city centre he leaned forwards to ask the driver the time.

You going up the club? asked Tammas.

Naw son I dont think I'll bother. There'll be nothing doing there anyway.

The *Royal*?

The *Royal*? Are you?

Tammas indicated the clothes he had on. I'd have to go home and get changed first.

Ah, I wouldnt bother . . . Deffy sniffed and folded his arms. A moment later he leaned forwards again. Heh driver, he said, go up St Vincent Street will you.

On the brow of the hill he told the man to pull into the kerb, and added, Two minutes I'll be.

When he got out he did not say anything to Tammas, nor did he look in his direction. He walked off across the street, tugging at the brim of his hat, and on up one of the side streets towards Blythswood Square. He reappeared holding a woman by the elbow. He opened the door of the taxi for her. Tammas moved to make room, noticing the driver's eyes in the rearview mirror. The woman sat down next to him. Deefy pulled open the folding seat and he sat there staring out the window.

They arrived outside Tammas's close first and he got out, taking the wad from his pocket, preparing to pay something but Deefy waved him away. Once the taxi had moved off again he could see Deefy shifting from the folding seat into the back seat to sit beside the woman. He continued looking after the taxi until it was out of sight, then he crossed the street and walked along to *Simpson's*.

•••

Margaret had called him ten minutes ago. He was lying on his side in bed, with the blankets to his chin. When the sound of cutlery and crockery had become less audible he threw back the blankets and got out; he was wearing his ordinary clothes. At the window he pulled open the curtains, he yawned and shivered, went into the bathroom to urinate and wash himself before going ben the kitchen. Margaret and Robert were still eating at the table.

His food was being kept warm beneath the grill. He sat down at the table where his place had been set and began to mash the potatoes into the mince and gravy. Robert was now about finished eating, wiping his plate clean with a slice of margarined bread: he left the kitchen without speaking. Then Margaret had finished, as she rose to carry her plate to the sink she glanced at Tammas. Since sitting down he had barely touched his food. And he said, I'm no that hungry Margaret.

She nodded. She began to stack the dirty pots and crockery on the draining board. Tammas turned and said, I'll wash.

It's alright.

Naw. He smiled: I'm washing.

She shrugged. She dried her hands on the small towel.

Did you see Grannie then?

Yes.

How was she?

Alright, the usual . . . Margaret lifted the kettle as it began boiling and she poured the water into the teapot.

Did you talk to any of the women?

No. Margaret lifted the towel and dried her hands once again. She brought teacups out of the cupboard and laid them on the table.

I'll bring it ben, said Tammas.

Mm . . .

When she had closed the door behind her Tammas scraped the rest of his meal into the bin, dropped the plate into the washing bowl in the sink. He washed then dried all the dishes, pots and crockery, took the two cups of tea into the living room. He carried his own through to his bedroom. He put it on the cupboard beside his bed then propped the pillow and rearranged the quilt, put some books next to the teacup. He read for a time, later he dozed and had a fit of shivering when he awakened.

Robert and Margaret were watching television when he entered. Anybody fancy a coffee? he asked.

After a moment Margaret replied, We've just had tea.

Fine. He made himself one and returned to the front room, sitting down on the settee. There was a news programme showing. He watched it for a few minutes. Then he said, O by the way, that guy McCann I told you about, him that drinks in *Simpson's*, he was saying the Peterhead job's going to be starting quite soon. A couple of months at the most.

O. Margaret nodded.

He thinks there'll be no problem, getting a start and that. He's an electrician and he says he'll get me labouring to him. Big wages. Bonus it is they're on.

That's nice, said Robert.

Tammas paused. He looked at the floor to where his cigarette packet and matches were lying. Aye, he said, eh, the . . . He rubbed his eyelids before continuing. A place near the site, where you sleep and that.

A hostel.

Naw, it's no a hostel I dont think I think it's a eh . . .

A hotel? Five star probably . . . Robert had turned his head to look at Tammas while speaking to him.

Tammas sniffed. He collected his cigarettes and matches, lifted the coffee from the arm of the settee. He walked to the door. Margaret was staring at the television screen while Robert had opened the pages of a paperback. Just as he clicked open the door Margaret shifted round on the settee. She said: I thought Billy's dad was going to speak for you in the copper place, the factory?

Aye, he's getting me the application form.

Well then . . .

Tammas shrugged.

D'you no want a job there?

Eh, no really.

O.

Robert's head was bent over the book he was reading.

I just think I'd prefer something in the open air.

Margaret nodded. She shifted back round on the settee again, facing the television screen. After a few moments Tammas opened the door and stepped out into the lobby.

During the night he kept wakening, his body sweating; the bed seemed to be confining him far too much. It was far too narrow a bed and there always seemed to be too many quilts and blankets stifling him. His forehead felt damp and cool. He was shivering again. There was a dream he had been having. More of a nightmare maybe. He turned onto his side, tugging the bedclothes to his chin, and then over his head; but eventually he got up and searched about in the cupboard drawers, till he found his pyjamas. Throughout the night he kept dozing, and in the morning he wrote a short note to Vi which he posted in the pillarbox along at the street corner. He returned upstairs and went back to bed.

•••

He was off the platform and running before the bus had stopped and he was still running when he arrived inside her close; he walked up the stairs two and three at a time and he chapped her door then flapped the letterbox. And when he heard the kitchen door open he bent to shout through the gap: It's me.

Tammas! She laughed, unlocking the main door.

Inside the lobby he clasped his arms round her; her head on his shoulder. Is it okay to come in? he said.

She slapped his chest and he picked her up off the floor, she was laughing, carrying her into the kitchen. Put me down ya idiot! Then she whispered, Tammas, you'll frighten her.

He let her down, kissed her on the mouth. He winked across to Kirsty who was sitting on the floor near the fire surround.

Are you hungry? There's still some mince in the pot.

Tammas grinned.

D'you want some?

Naw, I'm full up.

You're the man that's always starving! Come on!

Honest Vi.

Honest Vi! She smiled, shook her head at him.

I'd take a coffee right enough.

O would you!

Tammas was smiling at her. It's really great to see you Vi. All the way here I was thinking she'll no be here she'll no be here! And then – Christ!

Sit down.

He laughed, stepped round to sit on the edge of the settee, glancing back at her, then at Kirsty, winking at her again.

Take off your jacket . . . As she spoke Vi had crossed to the sink and she filled the kettle, prepared two cups of coffee.

It's a jerkin, he said while unzipping it; he took the cigarettes and matches from the pocket.

How's your cold now?

Okay. Actually it was the flu I think.

O, pardon me!

He grinned. Kirsty was watching him. She rose from the floor, facing down the way and pushing herself up with both hands. She toddled to the cot and stood there, holding onto the bars. When she glanced at him he winked again. Hullo Kirsty! She turned away. And he opened his cigarettes. He said to Vi: You still no smoking?

I'm still no smoking.

That's good.

Bloody awful! Vi was leaning with the small of her back against the sink, her arms folded; she was smiling. She turned and lifted the kettle, set it back down again.

Tammas inhaled on the cigarette, flicked the flame out of the match, dropping it onto the ashtray. He said: It's really great to see you.

She smiled. You've said that already.

Naw but . . .

Hey! Tammas! Vi clapped her hands and came forwards, bent to lean her elbows on the top frame of the settee, grinning at him, her face less than 12 inches from his: he moved to kiss her. Will you take me to the pictures?

What?

Eh? D'you no fancy it? She kissed the tip of his nose.

The pictures?

Please, eh? Come on . . . She was gazing right into his eyes, very close to him, now smiling. Eh?

The pictures?

She laughed and stood up. The bloody pictures! And she was returning to the draining board and the two cups, reaching for the bottle of milk. I've no been for ages. Honest Tammas, I cant remember the last time. I've even stopped reading the entertainments' page in the papers. I used to ask Milly if she would go but she was never interested. Vi paused to look across. D'you no fancy it?

What about Kirsty?

Aw Cathy'll babysit, no bother. I mean it's no as if we'll be late back either – I'll go and tell her eh?

He shrugged slightly. Vi was already walking to the kitchen door. He smiled at Kirsty who had been watching him but she cried out and rushed to the door after Vi.

Soon Cathy's door was opening and shutting. Tammas got up, he walked to get one of the coffees. He peered out the window, down into the backcourt. When he heard Cathy's door open he returned to the settee immediately.

Vi had Kirsty in her arms and she put her onto the floor, saying: Get your dolls now Kirsty . . . And she added: Tammas, you've no even looked at the paper.

The paper?

The paper! Vi marched to beside the television where a copy of the *Evening Times* was lying, and she gave it to him: You look while I'm getting her ready.

He nodded.

God you're no very enthusiastic.

Enthusiastic?

Aye I mean . . . tch. She shook her head, opening it at the entertainments' page, handing it over to him. She went to the cupboard and tugged out a drawer, collected a packet of paper nappies. Then she smiled and muttered, You dont really want to go do you!

What?

D'you just no fancy it?

The pictures?

Vi glanced at Kirsty who was kneeling at the foot of the bed where a toy pram lay. She turned back to Tammas. We dont have to go.

After a moment he said, It's just I'm skint Vi.

Aw God.

I only had the busfare and the ten fags. Had to tap the sister for it.

Tch, Tammas. Vi marched to him and put her arms round him and they kissed. She clung into him. He moved a little away from her, but she pulled back into him; they were still kissing. We'll be early home, she whispered.

•••

It was no longer pitchblack when he wakened. Vi's arm lay over his shoulder, and he lifted it, laid it on the pillow. He manoeuvered himself to the edge of the bed, sliding out from the blankets carefully. The alarm clock was on the mantelpiece. Vi kept it there so she would always have to get out of bed to switch off the alarm. Ten minutes to 6 am. Another hour and she would be rising for work.

He went to the lavatory. On his return he halted by the cot. Kirsty was lying on her back with the bedclothes near her waist. Tammas stared at her for several moments, and then he raised her vest and peered down at the scratches on her belly. They were more like scars. There were four of them and they were as though parallel, just beneath her navel. He lifted the vest down to cover them. Her arms were bent at the elbows, the forearms lying vertically. When he raised the bedclothes past her shoulders she made a sighing noise and she turned onto her side, looking towards the wall.

Back in bed he lay for quite a while with his hands behind

his head on the pillow. Vi's arm came onto his chest. Eventually he began stroking it. He turned a little so that he could touch her breasts and he stroked them around the nipples until she was awake, and he slipped his arm beneath her shoulders: Fancy taking the day off?

She chuckled. What time's it?

Only about 6.

6?

Aye. He turned onto his side, facing into her, the warmth of her, pulling her in to him.

•••

The photographer motioned them in closer together then waved them to the side a bit and back a step. Taking the camera away from his face he straightened up, shaking his head. Naw, he said, it's no good; yous'll have to get closer than that.

There was a burst of laughter from the little crowd gathered some twenty yards off by the church wall. Tammas put his arm round the best maid's shoulders and somebody shouted: No flies on him anyway!

And then came a cheer when Rab drew Rena closer into him, his arm round her waist as she clutched the small bouquet. The photographer was waving his hand about and saying, Fine, that's fine; now hold it there, fine. And another – fine now fine, and just . . . fine, and another. Fine.

Rab edged sideways as if set to say something to Tammas but the man stopped him by raising his hand and signalling . . .

Just you and the lassie now son – just you and the missus –
a nice yin. One for the grandweans!

Another roar then more laughter from the spectators. Rab
blushed and he glared at the man. Shoosh, whispered Rena.

I never said anything . . . He was shaking his head, he
glanced at Tammas.

Tammas shrugged. He and Julie retreated to the edge of
the crowd, standing next to the two wee girls who had been
bridesmaids.

The reception was being held in the home of Rena's parents.
It was a first storey flat in a red sandstone tenement they lived
in, less than two miles from where Rab's own parents stayed.
Once the guests had assembled an uncle of Rena asked for
quiet. And he nodded to Tammas.

Well everybody . . . Tammas cleared his throat.

Another man called: A bit of order now for the best man.

Tammas waited until the talking stopped. Well . . . He
cleared his throat again. I'd like to toast the bride. She's the
best looking bride I've ever seen. He turned to her and said,
Honest Rena, I really mean that. All the best to the two of
yous.

He raised the tumbler of sherry he had been given aloft.
There was silence, the faces in the room all gazing at him. It
was crowded. The door open widely and people standing
visible out in the lobby. Here's to Rena! he cried, and he swallowed the sherry in a gulp.

Somebody called: To Rena!

Then others were saying her name and the toasts being
made. Rena's mother was looking at him. He stepped to the
side, leaning to whisper to Rab, I'm needing a slash man be
back in a minute.

He kept his head bowed while making his way through the folk in the room. Betty was by the doorway, standing just to the side of an old lady who stared at him. Hullo Betty, he said.

O Tammas . . .

Nice wedding.

It was really beautiful.

Aye. He nodded, took out his cigarettes. The old lady was still staring at him. He smiled at her and turned slightly, scratching at his ear.

You didnt say very much for the speech.

I know. Hh. Have you seen Billy at all?

Billy. I'm no really sure if I know him Tammas.

O aye. Tammas returned the cigarettes to his pocket; he fingered the lapels of the dress jacket. Have to change out of this stuff. I better eh . . . this blooming bowtie!

I think it looks nice.

The bowtie? Tammas frowned at her. It feels like a wind-mill or something. And the trousers they gave me; could hardly get my legs into them they were that tight!

But it'll be nice for the photographs.

Aye, I suppose so. Listen Betty I'll see you later on and then – maybe have a dance if it's okay. He frowned. I'm supposed to look after the best maid.

Betty nodded. Wee Julie, she looks awful thin in the dress. It's nice right enough but she was really shivering for the photographs.

Aye . . . Tammas took out his cigarette again. After a moment he touched her on the side of the arm and said, I'll see you later Betty.

A large walk-in press was being used as a cloakroom. There was no snib on the door and he had to grip the handle while changing trousers. When he had his own suit on and the dress one on the hanger, he pushed open the door and peered out.

A group of kids was clustered by the bathroom door; also a young woman with a baby in her arms. She glanced at him as he passed along, and he nodded to her, before opening the front door and stepping out.

There was a pub about two hundred yards down the street and he sat in the bar for more than forty minutes, sipping at a pint of heavy, watching television.

The guests were queuing for food when he arrived back, a line of them filing along the lobby and in through the kitchen doorway, passing the tables where all the bowls and plates of things were heaped. Folk were either serving themselves or being given selections by two middle aged women. John was near the head of the queue and he waved to Tammas. Tammas returned the wave but continued along the lobby. In the front room different groups had formed, people chatting together while eating or drinking. Over near the bow windows Rab and Rena had been surrounded, mainly by younger folk, including both Betty and Julie. Behind them Tammas could see Billy listening to something Mrs McCorquodale was saying.

And Uncle Gus was gesticulating at him from the side of the room and calling, Hey . . . psst – Tammas.

He was standing next to a display cabinet. A bottle of sherry and a half bottle of whisky plus a few empty tumblers were on top of it, also a big plate in use as an ashtray. Uncle Gus was pointing at the sherry: Hope you can drink this cause the whisky's done and I dont see much else.

There's a boozer down the street, said Tammas. Nick out for a pint; that's what I've just done. They've got an *off-sales* as well.

An *off sales* . . . mm, aye. Uncle Gus nodded. Seems a bit out of order but: bringing a carry out to a wedding! Still, a bottle of bloody sherry'll no go very far.

Biblethumpers, muttered Mr McCorquodale, appearing suddenly. What else d'you expect?

Hey Boab, he's saying there's a boozer just down the street a bit.

Good. Mr McCorquodale glanced at Tammas: Son, d'you know what a biblethumper is?

Sssshh Boab . . .

And by the bye, you should have been getting things organised, no skipping out for pints. Mr McCorquodale poured himself a sherry then topped up Uncle Gus's tumbler.

Tammas nodded.

And did you just forget it or what? the speech . . . Mr McCorquodale was returning the bottle to the display cabinet.

I didnt really have it worked out properly.

Ah well you should have shouldnt you.

Leave the boy alone, said Uncle Gus, I've done the same myself.

Have you? When was that?

Och! Uncle Gus shook his head, pursed his lips and drank some sherry. Plenty of times.

Plenty of times?

Och aye, Christ.

Hh! Mind you . . . Mr McCorquodale smiled, It probably saved us getting a bloody sermon, if the speeches had all carried on.

Tammas glanced at him: Did they no?

Naw. Ended up everybody thought they were just to start eating! Mr McCorquodale shook his head.

It's no your fault, said Uncle Gus.

Whose fault is it then? Mr McCorquodale asked.

No his anyway, one of them could've said something.

Aw aye, I see.

Well they bloody could've. Uncle Gus frowned and swallowed his sherry in a gulp.

Cheers to you too, said Mr McCorquodale and did like-wise then reached for the bottle again. It's hell of a sweet this stuff isnt it? Effing syrup it tastes like!

Ssh.

Sssh yourself. Mr McCorquodale topped up his tumbler and then he glanced at Tammas and offered him one.

Naw no thanks.

Wise man.

Tammas smiled; he brought out his cigarettes, but paused: along at the group where Rab and Rena were, Julie was standing to the side and looking down towards him. She raised her left hand and touched herself at the back of the neck, seeming to smile at something one of the group was saying. Then she looked back along at Tammas again.

He's no listening to you, said Mr McCorquodale, he's watching that wee lassie.

I dont blame him.

Ah well it's better than watching you right enough I'll give him that.

Tammas sniffed, he cleared his throat and opened the cigar-ette packet.

I'm saying is there any jobs on the horizon son . . . ? Uncle Gus smiled.

Eh naw, no really, I'm thinking of maybe going away.

Going away?

I'm no sure.

What're you fed up?

Aye, a bit.

Mr McCorquodale was nodding. If you ask me you were a wee bit previous jumping on the broo when you did.

Probably.

Probably!

Aw Boab give the boy a break!

Mr McCorquodale pursed his lips and winked at Tammas: I've to give you a break!

Tammas smiled.

Well you're picking on him.

I'm no picking on him.

You are.

Tch, Christ. Mr McCorquodale shook his head. Am I picking on you Tammas?

Tammas smiled. Actually, he said, I better go . . . He turned from them and stepped towards the doorway.

Julie was coming in the same direction. He paused to strike a match, lighted a cigarette, and followed the girl out into the lobby. She led him into the doorway of the end bedroom. Thank God, he said, getting me away from Rab's auld man!

Julie nodded.

Naw, I'm no kidding ye!

It's cause Rab told me to. Did you no notice the time? I was trying to tell you when we were in there – it's half six.

O Christ that's right, the taxi.

You've to get it as soon as you can. As soon as the coast's clear they want to skip away.

As soon as the coast's clear?

Aye.

What d'you mean?

Pardon?

What coast you talking about?

Julie breathed in deeply and frowned, and Tammas grinned. She turned her head from him . . . You were supposed to toast me you know. I waited all week for it.

I'm sorry.

Mrs McCorquodale says she's going to give you a doing.

Hh.

She is . . . Julie continued to look away from him. She was

holding a slice of currant cake in her hand and she broke a piece of it off and put it in her mouth.

Tammas nodded.

But it was nice what you said about Rena.

I should've said it to you as well.

Tch, I wasnt meaning that.

Naw but . . . he shrugged. I'm sorry.

It doesnt matter. I wasnt meaning that.

Aye but that's some dress you're wearing; it'll look really great in the photographs.

Tch . . . Julie shook her head, still looking away from him.

Honest, I'm no kidding ye.

Tch. She shook her head again and began walking off.

Naw, he said and he whispered after her: I mean it Julie.

He waited until she had returned into the main room then walked down the lobby.

There was a telephone in the house but it was situated across from the bathroom and a crowd of kids and some adults were standing about. He continued on and out, shutting the front door behind himself, and he checked his cash while crossing the street to the pub. He had enough for one more pint and after he had made the phone call he stood by the exit, drinking it, peering out the door every so often. When the taxi arrived he raced over and told the man to wait a minute.

Rab's young brother, Alec, was waiting for him back in the house and he led him straight into a bedroom where Rena sat on the bed. With her were Betty and a couple of other girls. She now had on her ordinary clothes and the white wedding outfit was on a hanger, hanging from the top of a wardrobe door. Thank goodness, she said and laughed briefly. Is everything okay?

Aye, great, the taxi's down there.

Rena was onto her feet and bending to drag out a suitcase from below the bed. Moments later the door opened and in came Rab and he was in his ordinary clothes now as well; and behind him Billy and John, both grinning and holding plates of salad. Then Julie appeared, still dressed in the best maid's outfit.

Rab said, Naw, naw, it'll no do, there's too many of you; they'll twig something's up ben the room. Come on now . . . He glanced at Billy. Eh man?

Billy grinned and backed off. John edged out in front of him, also grinning. Rab was glancing at Betty and the other two girls: Eh? D'you mind?

And when they had gone he said to his young brother: You as well.

Aw Rab.

Naw, come on!

Let him stay, said Rena.

Naw.

Yes.

He'll be seeing us next week when he comes down to England.

Rab! Rena smiled and she shook her head.

Okay okay but it means the likes of my auld man'll know because we're all missing at the same time.

It doesnt.

Okay, okay.

Alec said, He's bloody terrible so he is Rena, he's always like this.

Shut up, muttered Rab, we've got no time for any carry on – eh Tammas?

Tammas nodded; he stepped to the door and clicked it open, peered outside.

It was arranged that Alec went first and stood guard by the

front door. Next out was Rab, followed by Julie, and Rena, and Tammas was coming last, with both the suitcases. And he waited until the front door had closed behind Rena before leaving the bedroom. But Mrs McCorquodale appeared from the kitchen. Her face was red and she whispered, Tammas.

Eh . . .

It's alright son I know what's going on. She stuffed money into the top pocket of his jacket . . . Just take it now cause you're doing fine you're doing fine.

Mrs McCorquodale . . . he began.

Naw son you're doing fine, away you go, come on. She waved her fist at Alex who was laughing at them from the landing outside, holding the door ajar.

Tammas nodded, he strode down the lobby and out, kicking the door shut behind himself.

Down on the street the driver was standing by the passenger entrance of the taxi, a cigarette poking from the corner of his mouth and he came forwards to grab the two suitcases, and slide them in next to Rab and Rena's feet. Alec and Julie were shaking hands and exchanging kisses with the two of them and the driver was now slamming shut his door and starting the engine and glancing over his shoulder. Tammas moved to the window and shook hands with Rab and kissed Rena. Good luck to yous, he said.

Rena laughed.

It was a great wedding, he said.

Worst fucking speech I've ever heard! cried Rab.

From behind Alec shouted: I'm telling mammy you swore! Punch him on the mouth for me Tammas!

Okay.

And thanks, cried Rena, reaching her hand out to him.

Tammas laughed.

O God! cried Julie.

And the taxi was moving off from the kerb. And loud cheering coming from the upstairs windows of the building. John's head could be seen and also Rena's mother staring down. And then a clattering of feet and folk emerging from the close and chasing after the taxi, a couple of them tossing confetti. The taxi slowed to do a u-turn and the cheering was loud once more as it trundled past them all, with Rab and Rena's faces at the window, laughing at everybody. Some of the guests started trotting behind it, waving and shouting Good luck and All the best. Tammas went with them and then Julie was beside him and they laughed at each other, and he paused to encircle her waist with his right arm, and squeezed her, half lifting her from the ground. Ahh! The breath came from her in a gasp and he let her go. She continued waving but was breathing quite harshly, now holding her waist with her hand. Christ, he said, sorry Julie . . . He shook his head, gazing after the taxi; it was nearing the end of the street, turning, out of sight. Sorry, he said.

You just caught a muscle I think . . . She peered down at her waist, rubbing it.

I'm really sorry.

The other guests and relatives were returning into the close now and he waited a moment before sticking his hands into his trouser pockets and strolling after her. There were still faces to be seen at the upstairs window, and also at other windows in the tenement building. He walked to stand near Billy and Alec. Julie was speaking to a girl who looked as though she was not one of the actual wedding guests, and there were others – mainly elderly women – who were standing looking on. A boy said to Tammas: Hey mister was there a scramble?

Tammas did not reply. Billy was saying, You going up the stair?

Aye in a minute . . . He nodded in the direction of Julie.

O aye . . . Billy sniffed. I'm wanting to see you but man, it's about the factory and that.

Tammas nodded. I'll be up in a minute.

My da's getting the forms, if you're still interested.

Aye. Christ.

I'll see you when you come up then . . . Billy turned and walked after Alec who had already gone into the close.

Eventually Julie came, accompanied by some wee kids who were staring at her dress.

Tammas asked, You going up the stair?

Going up the stair . . . ?

He shrugged.

Are you no?

Julie frowned.

Eh . . .

They'll be starting the records for dancing.

He nodded, offered her a cigarette.

I dont smoke.

O aye, sorry. He sniffed and went on: Listen Julie I'm sorry and that I mean lifting you like that, hurting you, it was really stupid – I didnt mean it I mean Christ, if I hurt you. He shook his head.

Dont be daft, you just caught a muscle.

Naw but . . .

It's alright. She smiled. They'll be expecting us up the stair.

Aye . . . He took out his matches, struck one and waited a moment before taking a light; he blew out smoke.

Julie moved slightly in the direction of the close. The kids were still there and a couple were standing in front of her. She scowled at them: Away yous go and stop being so nosey!

But they continued to stand there, giggling, until Tammas suddenly leapt at them making them jump and they shrieked laughter and rushed along to the next close.

Julie was staring in the opposite direction. I was looking forward to the dancing . . . I was, I was looking forward to it.

Were you?

Yes. She made a shivering sound.

Fair enough . . . They stared at each other for a brief period, both looking away at the same time.

Betty thingwi's got a face down to the floor.

What d'you say?

Julie was gazing back down the street as she replied, She's got a face down to the floor.

What d'you mean?

You know fine well.

He shrugged, smiled very slightly. The silence continued for perhaps as much as half a minute. Then he added, I'm not going with her you know.

Mmhh.

I'm no . . . He puffed on the cigarette.

She nodded, she was biting on the corner of her lower lip; now she crossed her elbows over her breasts, her hands gripped the sides of her arms, just below the shoulders. She shivered. She said, I think we should go up the stair. Eh, you coming up? It's really freezing.

He nodded but made no other movement.

Eh Tammas?

What about a pint first? he jerked his thumb in the pub's direction. No a bad lounge. Fancy going over for a minute?

Tch! I'm no going into a pub like this!

You look fine. Honest I mean . . .

Julie paused before saying, You dont go into pubs dressed like this but.

It's a lounge.

Doesnt matter.

It's quiet; it's really quiet.

Julie stared down the street without replying.

Could you no go up and get a coat?

She glanced at the close mouth.

Eh Julie?

I dont know.

Just for a pint, come on, I'll wait for you.

She turned and said: What did you forget your speech for?

I dont know, I just – I forgot.

Julie shook her head.

Honest.

Tch.

Tammas sighed. He smiled. Come on, come on we'll go.

I'll need to change first.

I'll wait for you here.

She nodded quickly and walked into the close, and kept walking along, to the foot of the staircase, where she glanced back over her shoulder. Tammas pointed to where he was standing inside the entrance and whispered loudly: I'll just be here.

About ten minutes later the door on the first storey opened and footsteps down, but it was Alec who appeared. He stolled out with his hands in his trouser pockets. She told me to tell you no to wait Tammas. She says you've to come up the stair, she'll see you in the house.

Tammas nodded.

You coming?

Eh I'll be up in a minute. I've got a splitting head. Hey, fancy a pint?

Alec frowned. Whereabouts?

Across the road.

Aw naw man they're too strict in there they'll no serve me. You sure?

Aye, fucking, they're really strict man.

Aw.

A moment later Alec shrugged. Anyway, they're about to stick the records on. All the Scottish stuff first but they'll be dancing after that.

Tammas nodded.

It'll be a good laugh.

Aye. I'll just have a quick pint.

You'll come up but?

Aye, course.

Okay. Billy was wondering where you were as well.

I'll just be a minute tell him.

Okay.

Tammas turned immediately, left the close, crossing in the direction of the pub, but he carried on walking beyond it. A taxi had pulled to a stop at the traffic lights; he rushed up to it and climbed in. The driver was waiting for him to speak. Sorry, he said, Shawfield, Shawfield jimmy.

•••

There had been a slight flurry of snow when they boarded the bus and now, as they alighted, it was coming down quite thickly and beginning to lie. He stepped from the platform first, turning to give Vi his hand; she was holding the wee girl. Along the pavement they walked carefully, the stonework slippery in places. At the close before the corner of her street Vi paused, sheltering while opening her handbag, taking a £5 note from the purse inside. Get us a couple of fish suppers from the chip shop, she said, it'll save me having to cook.

Sure?

Vi grinned: I'll race you as well. I bet you ten pence I've got Kirsty down before you get back!

Ha ha!

I bet you! she cried, and was already out the close and walking in a hurry.

Watch you dont fall!

But Vi continued on without glancing back the way and Tammas laughed and started running over the road towards the chip shop.

By the time he arrived up the stairs Kirsty was in her pyjamas and sitting up in the cot with a picture book on her lap, eating a digestive biscuit. Vi had set out two mugs and was pouring the tea. Her back was to him but she could be heard chuckling. On top of the table were the salt, the vinegar and the tomato sauce, a teaplate of margarined bread.

That bloody queue, he said.

Ha ha.

Naw but no kidding it was right out onto the pavement.

Tch! He cant even admit he's lost!

Naw but no kidding! Tammas stepped quietly to her and kissed her on the side of the face. He placed the parcel of food on the table, and the change from the £5 on the mantelpiece.

I hope my ten pence is there as well you!

Tell you what, a double or clear.

A double or clear?

Aye, plus the dishes. Whoever eats their grub first wins.

You kidding! A gannet like you! Think I'm daft?

Naw but a fair bet.

A fair bet! some hopes!

He laughed then he rubbed his hands briskly. Christ Vi I'm starving!

You're always starving – it was the same in the pictures

that time; after refusing my mince I had to sit all night listening to your stomach rumble! All through the bloody film as well!

Rubbish, that was yours!

O uh . . . She turned to Kirsty: Hear this big liar hen? Wont his nose start to grow!

Tammas was unscrewing the sauce bottle and pouring some onto the edge of his plate, sprinkling the salt then the vinegar. And I'll tell you something, he said, see when you went to the *ladies*; I told that auld woman sitting in front that it was you to blame.

Tch.

I did, honest.

Rubbish!

He had taken a mug of tea across to her, laying his own on the tiled fireplace; returned with his fish and chips and the margarined bread. And when he sat down he shook his head and sighed. This is great.

Dont be daft.

Naw, I mean it, honest.

Shut up.

He sniffed. He forked a chip into the sauce. Kirsty was looking at him and he winked at her. She said, Biscuit!

I'll give her one? he asked.

Vi nodded. He rose, laying his plate near to his tea. The packet of biscuits was in the cupboard. When he held one out to her the girl shook her head slowly, staring at him. He smiled. Okay Kirsty? And set it on the quilt beside her. She looked away from him, her attention reverting to the book.

Vi had been watching. While he collected his plate and sat down she said, Sometimes she can be funny.

He nodded.

But if she is dont take it personally.

Naw.

Okay?

Aye. He smiled at her; he was cutting a piece of the fried haddock, forking it into his mouth. He reached for the mug, sipped at the tea. Vi was also sipping tea and their gazes met.

So the wedding turned out okay after all?

Aye it was fine. Tammas shrugged. Everything just seemed to pass in front of my eyes. One minute I was getting the ring off Rab in the morning; next thing him and Rena were in the taxi and we were waving cheerio. It was a strange feeling.

Even stranger for them . . .

Aye, hh – and Rab but he had everything happening at once, rushing back up from Hull on the Friday afternoon and then having to leave first thing on the Sunday morning; plus it's his birthday next week, he's twenty.

Vi frowned.

Tammas had sniffed and he looked at the plate, dug the fork into a large chip, dipped it into the sauce.

Vi now smiled. She shook her head and laid her knife and fork on the plate. Aye, she said, I knew it. And yous grew up the gether didnt you?

What?

You and your pal Rab, you're the same age. Ho, God, I knew it. Milly and Joe were wrong and I was right. So what is he older than you or what?

What?

Your pal Rab, is he older than you?

What d'you mean?

What're you blushing for Tammas?

What?

Your face – it's bloody scarlet so it is!

He made no reply. He was balancing the plate on his knees, holding the knife and the fork in either hand. Eventually he gazed at her. Well what would you've done if I'd told you the truth? Hh, you wouldnt've bloody looked at me.

Vi sighed, shaking her head. You really have got a cheek but I'm no kidding you. She stared at him: Are you only nineteen?

Naw, twenty.

Twenty. So you're older than him are you?

About six months.

Is that the truth?

Christ sake Vi.

Well sometimes you dont know with you.

He sniffed and stared away, soon he dropped his gaze to the fireplace. There was a chip on the end of his fork; he ate it, glancing sideways. Kirsty still seemed to be engrossed in the picture book. And Vi had resumed eating. Listen, he muttered, you're only two years older than me.

Am I?

Aye.

How do you know?

I just know.

Who told you?

He shrugged.

Who told you?

Vi, there's no point worrying about ages.

No point worrying about ages? what you talking about?

There's just no point worrying about it.

Who's worrying about it?

You are, Christ, the way you're going on. I knew it was you when Joe asked me right away back when we were up the *Royal*, I knew it, I twigged right away. Tammas shook his head and he lifted the plate from his knees and laid it on the fireplace. He reached for his cigarettes from the mantelpiece.

Vi was watching him. You've no finished eating yet.

I know.

Tammas, dont act like a wean.

I'm no acting like a wean. It's no me that's bloody – Christ! He shook his head and stuck the cigarette in his mouth and fumbled open the matchbox. It's no me, he said.

Tammas, you've hardly touched your food.

Sorry.

It's a waste of money but so it is.

He nodded. I'll pay you for it next time I'm over.

O. Vi sniffed and she stood up, gripping her plate and cutlery. She stepped round in the direction of the sink. Tammas sat smoking and staring at the electric bars glow. And when is the next time you'll be over?

Pardon?

Quite plain.

He swivelled and made as though to stand to his feet but she waved him back down and he continued to sit as he was. Quite plain, she said: When is the next time you'll be over?

The next time?

O God the bloody next time, the N.E.X.T., the next time, the bloody next time!

The end of the week. I'll be over the end of the week. Christ, I'll just . . . the end of the week.

She had raised her arm and shut her eyelids and he got up and went over to her but he did not touch her. She opened her eyelids and said: You're blocking the view.

Vi.

You're blocking the view.

He stepped to the side, leaned his hand on the back of the settee, staring at her. Vi turned to face the sink. She lifted the teapot and asked, Want more tea?

No really.

She nodded.

I dont feel like it.

She nodded again. Maybe you're as well going.

D'you want me to?

O God . . . She put down the teapot.

Do you want me to go?

Do what you bloody like, she said and turned abruptly, walking past him to sit where she had been sitting before.

Tammas waited a moment then he coughed and he stretched across for his cigarettes and matches.

Kirsty was looking at him, the biscuit showing in her hand.

Then Vi muttered, Remember your jacket.

He walked to the door, into the lobby, uplifted the jerkin from the peg there, having left the door ajar. He hesitated but only a moment, he unlocked the front door and stepped outside onto the landing, and closed the door, staring at the letterbox. He went downstairs quickly though only one step at a time and on arrival at close level he paused, and stayed, facing back up the space right the whole way up to the top. When he reached the closemouth he stopped again; he shook his head, sighing, and he muttered, For fuck sake . . . and rubbed the corners of his eye sockets with the thumb and forefinger of his left hand. Then he felt into each of the pockets in his jeans and then the same with his jerkin. Snowflakes were landing inside the close. He zipped up the jerkin.

It was lying quite thickly, making the different sounds dull so that when a vehicle passed it seemed to do so in silence. When he stepped off the pavement a faint crunching noise came from the snow drifted in at the kerb.

He was walking at a steady pace, head bowed into the swirl and keeping tight in to the tenement walls. Every so often he shook the snow off his jerkin and head but his hair was soaking now and his wrists always wet at the gap between the jerkin cuffs and edges of the pockets. And his cigarette packet was also wet. He brought it out as he went, checking the actual cigarettes were dry, then paused by a shop doorway to light one. A policeman stepped out of the next close, hands in his coat pockets and no snow covering his cap. Tammas continued walking, staring straight ahead, replacing the cigarettes in his pocket.

As he passed a corner he saw a clock on the interior wall of a bank: quarter of an hour since he had left Vi's house.

The Clyde was not too far distant now and wide gap-sites had appeared. On one of them stood a pub, its brickwork showing it was once the ground level of an ordinary sized tenement building. Music was coming from it and it seemed to be 'live'; a sort of folk music. He cut in at its rear to shelter while getting a cigarette alight. He kept the cigarette fixed in at the corner of his mouth but as he crossed the bridge the wind was fierce, making it burn quickly and he nipped off the ash and returned it to the packet. There was a slope down the other side and his left shoe skidded as he turned the corner and he seemed set to do the splits but just managed to grab a hold of the railings and stop himself, his right hand onto the ground to be balancing. Fucking bastard, he cried, and he glanced around. Three guys stood across the street, in an inshot near to another pub, talking away, not appearing to have noticed him at all. He wiped his hands on his jeans, shaking his head, muttering, Fucking bastard.

He started walking quickly then began to trot, attempting to land each foot on the ground as flatly possible, his left arm swinging freely while his right hand gripped the cigarette packet in the pocket of his jerkin, and he was making a groaning noise which was gradually becoming louder till it changed into a continual grunt of Ya bastard Ya bastard Ya bastard Ya bastard, each Ya bastard simultaneous with his foot hitting the ground. Another twenty minutes and he was thudding into his own close and leaning against the wall, his forehead resting upon his right forearm, his breathing harsh, a raking screeching sound.

After a time he pushed himself away from the wall, bending half over and placing his hands on his knees, taking longer, more controlled breaths. Down the middle of the concrete floor was one long wet patch where folk had passed on their way up the close. His eyelids shut. There was a throbbing at his right temple. He raised his hand and kept it there, feeling the bone at the side of his skull. He covered his eyes with both hands and straightened, turning side on to rest his shoulders against the wall, his hands dropping. Eventually, stepping nearer the closemouth, he cleared his throat and sucked in a breath of air, before blowing a mouthful of catarrh towards the street. And he brought out his cigarettes and withdrew a whole one and smoked it there.

•••

An old guy who was needing a shave was sitting on the floor with his back against a radiator, his legs splayed open. Tammas looked away as he passed on along the corridor and into the ward where his grandmother was. She was asleep, seated on an armchair by a window with a blanket tucked about her legs. There was another old woman in the next bed and she was awake and watching him although she seemed to be lying in an awkward position, as if she had been propped to sit upright and then toppled sideways. Hullo, he said and when she made no answer he turned from her and lifted a chair out from a stack, placing it carefully about three yards from his grandmother, in such a fashion that his view out the window was unrestricted. Across the way was the Nurses' Home and occasionally nurses did appear, normally in twos and wearing capes, their arms linked and chatting together, walking quite fast. Layers of grey clouds in the sky. His grandmother was looking at him. He smiled. Hullo grannie. How you doing, you okay?

I'm fine.

He nodded. She was still looking at him and he smiled. No as cold now as it was . . .

She gestured at the mobile cabinet near to the top of her bed; there was a jug of water on it.

D'you want a drink?

Yes. She was pointing to the cabinet drawer and he reached over to pull it out. Some plastic cups were inside. He poured her water into one and gave it to her and she took it in both hands; she glanced towards the ward door before sipping.

I'm maybe going up to Peterhead to work, he said. There's no anything doing here at all except for maybe a job in a factory I could get. But I'd rather be out in the open air . . . He grinned.

She sipped at the water again and made a slurping noise.

And are you eating your food alright?

No . . . She smiled, shaking her head.

Margaret was saying it's better now – because that wee highland nurse is back and giving them all what for!

His grandmother smiled.

From the next bed the old woman called: Hullo.

Hullo. He smiled.

She pointed at his grandmother and asked, Is she a relation?

Mm. She's my grandmother.

That's nice.

Tammas nodded and looked back to his grandmother who was sipping at the water but moving her left hand at him; wanting him to take the water from her now, holding the cup towards him. He put it back onto the cabinet. She placed her hands in her lap and raised her eyebrows. He smiled.

And are you married? the other old woman said.

No, hh!

Have you got a girlfriend?

Tammas smiled at her and then at his grandmother who was watching him.

Tch! The old woman shook her fist at him, chuckling. Then she added, She's your grannie? That's nice.

Aye. He said to his grandmother: Mrs Brady was asking for you.

O.

She was saying she'll take a trip out to see you when the better weather comes in. Her legs are no very good either.

His grandmother nodded. She shifted slightly, looked towards the ward door. Another visitor was coming in, an elderly man with a bunch of flowers. And a woman followed, going to a different bedside, holding a couple of shopping bags and breathing noticeably, as if she had been hurrying.

Have I seen you before? asked the old woman in the next bed.

Tammas smiled. I'm no sure; it's usually my sister that comes.

O.

Aye, Margaret, you've probably seen her.

O.

She usually comes a couple of times a week.

O, that's nice.

Tammas nodded. His grandmother was still gazing towards the door. Outside two nurses had appeared from beneath the window, arms linked and heading across the grounds in the direction of the Home. One of them was smoking a cigarette and looked a bit like Betty from the back.

...

He joined the queue at his signing on box but when he reached the counter the clerk told him he would have to go to the *inquiries* desk because he was nearly half an hour late. Three benches were in use here and he had to squeeze in on the end of the third, next to a woman of about 30 who was fidgeting with a handful of documents. She was smoking and chewing and smelled strongly of perfume and every so often she nibbled on the skin at the corners of her right thumbnail. When she finished the cigarette she dropped it to the floor but did not stub it out and she lighted a fresh one immediately. The other one smouldered where it had landed. She returned the lighter and cigarette packet into her handbag then put in the documents as well, and withdrew a paperback book, flipped through its pages. Soon she was engrossed in reading, the smoke from the cigarette drifting straight into Tammas's face.

The next in line was called to the desk and slowly the queue edged along each bench until Tammas was able to move. A man squeezed in next to him. He was middle aged, wearing a camel coloured overcoat. A minute or so passed, and he said to Tammas, Excuse me eh do they take a while here? I've actually got an appointment and I was wondering if they let you go to the front – if you've got a real you know, a real reason, if you actually do have an appointment.

Tammas cleared his throat before saying quietly, Naw.

O, I see. The man smiled: It's like that is it! He opened his coat and brought a *Glasgow Herald* out of an inside pocket and, turning to the backpage, folded it at the television section. On the other side the woman was opening her handbag again; she took out a tube of a sort of medicinal sweet, unwrapped one and put it into her mouth, snapped shut the handbag. Tammas had his UB40 in the back pocket of his jeans and he manoeuvred it out, began to read it. It was more than half an hour before his turn came.

Outside rain drizzled. He strode along to the top of the street and crossed at once, not waiting for the lights to change, having to dodge past traffic. Just as he reached the opposite pavement his name was shouted: it was McCann – waving to him, coming from the direction of the job centre. And he shouted again: Hey Tammas!

He waited.

McCann was smiling when he arrived. How you doing? stranger! Where you been hiding?

Tammas shrugged.

Billy was wondering and all – he was down the job centre earlier on. What're you chucked drinking or what!

Naw, just – fucking skint man!

Aw, aw aye, aye, I know the problem!

Any smokes?

Hh! And as they began walking McCann added, I was through every fucking pocket in the house there before I left – nothing! no even a fucking dowp! And that wife of mine, Christ Almighty, she's started planking the fucking purse!

Tammas smiled. Anything doing down by?

Fuck all! Catering job in the Channel Islands right enough, if you're interested – commis chef.

Commis chef?

That's what they call a learner. Bum wages but the conditions arent too bad. Bags of fucking sun and all that, plenty of nooky! They'll give you it all except the fucking cash!

Tammas chuckled.

I'm no kidding ye Tammas – a brother of mine used to be in the game and he told me all about it. Like a fucking concentration camp so he says, these hotels.

Hh . . . They continued along in silence for several moments. Tammas sniffed and said: Any word of Peterhead yet?

Naw, just the same Tammas, mainly concreters and brickies they're starting; they're no really fucking interested in sparks; no yet, no for another month or so.

Is that right?

Aye, Christ, you know what like it is.

Tammas nodded, pursing his lips. And after a few moments McCann went on, That's how I was wanting a word with you, about that other thing, that bit of business I was telling you about.

Tammas glanced at him. McCann had slowed his pace a little and now he paused and stopped outside a newsagent whose side window was full of advertisements written in ink on the backs of postcards. Naw it's just eh . . . McCann lowered his voice, It's just the fucking debt and that Tammas. I wouldnt want to fuck off out the road and leave her having to face it all on her tod. She'd wind up getting hit for plenty, and I'm no kidding ye.

You'll be sending her money but surely?

O aye fair enough but by the time you get settled in and all that. You'll have your fucking lying time, paying off your subs – takes a while to get sorted out I mean fuck sake Tammas it's no just a case of walking in and that's you.

Aw I know that.

Ah well . . . McCann shrugged.

Tammas cleared his throat, he turned slightly, dropping a mouthful of spit to the pavement, rubbing on it with his shoe. They continued looking at the advertisements for a while, until McCann muttered, I'm getting wet . . . and they carried on walking. Both had their hands in their pockets, shoulders hunched, occasionally parting company to keep from obstructing oncoming pedestrians. It was Tammas who broke the silence. There's a cunt owes me a score, he said.

Eh?

Aye, bastard; owed me it for fucking ages so he has. I cant get it off him at all – pleads poverty every time I see him.

McCann nodded.

The last job I was in – that factory, we used to play cards on the nightshift, Fridays it was for dough, we all had the wages and that, pontoons, fucking great man, once we had done the quota and cleaned the machines, out came the cards – and you could fucking win a few quid as well! Tammas had turned to glance at McCann as they walked: And I'll tell you something man, if it hadnt've been for that fucking – the cards man, if it hadnt've been for the cards . . . Hh!

McCann nodded and chuckled. Peterhead'll definitely suit you then Tammas, the fucking cards up there!

Aye, you were saying.

Fuck! they're mad – crazy! you know what like it is in the building game! Plus cause they're all staying in these fucking dormitories Tammas they're all just sitting there, the wages in the pockets and all that, trying to stay out the boozers. No wanting to wind up fucking alkies so out comes the fucking cards and all that – all sorts of schools, brag and poker and fucking ponnies. You name it. Big money too. You've got to be fucking careful but, a lot of sharks so there are, cut your bolls off if they catch you pokling.

What?

No holds barred, anybody they catch at the pokle Tammas.

Aw thanks!

Naw, what I mean, even a cunt like Auld Roper, snatching a wee look at your dominoes – he'd get that fucking stick of his broke over his head!

Ah come on!

Naw, Christ Almighty, it's fucking serious stuff.

Hh!

And I'm no fucking kidding ye!

Tammas nodded.

They had reached a junction beyond where McCann normally split off to travel to his own street. As the lights changed and they crossed he sniffed and said, Fancy a coffee?

A coffee?

A coffee, aye, up in my house – the wife'll have brought in some fags; she'll have been at the post office.

Aw.

Aye so . . . you're welcome.

Tammas shrugged. I've got a message to go, otherwise I . . . thanks but.

Naw, it's only I was wanting to have a wee word with you and that.

Aw aye.

About that other thing.

Tammas nodded.

I mean, you've got to think about it.

I know – Christ, I have, I have been.

McCann sniffed. He glanced to the side, cleared his throat, then indicating the nearest close he started heading towards it, and Tammas followed a moment later. Naw, he said, that guy I'm talking about, Kenny, he's gen, straight down the line. And it's me and you and him just, the three of us, and he says its about fifteen hundred. I mean – it's good dough Tammas.

Aw I know, I know that.

See that's how . . . McCann stopped. He frowned: You worried about it?

Aye, fuck, hh.

Well you dont have to be.

Tammas shifted his stance, he stared out the close.

Come on we'll go for a coffee . . .

Naw honest Brian, I've got that message, it's for the sister.

McCann shrugged: Suit yourself cause I mean the wife'll have been out to the post office and all that.

Tammas nodded. Naw, he said, I really better eh . . .

Fine; nobody's forcing you Tammas.

Aw it's no that man it's just the sister and that she's expecting me back I mean Christ, otherwise . . .

No problem; no problem. McCann had nodded, then he went on quickly: See it's just the debt and all that Tammas normally I'm fucking – no kidding ye! but see this past while? Naw, once you get married and all that. The fucking weans too! And the way I'm thinking – straightforward, just fucking – get a few quid, just fucking get a few quid, pay off the debt, get a bit of gear the gether, then off up north, Peterhead, no worries – no worries Tammas, the wife and the weans and that, fine. See I mean that guy I was telling you about he's gen, he's gen; I'm no kidding ye – I used to work beside him in the yards. Gen, he's fucking, straight down the line.

Tammas nodded.

Cause I'll be honest with you – and I mean it Tammas – if I could get this debt cleared off I'd be away the morrow morning, the morrow morning.

Mm.

McCann was looking at him.

I dont know man, I dont know. I just eh . . .

Look, every cunt gets worried about something like this. But when the time comes you're fine, you fucking handle it I mean, Tammas, I'm no fannying you.

Aw I know, I know that; but it's just – I dont know man.

What? What d'you mean?

Naw, just . . .

What? What you thinking? Tell us.

Tammas nodded then he sniffed.

Come on, tell us.

Aw Christ man I dont know.

Is it just cause it's thieving and that? Is that what it is? Because it's thieving?

O! Aye, Christ, I mean, I've never fucking done anything like that before I mean Christ screwing a place man, never. Hh! Tammas laughed briefly. He shook his head, cleared his throat. And he stepped to the closemouth to peer outside, before taking a deep breath and blowing the spittle right out towards the gutter. He cleared his throat again, glanced back at McCann . . . Did you no think of asking Billy?

Billy?

Aye.

Naw, no really.

O fuck!

Dont worry about it.

Naw it's no that man I'm . . . He shivered suddenly. Wish to fuck I had a smoke!

That's what I'm telling ye Tammas the wife'll have some up the stair.

Mm. He began shivering again, and his teeth then chattering till he had to shut his mouth, and he laughed in a sort of fit of gasps for some seconds. He walked a few paces down the close, stopped and turned, shrugging.

McCann said, Be a lot of dough as well Tammas; maybe the five hundred apiece.

Hh.

McCann nodded, looking at him.

Mm.

Good dough.

Aye.

I mean I'll be frank with you Tammas I'm giving you the option cause we're supposed to be going up to fucking Peterhead the gether – to give us a fucking start – that's what I'm talking about, to give us a start.

Tammas nodded.

I mean fuck sake, I could go walking into *Simpson's* right now and pick any one from ten. Eh – I mean you know what I'm saying?

Aye.

Aye . . . McCann stared at him, then he turned and spat to the front of the close.

Tammas coughed, he rubbed his hands together with a slapping sound, his shoulders moving in a circular manner. Then McCann glanced at him and asked, Well?

What?

Well. What d'you say?

How d'you mean like?

Tch. McCann shook his head and turned away.

Naw I mean eh just – can I think about it?

Aye but fuck sake Tammas I told you about it a while ago.

Tammas nodded.

McCann held his hands out the way, palms upturned. Know what I mean?

Aye.

Aye – hh! McCann shook his head.

I'll tell you soon.

Aye well fuck, Tammas, it'll have to be – otherwise . . . He shrugged.

Tammas nodded.

•••

Eventually the outside door banged shut. Margaret was off to work. Once he had dressed he switched the radio on ben the kitchen, but not to play too loudly, and he sat at the table drinking tea and reading last night's *Evening Times*, the racing page. Then the footsteps on the landing and he was onto his feet and into the lobby as the mail came flying through the letterbox. Two of them; his giro plus an electricity bill addressed to Robert.

In the bedroom he checked the pawn tickets in the corner of the bottom drawer in the cupboard but he left them there. On his way out he emptied the last 10 pence coin from the meterbowl. It was just after 8.30 am and the cafe would not open for a while yet. He went to a general stores a couple of streets away, bought a single and a box of matches; and he was striking the match and lighting up before being returned his change from the man behind the counter. He stood in the doorway outside for some moments, watching a group of primary schoolchildren pass by; and then two women, one of whom he knew. They exchanged Good mornings. He walked along to join the queue at the sub post office and once the cheque was cashed he bought a copy of the *Sporting Life* and a packet of cigarettes from the newsagent in his own street, getting an extra £1's worth of 10 pence coins in the process, before going home.

•••

This hammering, it seemed to have been going on for ages. Moving onto his side again he tugged the blankets over his head, then he moved onto his front, face down on the pillow, closing its material over his left ear and a loud roaring noise like listening to a shell at the seaside. He only stayed on his front for a few moments after the hammering had stopped.

He sat up with his back against the bedhead, reached to the cupboard for the book and the cigarette packet, blinking into the bedside light. A piece of silver paper was marking his place and he turned the pages to it, looked at it a moment; he took out a cigarette, leaving two inside. The hammering resumed. It seemed to be coming from through the wall, from the adjacent flat up the next close. He gazed at the wall. He looked back to the book, and then returned it onto the cupboard, returned the cigarette to the packet and laid it on top of the book, and reached to switch off the light. He was lying on his side with the blankets to his chin when he heard footsteps in the lobby: Robert – going to the bathroom. Soon the cistern was emptying, refilling, and then a creak outside the door and Robert chapped and called: Heh Tammas!

Aye?

Okay?

Aye!

Can I come in?

Just a minute! He slid out of bed and pulled on his jeans and socks and was tugging down his jersey while going to the door. I was just reading, he said.

Robert nodded.

Tammas jerked his head in the direction of the bedside lamp: I just put the light out a minute ago.

Aye. Robert sniffed: Just making a bit of supper and that you coming ben?

Eh . . .

The football's coming on the telly.

O aye, aye. Hey d'you hear the hammering?

Ah it's only the house falling down!

Hh.

Dont worry but it's no serious.

Tammas grinned.

Hey how did Hull do by the way I never heard the results?

Two each.

Aw good – away from home too?

Aye. Tammas nodded. Trouble is you dont even know if Rab's playing cause there's no reports.

Och he'll be playing!

You never know right enough.

Come on. Robert paused a moment then turned to leave, adding: Beans and toast in five minutes.

Tammas called: Dont burn it!

You're worse than your sister!

•••

Billy came up for him at 10 minutes to 7 on the Monday morning. Tammas was already up and in the kitchen, eating the bowl of porridge Margaret had made for him. She offered Billy one but he shook his head. I'm on a diet, he said.

Ha ha! Margaret raised her eyebrows. If I was as skinny as you!

Billy laughed, sitting down opposite Tammas, and he said: It's nothing personal by the way, coming up as early as this man!

But you're quite right, replied Margaret. If I hadnt been here he'd have slept in.

Tammas continued eating, adding more milk to the bowl.

And are they sticky about time? asked Margaret.

No half! 3 minutes and you're quartered – an hour and you're sent home.

Honestly?

Aye. I was late twice that first week – gave the auld man a right showing up – he's no been quartered for twenty years!

Margaret smiled; she was pouring tea, getting out an extra cup for him. And later, when they were set to leave, she palmed Tammas a pound note. The front door was open and Billy had stepped out onto the landing. Tammas whispered, Aw thanks Margaret.

She shook her head slightly, frowning.

Naw, he said, thanks.

She closed over the door.

For the first six weeks he would be training on the job and if proving satisfactory he would be given a place on the line. Until then he was to be kept on constant dayshift. Billy had started the fortnight before but in a different section. You're in the rolling mill, he said, it's supposed to be a bit of a bastard.

Tammas followed him into the factory and on to where the gaffer of the rolling section had his office. Billy grinned and left him standing at the door. See you at the canteen!

Tammas watched him walk quickly off and round a corner. It was quite a few minutes till the gaffer came out and opened the door, beckoning him to come in. He explained briefly what the job was about then led him to the floor where the rolling machine was situated. Hey Peter! he shouted to a man. The man came across. This is the new fellow . . . The gaffer nodded at Tammas and went away.

Tammas followed Peter to behind the roller. Peter indicated where he wanted him to stand and he said: Stay there and keep your eyes open. And I might as well tell you, they shoes you're wearing, they're fucking no good. Surprised the gaffer didnt tell you.

He never mentioned it.

While he was talking Peter had picked up an enormous pair of heavy-duty clamps, positioning himself at a point to the side of the roller. There was a younger guy now standing on the other side of it. Tammas could see his head on occasion, bobbing about. A banging sound from the roller. Peter was now crouching. A white hot copper bar of around 6' in length and maybe 8" thick issued from it. Peter caught the end of it with the clamps, brought it forwards to the edge of the machine; he allowed it to drop a short way onto a wee mobile iron trolley. He steadied it, still gripping the clamps at its tip, and swung it sideways a little, pushed it into another part of the roller. Then he moved a couple of yards to his left and waited. The banging sound. He crouched, he was farther back from the machine than previously. The copper bar issued. It was now about 12' in length and maybe 4" thick, and was an orange colour. Peter repeated the process with the wee trolley. And once he had pushed the bar back into the roller he turned to

Tammas, wiped the sweat from his brow with the back of his right wrist, but said nothing. He lifted a smaller pair of clamps and stood as before, though farther back again. The bar was much longer now, a grey red in colour, and he used a much smaller trolley to manoeuvre it back in. For the next stage he went right up close to the machine and stood facing away from it, but looking down to between his knees, to where he was holding the clamps apart, just out from a wee hole the diameter of a golf ball. He glanced at Tammas just as another banging sound came and suddenly he had clamped onto the end of the issuing copper wire and was running with it, heading diagonally, making towards a thing like a kerb across the width of the floor, and behind him the wire still issuing, and he was shifting a bit as he ran, and steadying the clamps, to go thrusting the end of the copper wire straight into a narrow gap tunnelled through the kerb. And as he thrust it in Peter was jumping over the kerb. The gap was angled so that the wire darted out directly in line to a guy who was working a different sort of machine away up in the corner, a big circular device with a sort of cranking handle attached.

Peter stepped back over the kerb, putting the clamps in their place. Wiping his brow he said to Tammas, It might look easy but it isnt.

Tammas nodded. Peter was taking out his cigarettes and he lighted one for himself, tossed the packet onto an upturned oil drum near the wall. He asked, You done anything like it before?

Naw, no really.

Tch. Peter shook his head, and he walked to the machine and picked at something; he bent to lift the heavy-duty clamps, positioned them upright at the point where the bar would issue firstly. He called: I'll give you a shot before the break. Just watch till then. Where's your gloves?

Gloves?

Jesus Christ. You cant expect to work the fucking clamps without them – I do it but I'm fucking used to it I mean it takes a fucking while to get the heat. You'll no manage without a pair in the beginning.

He never mentioned it.

Peter shook his head. He went behind the roller and began to speak to the other guy. The two of them returned. Tell him, said Peter.

What?

Tell him, about the gloves and that.

Naw just, the gaffer, no mentioning them.

Fuck me!

And the helmet, muttered Peter, tell him about the helmet.

Aye, he never mentioned it either. And the shoes, nothing about them. Tammas sniffed, he took his cigarettes out and lighted one.

The other guy said, Might be a spare pair in the locker-area.

Boots?

Naw Christ I'm talking about gloves. The man grinned, You'll have to get yourself a pair of boots. The first-aid, you'll get them there – deduct it off your wages. Some no bad styles they've got. Eh Peter?

Suede. The fucking lot they've got. Wear them up the fucking dancing if you like!

Wouldnt be the first time, laughed the other guy.

Peter nodded. Anyway, time for another . . .

Tammas followed his gaze, seeing the overhead crane down at the very far end of the floor; a big furnace door had been pulled open and the next copper bar was being dragged out in a shower of sparks.

He positioned himself nearer to the roller this time,

watching everything Peter was doing. Peter made no acknowledgment till he had taken the stance with his back to it, set for the last issue. He called, Watch this yin specially, you've got to be fucking careful. If you pull at it you'll fucking stretch the bastard and that's it a binger. You've got to let it carry you along. If you go too slow you're fucked, cause what'll happen it'll fucking bend right up behind you and it'll fucking jam, it'll no go through, and that's you, another fucking binger! Peter shook his head. His cigarette was in the corner of his mouth and he moved it across to the other corner without taking his hands from the handles of the smaller clamps, not looking from the gap between his knees. Then the bang; and he was running.

By the time tea break arrived Tammas was still waiting to make his first attempt. He walked behind the machine and sat up on the oil drum. Then Peter appeared and handed him a pair of big gloves. The tips were missing on most of the fingers. He shrugged: It's the best I could find.

Tammas pulled them on without replying. Peter pointed to the clamps and said, The main thing is no to panic.

When the bang came and the bar issued Tammas raised the heavy-duty clamps, getting them round the end as it came slowly out the roller, and he gripped them there and tugged it slightly, lowering it off but it dropped down onto the trolley and angled a bit and he had the clamps still firmly there but moving as it continued to angle then roll and his fingers were poking out the gloves and he let the clamps go and the copper bar crashed down and bounced and he had to jump up and to the side to get out its path. Peter also had to jump. He shook his head and cried: I told you no to fucking panic!

I didnt panic, cried Tammas pulling off the gloves, my fingers were fucking burning!

Fuck sake! Peter was glaring at him. Then he shook his head again and he turned away; he walked to the end of the machine and gave a piercing whistle down towards the furnace. He roared: Hey Willie! Willie! Willehhh . . .

The overhead crane started to move. When it reached the rolling machine the guy who worked it pressed the button for the huge hook to descend. Peter wangled it around the tip of the copper bar which was much duller in colour now. Okay Willie! he called. And the cranedriver raised the hook just sufficient for Peter to slide the mobile trolley in below it. Peter then waved and Willie drove the crane back down towards the furnace. He glanced at Tammas, indicated the clamps and added: Okay, carry on.

Tammas got the clamps round the end of the bar and pushed forwards, working the bar on the trolley to the place it entered on the roller but in the process he nudged at the bar with his foot and the shoe burst into flames. For fuck sake! He jumped back the way, stubbing and stubbing his toe at the floor to put out the fire. Meanwhile the copper bar had rolled off the trolley and was lying flat on the floor again. Peter did not say anything. He walked to the end of the machine and gave the piercing whistle . . . Willehhh! And then he cleared his throat and spat, and he turned to Tammas. I told you ye needed boots.

When the crane arrived he beckoned Tammas forwards while he motioned the driver to lower the hook; but the driver called to him: No fucking good Peter, bar's too fucking cold.

Jesus Christ! Another bastarn fucking binger! Peter shook his head; he wiped his mouth with the back of his right wrist.

The guy from the other side of the roller had appeared. It'll be okay, he said, they know we've got a learner; we just dock it off the time sheet.

Peter nodded.

The younger guy grinned at Tammas: Hot in here son eh! Mon we'll have a fucking bevy!

Tammas looked at him. But the man was waving him to follow him and he shrugged and walked after him. Soon the overhead crane was returning with the copper bar, to put it back into the furnace.

Peter joined them. The other guy had opened a metal cupboard, bringing out a brown bottle; its glass was thick and mottled and its size was about that of an ordinary whisky bottle. He swigged a mouthful and handed it on to Peter who swigged some and handed it to Tammas. Dont drink too much, he said.

Or you'll get a dose of the skitters, chuckled the other guy. It's given to us for the sweat we lose. It replaces it. Undiluted; a kind of lime.

Tammas drank some. No bad, he said.

Good with vodka! Bring in a bottle the morrow and give it a buzz.

Wouldnt be the first time! muttered Peter.

Tammas smiled. He took out his cigarettes, lighted one, then offered to the other two; they both took one and he struck the match. Then the sound of the overhead crane starting up. Peter said: Okay that's us. Ready for another crack?

Tammas looked at him.

Eh?

Just now you mean?

Got to get the hang of it sooner or later.

Peter's right.

Hh!

Peter exhaled smoke, glancing at the approach of the crane. And the other guy said, You're definitely better to go straight at it.

Tammas shrugged and pointed at his shoes. No with them, they're useless – and the fucking gloves as well I mean, Christ!

327

You've got to learn but.

Aye I know.

Well.

Once I've got the proper gear.

Go and see the gaffer then, muttered Peter. It's fuck all to do with me.

I will.

Aye well fucking go then!

What d'you mean the now?

No point hanging about here, no if you're no going to fucking even attempt it.

Well I would if I had the proper gear to wear.

Ah you'll be alright, said the other guy.

No without the proper gear.

Go and tell the gaffer then.

Aye, okay. Tammas shook his head and left them there, and he walked straight down to the gaffer's office. A girl was in with him. She had a bundle of papers under one arm and was leaning over his desk, pointing to something on a paper he had in front of him. She was wearing a blouse and a skirt. He waited until she exited then chapped the door and entered. The gaffer gazed at him. My shoes, said Tammas, they're useless. Look . . . he displayed the toe of the burnt one. It went in bloody flames, just touched the bar and it went on fire. I need steel toe-caps.

Mm.

And the gloves as well. That guy Peter got me a pair but they're all holes and the heat comes through. Murder when it touches the bare skin, the clamps.

Aye well you get all that stuff in the first-aid. Did Peter no tell you?

He says I've to see you.

Christ I dont have it. I dont have anything here, it's all kept in the first-aid.

I've actually got a pair of boots in the house with steel toe-caps.

Have you?

Aye.

The gaffer nodded.

I'll bring them the morrow.

Fine. The gaffer nodded once more . . . Okay then?

Eh aye, but what about the gloves and that will I go to the first-aid?

O Christ aye, go ahead, you better get them.

And the safety helmet.

The safety helmet's really important, aye, mind and get yourself one. And tell Peter and them cause whenever I fucking pass I dont see them wearing it. And it's the safety code in here to wear it. Okay then?

Tammas nodded. I'll just go up the first-aid.

Aye . . . The gaffer sniffed. Then he added: Mind you and tell Peter and them about they bloody safety helmets.

The first-aid room was across by the administration offices in a different, more quiet, part of the factory. Once he had collected a new pair of asbestos gloves and a safety helmet he returned to the rolling mill. Peter was busy with a new copper bar. Tammas called, I've just to watch till I get my boots the morrow morning.

Peter nodded, not looking at him.

O aye and the gaffer told me to tell you to mind about the safety helmets.

Peter made no acknowledgement.

At noon the younger guy appeared and told Tammas it was dinner time. Peter had walked off, not having spoken to him since his return from seeing the gaffer. But the two men were not having their breaks then, they had eaten earlier, during the tea break. They were on the early shift from 6 am to 2 pm and were paid straight through the full eight hours. Workers on the ordinary day shift were there from 8 am until 4.45 pm and received a full forty five minutes at dinner time.

When he had found his way to the canteen he saw Billy sitting with a wee group of other men at a corner table. They were laughing. Billy turned to wave him over and he squeezed in beside them. The rest continued their own conversation while Billy asked, How's it going?

Tammas looked at him.

What is it as bad as that!

Bad as that! Tammas raised his right foot, displaying the scorched shoe. Look at the fucking state of this!

A burst of laughter from the others at the table – Billy's maybe louder than anyone's. We heard! he cried. We heard! They've nicknamed you Hotfoot!

Tammas shook his head. He opened his cigarette packet and gave one to Billy, lighted his own and put the packet back in his pocket.

One of the men, still chuckling, said: Ah you'll be alright son dont worry about it! Best job in the place once you get to know it – best fucking bonus and all! without a fucking shadow of doubt!

Tammas shrugged. He inhaled on the cigarette, staring over to the counter where a long queue of men in dungarees and boiler suits had formed.

Once the others at the table resumed talking Billy murmured, He's right but man that's what I've heard as well, them on the roller, they earn a fucking bomb so they do. Bags of overtime as well. They're in every fucking Sunday, my auld man was telling me.

Where you working?

The pattern shop.

The pattern shop?

Billy shrugged. It's difficult to explain; it's cutting and things.

Aw.

Influence!

Tammas nodded. Billy had a copy of the *Daily Record* in front of him on the table and he asked, Can I have a look?

I'm studying myself, replied Billy, opening it at the racing page and holding it so that Tammas could see it with him. There's a boy carries bets.

Is there?

Aye.

Great. Tammas was nodding as he spoke, gazing at the programme of races. I dug out a couple of big outsiders last night in the *Times* . . . He shifted on his seat, put his hand into his jeans' pocket and checked the money he had left. You got a pencil and a bit of paper?

The boy'll have it . . .

The two of them continued reading the racing pages, barely talking, until eventually one of the teaboys entered. When he came to their table he gave out betting slips and he also had a pen which each person who wanted a bet used in turn. Tammas backed a four horse *comedy* for 55 pence, and he paid the additional coppers in tax.

Around half past twelve the canteen was emptying as the men returned to their parts of the factory and Tammas sat on with Billy for a few minutes. As they were leaving a queue of office workers formed; both males and females, the former in suits or jackets and trousers, and wearing shirts and ties. They filed in as the last of the hourly paid men went out.

At 2 pm Tammas was sitting in the smoke-area while the back shift men prepared to start work. Peter and the younger guy had gone to clean up about five minutes ago. Then he spotted Peter, away down near the exit, talking to a man and gesturing in his direction. Tammas sniffed and glanced at the roller, he rose, lifting his cigarettes and matches, and walked over to behind it.

He was watching the backshift man who was doing Peter's job when the teaboy appeared. The man was on the bit where he allowed the bar to drop down onto the mobile trolley. The teaboy also watched for a time, then he called, Heh jimmy that's some start to your line you've got, eh!

What? Tammas frowned at him.

Nobody told you yet?

Told me?

Aye your fucking line, the first two man they've stoated!

What?

Aye! The teaboy laughed: 20's and 16's!

What?

Aye, your first two!

Ye kidding?

Naw, honest! The teaboy laughed at the guy with the clamps and jerked his thumb at Tammas: He doesnt fucking believe me!

Hh! The guy smiled.

20's and 16's? said Tammas.

Aye. Nearly eighteen quid you've got already!

Tammas nodded and then he sniffed: Time's it?

Three o'clock.

Tammas pulled the safety helmet from his head and sticking it on top of the oil drum alongside the new asbestos gloves he glanced at the man with the clamps: I'm away, he said.

A male office worker was in the gaffer's office, sitting on a chair facing him across the desk. Tammas chapped twice on the door and walked straight in. Can you make up my cards? he asked.

What?

It doesnt . . . I'm no suited . . . Tammas was shaking his head as he held his foot up, showing the shoe. Nearly burnt the foot off me this morning!

Aye but you're getting your boots, said the gaffer, after a pause.

Ach naw I just – I'll just lift my cards.

But it's your first day just. Hh! The gaffer was holding a cigarette in his hand and he gestured with it at Tammas while addressing the other man: There you are; it's his first bloody day and here he is wanting to wrap it.

The man made no comment.

I'm no used to the work, said Tammas.

Aye but you've got to learn it!

Naw it's . . . Tammas shook his head. Just make up my cards.

What d'you mean make up your cards – I cant just go making up your cards. It's too bloody late anyway and it's got to get done through the bloody office. No chance! The gaffer inhaled on the cigarette and blew out the smoke immediately.

You can send them on then or else I'll pick them up.

Whatever you like.

Okay, said Tammas and he turned and left the office, pausing to call: I'll get them the morrow morning.

Collecting his jerkin from the locker-area he raced on to the exit and right out and up the road to the betting shop. The boardman was marking up the results of the race his third runner was in, its name being marked up, into the first position, 9 to 1. His third runner had won at 9 to 1. Nine to one. Tammas closed his eyelids. 20's 16's and 9's; 50 to 20 was 10 plus the 50 is 10.50 at 16's; 10.50 at 16's. He walked to the counter and got a pencil and a betting slip and went to one of the wall ledges to check the figures. As far as he reckoned he had £178 alone for the treble, £178 going on to his fourth

333

and final runner, £178. That was a lot of money, it was fine, good money, plus the doubles, even if it lost, the fourth runner. Tammas nodded. It was good money – plus the three doubles, the 20's and 16's and the other two. Win lose or draw he had £178 plus three doubles – about another thirty or forty quid. Two hundred quid minimum. He opened the cigarette packet, put one in his mouth and looked for his matches, he did not have them, he must have left them on the oil drum or someplace. He walked to the counter and asked the woman cashier for a loan of her lighter. She pushed it beneath the grille to him. A sweetish taste in his mouth. He examined the betting slip once again and dragged on the cigarette. The taste had been there all day, to do with the heat probably, and the copper bars. The fourth runner was forecast favourite and favourites always had a favourite's chance, the most fancied horse in the race, the best fancied horse in the race, the horse with the best chance of winning – the horse that always let you down. It did not always let you down. Sometimes it won. Just not often.

He walked across to one of the walls where the formpages were tacked up but he stopped. He knew the betting forecast on the race, the favourite being reckoned an even money chance. There was nothing else he needed to know. Not now. He had backed it and that was that, the money was running on and there was nothing he could do about it, either the horse would win or it would lose. There was not anything in between.

A hundred and seventy going on to it, it was good dough. And win lose or draw there was still a return. He would receive cash in exchange for the slip of paper; and that is what it is about.

A show of betting was coming through the extel speaker. The fourth runner in the accumulator was favourite as forecast. They were making it a 13/8 chance. To a hundred and seventy eight was 356 plus 3/8ths say about sixty quid. No – 5/8ths; 356 plus 5/8ths, about another 100, say about another hundred quid, about four hundred and fifty all in – plus all the doubles – and the trebles, the trebles alone, amounting to a fortune. A fortune. No point in even reckoning such a sum, not until it had won – either, or lost. Yet it had to be close to a grand, the thousand – it had to be close to a thousand, the thousand quid, it had to be.

He left the bookie's and crossed the road and stared into the window of a shop. It was glasses, a display of glasses, a display of glasses, it was an optician's shop, all fancy types of spectacles. The favourite was on its own. There was no question about that. It was a race for novice chasers over 2½ miles. Some people would call it a bad race to bet in but sometimes it could be a good race to bet in. And the favourite was favourite because it was the best horse in the field, because of its good form over hurdles; this was only its second race over the bigger obstacles. That sweetish taste in the mouth when he inhaled on the cigarette. It would have to do with the copper. The copper and the smoking together.

A loud voice from across the road. Two guys laughing about something at the entrance to the betting shop.

He nipped the cigarette and walked back over.

The favourite was now in to 5/4 which was good or bad, good or bad, depending. Yet it did not matter. None of any of that really mattered. And if the horse stayed on its feet it was a certainty. That was the fact. The only gamble: whether it would jump the fences. Tammas reckoned the horse would have been about 4 to 1 on if the race had been over hurdles. Just before the *off* the last show of betting had it in to even money.

It fell three fences from home. It seemed to be in a good challenging position at the time, before it toppled, before it fell.

...

He stepped back a couple of yards, squinted up at the high windows. Lights were on inside. A lollipop-woman was watching him. She frowned at him. The bank doesnt open till half nine, she said.

Aw. He nodded.

There was a grocer's along the road. He bought an orange and a bar of chocolate, peeled the orange skin as he returned, dumping it into a wastebin at the corner where the bank was. The doors had opened already and two people were in in front of him but when it was his turn he pushed the wad of notes under the grille and said to the clerk: I want to open an account for a hundred and twenty pounds.

Is it current or deposit?

Eh deposit.

Deposit. Fine. The clerk began counting out the money.

He went to the broo afterwards and reregistered; and then to the pawn where he redeemed all the stuff he had outstanding. Back in the house he laid the things on the bed and placed the bankbook upright against the alarm clock, the new UB40 balancing against it. He had paid Margaret rent money in advance and now, from the corner of the bottom cupboard drawer, he brought out a bundle of notes and separated them into their denominations. There was more than £50. Unfastening his wristwatch he laid it on the money, and went into the bathroom, and began filling the bath from the hot water tap.

Around dinner time he walked into town and watched snooker for about an hour, then he went to the pictures. He stayed out afterwards, eating in a Chinese restaurant and sipping two pints of beer in a lounge in the city centre. He finished up in the *Royal* casino but only gambled £5 on the tables. Next morning he remained in bed until late, spent the afternoon in a different cinema; he ate in a chip shop in the evening and again went to a pub and on to the *Royal*, this time without gambling at all. It was after 2 a.m. when he got home and there was a light on in Margaret and Robert's bedroom. He clicked shut the outside door and stayed on the spot for several seconds. He walked very quietly to his room.

The following day, at around 1 pm, he was standing spectating in the snooker hall. He had been there nearly an hour and it was becoming extremely busy. When he was returning from the lavatory one of the elderly attendants was just hanging the full-up notice on the back of the swing doors. He walked to the top table where a tournament was in progress and found a spare place to lean against a pillar. He took out his cigarettes, put one into his mouth; then he took it back out and turned and headed towards the exit, nodding to the old guy on the door. Up the stairs he paused to glance at his wristwatch but continued on, past the pub where he occasionally went for a pie and a pint, down across Argyle Street, in the direction of the bus terminal.

•••

Vi was not in. She would be out at her work. She worked during the day. There had only been a very slight chance that she would have been in. He flapped the letterbox and rang the doorbell again. Nothing. And it was black inside. Vi always closed the kitchen door and the lavatory door so that nobody could see anything by looking through the letterbox.

Tammas was smoking. He took one more drag on the cigarette and then nipped it and stuck the dowp back in the packet, and stepped to the staircase but turned and crossed the landing and chapped Cathy's door.

It's you! she said. Vi's at her work.

Aye. I thought she would be. Will she be back later?

Yeh, come in.

He shrugged.

Come on in, she said, opening the door more widely for him.

Ah well, if it's okay.

Of course.

Kirsty was in the kitchen; she was sitting in one of the armchairs with a pile of toys. Cathy's own baby was asleep on the bed in the recess, lying on top of the cover with a patchwork type of blanket tucked about it.

He waved to the girl: Hullo Kirsty! How's it going? He smiled and took a packet of sweeties out his pocket. This is for you, he said.

She gazed at him.

D'you want them?

She glanced at Cathy then back to him.

Cathy whispered, She wont go near a man hardly – even George; and she knows him well. If he tries to lift her!

Tammas nodded.

Cathy smiled and waved him onto the settee: Sit down, sit down! Tea or coffee?

Thanks.

Tea or coffee!

O aye eh whatever you're having yourself.

Tch!

Well eh . . .

Coffee?

Aye, coffee'd be great . . . He winked at Kirsty who had glanced across at him, and he said: Hey Cathy I thought you had two weans?

I have, the girl's at school.

School?

Cathy grinned: I know, I was married young! Pregnant at 16 married at 17; I thought I was going to be dead at 18!

He laughed.

I'm no kidding ye! And she's just turned 6, the lassie, I'm no that old!

O I know, I know I mean it just seems funny, having a wean at school.

Seems funny to me as well. But never mind.

I meant to ask you, did you wind up getting drunk at Hogmany after all?

Cathy made a face. No, no really, it wouldnt have been appreciated. That family of George's! what a shower. Over they come every New Year and all they do is sit there moaning and talking behind each other's backs. It's his fault but – George; he's too soft. God, I cant stand them – sometimes I think you're better off without relations all the gether! Cathy shook her head and grinned: It's mutual right enough, ever since we met. Because I was too young for George. The wee girl they called me! George's wee girl. Even in front of my face! Does George's wee girl want another cake. Is the wee girl wanting another cup of tea.

Hh!

It was to each other they said it. Anyway, it was my own fault. I let them get away with it. I shouldnt have. I should just have told them straight out from the beginning. Tch, who cares!

Cathy gave her attention to the coffee, making it in two large mugs which she carried and placed on a coffee-table with a glass top. It was between the settee and the other armchair and it was on the other armchair she sat down herself. She was wearing jeans and a jersey and she sat with her legs tucked beneath her. Do you go up the dancing much? she asked.

Naw no that much. Sometimes.

She nodded. It's eighteen month since I've been there. It was a staff dance. I never went to the last yin because of the baby; I was like the side of a house. They'd all have been looking at me, them in George's work – a bunch of right toffee noses so they are.

Okay if . . .

It's because they work in an office Tammas. They think they are something.

He nodded. Hey is it okay if eh . . .? He had the cigarettes in his hand.

Of course. It's about time for Kirsty's nap anyway. Isnt it Kirsty! Kirsty! You ready for your nap? Cathy winked at Tammas and went on: Yes now time for your nap Kirsty, a wee baby sleep; you going into the pram?

Kirsty was smiling at her.

I'm going to put you into the pram! And David can stay on the bed. Or will I give him your cot? Eh will I give him your cot? and you can have his pram? Eh? Will I? Cathy had moved from the armchair onto her feet and she was crouching as though about to spring at the girl who laughed aloud and moved back the way in anticipation and then Cathy lunged forwards and grabbed her up, tickling her and making her laugh loudly. And she held her out to Tammas. A kiss for Uncle Tammas?

Kirsty jerked her head away, to peer back over her shoulder.

Come on now Kirsty!

Tammas said, It's alright Cathy.

Tch! Come on now Kirsty, a kiss for Uncle Tammas! She held the girl out to him and he touched her on the cheek with his nose.

That's a nose kiss! he said.

A nose kiss! Cathy shook her head.

Kirsty was gazing at him and he winked and pointed at the sweeties on the mantelpiece. They're for you!

Tch, you'll spoil her! And as she walked to the door she called, Come on, you bring him!

What?

Cathy paused by the door, jerking her head at the bed: The baby!

Me bring him you mean?

Cathy grinned at Kirsty: Silly man! Isnt he? a big silly man!

Naw but you want me to bring him ben like? he said, half rising from the settee.

Of course.

He continued on across to the bed. The baby was lying on its side, the head at an angle as though looking up the way, and the left arm was up to the face, the fist clenched. Hh! Tammas glanced at Cathy and smiled. What do I do?

What does he do!

Naw eh . . . He grinned, rubbed behind his ear. Do I just actually lift him up?

Yeh, of course, but just mind his head and neck, just put your hand under his head, to support it. He'll no wake up anyway as it happens – he's like his father, he'll sleep forever!

Tammas hesitated a moment. He reached down and laid his right hand behind the baby's head and neck and his left hand onto the shoulder, and lifted him straight up, with the blanket hanging. What about this blanket? he asked.

Just leave it.

He moved the baby out from him and the blanket dropped onto the bed. The baby's eyelids flickered open. He stared at the face; he was still holding the baby with his right hand behind the head and neck and the left hand balancing at the shoulder.

The door had opened. Cathy was standing in the doorway with her back to it. Come on, she said.

He turned and watched in front of his feet as he followed her out and ben the lobby and into the front room, and he waited while Cathy prepared Kirsty in the cot. So it's two rooms you've got? he asked.

Yeh, and a shower. George put it in two years ago. It adds on to the value if we want to sell it.

It's a single-end Vi has . . . Tammas stared at the baby's face while speaking.

I know. We're keeping our eyes open but. Course she's rented you know Tammas and she was lucky to get it – it was him spoke for her, Milly's man, what do you call him?

Joe?

That's right. She was really desperate at the time because of Wylie. He was going to get her. He told everybody he was going to break out and come looking. She was terrified. Terrified! Hh! Vi. You know what like Vi is. Imagine her being terrified!

Cathy had lain Kirsty in the cot and tucked the blankets about her and she laid her hand flatly on the girl's forehead, keeping it there as she said quietly, A nutcase he was. The whole family. Bloody guns and knives and . . . She shook her head. All nutcases.

Tammas sniffed. Cathy was gazing at Kirsty who was not returning the gaze although her eyes were open; but she was almost sleeping; and now her lids closed over. Cathy turned and took the baby from him and she stepped over to put him down into the pram.

Nothing more was said until they had returned to the kitchen. Tammas sat down on the settee. What about that guy Stan? he asked. I mean he seems to do alright by her and that I mean he doesnt seem anything – no anything bad I mean.

He just fancies her Tammas.

What?

He does, yeh. Anyway, she has to keep on his right side.

Hh.

Cathy glanced at him. What is it?

He shook his head. Nothing . . . After a few moments he reached for his cigarettes again.

You smoke an awful lot.

Och, no that much.

How many a day?

Depends. He struck a match, inhaled and exhaled. Sometimes I dont smoke any.

Honest?

Aye, when I'm skint!

Aw, tch! Cathy laughed. She leaned over to punch him on the shoulder. That's because you're a gambler! Vi told me.

She seems to tell you a lot!

She doesnt; no really, just sometimes, sometimes she talks about what like Wylie was.

Mm.

Cathy smiled. And Stan, hanging about her like a big sheepdog! She gets them so she does!

Hh, thanks a lot.

No I dont mean you, just these Wylies. But Stan's different

anyway, he's no like his brother at all. In fact he might no even be his brother, he might be his cousin or something.

After a moment Tammas said, How d'you mean? did Vi say that?

No, I just think it myself.

He nodded.

You never know what Vi's thinking anyway. Even what she tells you. And it's like trying to get blood out a stone. Honest, if you've ever got a secret go and tell her because she'll never let it out.

Mm. Cathy . . . he dragged on the cigarette before asking, What did you mean when you said she has to keep on that guy Stan's right side?

No I just meant that in case he told him where she is, Wylie I mean.

In case Stan told Wylie?

Yeh.

D'you think he would?

I dont know, I dont think so, he doesnt seem like that. You've met him but what do you think?

Hh, I dont know . . . Tammas had been resting back on the settee; now he leaned forwards, his elbows on his knees, gazing into the electric fire.

Cathy stood up from the armchair. I'll no be long, she said, walking to the door and leaving, shutting it behind herself. Tammas glanced at his watch. There was a stack of magazines on the shelf beneath the glass top of the coffee table and he lifted a few out. They were mainly for women and he leafed through them quickly, pausing to read a couple of pages with letters on personal problems. Then he discovered one which had an article on the wives and girlfriends of National Hunt jockeys. He was still reading it when Cathy came back in. They're both sound asleep, she said as she closed the door. She had changed out of the jeans and jersey and now had on a skirt and a sort of blouse. She shrugged: When you're stuck in the house all day you just end up wearing anything. I feel as if I've been living in these jeans!

He nodded.

It's this weather; you feel as if it's going to last forever.

Ach it'll be spring soon now Cathy, and you'll be out and about. There's that big park up the road.

Mm . . . She glanced at her mug of coffee and lifting it to show him she said, Cold as usual look! She walked to the sink and refilled the electric kettle: Want another yin?

Eh . . .

I'm making it for myself.

Okay, he smiled, passed her his mug.

Those presents you got Vi and Kirsty at Christmas, they were lovely so they were.

Ah!

No, honest, and that bracelet!

Hh – she never wears it!

Because she's scared of losing it; she's accident prone – or so she says. It must've cost a fortune though!

Och!

Cathy left the sink, returning to the armchair; but after a moment she got up and picked the cushion off, putting it on the carpet, and sitting down there, arranging the cushion between her back and the front of the chair. She sighed, kicking off her shoes. It's good to relax at times.

Aye.

With the kids you dont always get the chance.

He nodded. When the kettle of water began boiling he rose: I'll do it . . . D'you take sugar?

No just milk.

She had already put the coffee into the mugs and he poured on the boiling water, the milk; the sugar into his own. Then he handed hers down, carefully, leaning over the top of the settee. As he sat back on the settee with his own mug he said, Were you wearing that skirt at the New Year?

The skirt?

Aye, I seem to remember it.

No. Cathy smiled. I wore a dress. She looked at her skirt and smoothed it out. I've had this yin for ages.

I thought you were wearing it.

No, definitely, I wasnt. I know the dress I was wearing, it's one I dont wear very often.

Mm.

I keep it for best really.

Aw aye. Tammas grinned, And you didnt even end up getting drunk either eh!

I didnt, no.

Ah you let me down – Hogmanay!

Hogmanay, yeh, and you let me down!

Tammas smiled then added: How d'you mean? let you down?

Well, you said you were going to come back!

O aye – and I would've!

No you wouldnt've!

I would've, honest!

Cathy laughed.

Tammas nodded. If I hadnt've found Milly's place. Honest, honest Cathy, I would've.

You wouldnt even take a drink!

What!

Well you wouldnt! I offered you one and you wouldnt take it.

Naw, because I didnt want to get involved in the company. You know how it is.

Cathy looked at him. I'll believe you this time!

Well it's true. He grinned: And you were calling me Thomas.

I thought that was your name though.

Did you . . .

Yeh.

Honest?

Yeh, of course, what d'you think?

I dont know what to think!

Cathy frowned then grinned.

Tammas laughed and lifted his coffee from the table. Cathy lifted hers from the floor. She shivered suddenly, replaced the mug where it had been; she stretched forwards a little, to put her hands closer to the fire, and she switched on the other electric bar.

It'll be too hot, he said.

Cathy shook her head. This place is always freezing. I had the two bars on just before you came in. And sometimes I put the oven on as well.

Christ!

It's damp, the whole building. That's how I go about looking like a tramp all the time, it's to keep warm.

He nodded.

After a moment she asked, D'you no feel it cold?

Naw, no really.

Well, men dont get as cold as women.

He looked at her.

It's true.

What!

That's how little you know.

Hh! He chuckled.

Honest Tammas I'm no kidding, feel my hand! She moved to kneel, putting forwards her hand and he took it in his and held it for a few seconds, gazing at the fireplace. She asked, Well?

He nodded.

She gave him her other hand and he took it, and she withdrew the first. And eventually she asked, Well?

Aye, hh. He opened his hand and she withdrew hers, placing

it on the edge of the settee, balancing herself; then she rested back the way, sitting on her heels. He reached forwards to her and said, Give us your hand again . . . just till I see . . .

When he took her hand this time he cupped both of his round it. She stared at it. He looked at her but she continued to stare at her hand inside his two. Then he opened them and she withdrew it again, and she sat back against the armchair once more. He picked his cigarettes up from the coffee table, lighted one.

Vi's started again. Smoking I mean.

Has she?

Cathy nodded, shifting her position a little, stretching to hold her hands to the fire. Even more now than she used to . . . or so she says.

Hh.

Cathy was gazing into the electric fire, and without taking her gaze from it she asked, Can I make you a sandwich?

He cleared his throat. Naw it's okay.

Sure?

He nodded. He glanced at his wristwatch: Actually I better be going.

Are you sure you dont want something?

Honest, I had quite a big dinner – a pub lunch; soup and all that.

It wouldnt be any trouble.

Naw, thanks but. He drank a mouthful of coffee and then collected the cigarettes and matches and got to his feet.

Cathy also stood up. D'you want me to give her a message?

Naw eh . . .

Just tell her you were here like?

Aye, that'll be fine, ta.

It's no bother . . .

Out in the lobby he paused as she opened the front door

and stood aside for him. And remember, she said, if you come up and she's no in again just knock the door and you can always come in and wait.

Thanks.

It's no bother. I'm nearly always in.

Thanks . . . He nodded. Cheerio then.

Cheerio. Cathy shut the door immediately.

•••

The wad amounted to £40 of which £10 was to play about with forecasts as well as pay expenses; the other thirty was for the nap. He arrived in plenty of time for the first race. The nap would not be running until the third. While the dogs were being paraded he wandered around, glancing at the *Adviser* and the tips in the *Evening Times*. Most of the runners in the first were returning after lengthy absences and their fitness had to be taken on trust. He laid a small bet on the tote for a forecast, choosing the two dogs he expected to be the biggest outsiders. He placed a similar sort of bet on the second race. A couple of minutes before the *off* on the third he finished the export he had been drinking and strolled out of the bar and along to the betting enclosure. The bookies were making his nap a 4 to 1 chance and he moved up immediately, gripping the wad as he went, and bringing it out and passing it up to the bookie: Four thirties the bottom, he said quietly. And the bookie had taken it without returning him a betting-ticket and repeated the bet to his scribbler while dropping the notes into the big money bag, and he said, Down to Tam. He turned and glanced along the row, rubbed out the chalked 4/1, leaving the space blank. But shortly before heading up the Stand Tammas saw the guy chalking the 4/1 back in again.

He read the *Adviser* while climbing the steps. He had napped the dog the previous night and reading today's newspapers had only strengthened his conviction. It was running from trap 5 and going from its best handicap in weeks; but even more importantly, there was a 3 yard gap between it and the 4 dog. 4 dog was much the faster out of the boxes and would be up with 5 at the 1st bend, but getting this 3 yard start meant 5 would have started racing by that time, and if it managed to keep 4 off round the 1st bend then it had a great chance of maintaining its head in front till the winning post. Anyway, dog 4 was not the real danger. The real danger was the 2 dog. If there was any trouble in running at all then this one's chance was outstanding. But they were making dog 4 the favourite, in the belief it would lead the 1st bend.

The wee man with the spectacles was standing below him, puffing on a roll-up, listening to a guy beside him while studying the *Adviser*. Tammas reached to tap him on the shoulder: What's the dangers Shuggie?

The bottom.

I've backed it, said Tammas.

Have you Tam aye it's the worry, the worry.

D'you no fancy 2?

Aye – strong! Fucking flying machine Tam, if it gets the luck – see it on Tuesday night! Fuck sake! it walks out the boxes and it's beat a short head! Fucking hell! I couldnt believe my eyes! No kidding ye!

Have you bet it yourself?

Nah I'm on the 4 Tam, if it beats 5 round the 1st it's a fucking stonewall.

Tammas nodded, stepping back up, taking the *Adviser* back

out of his pocket for another look. But the lights had dimmed and the hooter was sounding and Tammas was rapidly extracting a cigarette from the packet and getting it alight and exhaling as the traps opened and 5 had missed the break. Somebody nearby cried: 5's fucked!

But Tammas roared: You're still a good thing 5! On ye goooooo . . . Eeeassayyyy, eeeaaasssayyyy the 5 – ah bastard! look at 2, look at 2, 2's a fucking . . . ah! bastard! bastard . . . Tammas nodded.

Below him Shuggie was shaking his head and turning to exclaim: I thought you were a fucking certainty there Tam! The way 5 shook off the 4 coming round the 1st – I mean that 4! Fucking favourite! He's shot the boxes and still got beat! Hh! Fucking hell! I'm sick backing the bastard – owes me a fucking fortune so it does!

Aye.

And that 2 dog too d'you see the way it finished? Eh? Fuck! No kidding ye Tam that's a fucking flying machine so it is.

Tammas nodded. After a moment he stuck the *Adviser* into the inside pocket of his jacket and started walking down the steps.

As he crossed out through the parking area he chipped away his cigarette, checked the change he had in his trouser pocket, before heading along and up towards Bridgeton Cross.

•••

An old woman walked past him, round the corner and along to the grocer's shop, and when she came back she stared at him. This was the second time she had been out to the shop since he had been standing there, almost half an hour. It was after 6 p.m. and Vi was late. When a bus stopped to let off passengers at the stop nearby he was unable to see who was there until after it had moved away. And when Vi appeared at last he hurried out of view, dashing through the next close and across the back-court and into the close next to her own. He keeked out, seeing her turning the corner, carrying the big cardboard box, the top of a cornflakes packet showing. He waited until she was passing the close and he stepped out immediately behind her, going on her outside. Hullo, he said.

Tammas! She stopped walking. What you doing here?

Eh . . . he sniffed and put his hand to her elbow. Can I carry your messages?

No, it's alright, I can manage. She frowned: What you doing here?

Nothing. I was wanting to see you again.

You must be winning then. Or losing . . . I can never work it out . . . Vi started walking away and he walked after her.

You sure I cant help with the box?

I can manage.

It looks heavy.

That's because it is heavy. She stopped just inside her close and she frowned again. I'm just going up the stair Tammas I'm in a bit of a rush.

I was wanting to see you.

What about?

Can I no come up, and tell you inside?

No.

Aw, hh. He nodded.

I'm in a rush. I've got to get Kirsty fed and then take her over to my mother's.

Mm.

Vi had been standing side on to him; now she turned a

little to look straight at him. You were up yesterday. Did you no know I would be at my work?

Ah I just took a notion, just in the off chance . . . He sniffed, gestured at the box of messages: Let us hold it for you a minute Vi.

I'm going up the stair.

Aye but I want to see you.

What about?

A couple of things. I'll no keep you back.

You'll no keep me anything Tammas I just dont have the time, I've got to get ready and I've got to get Kirsty fed and everything. Honest I really dont have the time.

He smiled. What're you going out with somebody?

Yes.

Aw. He looked at her.

I'm going out with Stan. And I dont know why I'm even bothering to tell you. Look, I've got to go up and get ready.

I thought you didnt like going out with him?

I'm no even going to answer that.

Cathy says he fancies you.

Well Cathy's got no right saying that cause she doesnt bloody know!

He continued to gaze at her for a moment, then took out his cigarettes, offered her one which she declined, and lighted one for himself. You still off the smoking? he asked.

Is it anything special you want to see me about?

I'm going up to Peterhead.

What?

Peterhead, I'm going up to Peterhead, to work.

O.

He nodded, gazing at her. Eventually she changed her stance, adjusting the cardboard box, and he moved to her. Eh Vi let us hold it a minute . . .

What're you going to work at?

It's a guy I know that's fixing me up, he's a spark – an electrician – he's going to get me in labouring to him. He glanced along the close in the direction of the staircase; a door had opened and banged shut somewhere above. Eh Vi can I tell you up in the house?

She made no answer. A person was coming down the stairs, a woman; she came walking through, head bowed, muttering, Hullo Violet.

Hullo.

When the woman had gone Tammas pointed at the cardboard box but Vi shook her head, leant her shoulder against the wall, readjusting the weight distribution. And she said, When you coming back?

I dont know. No that long I dont think – it depends.

She nodded; and sighed.

If it's rubbish I'll no stay.

Is it the North Sea?

Naw, it's just a building site – a big yin right enough. I'm no sure what it's for.

Maybe it's another prison.

Hh.

And do you want to go?

He shrugged.

Is the money good?

Supposed to be, aye. He sniffed. D'you have to meet Stan?

He's expecting me.

Could you no phone him or something?

No, no really.

Aw . . . he moved a step to her, put his hand up to her face, curved onto her cheek; when she looked at him he bent to kiss her on the lips. Soon she broke from him.

O Tammas. She closed her eyelids, shaking her head slightly.

He glanced away, inhaled on the cigarette.

When is it you're leaving?

I'm no sure. Soon.

How soon?

I dont know – just depends. The guy . . . He glanced at her: What time'll you be back at? The night I mean.

Vi did not respond for a while, then she sighed and looked out the close

I could come back later.

No.

Hh; Vi . . . He shook his head and he moved to her again, putting his right arm round her shoulder, standing side on to her, and then leaning to put his cheek to hers. She made no movement, still looking in the direction of the street. You smell great . . . he whispered.

Vi began to say something but did not.

Have you got to go out with him?

She nodded.

Could you no phone him?

No.

You sure?

Honest Tammas.

Okay. He raised the cigarette to his mouth and dragged deeply, and as he exhaled he moved away from her. She shifted the weight of her body onto the other foot, adjusting the cardboard box in her arms. And she said, I better go up.

What about the morrow night then?

Okay.

Okay?

Aye.

Hh. He grinned. The morrow night?

Okay, She nodded, smiling.

The morrow night? It's a Saturday remember!

Aye, okay.

Hh. He grinned, shaking his head.

What time?

What time? Eh . . .

I'll be home about sevenish.

Sevenish?

Aye, we're always later on Saturdays. You could just come up then, say about half past.

Aye Christ.

She smiled as she walked past him and he watched her to the foot of the stairs where she half turned to smile again.

•••

He went into the cafe on the way home, buying a sausage supper to take up the stair with him. The lobby was in darkness, no lights showing beneath any of the doors. He switched on the radio and made a pot of tea, ate the sausages and chips off the greaseproof paper wrapping, the *Evening Times* spread out on the table at the sports' pages. Some dirty crockery and things were on the draining board and he stacked them in the washing-up bowl and boiled water. He was at the sink when the front door opened. It was Margaret and Robert; they went straight along to their bedroom then one of them came out and across to the bathroom. A few minutes later Robert appeared in the doorway, calling: Hullo.

Hullo . . . Tammas glanced round at him, his hands still in the bowl of sudsy water. And when his brother-in-law gave an exaggerated sniff he said, I've just finished my tea – chips I had; a sausage supper.

Mm, smell it a mile away. I'll just see if eh . . . Robert nodded, backing out and shutting over the door.

Tammas frowned; he stared at the door, puffing on the cigarette, using two fingers carefully on the tip while withdrawing it from his mouth. He carried on washing the dishes with the cigarette wedged in at the corner of his mouth, screwing his eyebrows upward to avoid the drifting smoke.

The two of them entered together, Robert sitting down at the table and Margaret coming to the sink area and lifting a kettle. Tammas stepped to the side to allow her in to the tap. There's some tea in the pot, he said. Probably only lukewarm now right enough.

She nodded.

Were yous out?

We went for a meal, called Robert; that new steakhouse place at Charing Cross.

Aw. Any good?

No bad. A wee bit pricey but I thought.

Margaret was standing with the teapot in her hand. Can you let me in to rinse it? she asked.

Sorry . . . He lifted the bowl out to make way for her.

Have you ever been in it yourself? called Robert.

Once or twice, aye.

How long's it been open then?

Eh, I'm no sure. About six month maybe.

Robert nodded; and while Tammas moved to return the bowl his attention was attracted to the *Evening Times*. Tammas said, I think there's no a bad picture coming on . . . He had his hands back in the bowl now then he lifted over a dirty pot and dipped it in, reached for a brillo pad.

No, said Margaret, it's non-stick, you'll just scratch it.

Aw aye, sorry.

You're best just filling it with water and leaving it to soak – it's the porridge one anyway isnt it?

Aye.

Well just leave it to soak.

Okay. He puffed on the cigarette and some ash fell into the water. There was another pot on the draining board with the remains of scrambled egg on its inside. He dried his right hand on the teatowel and took the cigarette out his mouth, inhaled and exhaled, tapping ash into the rubbish bin. Then he filled the other pot with water and muttered, I'll just leave this yin to soak as well I think.

Margaret and Robert had been exchanging looks. And it was Robert who said, Aye eh could you sit down for a minute Tammas, me and Margaret, we were wanting a word with you.

Aw aye.

It's nothing bad.

Tammas sniffed. Margaret was looking at him. He nodded, but continued to stand there, the small of his back leaning against the sink. Shifting his weight onto his right foot he folded his arms. Robert said, D'you mind if I turn the radio down a bit?

Naw – turn it off all the gether if you like.

You sure?

Tammas shrugged. He had a last couple of puffs on the fag before dousing it in the sink and sticking it into the rubbish bin. The kettle of water began boiling; he filled the teapot. Margaret said, Tammas . . . and then stopped.

Robert glanced at her.

Tammas asked, Is it to do with the job? I mean because I chucked it and that?

Well . . . Margaret sighed. It's no really only to do with that Tammas.

Cause it was really terrible you know I mean God sake, hh, terrible. You'd have to be crazy to work at it, that rolling machine – terrible!

Robert shrugged.

Naw Robert I'm no kidding ye.

Aye fair enough I'm no saying anything, except maybe if once you'd get used to it and that.

I would never've got used to it.

Robert shrugged again.

But what about Billy's dad? Margaret asked. Is it no a showing up for him after getting you in like that?

Well Margaret he never really got me in so much as well just the form and that I mean so I could fill it in.

She nodded.

It'll no really matter.

Are you sure?

Aye. Billy's da's a good auld guy; he doesnt really bother about things.

After a moment Robert shook his head and smiled briefly. Aye but Tammas that's no the way to look at it. I mean you dont look at it like that – his da's a good auld guy and so you dont bother – I mean if anything that's more of a reason for sticking the bloody job, no chucking it.

Margaret was nodding.

No think so yourself?

Eh, aye, to some extent, probably.

Surely it's more than to some extent? said Margaret.

Tammas sniffed.

Eh? is it no more than to some extent?

What do you want me to get my foot burnt off for the sake of Billy's auld man?

There's no need to be cheeky about it Tammas.

Och I'm no being cheeky Margaret, it's just – God sake . . . He turned and faced the window above the sink.

It's you she's thinking about, said Robert.

Tammas nodded. He turned back again: Actually I didnt really want the job in the first place. I dont really want to work in factories any more.

Hh! Robert grunted, I doubt if you're going to have any say in the matter the way things're going!

Tammas shut his eyelids; then he glanced about for his cigarettes and matches, collected them from the table. Margaret sighed and said, We just want to know you're going to be alright.

Alright?

Well, God, Tammas, we dont know anything really, not about what you're doing – just suddenly you've got piles of money and we dont see hide nor hair of you for days.

What?

You know what I'm talking about.

I dont.

Tch Tammas, you paid all what you owed and then gave us a month's rent in advance!

He shrugged.

Well it's a lot of money.

It's no that much.

Yes it is, it is.

Margaret, God sake, I just won a few quid on the horses.

Hh! Robert grinned.

Margaret was shaking her head. It's just too much, she was saying, it's just too much.

Too much? what d'you mean?

It's too much, the money, to win on the horses.

Tch Margaret, for goodness sake.

Well it is.

Naw it's no.

It is.

It isnt but, honest – Robert! Tammas gestured at him.

What?

Naw I mean just, will you tell her?

Tell her?

Naw just Christ the money and that, the horses, if she thinks I'm thieving or something.

She doesnt think you're bloody thieving! Dont be daft.

Well, Christ . . . Tammas had blushed; he inhaled deeply on the cigarette, flicked the grey ash into the sink. He glanced at his sister. Honest, I just won the money on the horses.

Tammas . . . Margaret shook her head, stared at the floor.

I'm sorry.

I'm no wanting you to be sorry.

Well what? Hh, I dont know.

Robert frowned at him.

I'm sorry I mean I'm no being cheeky I just dont know, I dont know what I'm supposed to do, I mean, what I should be saying and that.

Look Tammas all your sister's wanting to know is you're going to be okay. That's all; she's just bloody worried cause of the way things are going. Let's face it, they're no going that good. You cant deny that.

Tammas shrugged.

You chucked your job on the first day; you never gave it a chance. It'll get kept against you. It'll be down in black and white.

Mm.

It will but Tammas that's what bloody happens I mean we just want to know you're going to be okay. And I'm talking about the future.

I'll be fine. He glanced at Margaret: Honest, I'll be fine. I've got a girlfriend by the way.

God Tammas we know you've got a girlfriend.

Aye well . . . sometimes that's how I'm away.

Margaret nodded. It's good you've got a girlfriend; we're no saying anything about that.

Mm.

But in some ways that just adds to it Tammas. Cause how're you going to live? That's how I end up getting worried. You're my wee brother ye know!

Tch Margaret, God sake.

Well, you are!

He dragged on the cigarette, turning to face the window as he blew out the smoke. It was dark outside, light glinting on the wet roof opposite. He dragged on the cigarette again, started gnawing at the edge of his right thumbnail.

It's a big world out there you know!

It was Margaret had spoken. She was smiling. Tammas smiled back at her, and he added: To be honest, I'm going to be going away quite soon.

Are you?

Aye. He shrugged.

Margaret was gazing at him.

Robert glanced at her before asking, Whereabouts?

Eh, Peterhead probably.

Probably?

Tammas nodded. He lifted the teapot, put it back down again. I've been considering going to England as well – Manchester.

Manchester? said Margaret.

Aye.

What for?

To work. That's where John is. He's been trying to get me and Billy to go and stay with him. There's bags of jobs down there he says. Mainly factories right enough. That's how I'd rather go to Peterhead, because of the actual job. Getting into the building game I mean I'd really like to get into it. You make good money and then you can move about as well. Plus cause you're up there you might hear about the North Sea.

Are you talking about the rigs? said Robert – cause if you are you're talking about really hard graft. Really hard graft. Aye and the conditions arent that good either!

Tammas nodded, he cleared his throat.

It's no all it's cracked up to be, that's all I'm saying.

Are you just going to go yourself? asked Margaret.

Eh, naw I'll probably be going with somebody. No mind? I was telling you a wee while ago – a guy called McCann.

O. Is he working?

What do you mean just now?

Margaret nodded.

Naw, he's been on the broo a few months. That's how he's looking for a job. He's an electrician.

Mm, I see.

Robert said, What's his name again?

McCann; I'm no sure if you know him. He drinks in *Simpson's*.

I might've seen him around.

Probably have.

Robert nodded.

Tammas inhaled on the cigarette, tapped the grey ash into the rubbish bin, and he said, I think I'll go ben the room . . . Okay?

Margaret shrugged after a moment.

•••

He had waited until past midnight before leaving the house and he left without bidding Goodnight; his sister and brother-in-law had been watching a picture on television.

Although the rain had stopped the street was wet, quite a few puddles on the pavement. At the corner he bought a *Daily Record* from a paperboy and he got a taxi in less than five minutes. When he arrived down the lane the door of the club opened and two guys came out. They seemed a bit drunk and were talking back to Deefy. But Deefy was not paying much attention. He spotted Tammas and called: How's it going son?

No bad Deefy, no bad – how's yourself?

Deefy shrugged, pursed his lips. He stared after the two till they reached the end of the lane, before replying. Fucking horses! He stepped back inside the doorway, staying there until Tammas had entered . . . See the results the day!

Naw, I never had a bet.

You never had a bet?

Naw.

Wise man – fucking murder! He followed Tammas along the corridor and into the snacks' room. It was quite busy, a few men but mainly women. Deefy had paused to speak to an old fellow Tammas recognised as a newspaper vendor who had a pitch near Queen Street Station. He carried on, straight through into the gaming room. It was busy here also and he could see Joe standing over by the corner of the horseshoe table, on the fringes of the spectators; he was smoking a cigar.

There was a man beside him and whispering something to him. Joe's head was lowered as he listened, one hand in his overcoat pocket, the other holding the cigar behind his back. It seemed as if nobody else was talking in the entire room.

Tammas waited a short period. He crossed the floor to the corner opposite where Joe was; and he nodded to him but Joe appeared not to notice. There were no cards out on the table. They were all in the shoe. And the dealer was sitting back on his chair, arms folded, a cigarette dangling from the corner of his mouth. He had on a waistcoat which was unbuttoned and his braces were showing, old fashioned ones that functioned with buttons instead of clips. His two workers were both sitting with their hands clasped on the table and not looking anywhere in particular. Eventually the dealer yawned and said: I'll wait here all fucking night.

Nobody answered.

The dealer was gazing at the ceiling when he had spoken, but now he unfolded his arms and took the cigarette from his mouth, inhaling as he did so. He looked round the room and sighed, and he put the cigarette back into his mouth and clasped and unclasped his hands; he looked at a man sitting amongst the players and said: See Jimmy I know it was you.

It wasnt me Jake.

Jimmy. It was you. I fucking know it was you.

It wasnt.

The dealer sniffed and muttered, It fucking was you.

Honest Jake it wasnt.

The dealer shook his head and he sighed, and he clasped his hands and stared straight at the man. The two boys had their money out on the fucking table, he said. And they had a fucking tenner. Next thing it was a fiver. And it was you that fucking took it.

It wasnt me at all.

It fucking was Jimmy.

It wasnt but honest, honest Jake.

I dont believe you. I just dont believe you – they werent that fucking drunk! The dealer continued to sit looking in the direction of the man. And the silence continued for several seconds. Eventually he said, I think you should just go home out the road Jimmy.

But I never fucking took the money.

Course you fucking took the money! The dealer smiled and sat back on the chair again. He folded his arms and glanced at the worker to his right. Then he sniffed and took the fag from his mouth and he jerked his thumb at the door into the snacks' room. Jimmy, he said, fuck off.

The man cleared his throat as though about to reply.

Okay? Just fuck off . . . The dealer turned his head away, his eyelids flickering shut. He dragged deeply on the cigarette, gazing vaguely in the direction of where Tammas was standing.

Suddenly the man stood up from his seat and the guys behind stepped out of his path as he strode to the exit, staring straight ahead.

Somebody strolled to close the door behind him. A moment passed, then several conversations broke out. The dealer was muttering to the worker on his right: It fucking sickens me when that happens but I'm no kidding ye, it just fucking sickens me.

Should've his fucking hands cut off.

The dealer nodded, reaching to the shoe; and he began lifting out all the cards. Here, he said, shuffle them for a new deck . . . He glanced towards the punters and asked, Where's the bank got to? I've bloody forgot with all this carry on.

There was some laughter. Eventually it was sorted out. The two workers were still shuffling the cards and different conversations continued. Across the other side from Tammas Joe was moving away and he and the man with him walked to the door. Tammas stepped out from the row of spectators and gave him a wave. Joe grinned. How you doing Tammas?

No bad, yourself?

No complaints . . . he introduced the other man as Eric. We're just heading up the *Royal*, he said, this place gets too noisy sometimes.

Eric grimaced, shaking his head.

Tammas smiled.

Come with us if you want.

Nah it's okay Joe thanks.

Naw, come on, you're alright.

Ah well okay.

Be a game of poker later on . . . Joe held the door open for him and as they walked behind Deefy to the exit he asked, Still seeing wee Vi?

Aye.

Joe glanced at Eric: He's winching wee Vi Wylie.

Is he? Eric peered at Tammas and said: Are you?

Well no really winching I mean we're . . . he sniffed. We're seeing each other right enough.

Nice wee lassie.

Tammas nodded.

No out with her the night? said Joe.

Naw.

Course she's got that wee wean to look after.

Aye.

Tricky and that for babysitters? asked Eric.

No too bad.

Eric nodded. Deefy was holding the outside door open for them and the trio exchanged Goodnights with him.

The *Royal* was also busy. In the coffee lounge Tammas ordered an omelette and chips. Joe and the other guy had coffee and they sat drinking it with him while he waited. When the woman appeared with it from the kitchen he got up and so did the other two. See you when you come ben, said Joe. He and Eric walked to the door through into the casino but then he turned back alone and he said quietly, Hey Tammas you okay for the poker?

Aye.

About cash I mean. Sometimes on a Friday they make it a fifty sit in.

A fifty! Christ, I thought it was just twenty.

Sometimes, aye. It depends. Not if there's money about.

Tammas shrugged.

Wee Vi'd give me a doing if she thought I was leading you astray! Joe grinned, speaking quietly.

D'you think it'll be fifty the night like?

Could be. And it's stud they play. No quarter!

Tammas looked at him. The woman was returning him his change: Just keep it, he said, lifting his plate and reaching for a knife and fork. He glanced sideways. I'm alright Joe.

Fair enough, aye. Joe tapped him on the shoulder, turned to leave.

Eh Joe . . . Tammas paused with the plate and cutlery in his hands. That guy Stan's no in the night is he?

Stan? Naw – no Stan; he never comes – no unless the women are here or something.

Aw.

How? D'you want to see him?

Naw.

Joe nodded. He was looking at Tammas: Okay?

Aye, Christ, fine.

Stan's alright.

Aye.

A nice big guy. Joe grinned: You dont worry about him do ye!

Naw.

Good. Okay . . . Joe patted him on the shoulder before leaving.

He took his time in eating the omelette and chips, gazing at the following evening's dog card at Shawfield. There was one going he fancied quite strongly. He had backed it last time out and it had just failed to get up on the line. Now it was getting an extra yard in the handicap and had to have a chance. He put a tick against it with his pen, then ate the last couple of chips, finished off the coffee, strolled through to the gaming section.

He had £52 of a wad, enough to play poker and just about be comfortable with, but not much more than that. But there was no point trying to improve it on the tables. That was how it got frittered away, the quick route to going skint. According to Joe the only game worth playing was chemmy – except for poker. And all you had to do was look at the kind of folk playing here in comparison to those back at the club. There was money but not much else. Real punters like Deefy and them would hardly watch roulette never mind play it. Tammas had never seen Joe gambling at any of the tables, just occasionally standing by one while talking to somebody. And it was very seldom he ever went near at all when Milly was playing. She always played roulette, nearly always at the same table, and she tried to sit next to the wheel. There were two women sitting at her usual place just now. Tammas recognised them vaguely. Both were wearing long dresses of a style similar to the one Rena's best maid had worn at the wedding, the dresses stopping short at the top of the breasts so that the cleavage was quite easy to see. When Vi was in with Milly what she did was stick to the even money bets. And occasionally she won, and would stop while ahead. There was a Chinese guy on the opposite side of the table. He was betting after the same sort of method. He had a card and he was marking in numbers, he was in the midst of a winning sequence. The *19–36* he was gambling. Tammas watched him win four times in succession and on each occasion his bet was six £5 chips. The sequence ended when number 11 appeared. And he did not bet in the next, nor the next. Tammas lighted a cigarette. The two women were using the individually coloured chips, spreading them about on single numbers. That was the way Milly gambled. They were not talking to each other while they were doing it. One of them seemed to be winning a lot. The Chinese guy was now making a bet – the *odd* column, again for the six £5s. The metal ball was spinning and some latecomers were putting down bets quickly and methodically. Number 33: and the Chinese guy was a winner. So too the woman who seemed to be winning a lot. The croupier stacked out the chips for her and then for him. He lifted six and left six, and lighted a plain cigarette. There was a brief pause. Then the croupier was whirling off the wheel with his left hand while flicking the ball in with his right, and leaning back a little, listening to something being whispered by another of the casino employees. And again people were stretching to make their bets and Tammas also was leaning forwards and he dropped £50 down onto the *black* bed, and stepped back, folding his arms and holding the cigarette to his mouth with his left hand. The croupier glanced at him then exchanged the notes for ten £5 chips, stuffing them through a slot to the side of the wheel; and the smooth whirr of the ball spinning was becoming a rattling noise and the croupier called, No more bets. The ball settled into a red number. It was also an odd number and the Chinese guy was a winner. Tammas nodded slightly, inhaled on the cigarette. And he waited there until the ball was spinning once again.

Eric was across at the craps table, leaning his elbows on the rim of it, totally engrossed in the play. Joe was nowhere to be seen.

On his way out Tammas stopped and went into the coffee lounge. A man was sitting at the table he had been at before and was reading the *Daily Record*. Tammas said, That's mine – I just left it there.

The man shrugged, he closed it over and passed it up.

I've no finished reading it myself . . . Tammas sniffed. He rolled it up while heading to the exit.

•••

If I was drawing you, he said, moving his right forefinger down over the bridge of her nose and her lips, and down and along the line of her shoulder to the top of her arm; he tugged the blankets down a little, continuing the line round the curve of her left breast, moving his finger beneath and lifting it slightly, now moving the back of his hand in beneath it and he stared at her until she glanced at him out the corner of her eye. Sometimes eyes look like fish.

O thanks, thanks a lot.

Naw, just from side on like this when you're looking . . . His head was resting on the palm of his left hand, propping himself on the elbow. He withdrew the hand from beneath her breast and she shifted her position a bit, still lying quite straight on her back with her right arm beside him, the hand on his left thigh. He returned his forefinger onto her forehead again, retracing the outline of her profile, this time bringing the tip of his finger round the lines within her left ear.

Watch my nose with your elbow, she muttered and half turned her head, her hand also moving away but it resettled on his thigh again.

He placed his right hand on the other side of the pillow, manoeuvering himself to kiss her on the mouth. Vi, you're really beautiful. I'm no kidding.

Tch, shut up.

Naw, honest. He moved a little away and stared at her. You are. I'm no kidding.

You've said that.

I've said that?

She shook her head, smiling, moving to kiss him. It's alright, I dont mind you telling me I'm beautiful.

Christ Vi. He kissed the tip of her nose, shifting his right leg over her left leg, the knee resting between hers, and she put both her arms round his back, raising herself up into him. Soon he was hard and she lay for him to push entry. He whispered, I really love that feeling. She was looking at him and she nodded; her eyelids opened and closed. He was inside her now and stretching, then he lay taking the weight on his elbows. She was looking at him and he smiled and her eyelids shut, and he started the thrust.

When he had come he remained inside her. She kissed him, pulling him down on top of her and she said, Just lie.

I'll flatten you.

No you'll no.

You sure?

She smiled, knocking at his arms until he took the weight off his elbows and settled onto her.

I'm squashing you.

You're no.

Hh.

I like feeling you.

He smiled and altered the way he was lying just sufficient to face into the hollow of her neck and shoulders, the side of his head resting on the pillow.

Mm.

What is it?

This is nice.

Hh, aye.

And soon she was moving, a sort of circular motion, still with him inside her although still soft. She kept the movement going for a while, until he had become semi hard and able to continue alone, and she shut her eyelids and kissed him on the mouth and he stretched, grinning down at her, now kissing her on the forehead, and her intake of breath when he started thrusting a bit more deeply.

It's nearly eleven!

What . . .

She was reaching across and switching on the bedside lamp. She clambered over him and off the bed onto the floor, and she dressed quickly.

D'you mean in the morning?

It's no funny. Cathy'll be wondering if something's up.

Och naw she'll no.

She will but you dont know her! Vi was buttoning up her blouse, tucking the hem of it inside her skirt waistband. I'll need to tell her something . . .

Tell her we're having a marathon!

It's no funny I'm saying . . . Vi had walked to the sink and she turned on the tap. Kirsty as well, she'll be wondering. And sometimes Cathy's kids pick on her a wee bit . . . She was rubbing her hands on the towel, dropping it onto a dining chair as she passed to the kitchen door. D'you mind getting up?

O aye, sorry.

Naw it's just . . . Vi paused, she smiled. It's just Kirsty I suppose I just . . . She smiled again, shrugging.

Of course – sorry.

Naw, tch! She opened the door and went out.

He got up and put his clothes on. Vi had cooked food for them earlier and all the cutlery and crockery and stuff were still lying about the oven and the sink and on the coffee table beside the settee and armchair. He filled a kettle to start the washing up, and he made himself a cup of coffee. He moved quickly about the place, lifting Kirsty's toys and putting them in one heap beneath her cot.

The washing up was finished and he had switched on the television by the time she came back. Kirsty was in her arms, thumb in the mouth and eyelids flickering but she stared at Tammas when she saw him.

Vi glanced about at everything and smiled at him. No comment, she said and he grinned and offered her a cigarette. Then she frowned: You could at least have told me I'd forgot to put on my tights!

What?

I forgot to put on my bloody tights! she said, mouthing the last part of the sentence.

Hh.

Aye I know, hh!

He was smiling at her. Want a coffee or tea?

Naw, I had to take one in with Cathy.

Did she say anything?

Naw. But she knew.

She knew?

Vi raised her eyebrows at him and started preparing Kirsty for bed. Aye she knew!

What're you talking about, knew? Knew what!

Vi looked at him and he laughed.

He peered down at her when she spoke; he had his hands beneath his head on the pillow and she with her head on his chest, lying almost on top of him. About the crisps, she said, that first time we met – what was it you said again?

Pardon?

Vi was grinning. You said something when you dished out the crisps, that first time we met, down at Ayr Races. Remember? You went up and bought a round of drinks for everybody and then dished up a pile of crisps. Vi laughed. And you said something – I dont remember. Just the way you said it but. You should've seen Charlie's face.

How what d'you mean?

I dont know, it was just funny.

What I said?

Well aye, and the way Charlie looked. And he made a face behind your back.

What?

Honest! Vi laughed.

Christ. He had shifted to see her more fully: What kind of face?

It was as if he thought you thought you were somebody, because you'd won the money.

Hh! That's f – that's terrible.

Vi chuckled.

Naw, Christ, all I did was buy a round up.

I know but it was the way you did it, and all these crisps!

Christ. Tammas shook his head, and he twisted sideways, leaning out the bed to collect the cigarettes and box of matches from the floor.

It's okay; it was just funny.

She had her hand on his back as he struck the match, keeping the action outside of the bed, and he blew out the flame while lifting the ashtray to dump in the spent match. He lay higher up on the pillow, his head against the headboard. Who is that guy anyway Vi?

Charlie you mean? I dont know really. He's married to Ann – she's a good pal of Milly's.

So he's no actually mates with Joe?

I'm no sure. How?

He shrugged.

Maybe he is. What do you want to know for?

Naw I was just wondering.

Vi gazed up at him and indicated the cigarette; and he gave her a drag of it, holding it for her.

I was going to ask you, he said, and he sniffed . . . It might sound daft. It was just – see Joe and that? Tammas inhaled on the cigarette; he exhaled and asked, What does he actually do?

Joe?

Aye I mean just how he, I was wondering, how he makes a living and that . . .

Och he does different things.

Tammas nodded.

Vi was lying side on to him once more, her left arm on his chest, looking up at him. He just does different things.

What like but I mean?

Vi chuckled.

Naw I was just wondering . . . He leaned to flick the ash down into the ashtray on the floor.

I dont know.

You dont know what he does?

No really, no.

Honest?

Aye honest, of course honest! Vi slapped him on the chest.

He smiled, holding onto her wrist.

Well – I'll bloody honest ye!

Sorry!

You should be and all! She slapped him on the chest again.

Ssshh . . . he pointed over to the cot.

And you should be glad anyway, cause he sticks up for you.

Joe?

Aye.

Hh.

He says you're just young! Vi laughed.

Tammas looked at her.

She slapped him on the chest: Milly doesnt think I should be seeing you. She says you're a chancer.

What?

Vi laughed.

But he shook his head. That's terrible. Naw, no kidding ye Vi . . . He shook his head again.

She was still laughing.

Naw, he said, hh, that's really terrible. I mean she doesnt even know me Christ, that's no fair. It's no.

Vi was smiling.

Naw but . . . It's just no fair.

O come on! dont worry about it – that's just Milly! Tch! Vi gripped him by the arm; and he leaned to stub the cigarette in the ashtray. She just looks after my interests. She worries about me.

Tammas exhaled the last puff of smoke and sat back.

It was her got me this place you know. And she's done other things. She's been good; a good friend.

Fine, I'm no saying anything . . . He lay down with his head on the pillow. He slipped his arm under her neck and she rested her head on his chest, turning side on to him; he took her hand in his.

She helped me out when I was in trouble. And I mean trouble! Vi peered up at him and he nodded.

They were silent for a while. Vi's eyelids were closed. Tammas had been staring across at the sink; now he shifted position slightly and he murmured, I'm no hurting you?

No.

He cupped his hand in below her left breast and raised it a bit. It's really soft, he said, and yet it's heavy at the same time.

Mm.

And these wee kind of bumps round the nipple.

Thanks.

Naw Vi, just the way – just the way . . . Hh – even your actual skin feels different.

She nodded.

Naw I mean . . . He had his left arm round her back and he started smoothing the palm of his hand up and down her side, between her thigh and shoulder blade and eventually she sighed and yawned. He squinted across at the sink, to where the light had changed at the sides of the venetian blind. Dawn's coming, he said.

Vi smiled, her eyelids shut.

This room's different from mine, where it's facing; you'll get the sun in the morning, I get it in the afternoon. Sometimes I just lie on my bed looking out, keeping the curtains open to see the sunsets, the way the sky goes, although you cant see the stars properly. But here you'll get good dawns, sunrises.

He began smoothing her skin again, still gazing across.

...

Kirsty was rattling the frame of the cot. When he stared at her she looked away but continued pulling and pushing at it. It was just after nine o'clock and the shop round the corner would be selling Sunday papers. But his clothes were lying over the back of the settee and it was not possible to get there without being seen by the wee girl. Single-ends were hopeless. She should at least have had a room and kitchen. Plus that heavy smell of dampness at times, especially over at the corner of the room near the sink – in fact the whole window area. Even a good lick of paint might have helped. And getting rid of the striped wallpaper. A fresh gloss on all the woodwork. There were other ways of brightening the place up. The venetian blind for instance, it only stopped the light coming in.

Kirsty was now rattling the cot frame quite loudly and he whispered, Ssh! But she continued doing it and there was a movement from Vi. She was on her side, facing away from him into the recess wall. He turned over and snuggled up onto her, got an erection and backed off. What time is it? she said.

Mummy!

Shut up Kirsty.

Mummy. And she began rattling the frame even more loudly.

You're a pest. Shut up.

She's been awake for ages, whispered Tammas.

She's a pest.

Kirsty continued rattling the frame till soon Vi sighed and turned, rising halfways up and calling, Shut up. Just shut up. Lie down and read your book.

No.

Just do it when I tell you Kirsty come on now, lie down – eh? Just till Mummy's ready?

No.

Come on, just for a wee while . . . Vi lay back down and Tammas laid his left arm out as she did so; they settled in close together. And he whispered, You could do with an extra room eh?

Mm.

Could you no apply for a council house?

Mm, suppose so.

All you need to do is put your name down, just wait your turn.

Mm.

I mean you'd get a bathroom and that, a separate room for Kirsty.

I know.

Well?

Well what?

You should put your name down.

O, thanks for telling me.

Well you should, you'd get a house sooner or later.

I know I'd get a house sooner or later, God – I know better than you. I mean tch, d'you think I dont know!

He nodded.

God sake Tammas.

He nodded again.

I'm sorry, she said, it's just – Tammas, I dont want my name down on any lists if I can help it.

Hh.

Naw, I mean it, because of him.

Aw.

That's how.

Aye . . . He was silent for a few moments. But they dont hand out names and addresses to anybody that asks.

Mm.

They dont but, surely.

Vi shrugged. She moved off from his chest, saying: Pass me a fag . . . And she tugged the sheet up over her breasts, sitting up a bit, her shoulders against the bedhead.

When they were both smoking he said to her: Is it true he's going to come after you when he gets out?

Vi was staring at the wall opposite. She shrugged. He said he was.

Tammas nodded.

But he's got a screw loose, you dont always know.

He held the ashtray out for her to tap in cigarette ash: D'you think he will?

I dont know, he might.

Tammas inhaled on his cigarette and he blew smoke sideways, and turned, about to say something; but Vi said: I dont like talking about him with you.

Ah, sorry.

Naw Tammas, I just dont like talking about him with you, cause it's you.

He sniffed.

She smiled at him. Okay?

Aye, Christ. He cleared his throat and swallowed, inhaled on the cigarette again. Maybe your best bet's getting out of Glasgow all the gether.

O to Peterhead I suppose!

He grinned and she laughed. And he cleared his throat again, before saying, Naw, actually I'm being serious.

She smiled, shaking her head.

D'you no fancy it like?

Vi shrugged, puffed out a cloud of smoke and tapped ash onto the ashtray.

There's big money on this job you know – 12 hour shifts they're working I mean it wouldnt be long till I was able to bring yous up, the two of yous, you and Kirsty.

Mm.

And you wouldnt need to work.

But I like working.

Okay.

I hate being in the house all the time.

Fine I mean . . . he shrugged.

God Tammas Wylie never liked me working either. He always thought men were looking at me. Even before we got married he was wanting me to stay at home in my mother's – imagine! All day – sitting in the bloody house!

Hh.

God.

I wouldnt mind you working at all.

O thanks, I'm very grateful.

He looked at her.

Naw really, I'm very very grateful.

Christ Vi sometimes you take the needle hell of a quick.

I take the needle!

Well so you do, Christ, sometimes I can hardly get talking.

Aye well no bloody wonder. It's bad when men expect you to stop work just to suit them.

Okay.

I know it's okay.

Aye well, sorry.

You dont have to be sorry I'm no asking you to be sorry.

He sniffed and dragged on the cigarette.

I just think it's out of order, the way men expect that. D'you no agree?

He nodded.

Are you sure?

Aye Christ.

Well you dont seem too bloody convinced!

There was a brief silence. Kirsty called, Mummy!

And Vi looked over towards her and waved: It's okay pet, I'll be getting up in a wee minute.

Tammas muttered, Sorry.

Tch, I dont want you being sorry, there's nothing to be sorry about. It's just . . . och. She shook her head and sighed, and motioned for the ashtray, stubbed out the cigarette. I think it's time for a coffee, she said.

Aye, I'll make it.

Or would you rather just have a breakfast?

Eh naw, it's okay, it's up to you.

Tch come on, you're always starving.

I'm no always starving.

Aye you are!

I'm no Christ.

Dont go in the huff.

I'm no going in the huff.

You are.

I'm no. He inhaled on the cigarette; and he glanced at her while exhaling. I'm no.

She nodded.

D'you still feel like a coffee?

Aye, thanks.

Aw. Tammas paused. Sorry – you'll have to do it . . . He indicated the cot. I've got no clothes on.

Vi frowned.

Naw, honest, if it wasnt for that. Definitely I mean . . . he shrugged.

Vi glared and slapped him on the chest. You're no getting away with that! she said. I'm going to get you your trousers!

Tammas laughed.

Mummy! called Kirsty

It's okay pet it's okay, I'm getting up in a wee minute!

Tammas waved to her: It's okay Kirsty! He stubbed the cigarette out in the ashtray and leaned to place it on the floor. And he put his arm round Vi. The two of them lay back down again, her head on his chest. Kirsty was standing up, holding onto the top of the frame and gazing across at them. Tammas winked at her and she frowned, and after a moment she bounced along on the mattress and lifted a toy from the other end. Tammas had increased the pressure of his arm round Vi and she looked up at him. He smiled. And she said, What is it?

Nothing.

Nothing?

Aye, nothing.

Mm. It's a funny nothing.

He sniffed and shrugged, then suddenly frowned and glanced sideways, he frowned again.

What is it now?

Eh nothing, naw . . . Hh. Christ! He grinned and shook his head.

What is it?

Naw, it's just – I could actually just go myself. To Peterhead I mean.

Mm.

He grinned. I dont actually need anybody to go with Christ I mean I can just bloody go myself.

You've said that.

Hh! He chuckled. Ah! He gazed at the ceiling: Ya beauty! Ya beauty! Then he clenched his right fist and began punching the air and grunting: Pow pow pow, pow pow pow.

Both Kirsty and Vi were watching him. Vi was smiling.

Look Vi, would you really consider coming with me? I mean really – once I'd got settled in and that, once I'd got a place?

Would I consider it?

Aye.

She nodded.

You would consider it?

Aye, okay.

Honest?

Honest – aye, okay.

Christ.

I'm just saying I'd consider it but Tammas, that's all I'm saying, I would consider it.

Aye, Christ . . . he grinned and kissed her on the forehead.

•••

£65 was left in the bank account. He withdrew twenty one of it and stopped in at the newsagent to buy 20 cigarettes; there was a spare *Sporting Life* on the counter. When he returned upstairs Robert was still in the house, sitting reading a book in the living room. Tammas made a pot of tea and took him ben a cupful. Thanks, he said, barely glancing away from his page.

Tammas nodded. Through in his own room he spread the

Life across the bed. He had just lighted a cigarette when Robert could be heard coming out and down the lobby, and chapping the door: Hey Tammas! Can I come in a minute?

Aye.

He remained in the doorway with his hand on the door handle. Naw, he said, just to tell you, that fellow McCann, he was up at the weekend there.

Tammas did not answer.

Saturday it was, just after teatime.

Tammas dragged on the cigarette. He had been lying on his side and now he sat up and swivelled to tap ash into the ashtray on top of the cupboard, facing away from his brother-in-law. And his brother-in-law was yawning and saying, You still thinking in terms of Peterhead?

Aye. Tammas sniffed; he cleared his throat while turning to look at him. Maybe next week; I'm no sure.

Good, good for you; I really think you're doing the right thing. That's eh . . . I was wanting to say, just that I mean this room and that, it's yours, if the job maybe doesnt work out, you know, it's here for you, it'll be here for you – when you come back and that I mean you knew that anyway I hope.

Aye, thanks.

Well God sake it's your room! Robert grinned. We'll no take in any lodgers, it's alright!

Tammas smiled, he inhaled on the fag and flicked ash over into the ashtray again. Robert was smiling too. Then he glanced at his wristwatch and shook his head: Soon be time soon be time!

Backshift eh!

Aye, tch – I even prefer nightshift! Robert raised his eyebrows and grinned, his hand still on the doorhandle. He indicated the *Life*: Still punting the horses!

Aye.

By the way! That was a good score for Hull! Three nothing?

Aye, great.

Probably Rab got the hat-trick!

Aye. Tammas smiled, dragged on the cigarette and exhaled, and he said: Even if he was just playing but – in the first team.

Aye. Robert nodded. You're no kidding. Anyway – see you later eh! He closed over the door, clicking it shut.

Tammas glanced at the door for a moment and then at the window, and to the cupboard. The alarm clock was not going. He wound it up and set it to the time on his watch, and got up and walked to the wardrobe. He opened it, gazed inside and to the bottom, at his boots. The cigarette was in his mouth and he withdrew it without inhaling, drawing the knuckle of his right forefinger across the corners of his mouth. He went to the window, seeing the close opposite where two old men were standing chatting just out from the entrance; one of them with his hand on the other's elbow, his head tilted, listening; he looked to be laughing. Both of them wearing bunnets and overcoats and the one doing the laughing wearing a tartan scarf. And now a woman appeared from the close, bare arms folded and peering from left to right along the street, the men remarking something to her and her shake of the head, returning back inside.

He sniffed and moved back to the bed, shifted the newspaper, making space to lie stretched fully out, crossing his feet at the ankles, left hand behind his head. Then he raised himself up a bit and got his tea from the top of the cupboard; it was lukewarm and he swallowed it down. He manoeuvered the money out of his pocket, the four £5s. They were crumpled and he smoothed them out and placed them flatly, next to the alarm clock. He got up and returned to the window but then came back again and sat on the edge of the bed, picked up the *Life* and turned to the results from Saturday. The dog he had napped at Shawfield had won at 2/1. 2/1 was a good price and it would have been worthwhile making the journey for it alone. In that morning's *Daily Record* they had forecast 5/1 but Tammas had known it would never have been that – 2/1 was much more like it. Although of course if he had of made the journey it would probably have got beat. Nothing surer. That was the way things happened. There again, he had been skint on Saturday and the bank was shut. That was one of the inconveniences about banks – just like if you needed dough and it was after 3.30 in the afternoon. Or if you had left the bankbook in the house by mistake.

Some ash fell onto the page and as he made to lift it it rolled onto the bedclothes.

Monday was nearly always a bad day for betting; generally speaking the racecards were second-rate efforts – a bit like the opening race at a greyhound meeting, a time for looking on and taking notes, not for getting the money down. But it was still possible to back a winner. He continued studying the form till approaching half past one. He found two horses he fancied quite strongly and a third which had a reasonable chance. But nothing worthy of going nap on. It was probably a day to go to the pictures.

On his way out he made a piece on jam and he ate it while walking downstairs and along the street to the betting shop. He knew the boardman and they exchanged hullos. The boardman was eating a sandwich and drinking tea and he offered Tammas a mouthful. Naw, no thanks. Tammas said, Auld Phil no in the day?

Naw. He was in on Saturday.

Tammas nodded, strolled to a wall to read a formpage. It was from the *Sporting Life* and he had read it many times already. He was going to stick to the three he had selected upstairs, and back them in 3 x £1 doubles and a £1 treble,

and also back the two he fancied strongly in singles. He had
£20 and £4 away left £16 – unless he paid tax in advance.
Sometimes he did and other times not. It just depended on
the dough he had in his pocket, on whether the sum was
round or not. And £16 was round; it gave eight on each single,
or less, if he wanted to keep a couple of bob for a pint later
on. There again, it might have been worthwhile considering
doing single bets on all three. That meant £15 would be round,
three bets at a fiver each. One thing was sure, if he backed
two out the three the only winner would be the third, the one
he did not back. Plus of course if he only backed the third
the other two would win. That was why it was usually best to
get the one, to select the nap and stick to it, and if it lost there
was always tomorrow. But none of the three was worthy of
the nap. Maybe it was best just doing the doubles and the
trebles and leaving the singles alone altogether – do the 3 x
£1s and the £1 treble, and just go up the town to the pictures.

The first of the three runners was going in the 1.30 at
Wolverhampton, a race for 4 year old novice hurdlers. He
moved to a different wall to have a look at the formpage here,
it was from the *Express* and did not give the actual form, only
what the tipster had to say about it. But Tammas knew its
form inside out anyway and the main thing was that it would
win or it would lose. Or it could be placed. There were eight
runners and its price was forecast at 6/1. 6/1 represented good
each way value. Maybe the best thing was to stick the whole
score down as a tenner each way, the safety first bet – and
even if it finished third he would still be a winner, he would
still be receiving cash in exchange for the betting receipt.
Although there again, if he backed it each way the only
certainty was that it would finish fourth. Or else win maybe.
He was probably best just sticking the lot on as a win. But
that was daft because it was not a nap. He did not fancy it as

strongly as all that. And yet either it would win or it would lose and even if it did lose he still had £44 in the bank. Which was not a lot. But it had come from nothing and it was a mistake even thinking like that. £44 was fine. Plus he still had the twenty in his pocket. And he was backing three horses. Win lose or draw. He fancied three, and two better than one; and he would back these two as singles as well as in the doubles and treble. And even if they all lost he would still have a few quid in the bank. Although probably he would have the one winner, the one he had not backed singly. But it was not possible to do everything. You had to make your selection and stick to it. There was nothing else you could do. There was nothing else, nothing at all. A mistake to even think like that.

A show of betting came through on the speaker and he turned to watch the boardman mark up the prices. Then the door opened and in came Billy. He stood for a moment before spotting Tammas, then he stepped back a yard and pointed his finger at him, and strode across with his right arm aloft, and slapped him on the shoulder: Ya sneaky bastard ye where've you been hiding!

Tammas laughed loudly.

Naw but where the fuck have you been?

Ah skint man, skint – keeping out the road! Hey what's up you're no at work.

I chucked it! Honest, I backed a winner and handed in my notice!

Ha ha, said Tammas.

Billy laughed and slapped him on the shoulder again. Hey, by the way, they're still talking about it in there! Naw – no kidding ye man – they are! They're fucking wanting me to get your autograph!

Tammas laughed.

Ya cunt ye how did you no wait for me that day? Or else

come up and take me out for a pint later on! Eh? Fucking terrible man!

Ah sorry.

Naw no kidding but I mean fuck sake – two hundred quid man and you dont even take your mate for a bevy! I've been sitting in the house for a fortnight!

You're right man sorry, I should've.

Fucking think so too! And Christ sake you're no telling me you're skint? Fucking two hundred quid!

Sssh . . . dont tell every cunt.

Okay. Okay. Billy grinned and went on: So what're you taking me for a pint or what?

You taking me for one?

Christ – Tammas, you've no lost it all back already, eh?

Tammas looked at him. Then he smiled: Come on ya bastard! He took his cigarettes out as he walked to the door and he handed one to him and struck the match. When they were both smoking Billy said, You putting a line on?

Eh naw, I'm no going to bother. Bad race for betting. What about you?

Ah fucking skint man. Serious, I just looked in to see if anybody was here.

Hh! And you found me ya cunt!

Billy laughed and pulled open the door, standing aside to let Tammas exit first. And out on the pavement Tammas started walking in the direction opposite where *Simpson's* lay. I'm fucking sick of *Simpson's*, he said.

Ach come on! Billy smiled. We'll get a game of doms. Auld Roper's in – I saw him fucking limping along ten minutes ago. And McCann'll be there as well.

Nah I dont fancy it man.

Ye kidding? What's up?

Fuck all up.

Well come on then!

Look Billy it's me that's fucking buying the drink . . . Tammas shook his head and turned away, inhaling on the cigarette.

Billy sniffed. He stepped to the edge of the pavement and spat into the gutter. He returned the cigarette to his mouth and put his hands in his jeans' pockets. Going to tell me something, he said, is this to do with McCann?

McCann?

Is that how you dont want to go into *Simpson's*?

Naw, fuck. Naw.

You sure?

Aye Christ – how?

Cause he thinks you're fucking avoiding him.

What?

Aye I'm no fucking kidding ye man, every time I bump into him, he's wanting to know if I've seen you!

If you've seen me?

Aye.

Hh, Christ sake.

Billy dragged on the cigarette and asked, Is it cause of Peterhead?

Peterhead. What d'you mean?

Billy shrugged. I dont know. Just cause you never went . . .

Never went! Fuck sake Billy it was me waiting for him, no the other way about. That's how I ended up taking the start in your auld man's place. Christ, I was getting sick of fucking hanging around.

Aw thanks!

Naw, sorry man nothing against the job or fuck all.

Billy smiled.

Naw, honest Christ I would've stuck it I mean . . . Tammas shrugged. It was just cause, ach, I dont know Billy I'm just getting fucking sick of factories, getting stuck inside all day. That's how Christ, Peterhead and that man I really fancy it – I do . . . Tammas had been about to add something but he stopped and moved out the way of a man who was hurrying into the betting shop. And he glanced along the road. Naw, he said, it's me that fucking wants to go but he keeps saying it's too soon.

Aye well maybe that's what it's about then, maybe it's time now.

Tammas nodded.

I mean he's saying he doesnt even see you at the broo whereas yous used to always go the gether.

Hh! Fuck sake. Tammas shook his head: I'm no even getting broo money.

Aye but you're signing on.

Aye, Christ but I'm no getting fuck all cause of that six week rule about chucking your job.

Aye fair enough but I mean . . . Billy shrugged.

I'm no even getting social security money.

Hh; how no?

Dont know man – it's just no coming through or something.

Mm. Billy nodded. He glanced sideways and sniffed. Where d'you fancy going then? The *Inn*?

Nah.

Where?

Tammas shrugged. I'm no bothered. If you really want to go to *Simpson's* then we'll fucking go to *Simpson's*.

Well I'm no desperate.

Naw but if you want to go we'll go.

It's alright.

You sure?

Billy shrugged. It's your fucking cash.

We'll go.

I'm no bothering but, honest.

I'm no bothering either. Tammas shrugged. It was just a change; I just felt like a change.

Aye fair enough. Billy stepped aside as another guy came rushing up and into the betting shop, and as the door banged open and shut the voice from the extel speaker was quite audible; the runners for the 1.30 race were coming *under orders.*

Come on, muttered Tammas, I dont want to hear this commentary.

Billy smiled.

•••

McCann was in. He was sitting at one of the rear tables, not far from the darts' area. Auld Roper was beside him; also a postman by the name of Freddie; and the three of them were playing dominoes. Tammas paused at the head of the bar to order the drinks but Billy continued on.

A moment later came the cry: Hey Hotfoot!

Tammas ignored it. The cry was repeated. It was Roper who was responsible. And when he arrived at the table with the two pints of heavy the elderly man again cried: Hey Hotfoot!

He laid down the pints and glanced at Billy: Thanks for telling every cunt in Glasgow.

Billy laughed.

Is that how you've stopped coming in? cried Roper. You've been feart to show your face!

Show his feet's more like it! The postman laughed and leaned over the table to see down at them. Are they recuperating?

Fucking patter! said Tammas. He rubbed his hands as he sat down on a spare chair.

Aye! Auld Roper pursed his lips and shook his head, he raised his half pint of lager and muttered, The copper works – no an easy job eh!

The postman nodded. I've heard that myself.

Billy grinned.

Then McCann was tapping the edge of the table and saying, Are we supposed to be playing fucking dominoes here!

Hh! Roper shook his head: Listen to moaning face.

Aye well I've fucking forgotten who's turn it is there's been that much fucking yapping!

Me it is ... The postman leaned to study the dominoes already lying on the board.

Tammas swallowed a mouthful of beer and sat back on his chair; he glanced at McCann and lifted his beer again, and he said, How's it going Brian?

Ah no bad Tammas no bad – yourself?

Aye, okay.

Nice wee turn you had the other week.

Aye.

And kept out of every cunt's road till he'd spent the money! grunted Auld Roper to the postman.

Ah well you couldnt blame him for that, replied McCann. No with a bunch of begging bastards like you going about!

Hh! Will you listen to who's talking! Ya cunt ye McCann the next time you buy anybody a drink'll be the first time. Eh? The elderly man glanced round the table at the others.

Billy grinned: This is getting serious.

You shut up and all, muttered Roper, taking days off your work when half the country cant fucking get any! Eh Freddie?

The postman shook his head. Keep me out it, I'm neutral.

Neutral! Hh! Roper reached for his half pint of lager and sipped from it.

After a moment McCann asked, Who's to fucking go?

Me, said Freddie.

Aw you're chapping ya cunt give us peace!

How d'you know?

Cause I fucking looked at your hand.

Aw, okay.

Auld Roper sighed and tapped his fingers on the edge of the table Going to get this fucking game moving eh! my rent's bloody due next week.

Tammas had grinned; he pushed back his chair and stood up swallowing down most of the remainder of his beer. What yous wanting? he asked.

Pardon?

What did he say?

Heh McCann . . . Auld Roper frowned: Did you hear that nice boy speaking there? I'm no sure if my ears were open or what?

Ears ya cunt? McCann cried: You've got fucking ears like Dumbo the elephant.

Auld Roper burst out laughing. Eventually he had to reach into his coat pocket and extract a big handkerchief and use it to wipe his eyes and blow his nose. The others, including McCann, were also laughing and some of the folk at other tables were looking across and smiling.

Okay then, said Tammas, last orders!

Last orders! The postman grinned.

Once he had got their orders he went to the bar and was joined soon after by Billy who was returning from the lavatory; the two of them carried the drinks back to the table. McCann had been shuffling the dominoes for a new game. And he said, Yous two playing?

Aye . . . take some money off yous! Tammas smiled.

Ho! Listen to the boy! Auld Roper shook his head as he reached to pick up his dominoes.

And the game began. When they had been playing a couple of rounds the postman glanced up from the dominoes he was holding and he said to Roper: Heh auld yin, d'you mind of a horse by the name of Hotfoot? Nightingall used to train it.

I mind of the horse, aye, but Nightingall wasnt the trainer.

He was.

He wasnt.

Aye he was. Dunky Keith used to ride it and all.

He never! Geoff Lewis rode it. And Ian Balding fucking trained it.

Tch . . . The postman shook his head and he sighed and looked at McCann: D'you mind of it Brian?

Nah do I fuck – I'm no an auld cunt like yous.

Hh, cheeky bastard . . . Who's to go?

You, said Tammas.

Chapping.

We all fucking knew you were chapping! Billy laughed and leaned to play his own domino.

Tammas was next and then McCann. Auld Roper followed, playing his last domino with a flourish. And he chuckled and reached for the empty domino box, upturned it for the five 10 pence coins. Contributions gratefully accepted, he said, contributions gratefully accepted.

Billy grinned. At this rate you'll be able to buy a round auld yin!

Roper gaped at him, stuck the money into an interior pocket; he peered round at the others and said Who's got the fags then? Eh McCann – still keeping them under lock and key!

Shut up ya pokling bastard.

Pokling bastard! That's the last thing I need to do to beat you son!

The postman laughed; he was unwrapping a fresh cigarette packet and he offered them about. Anybody got a light? he said.

Damascus is over there! cried Roper, gesturing over his shoulder.

Aye well I wish you'd catch a fucking train and go! McCann muttered.

I'd go in a fucking minute if I could get away from you! And anyhow McCann . . . I thought you and Hotfoot were catching a train up to fucking Peterhead to give us all a rest down here? Eh Billy? Auld Roper winked at him.

Billy smiled.

McCann sniffed and glanced sideways at Tammas, and jerked his finger at the elderly man: Listen to fucking Dumbo!

Naw but I thought you said you were.

What's it got to do with you?

What's it got to do with me? I'll fucking tell you what it's got to do with me . . . Roper lifted his half pint glass of lager and sipped at it, then he put it down and wiped his mouth with the cuff of his overcoat sleeve. I'll fucking tell you what it's got to do with me, it means I'll have to look for a new fucking mate at dominoes!

The postman winked at Billy: This is getting serious eh!

Naw, said Billy, it doesnt get serious till one of them starts buying a fucking round!

The postman laughed.

Auld Roper raised his eyebrows and he glanced at McCann: Eh? did you hear the boy there?

No respect for his elders.

Exactly what I was thinking. That's this fucking younger generation for you. That's what happens when you start drawing a pension – every cunt's out to stick the boot in. Fucking sad so it is.

Aye, said McCann, and I dont see him rushing to buy a drink either!

After a moment Billy replied, I'm skint but.

Well so are we.

Hotfoot's no, grunted Roper.

I'll tell you something, said Tammas, this Hotfoot patter's beginning to annoy me.

O o. Billy glanced at the postman. Now it's getting serious.

Aye well no fucking wonder, said Tammas. He stood up and swallowed down the last of his beer.

The postman looked up at him: Ah come on son it's just a bit of fun.

I know it's a bit of fun but I'm just fucking sick of it. Then he smiled, Plus it's costing me a whole round every time I want a pint!

Ah well I was just about to buy you one back I mean I'm no fucking . . . the postman shrugged. I was going to get you one back son.

Naw I know Freddie, sorry . . . I'm no meaning anything. Naw, I just want to go take a walk down the betting shop. Tammas sniffed and glanced at Billy: You coming man?

Eh aye . . . Billy had hesitated but now was reaching for his pint and drinking a large mouthful in a gulp, and standing up, taking his jerkin from the back of the chair.

McCann shifted on his seat, and he stared up at Tammas: If I'd had enough fucking money I'd have bought you a drink back as well, dont worry about that.

Tammas nodded. I know.

Aye well dont fucking start that with me then.

Start what? I'm no starting anything.

McCann was staring at him. Then he sniffed. I dont like

the way you said that, that's all. You knew we were fucking skint. No cunt was fucking forcing you to buy us anything.

I know.

Aye well dont fucking start then that's all I'm saying.

I'm no fucking starting.

I mean ya cunt ye two fucking hundred quid you win and you worry about buying us a pint! Jesus Christ Almighty.

Ssshhh. Auld Roper patted McCann on the wrist.

Well no fucking wonder, that's fucking out of order!

He's just a boy, muttered the elderly man.

Ah fuck sake but . . . McCann shook his head. There's no need for that. As if we were reneging on the fucking company man I mean Jesus Christ – eh! McCann sat back round and he glared at Tammas: I mean what's the fucking score at all eh! starting that kind of fucking patter with me and the auld yin! Eh? Giving us a fucking showing up like that!

I'm no giving yous a showing up.

You fucking are giving us a showing up!

Billy was now onto his feet, his hands held palms upwards and saying: Come on Brian eh? come on . . .

Naw fuck sake Billy! McCann waved him away. That's fucking out of order!

Okay. Tammas said, I'm sorry.

You're sorry.

Aye, I'm sorry. I've bought yous a drink as usual but I'm fucking sorry.

McCann bounced up onto the floor and grabbed Tammas by the neck and marched him backwards about four yards and he yelled: Ya wee fucking bastard ye ya wee fucking bastard I'll fucking murder ye man here and now, I'll fucking murder ye.

Tammas was choking and he staggered but had gripped onto McCann's wrist while stepping back the way. McCann let him go, and he stepped back another yard, rubbing his neck and coughing. A lot of the people in the pub were talking at once. And Billy had jumped round the side of McCann and was shouting: Dont fucking start that with Tammas ya cunt or you're in fucking trouble man, you're in fucking trouble . . .

But McCann had caught him by the shoulder and was pushing him on the way and he went staggering a couple of paces, catching onto a table, and two men who were sitting at it jumped quickly back out the road.

McCann stood staring at Tammas, his arms at his sides, both of his fists flexing open and shut, and his shoulders moving, and he raised his right hand, wagged the forefinger at Tammas: Dont you ever fucking do that again to me. Right!

Tammas said nothing.

I'm fucking warning you Tammas; dont you ever fucking do that to me again. Or you're fucking dead. Ye listening? D'you know what I'm talking about? You're fucking dead!

Tammas was gazing at him.

You hear what I'm saying?

Tammas made no answer.

Eh?

And Billy was now tugging at him on the elbow. Hey man hey come on, let's go, let's go man, let's go – out of this fucking place man, fucking bastards, let's go . . .

Tammas rubbed at his neck again and coughed. Over McCann's shoulder he could see Auld Roper making signs, gesticulating, pointing at the exit . . . He made no acknowledgment but continued gazing in the direction of McCann.

McCann was staring back at him.

And now Billy's hand was on his shoulder and pulling him backwards and he said, Aye, aye, I'm coming . . . And he saw the barmen staring at him and also a couple of guys standing up by the bar, all staring at him.

Outside on the pavement Billy took him by the arm. Tammas was shaking his head, still rubbing at his neck, Come on man . . . Billy was patting him now on the shoulder.

Fucking bastard, said Tammas, fucking bastard.

I know man I know he's a fucking, a fucking bastard man a bastard, you dont worry about him man a cunt like that, you dont worry about cunts like that man dirty fucking bastard.

Whhh Jesus . . . Tammas shook his head from side to side, making a grunting blowing noise, his eyelids shut and with his shoulder now leaning against the tenement wall; then he was seeing an old woman staring at him – she was standing some yards away at a bus stop, standing staring at him. He turned his head, putting his hand over his eyes, and walked on, Billy going with him.

They were walking in the direction of where Billy lived, neither speaking, not looking at each other till eventually Tammas paused a little bringing out the cigarettes, and they got them lighted, and then he led the way across the road and round the next corner. And Billy said, Going to the betting shop?

Aye. Tammas sniffed. A horse I fancy in the next.

You alright?

Aye.

Neck?

Aye, okay . . . Fucking nearly strangled me so he did.

Billy nodded. As they entered the doorway of the betting shop Tammas palmed him a £5 note but he frowned and muttered, What the fuck's this for?

Tammas shrugged.

I dont want it . . . Billy held it upwards as though to return it.

Och stick it in your pocket man it's just to have a bet.

Billy shook his head but he took the money and he followed Tammas into the shop.

It was very busy inside and each went to different form-pages. Then Tammas checked the previous races' results. Neither of the first two runners of the three he fancied earlier had managed to gain even a place. He counted the money he had left and then stuck it all onto the third one. When he was writing out the line he saw Billy across the room, also writing out a line. They went to different pay-in windows, then stood together to hear the commentary. The horse Tammas had backed fell at the 2nd fence. But neither he nor Billy had mentioned their selections to the other, and after a moment he muttered, I need a slash man . . . And he crossed in the direction of the lavatory, leaving Billy engrossed in the commentary. Outside he began running. It was after 3 o'clock. He ran over the road and cut through the back of a close, crossing backcourts to avoid passing *Simpson's*, and on to his own street and up the stairs to collect the bankbook.

The bank was almost empty. He scribbled a withdrawal slip for the £44. The clerk gazed at it and at the figures in the bankbook. Is that you closing the account altogether? he asked.

Well eh . . . Tammas sniffed. Naw, just give me the forty three.

The clerk nodded. But you'll need to alter it and initial it . . . and he returned him the slip.

Billy signalled to him when he arrived back in the book-maker's. D'you catch it?

Nah.

Billy nodded. No me either! First favourite of the day as well! Could've been backed.

Mm . . . Tammas had taken out his cigarettes; he offered Billy one but he declined.

I'm smoking too much these days, he said. And he glanced

at Tammas's neck and pointed at it: Alright man? Looks hell of a red.

Tammas nodded. A wee bit sore.

Fucking McCann! Billy shook his head, he cleared his throat and spat in between his feet, scraping his shoe over it. And when Tammas did not reply he added, Now I know how you were wanting to give it the go bye!

Tammas looked at him.

Naw I mean . . . Billy smiled. You werent wanting to go in the first place man it was me fucking dragged you – *Simpson's* I'm talking about.

Aw aye, hh. Tammas inhaled on the cigarette and a moment later he walked to a wall to look at one of the formpages.

•••

The bedroom door being opened roused him but the light was not switched on and he kept his eyelids shut and stayed in the same position, and soon the door closed, clicking shut.

Later on Margaret entered, she walked straight in and put her hand onto his shoulder, and he turned over to lie on his back. I didnt want to waken you, she said, but I know you never took your tea; and me and Robert's just about to have some supper.

Mm.

It's nearly midnight.

He sniffed and squinted at the alarm clock, raising himself onto his elbows.

You've been sleeping for ages Tammas.

Aye; I was tired.

She smiled. When he squinted over at the clock again she said, Will I put on the light?

Nah, I think I'll just stay here . . . He lay down and tugged the blankets up to his chin.

Are you okay?

Okay? Aye.

Are you sure?

Aye, fine.

You dont seem fine.

Well I am.

She nodded.

Honest. Honest Margaret.

It's toast and cheese we're having if you're interested.

Eh – naw, ta, I'll no bother.

Tch, Tammas.

Honest Margaret I'm just no hungry.

Well you'll take a cup of tea surely!

Aye.

Well thank goodness for that!

Once she had gone he waited a moment then sat up and reached to switch on the bedside lamp. He lifted the cigarette packet; only one remained inside. He left it on top of the packet and lay down again, but only for a brief period, then he got up out of bed and pulled the curtains open about a foot in width. Margaret's footsteps in the lobby. He jumped back into bed and tugged up the blankets. When she came in she was carrying a teaplate with a slice of toast and cheese on it, as well as a cup of tea. Dont eat it if you dont feel like it, she said.

He nodded. Thanks.

She paused by the door. Goodnight.

Goodnight.

She shut the door. Tammas sat up, punched the pillow in at his back, lifted over the teaplate.

•••

He was awake before the alarm went off. It was 5 am and some birds had been whistling for maybe twenty minutes although it still seemed dark outside. He waited until the click occurred just prior to the bell and quickly stretched across and tapped down the button, and he got out of bed immediately. Once he had dressed he opened the wardrobe door and took out his big travelling bag. It was already packed. He laid it on the bed. Beside it he laid the bankbook, the UB40, the cigarette and box of matches. He took his boots from the bottom of the wardrobe and placed them on the floor down from the bag, lifted his jerkin from its hanger and folded it next to the bankbook. Then he knelt and looked beneath the bed, and stood up and looked about the room, going into the drawers in the cupboard and checking along the window-sill and all other places where things could be lying.

And afterwards, he went into the bathroom for a piss and then washed and collected his toothbrush and shaving gear, and back in the bedroom he unzipped a side pocket in the travelling bag and stuffed them in.

There was enough milk for a bowl of cornflakes. But he did not make coffee or tea. He margarined a slice of bread then put some jam on it. He found a plastic wrapper to stick it into. Back in the bedroom he unzipped the side pocket once more and stuffed it in. He stepped to the window and stared out for a time.

It was cold but dry, and there was only a breeze. At the close-mouth he struck a match and lighted the cigarette. He swung the bag up on his shoulder while stepping out onto the pavement. There had been eleven 10 pence coins in the meterbowl, plus some coppers in change lying on the mantelpiece. He had taken the lot and left a note for Margaret.

When he reached the corner of the street a bus approached. He carried on walking, heading along towards Argyle Street. He kept on walking, passing through the centre of the city, on along to Bridgeton Cross, passing the turnoff to Shawfield and on towards Celtic Park. A transport cafe had lights on inside but its doors were still locked shut. He walked maybe two hundred yards beyond the Auchenshuggle terminus, and then put down the travelling bag and lowered himself down next to it.

A car was coming. He watched it pass, seated on the heels of his boots. And another was coming. He watched it too. Then a big lorry in the distance and he got up smartly, grabbing the bag and striding on, the thumb out. But the lorry did not pause at all. The next one did, it slowed to a stop some fifty yards ahead and Tammas started trotting after it, the bag swinging at his side. A big articulated lorry. He opened the cabin door and the driver nodded. Thanks a lot, he said. And he gripped the bar by the door and climbed the couple of steps up and in.

The driver was moving on now, his gaze to the rearview mirror. And as he increased the speed he was reaching into the top pocket of his shirt and bringing out a packet of cigarettes . . . Smoke?

Aye. Thanks.

The driver passed him one and lighted his own with a gas-lighter. Tammas struck a match for his. The driver glanced at him: Going far?

Eh, how far you going yourself?

Me Jock? London.

London?

Yeh . . . The driver nodded, his gaze returning to the road. Yeh, home and see the kiddies. Four days I been away Jock, four days – four days too long!

Tammas nodded.